THE CONTRIBUTORS

JULIE WILSON, the author of a book on St. Martin/Sint Maarten, is contributing editor for *Town and Country* and writes frequently for *Travel & Leisure*.

ANITA GATES is a travel consultant for American Express, contributing editor for *Frequent Flyer* magazine, and is widely published in major women's magazines.

JENNIFER QUALE, who has lived in the Caribbean, writes for *Travel & Leisure, Vogue, Food & Wine,* and other magazines and newspapers.

JESSICA HARRIS, the author of a book on African influences on New World cooking, writes for *Caribbean Travel and Life, The New York Times, Essence,* and other publications.

J. P. MacBEAN is the author of a guidebook on Puerto Rico, and has written for *Travel & Leisure, Discovery, Odyssey, Going Places,* and other magazines.

SUSAN FAREWELL is associate travel editor of *Bride's* magazine and writes frequently about popular honeymoon destinations in the Caribbean.

ROBERT GRODÉ, a journalist, reviewer, and longtime resident of the Caribbean, has written two books on the culture of the Caribbean.

JEANNE WESTPHAL, a trustee of the Society of American Travel Writers, has been a consultant to the World Tourism Organization, Organization of American States, and a number of Caribbean-island governments.

THE PENGUIN TRAVEL GUIDES

AUSTRALIA

CANADA

THE CARIBBEAN

ENGLAND & WALES

FRANCE

IRELAND

ITALY

NEW YORK CITY

THE PENGUIN GUIDE TO THE CARIBBEAN 1989

ALAN TUCKER

General Editor

PENGUIN BOOKS

PENGUIN BOOKS

Published by the Penguin Group
Viking Penguin Inc., 40 West 23rd Street,
New York, New York 10010, U.S.A.
Penguin Books Ltd, 27 Wrights Lane,
London W8 5TZ, England
Penguin Books Australia Ltd,
Ringwood, Victoria, Australia
Penguin Books Canada Ltd, 2801 John Street,
Markham, Ontario, Canada L3R 1B4
Penguin Books (N.Z.) Ltd, 182-190 Wairau Road,
Auckland 10, New Zealand

Penguin Books Ltd, Registered Offices:
Harmondsworth, Middlesex, England

First published in Penguin Books 1988
Published simultaneously in Canada

1 3 5 7 9 10 8 6 4 2

ISBN 0 14 019.900 4
ISSN 0897-6821

Printed in the United States of America by
R. R. Donnelley & Sons Company,
Harrisonburg, Virginia

Set in ITC Garamond Light
Designed by Beth Tondreau Design
Maps by David Lindroth
Illustrations by Bill Russell

THIS GUIDEBOOK

What do you really need to have a great vacation in the Caribbean? Money. A round-trip ticket. A toothbrush. Maybe a passport. Not much more.

But you also need information. What are some informed choices of good places to stay, and then some good places to eat, shop, sightsee, or maybe just hang out? Which island should you be going to in the first place?

Our Penguin Caribbean writers tell you what you *really* need to know, what you can't find out so easily on your own. Where are the interesting, isolated, fun, or romantic places to stay within your budget, for example? The hotels and resorts described by our writers (each of whom is an experienced travel writer who regularly tours the island or islands he or she covers) are the *special* places, in all price ranges except for the very lowest—not the big, obvious places on every travel agent's CRT display and in advertised airline and travel-agency packages.

The Penguin Guide to the Caribbean 1989 is likewise designed for use *on* the island—to identify the truly out-of-the-ordinary restaurants, shops, music venues, activities, and sights, and the best way to "do" the island—as much as it is for trip planning and for choosing and reserving the accommodations.

By being selective, we make it easier for you to find the information you do want.

This guidebook is full of reliable and timely information, revised each year from a computer database updated by our writers. We would like to know if you think we've left out some very special place.

The Penguin Guide to the Caribbean 1989 projects hotel and resort rates for fall 1988 through spring 1989.

We trust you understand that these rates may change after the book goes to press in late 1988. The rates given here are intended only as rough guidelines for trip planning; call the individual booking offices (we supply the telephone numbers) for detailed and up-to-the-minute rate information.

ALAN TUCKER
General Editor
Penguin Travel Guides

40 West 23rd Street
New York, New York 10010
or
27 Wright's Lane
London W8 5TZ

CONTENTS

*The destinations appear in the order in which they lie
in the Caribbean, from the northwesternmost
(The Cayman Islands) clockwise to
the southwesternmost (Aruba).*

This Guidebook	v
Overview	5
Useful Facts	12
Bibliography	13
The Cayman Islands	21
Jamaica	30
Haiti	52
Dominican Republic	61
Puerto Rico	70
The United States Virgin Islands	89
The British Virgin Islands	105
St. Maarten/St. Martin	118
St. Barts (St. Barthélemy)	127
Anguilla	135
Saba	141
Statia (St. Eustatius)	147
St. Kitts and Nevis	153
Antigua and Barbuda	164
Montserrat	173
Guadeloupe	179
Dominica	188

Martinique	196
St. Lucia	207
Barbados	219
St. Vincent and the Grenadines	231
Grenada	245
Trinidad and Tobago	254
Bonaire	266
Curaçao	274
Aruba	284
Index	293

THE
PENGUIN
GUIDE
TO THE
CARIBBEAN
1989

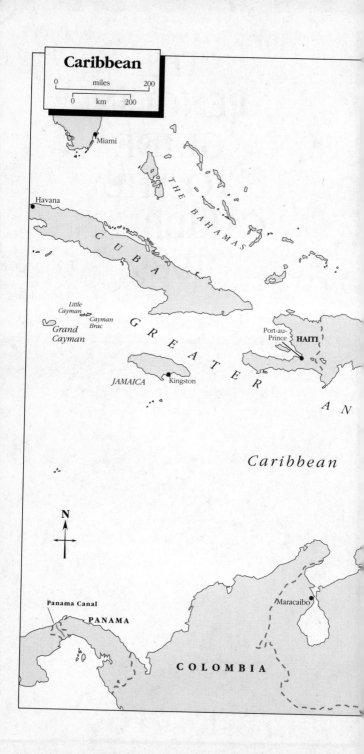

Caribbean

| 0 | miles | 200 |
| 0 | km | 200 |

Miami

THE BAHAMAS

Havana

CUBA

Little
Cayman

Cayman
Brac

Grand
Cayman

GREATER

Port-au-
Prince HAITI

JAMAICA Kingston

A N

Caribbean

N

Panama Canal

PANAMA

Maracaibo

COLOMBIA

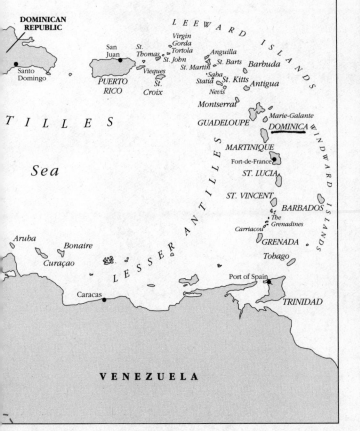

ATLANTIC
OCEAN

DOMINICAN
REPUBLIC

San
Juan

St.
Thomas

Virgin
Gorda
Tortola

St. John

LEEWARD ISLANDS

Anguilla

St. Barts

Barbuda

Santo
Domingo

Vieques

PUERTO
RICO

St.
Croix

St. Martin

Saba
Statia

Nevis

St. Kitts

Antigua

Montserrat

Marie-Galante

TILLES

GUADELOUPE

DOMINICA

WINDWARD ISLANDS

MARTINIQUE

Sea

Fort-de-France

ST. LUCIA

ST. VINCENT

BARBADOS

LESSER ANTILLES

The
Grenadines

Aruba

Bonaire

Curaçao

Carriacou

GRENADA

Tobago

Caracas

Port of Spain

TRINIDAD

VENEZUELA

OVERVIEW

By Julie Wilson

Julie Wilson, contributing editor for Town and Country *magazine, has written for* Travel & Leisure *magazine for over ten years. She has been food critic at* Connecticut *magazine and is the author of a book on St. Martin/St. Maarten.*

In a cold climate, where the winters stretch damp and chill to a distant spring, the most enviable of statements is, "I'm going to the Caribbean." The mental images are immediate and palpable—a blazing tropical sun, warm sand under foot, the gentle cooling of a tradewind, an infinity of stars in a night sky, coral reefs hiding colorful fish, hummingbirds and yellow birds darting among hibiscus and bougainvillea, rum punch at sunset, and palm trees stretching as far as the eye can see.

There's nothing wrong with the images; they're all valid. There is, however, something wrong with the enviable statement: The Caribbean is not an entity—it is a collection of separate, politically fragmented islands connected only by navigational charts and airline flight paths. Each island has a distinct personality, derived from its own particular history and defined by its geographical blessings and limitations. An island that once grew rich growing sugarcane is different from an island whose economy was based on smuggling and other methods of trade. An island colonized by the French has a different tone from an island colonized by the British or dominated by the Dutch. A flat, beachy island built up of coral has a different feeling from a lush, mountainous, volcanic island. To confuse the issue further, an island can be any, or all, of the above.

5

Nearly all the Caribbean islands were discovered by Christopher Columbus on his four New World voyages between 1492 and 1502. On his first, he discovered Cuba, the Bahamas, and Hispaniola (shared now by Haiti and the Dominican Republic). He also made contact with the Arawaks, peaceful Indians who lived in simple compounds and ate roots. On his second voyage, he may have wondered why he had been anxious to return—he discovered not only a lot of other islands but also the Carib Indians, warlike cousins of the Arawaks. The Caribs ate their captives. Nevertheless, Columbus persevered and discovered nearly all of the other islands in the Caribbean. Alonso de Ojeda, who sailed with Amerigo Vespucci, discovered Aruba, Curaçao, and Bonaire in 1499, while Columbus was busy up north. With more foresight than Columbus, Amerigo gave his name to everything on this side of the Atlantic north and south of the equator.

These islands were on the route to the riches of Mexico and Peru, and—what with countless sheltered harbors and hidden coves—they were a haven for traders, navies, smugglers, pirates, privateers, and buccaneers. The English, French, Swedes, Danes, Dutch, Portuguese—even the Latvians—squabbled over the Caribbean. The islands were treatied away, swapped, sold, fought over, fought on, bloodied, bartered, bargained off—always pawns in someone else's war. History's most romantic heroes and scoundrels sailed here: Sir Walter Raleigh and Sir Francis Drake, Blackbeard, Bluebeard and Captain Kidd, Captain Bligh, Horatio Nelson, and Peter Stuyvesant. Some islands changed hands so often that an eager colonial administrator arriving after a long sea voyage would find that his services were not necessary as the island would by then belong to another government.

The 17th century saw the beginning of the age of the planter, when great fortunes were made growing the sugarcane that Christopher Columbus introduced to the islands. Since the vast plantations required many workers, ruthless men also made fortunes by "trading around the Triangle." Whether the trader's home base was Europe or New England, the Triangle included a stop in Africa to pick up captured natives, a stop in the West Indies to sell those natives as slaves and pick up molasses, rum, or gold, and a trip back home to realize a fortune. Understandably, those years left a well-deserved legacy of resentment and mistrust. The planters also left the islands an architectural legacy—the colonial West Indian buildings that are today part of the Caribbean charm and the thousands of stone sugar mills scattered in open fields far behind the beautiful beaches.

With the abolition of slavery in the mid-19th century, agriculture became less lucrative than it had been. Nevertheless, agriculture (with mining and, later, oil refining) persisted as the economic mainstay for the better part of a century, until airplanes, tourism, and political independence shook things up. In the 1950s the Caribbean islands rapidly became a playground for wealthy foreigners, especially North Americans.

As more and more islands moved toward self-government, they became more self-absorbed while, paradoxically, absorbing the characteristics of the latest outsiders into their already separate cultures. Given the financial exigencies of newly independent nations, some of them traded away a newly discovered birthright to an international corporation.

The Caribbean islands now realize that financial independence—and clout—comes through unity, and they are making efforts toward practical regional cooperation.

Besides looking forward (politically and economically) the islands are also starting to look backward and inward, showing an interest in their own cultures and examining why they are who they are—both individually and collectively. Rediscovering their Amerindian heritage, they are protecting archaeological sites and establishing some extremely fine small museums. They are increasingly—and justifiably—proud of their West Indian cuisine and music.

The music of the Caribbean—the lilting, syncopated calypso, born in Trinidad and now universal—is instantly recognizable. Simple, musically unsophisticated, a tuneful narrative of local gossip, calypso is as slangy and catchy as the Caribbean voice, which, of course, varies from island to island. The accepted accompaniment is the steel drum, first hammered out of oil drums by the Trinidadians in the 1940s. Calypso was popularized around the world by Harry Belafonte, who sang about banana boats and about Matilda (who took his money and "run Venezuela") in the 1950s. To many, the New York-born Belafonte is still the ultimate Trinidadian. By the 1960s, when Bob Marley and other Jamaicans thrust into the public ear the revolutionary reggae (a kind of cross between calypso and rock, with a shuffle beat), West Indian music had crossed from folk over to mainstream popular music. Nevertheless, it still sounds best on its home turf. There are few travellers so jaded that they don't enjoy hearing "Yellow Bird" played on a steel drum on any island—even for the millionth time.

The West Indian, or Creole, cuisine of the Caribbean was for many years confined to home kitchens. As they dined on "Continental cuisine" in hotels, tourists could only imagine what those intriguing aromas wafting from home kitchens might promise. Now they know, for West Indian food has become easily available as the natives have discovered that tourists not only like it, they gobble it up. Each island has its own style of cooking, which, like the language, shows the influences of Africa, France, Spain, North America, Portugal, India, the Far Eastern ports of the trading ships—sometimes even the Arawaks.

As with most cuisines, West Indian cooking is based on what is readily at hand—and what is at hand is bountiful. From the sea come spiny *langoustes,* conch, red snapper, giant grouper, dolphinfish, and a raft of other fish. From the land come spices, pineapple, coconuts, limes, mangoes, breadfruit, papayas, christophines, eggplants, soursops, bananas, and avocados. From under the earth come sweet potatoes, yams, cassava, taro (also known as dasheen), and *bluggoe.* Nearly every fruit or vegetable has a different name on each island. The differences among these starchy vegetables are so interesting and subtle that West Indians find a foreigner's preoccupation with the potato quite perplexing. The potato is, to them, unchangingly uninteresting.

Variations aside, West Indian cuisine itself is pretty basic. Consider the ubiquitous hot sauce, a fiery and unsubtle condiment that adds piquancy when used sparingly and could lead to hospitalization if used unjudiciously. Or consider the *roti,* a distant, curried cousin of the Cornish pasty that looks like a pillowcase stuffed with laundry. Or the fragrant stews made of goat, pig, sheep, or free-road chicken; the variations on rice and peas; the stuffed land crabs; and the vegetable fritters. And remember that whatever the name, and whatever its island of origin, the dish will have been prepared with the uninhibited pleasure typical of the Caribbean.

Caribbean food and music come together at Carnival—the traditional hail and farewell to pleasures of the flesh preceding Ash Wednesday. But Carnival can occur at any time of the year throughout the islands, for it is primarily an island's celebration of itself . . . and an excuse to whoop it up. Many Carnivals are held in summer, when the children are home from school and off-island relatives can return on vacation. On southern islands, such as Aruba and Trinidad, Carnivals are nearly as lavish as Carnival in Rio; on small, less-Latin islands they may be very simple, hardly more than glorified bake sales. But almost anywhere, count on costumes, floats, local foods, and a jump-up.

Quintessentially Caribbean, a jump-up consists of steel bands swinging down the street, followed by a wild procession of everyone dancing, singing, clapping, and generally having the best time in the world. (Airline tickets may be scarce during an island's Carnival week. Unless the Carnival falls in February, during the high season, hotel rooms won't be a problem—those fellow passengers on the airplane are going home.)

But knowing the common culture and the common blessings (sun, sand, sea, and sports) doesn't explain why travellers often love one island above all others. The factors that go into that are as different as the range of human interests and inclinations.

Outstanding Characteristics of the Caribbean Islands

On most Caribbean islands you will find good beaches, plenty of water sports, a nice blend of European and North American cultural influences, West Indian ambience of some sort—in short, a little bit of everything. The following chart emphasizes the *special strengths of each island, as well as what you should **not** expect to find there.*

If an island destination comprises two or more places—as in Trinidad and Tobago—we have assigned numbers to each part. For example, in the shopping category, a number "2" is written in the U.S. Virgin Islands column, indicating that shopping is **outstandingly good** on St. Thomas—better even than the excellent shopping, say, on St. Croix.

Some islands are coded as follows:

1. Vieques	9. Trinidad
2. St. Thomas	10. Tobago
3. St. Croix and	11. St. Martin
St. John	12. St. Maarten
4. St. Croix	13. Nevis
5. Tortola	14. St. Kitts
6. Antigua	15. Carriacou
7. Barbuda	
8. The Grenadines	

	Cayman Islands	Jamaica	Haiti	Dominican Republic	Puerto Rico	U.S. Virgin Islands	British Virgin Islands	St. Martin/St. Maarten
Big-resort action		●			●			●
Chic and cosmopolitan								
White-sand beaches								●
Black-sand beaches								
No beaches								
Relative quiet							●	
Quiet								
Very low-keyed quiet								
Hiking and dramatic nature			●					
Birdwatching								
Yachting centers						●	●	
Especially good scuba diving	●					4		
Underwater snorkeling trails						3		
Surfing					1		5	
Especially good golf	●	●		●	●	4		
No golf								
Shopping (duty free)						2		●
Island arts and crafts		●	●		●			
Fine dining				●	●			●
Interesting local dishes								
West Indian music		●						
Casinos					●			12
No casinos								11
Spanish influence				●	●			
French influence			●					
Dutch influence								12
British influence		●						
Irish influence								
Luxury resorts on private islands							●	
Known for fine small inns								

St. Barts	Anguilla	Saba	Statia	St. Kitts and Nevis	Antigua and Barbuda	Montserrat	Guadeloupe	Dominica	Martinique	St. Lucia	Barbados	St. Vincent and the Grenadines	Grenada	Trinidad and Tobago	Bonaire	Curaçao	Aruba
•											•						
•	•			13	6								•				
			•	14		•											
		•															
					7			•		•				10			
		•	•	•		•						8					
							•	•		•			•				
								•						9	•		
					6							•					
		•	•													•	
	•													10			
							•				•						
											•						
•	•	•	•		7								15				
									•					9		•	•
•							•		•		•						
								•					•				
									•		•			9			
	•			•													•
•		•	•		7	•							•				
•							•		•								
		•	•												•	•	•
				•	•						•						
						•											
					6								•				
			•	•								8	•				

USEFUL FACTS

Local Time
With several exceptions, most Caribbean Islands observe Atlantic Standard Time, which is one hour ahead of Eastern Standard Time and four hours behind Greenwich Mean Time. Exceptions are the Cayman Islands, Haiti, and Jamaica, all of which observe Eastern Standard Time year-round.

Language
English is spoken widely on most islands. On the French islands (especially Martinique and Guadeloupe), a knowledge of French is useful, as is a knowledge of Spanish in the Dominican Republic and on parts of Puerto Rico. Every island has its local dialect or patois, made up—in different degrees—of English, French, Portuguese, Dutch, African, and Spanish.

When to Go
Generally, high season runs from December 15 through April 15. That's when most people want to go where it's 80 degrees and sunny, and consequently the prices are the highest. (Unless otherwise indicated, hotel rates listed in this book are double room, double occupancy, from fall through spring.) The weather in the fall months is likely to be unpredictable. Hurricane season is from August through November. Hurricanes occur infrequently—but when one comes, it's often a humdinger.

What to Wear
Although each island has its own degree of formality (covered at the end of each chapter), the general ground rule calls for loose-fitting sportswear, bathing suits, sunglasses, and a hat. Also sunscreen: the northernmost point of these islands (Port-de-Paix, Haiti) is only 20 degrees from the equator; the southernmost point (Galeota Point, Trinidad) is a mere 10 degrees from the equator.

Currency
Because currency varies among the islands, all prices have been listed in U.S. dollars for comparison purposes.

Nightlife
Except on some of the larger, more sophisticated islands, there is not much nightlife. After all that sun and daytime sporting activity, people are usually too bushed to stay up late. Some islands do have casinos, all the big hotels have evening entertainment, and even the smallest inn usually has a steel band in once a week.

Getting from Airport to Hotel
On some islands, you can pick up a rental car at the airport. On others, you'll have to take a taxi to the hotel, where a rental car will be delivered. On any island, it's a good idea to take a taxi first—if only to check out the local driving customs. Ask at the airport what the rate should be. And don't worry about finding a taxi; the drivers know when the planes come in.

BIBLIOGRAPHY
Some of the volumes listed below may be available only in the West Indies. Check with bookshops on the islands you visit for titles dealing with the area, local customs, and history.

General
QUENTIN CREWE. *Touch the Happy Isles* (1987). This British author takes the reader on a highly subjective tour of Caribbean civilization today.

PATRICK LEIGH FEMOR. *The Traveller's Tree: A Journey Through the Caribbean Islands* (1950). This richly detailed, insightful, and sensitive account resulted from the prize-winning author's now-classic journey through the Caribbean in the 1940s.

IDAZ GREENBERG. *The Guide to Corals and Fishes of Florida, the Bahamas and the Caribbean.* Indispensible guidebook to the area's teeming marine life, with color illustrations.

LENNOX HONYCHURCH. *The Caribbean People,* three volumes (1981). A lively, well-balanced history of the West

Indies by one of the leaders of the Caribbean's "New Historians."

IAN KEOWN. *Ian Keown's Caribbean Hideaways* (1988). Guide to the Caribbean's smaller hostelries by a longtime authority on these frequently overlooked tropical inns and guest houses. Up to date and reliable.

BOB SHACOCHIS. *Easy in the Islands* (1985). Short stories that vividly (and sometimes raunchily) capture the vitality and color of the tropics. Winner of the American Book Award for 1986.

KAY SHOWKER. *Caribbean Ports of Call* (1987). Well-researched guide for cruise-ship travellers.

SUZANNE SLESIN AND STAFFORD CLIFF. *Caribbean Style* (1985). Superbly illustrated photographic survey of West Indian domestic architecture from 18th-century estate houses to the hideaways of today's "beautiful people."

ERIC WILLIAMS. *From Columbus to Castro: The History of the Caribbean, 1492–1967* (1970). Scholarly, very thorough chronicle of the West Indies by the former prime minister of Trinidad and Tobago.

HERMAN WOUK. *Don't Stop the Carnival* (1965). Although set in fictional "Amerigo," this novel has attained the status of a classic throughout the Caribbean. Visitors inquiring about expatriate life in the tropics are almost certain to be asked in turn, "Have you read *Don't Stop the Carnival?*" Be prepared.

Aruba
JOHANN HARTOG. *Aruba*. History of the island that also provides valuable pointers on touring Aruba. Illustrated with color photographs.

Bonaire
JOHANN HARTOG. *Bonaire*. An armchair tour of Bonaire, illustrated with 90 pages of photographs by Chris and Donna McLaughlin. In English, Dutch, French, German, and Spanish.

JOHANN HARTOG. *History of Bonaire* (1975). Detailed narrative traces the island's rich past. Black-and-white photographs.

TOM VAN'T HOF. *Guide to the Bonaire Marine Park* (1983). Guide to the Park's marine and coral reef ecosystems. Detailed suggestions are given for diving and snorkeling at each site in the park. Photographs and maps.

PEER REIJNS. *Excursion Guide to Washington/Slagbaai National Park* (1984). Nontechnical guide to the park includes descriptions of the sites, plants, and animals to be discovered there.

British Virgin Islands

JOHN ROUSMANIERE. *The Sailing Lifestyle.* Quite technical in its approach, this should prove indispensible for those intending to explore the islands, cays, and reefs of the B.V.I. by boat.

ROBB WHITE. *Two on the Isle.* Charming autobiographical account of how the author and his wife discovered the British Virgins and set about building a home that eventually became Marina Cay Hotel.

Cayman Islands

PETER MATTHIESSEN. *Far Tortuga* (1975). Novel that deals with sailors and the sea and has been compared with the works of Conrad and Stevenson.

ROBERT LOUIS STEVENSON. *Treasure Island* (1883). Young Jim Hawkins, Blind Pew, Long John Silver, and all those "Yo-ho-hos."

NEVILLE WILLIAMS. *A History of the Cayman Islands* (1970). Overview of an island that is as popular with financial types as it is with sun seekers.

Curaçao

TOM VAN'T HOF AND HELEEN COMET. *Guide to Curaçao Underwater Park.* Comprehensive guide to dive sites, along with general information about the park.

GEORGE S. LEWBEL. *Curaçao Underwater.* Scuba and snorkeling guide to the waters along Curaçao's southern coastline.

PEER REIJNS. *Excursion Guide to the Christoffel Park.* Handy suggestions for three driving tours and one on foot that include information about flora and fauna that may be encountered along the way.

JOS DE ROO. *Curaçao—Scenes and Behind the Scenes.* General history of Curaçao, along with suggested walking tours of Willemstad and excursions into the countryside.

Dominica
LENNOX HONYCHURCH. *The Cabrits and Prince Ruperts Bay* (1982). The inside story of the restoration of Dominica's major historical monument.

LENNOX HONYCHURCH. *The Dominica Story: A History of the Island* (1984). Candid, no-holds-barred study by a member of a long-time island family.

JEAN RHYS. *Wide Sargasso Sea* (1982). In this fascinating spin-off of Brontë's *Jane Eyre,* Rhys recreates in fictional form plantation life in 19th-century Dominica.

ANTHONY TROLLOPE. *The West Indies and the Spanish Main* (1859). What Dominica was like in the mid-1800s; clear-eyed and, expectably, well written.

Dominican Republic
SAMUEL HAZARD. *Santo Domingo Past and Present; with a Glance at Hayti* (1982). Originally published in 1873, this captures the feeling of life in the area during the 19th century. Illustrated with exquisite line drawings.

Grenada
NORMA SINCLAIR. *Grenada, Isle of Spice* (1987). Helpful hints for touring the island, destination by destination. Some general historical and social background.

Guadeloupe
LAFCADIO HEARN. *Two Years in the French West Indies* (1890). Colorful descriptions of life on Guadeloupe and Martinique during the late 19th century.

SAINT-JOHN PERSE (ALEXIS SAINT-LEGER LEGER). *Anabasis* (1924). Modern verse of great emotional power by the Nobel Prize-winning poet born in Guadeloupe in 1887.

Haiti
AIME CESAIRE. *The Tragedy of King Christophe* (1969). Drama depicting the last days of Henri Christophe, must reading for anyone visiting the Citadelle.

HERBERT COLE. *Christophe, King of Haiti* (1967). Biography of Henri Christophe.

GRAHAM GREENE. *The Comedians* (1972). Novel depicting the dark days of the Duvalier regime.

SELDEN RODMAN. *Artists in Tune with Their World: Masters of Popular Art in the Americas and Their Relation to the Folk Tradition* (1982). Forty-page section on Haiti offers a comprehensive look at the "primitive" art Rodman himself did much to encourage.

Jamaica

LADY MARY NUGENT. *Lady Nugent's Journal* (1939). Intriguing insights into Jamaican life in the early 1800s, when "sugar, slaves, and sin" were as common as "sea, sun, and sand" today.

PHILIP WRIGHT AND PAUL F. WHITE. *Exploring Jamaica: A Guide for Motorists* (1968). An indispensible companion for those bent on discovering some of Jamaica's most out-of-the-way attractions. Thorough and, best of all, reliable.

Martinique

TRUMAN CAPOTE. *Music for Chameleons* (1975). In the title story, Capote captures in lyrical prose the beauty, strangeness, and sophistication of Martinique.

ANDRE CASTELOT. *Josephine* (1967). Biography of Marie Josèphe Rose Tascher de La Pagerie, better known to the world as "The Empress Josephine." Colorful and moving.

AIME CESAIRE. *The Collected Poetry* (1983). Translated by Clayton Eshleman and Annette Smith. Lyric verse by internationally acclaimed Martinique poet and mayor of Fort-de-France. (In French and English.)

EUZHAN PALCY. *Sugar Cane Alley* (*La Rue Cases Nègres*). Orion Classics film directed and adapted by Palcy from the novel by Joseph Zobl. Filmed in Martinique, a sensitive depiction of a boy's coming of age in the 1920s. (In French, with English subtitles.) Available on videocassette.

GORDON THOMAS AND MAX MORGAN WITTS. *The Day the World Ended* (1969). Riveting account of the events leading up to the Mont Pelée volcanic explosion of 1902 and the destruction of St. Pierre.

Nevis

JOYCE GORDON. *Nevis: Queen of the Caribees* (1985). Guidebook with an especially good coverage of the island's intriguing history—Admiral Nelson, Alexander Hamilton, et al.

Puerto Rico

OSCAR LEWIS. *La Vida* (1966). Poignant account of slum life in *La Perla* in Old San Juan.

Puerto Rico: A Guide to the Island of Boriquén. Excellent 1930s WPA-sponsored guide to the island.

Qué Pasa. Superb, free, monthly guide produced by the Tourism Office and an essential reference work for day-to-day events in music, dance, theater, art, sports, festivals, night spots, and holidays.

CHRISTOPHER RAND. *The Puerto Ricans* (1971). Beautifully written social study of the Puerto Rican people and their lives as new arrivals on the mainland.

Saba

JOHANN HARTOG. *History of Saba* (1975). Brief but always intriguing summary of three centuries of Saban life. (Illustrated.)

WILL JOHNSON. *Tales from My Grandmother's Pipe* (1979). Saban lore, charmingly recounted by one of the leading young authorities on the island.

St. Eustatius

YPIE ATTEMA. *St. Eustatius: A Short History of the Island and Its Monuments* (1976). A concise overview compiled by one of the authorities involved in the restoration of Fort Oranje in the early 1970s.

WOUT VAN DEN BOR. *Island Adrift: The Social Organization of a Small Caribbean Community: The Case of St. Eustatius* (1981). Scholarly, if sometimes over-simplified, study of the political, societal make-up of the island.

JOHANN HARTOG. *History of St. Eustatius*. Skimpy but interesting, nonetheless. His *Bovenwindse Eilanden* (1964) (only in Dutch, unfortunately) is far more informative.

ELEANOR HECKERT. *The Golden Rock* (1971). Historical adventure novel set during the late 1700s that captures much of the flavor of that boisterous period.

A. H. VERSTEEG AND F. R. EFFERT. *Golden Rock: The First Indian Village on St. Eustatius* (1986). Slightly stilted but comprehensive survey of pre-Columbian St. Eustatius.

St. Lucia
CHRIS DOYLE. *The Sailor's Guide to the Windward Islands* (1980). The author, a long-time shipper of the island, provides vital, often amusing—if not the most literate— information on getting around by boat.

HARRIET F. DURHAM AND FLORENCE LEWISOHN. *St. Lucia Tours and Tales* (1971). This homespun volume offers a charming but biased exploration of the island's histories and highways.

St. Maarten/St. Martin
JOHANN HARTOG. *St. Maarten, Saba, St. Eustatius* (1974). Written before tourism reached full flower on St. Maarten, this is somewhat dated in certain areas, yet nonetheless valuable for its historical and cultural background information.

St. Vincent and the Grenadines
BOBOROW AND JENKINS. *St. Vincent and the Grenadines* (1987). Lushly illustrated coffee-table book with informative introduction, plus selected verse by Canadian writer Margaret Atwood, a longtime island enthusiast.

EARLE KIRBY. *Guide to Selected Attractions on the Island of St. Vincent* (1987). The title tells it all; magazine-size scholarly Baedeker to historic sites and other attractions.

Trinidad and Tobago
David Frost Introduces Trinidad and Tobago (1975). Collection of articles written by authorities in various fields, subjects including steel bands, Carnival, natural history, sports, growing up in Tobago, calypso, and much more.

MALCOLM BARCANT. *The Butterflies of Trinidad and Tobago* (1970). Comprehensive, fully illustrated text contains information on more than 622 species. The author collected butterflies for almost half a century and has bred and cross-bred various species.

G.A.C. HERKLOTS. *The Birds of Trinidad and Tobago* (1972). Covers more than 400 species with more than 260 illustrations, most by the author. Essential for visiting birders.

V. S. NAIPUL. *A House for Mr. Biswas* (1962). Perhaps the best-known of the internationally acclaimed Trinidadian author's novels. Set on the island, it sensitively depicts life among the East Indian population.

ERIC WILLIAMS. *History of the People of Trinidad and Tobago* (1964). Written by Trinidad's first prime minister as a gift to the people on the eve of the country's independence (August 31, 1962). First full history of the two islands.

THE CAYMAN ISLANDS

By Anita Gates

Anita Gates, an author whose work has appeared in Travel & Leisure, Mademoiselle, *and other magazines, is a consultant to American Express and a contributing editor at* Frequent Flyer *magazine.*

There's a real sense of privilege about being in the Cayman Islands these days. Apart from the fact that half the people may be here just to visit their money, there's the basic issue of being able to afford the place. Not everything is expensive, of course, but the occasional paperback book with a hardcover price tag might startle a first-time visitor, just as the price of Scotch in Tokyo has taken foreigners aback for years.

The average Caymanian exudes a quiet, take-it-all-for-granted self-confidence, the sort of demeanor Americans used to see among 25-year-olds who had made a good deal of money on Wall Street. But then Caymanians have many reasons to feel secure. Their economy is strong, their political climate as stable as they come (it's a British Crown Colony), and the almost 500 banks here provide an enviable standard of living for residents as well as an "offshore financial center" (read tax haven) for outsiders. Tourism is just the icing on the cake.

MAJOR INTEREST

Underwater beauty for divers and snorkelers
Seven Mile Beach's calm, clear waters
A very civilized social atmosphere

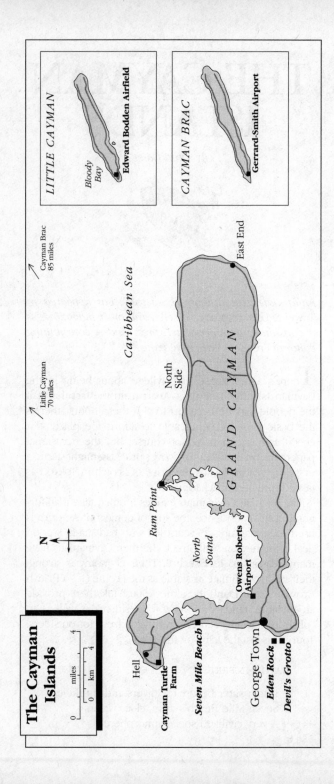

The Cayman Islands are less than 500 miles south of Miami, and about 200 miles northwest of Jamaica. The main island, 76-square-mile **Grand Cayman**, is by far the most popular destination. The two smaller islands, **Cayman Brac** and **Little Cayman**, are favored by serious divers and lovers of ultra-secluded—and that's no kidding—vacations, but everyone should see one or both at least once (each is a half-hour flight away, about $80 round trip).

The only question seems to be: if you're not a devoted diver or snorkeler, are the Caymans still a destination for you? Underwater—there's no argument—these are among the most beautiful islands around. Grand Cayman is actually the top of a huge sunken mountain. Visibility below is 100 to 125 feet year round, and snorkelers only have to go about 150 yards out to see some spectacular examples of what the rest of the mountain down here looks like. Diving instruction for beginners is widely available. On land there is an attraction, too: Seven Mile Beach.

Seven Mile Beach

Back in the 1970s, when tourism was just beginning here, the divers had their dive resorts and their live-aboard boats, and the financial types had their houses and condos. For the sun-and-sand vacationer, there were clean, pleasant hotel rooms—adequate but hardly luxurious. When the **Hyatt Regency Grand Cayman** opened in December 1986, all that changed.

The Hyatt, which sits across the road from Seven Mile Beach like a giant Wedgwood blue sculpture, was the first luxury resort to open its doors on Grand Cayman. Guests have gardens, pools, a swim-up bar, and restaurants, all set in a grand British Colonial atmosphere. A short walk away is the hotel beach club with its restaurant and water sports facility.

The **Grand Pavilion Hotel** next door has perhaps the most elegant rooms on the island, some decorated with Louis XV-style furniture and canopied beds. It was designed with business travellers in mind, but there's a courtyard pool and a beach-privileges arrangement with the Holiday Inn.

Before these hotels were built, vacationers looking for

luxury often rented apartments in one of the island's oceanfront condominium complexes. Renting is still a good idea, especially for those who want larger units. **Lacovia**, on Seven Mile Beach near the Hyatt, is one of the most elegant complexes. Those who prefer a more se-cluded, casual setting, but with resort extras such as pool, tennis courts, and sauna, favor **The Retreat at Rum Point**, located on the north central coast.

The **Treasure Island Resort**, just off Seven Mile Beach, opened in 1987, and brought a Nashville connection to the Caymans. Country singers Conway Twitty, Larry Gat-lin, and Ronnie Milsap are among the owners; fans are among the guests. The stars have been known to perform here, but it's hard to predict just when that will happen. The rooms are more functional than glamorous, but room rates are lower than the Hyatt's.

The best reason to go to Treasure Island, however, is to see Sons of the Beach play at Silver's. Their evening of fifties and sixties nostalgia eventually has almost everyone dancing and/or singing along to hits from their senior year—whenever it was. Friday night is the time to go. (Because of the Caymans' Sunday liquor laws, the last Saturday night drinks are served at midnight.)

Until Sons of the Beach came along, Barefoot Man's show at the Holiday Inn was the essence of island night-life. It's still the best spot to get a fix of "Montego Bay," "Yellowbird," and other quintessentially Caribbean fare.

Dining and Shopping

For a fashionable dinner, head back to the Hyatt. Its **Garden Loggia Café** is as likely to serve up lobster ravioli or whole wheat fettucine in jalapeño cream sauce as broiled turtle steak. The most formal French dinner in town can be had at **Le Diplomat** in the Grand Pavilion. For a romantic setting try **Chef Tell's Grand Old House** (owned by TV chef Tell Erhardt). It's set in the old Petra Plantation, a Victorian house with a big porch and sea views. Most people also drive out to the northwest tip of the island to **Ristorante Pappagallo** for northern Italian cuisine and seafood served in a thatched-roof Polynesian-style setting. Diners may find themselves surrounded by live (and often very vocal) tropical birds.

The **Cracked Conch** (just the sort of seafood place it

sounds like) and **Santiago's** (for Mexican food and marga-
ritas), both right across from Seven Mile Beach, are more
casual restaurants.

It may sound as though everything is within easy walking distance on Grand Cayman, and that's certainly true of
the Seven Mile Beach neighborhood. This is the heart of
Cayman Islands tourism, its main road lined with hotels,
condos, restaurants, and even small shopping centers. Yet
it's unlikely ever to become a "strip," partly because of
the law against high-rises. The pristine white-sand beach
is as quiet and laid-back as any escapist could want.
Downtown **George Town** is probably the best bet for
shopping. The local specialty is black coral, sold mostly in
the form of jewelry. This British Crown Colony's wedding
present to Prince Charles and Princess Diana was a black
coral cutlery set.

Around the Island

Grand Cayman offers limited sightseeing. The best-known
spot on the island is probably the "village" of Hell, near
Seven Mile Beach. A backyard-size landscape of jagged
blackened limestone formations, Hell has its own post
office from which visitors can send home postmarked
cards inscribed with clever comments ("Came here in a
handbasket," "Finally took your advice," etc.).

Nearby is the Cayman Turtle Farm, where thousands of
turtles are bred for turtle steak and tortoiseshell gift
items. If you're a U.S. citizen or just passing through the
States on your way home, forget the latter; it's illegal to
bring in turtle products. More ecologically responsible
visitors can arrange to have a baby turtle or two set free
(about $4 apiece). Sponsors don't actually get to see the
hatchlings let loose on the beach to fend for themselves,
but they are given Turtle Release Certificates to prove
good intentions. The survival rate, researchers say, is
pretty good.

One of the newest attractions on Grand Cayman is the
50-foot-long Atlantis submarine, which takes 28 passengers down 150 feet for a close-up view of tropical fish,
coral, sponges and undersea cliffs—all in air-conditioned
comfort. The night dives, illuminated by the sub's flood-
lights, are more colorful than daytime trips. The sub
leaves from George Town Harbour.

Scuba divers and snorkelers will find impressive underwater sites all around Grand Cayman. Some maps actually show dive sites instead of streets. Among the best sites: **Eden Rock** and **Devil's Grotto**, both off the southwestern coast just below George Town; and the wall at Little Cayman's **Bloody Bay**.

Fishing, catamaran cruises, swimming, parasailing, windsurfing, and virtually every other water sport known to man are available throughout the island. There are also tennis courts, and a golf course where players use the Cayman ball, which only goes half as far as the normal one. Jack Nicklaus designed the Britannia course (part of the Hyatt Regency complex), and it's described as "a tough nine but a forgiving eighteen."

Even the most gregarious of visitors should at least see the secluded but breathtakingly beautiful area of the island around **Rum Point**. It's a half-hour or so drive from Seven Mile Beach.

One of Grand Cayman's newest attractions is also one of its most popular: the Maritime Museum. Located at the edge of downtown George Town, it offers a well-done slide show on island history, a small but interesting collection of sunken treasures, and an unusual talking Blackbeard.

Pirates And Other Influences

The Caymans are one of the most pirate-oriented island groups in the Caribbean—the annual island celebration, originally organized to attract off-season tourists, is Pirates Week—and the local fascination with buccaneers is based on fact. Sir Henry Morgan first landed here in 1670. Edward Teach, the aforementioned Blackbeard, was doing dastardly deeds at Grand Cayman as early as 1717. As any reader of *Treasure Island* knows, it was Blackbeard who shot and lamed his gunner Israel Hands just for the fun of it. And Neal Walker stored much of his pirate treasure in a cache at Grand Cayman's East End.

Sir Walter Scott had a character in his novel *The Pirate* describe the mood of the islands in the 1720s: "Is he dead? It is a more serious question here than it would be on the Grand Caymains or the Bahama Islands where a brace or two of fellows may be shot in the morning and no more heard of, or asked about them than if they were so many wood pigeons."

The islands' most famous seafaring tale, however, has nothing to do with pirates. In 1778 ten British ships collided in the Wreck of the Ten Sails and Cayman citizens rescued all of the victims. The legend goes that King George III was so grateful he decreed that Caymanians would never have to pay taxes. (In reality, they still don't. The Caymans are virtually free from both personal and corporate taxation—and absolute financial secrecy is the law.) The real moral of the story is that Caymanians were, and are, mostly nice folks. Residents brag about the racial harmony here which, they'll explain, is the result of centuries of intermarriage. When black people with blond hair tell you this, it's convincing.

If Caymanians are tolerant, it is partly because they started out in the 1600s as a racial hodgepodge of settlers—Scots, Welsh, Jamaicans, Africans, and the British from Cromwell's army—who came to the Caymans to start a new life. If Caymanians are sophisticated, it's partly because Cayman men have always been seafarers and have brought a certain worldliness back home with them.

Today the Caymans are the picture of domestic tranquility, and the template of a virtually crime-free society. Be advised: The penalty for drug use is stiff. In fact, penalties in general are pretty draconian. One local homeowner, a transplanted European, tells of being slapped with a $500 fine and five years' probation for a speeding ticket.

USEFUL FACTS

What to Wear
Summer resortwear is appropriate year round.

Getting In
Most visitors enter the Caymans via the Owen Roberts International Airport outside George Town on Grand Cayman. Cayman Airways has nonstop flights from Miami, Houston, Atlanta, and Tampa, with special nonstops from several other North American cities during high season. Northwest Airlines flies nonstop from Memphis, and Eastern from Miami. Air Canada has flights from Toronto and Montreal to Miami. Qantas flies from Sydney to Los An-

geles and San Francisco, where connections can be made with a U.S. carrier.

Pan Am and Cayman Airways have also established an "air partnership" (feeder network), which means visitors can take any Pan Am flight from London or another U.S. city to New York or Miami and connect with a Cayman Airways flight. All ticketing, seat assignments, luggage checking, and the like are handled by Pan Am at the point of origin.

Entry Requirements
No passport or visa is required to enter the Caymans. U.S., Canadian, and British citizens need proof of identity only.

Currency
Cayman Islands dollar.

Electrical Current
Same as in the U.S. and Canada—110 volts, 60 cycles.

Getting Around
Cayman Airways links Grand Cayman with Cayman Brac and Little Cayman. Flights are approximately 30 minutes.

From the airport it's a $9–$14 taxi ride to most Seven Mile Beach hotels. Taxi drivers charge flat rates, so fares should be discussed at the outset.

Major rental car companies have offices here. Unlimited-mileage rates start at about $22 daily off-season. Cars are a necessity only for those staying or touring outside the Seven Mile Beach area. Buses run regularly along the Seven Mile Beach road to and from George Town.

Business Hours
Most businesses and stores operate on a nine-to-five schedule.

Festivals
The Cayman's major seasonal events are Pirates Week, at the end of October, and Million Dollar Month Fishing Tournament, an angling competition that lasts throughout June.

ACCOMMODATIONS REFERENCE

The rate ranges given here are projections for fall 1988 through spring 1989. Unless otherwise indicated, rates are for double rooms, double occupancy. The telephone area code for the Caymans is 809.

▶ **Grand Pavilion Hotel.** P.O. Box 69, Grand Cayman, BWI. $95–$225. Tel: 947-4666.

▶ **Hyatt Regency Grand Cayman.** P.O. Box 1698, Grand Cayman, BWI. $175–$350. Tel: 949-1234; in U.S., (800) 228-9000.

▶ **Lacovia Condominiums.** P.O. Box 1998, Grand Cayman, BWI. $200–$400 (all suites). Tel: 949-7599.

▶ **The Retreat at Rum Point.** P.O. Box 46, North Side, Grand Cayman, BWI. $160–$360 (all suites). Tel: 947-9535; in U.S., (800) 423-2422.

▶ **Treasure Island Resort.** P.O. Box 1817, Grand Cayman, BWI. $120–$210. Tel: 949-7777; in U.S., (800) 874-0027 (reservations); or (800) 251-3052 (information).

OTHER ACCOMMODATIONS

▶ **Southern Cross Club.** Little Cayman, BWI. $110, including 3 meals. Tel: 948-3255. Small (10 rooms), comfortable (bordering on rustic) hotel with scuba diving, deep sea fishing, and snorkeling. Does not accept credit cards.

▶ **Tiara Beach Hotel.** Cayman Brac, BWI. $70–$180. Tel: 948-7313; in U.S., (607) 277-3484 or (800) 367-3484. Small (58 rooms), less rustic than Southern Cross, with air conditioning, a pool, tennis court, scuba diving (of course), and snorkeling.

JAMAICA

By Jennifer Quale

Jennifer Quale contributes travel-related articles to Travel & Leisure, Vogue, Connoisseur, Food and Wine, *and other magazines and newspapers. She has lived in the Caribbean and reports on that area frequently.*

Jamaica is one of those places where you never want the days to end, where you never want to leave. Noel Coward never wanted to say goodbye forever, so he was buried there. Whenever Ian Fleming had to leave, it was always with a lump in his throat. Even Errol Flynn, despite his self-confessed "wicked ways," remained faithful to the end. And Bob Marley brought it all home. Unlike one-dimensional islands, Jamaica is—as the old advertising campaign claimed—more than a beach. It is a staggeringly diverse country of two million people, the most complex nation in the Caribbean—from its many-sided culture to its distinctive cuisine. The landscape is so varied, so lush, and so beautiful that you can't take your eyes off it. And the people, especially beyond the major tourist centers, are proud, engaging, and full of grave drama. Still, the best reason to go to Jamaica is to be captivated by the seductive rhythms that keep the rest of the world at bay.

MAJOR INTEREST

Jamaica's special seductive qualities
Jamaican art and music
The classic hotels
Rafting on the Rio Grande

The town of Port Antonio
Blue Lagoon
Noel Coward's house
Kingston
The Blue Mountains near Kingston
Good Hope Plantation
The South Coast
The beaches

Most first-time visitors land in Montego Bay, the island's primary resort area and second largest city, to stay
in one of the many beach-front hotels strung along the
North Coast—the Jamaican Riviera—from Negril to Ocho
Rios. But the intrepid traveller who wants more than to
bake on a beach might land in Kingston, the country's
capital and cultural mecca, cradled in the 7,400-foot Blue
Mountain range. From Kingston, it's a relatively easy two-
hour drive along the coast to Port Antonio on the north-
easternmost point of the island, the niche that Jamaicans
refer to as the "real Jamaica." The bare-bones adventurer
seeking something completely different, remote even by
Jamaican standards, will find it on the South Coast,
reached within a couple of hours from Montego Bay.
Although in a week's time it's possible to make a clean
sweep from Montego Bay and west to Negril, down to the
South Coast and back to the north to Ocho Rios and Port
Antonio, then on to Kingston, such a journey is not recommended. You would never get out of the car. It's best to
pick one or two spots and save the rest for the next visit.

The ideal way to get around is by rental car; on the map
distances appear to be short but roads are often winding,
skimpy, and clogged with life of their own (road life,
especially in the villages, is the soul of Jamaica). Then,
too, many of Jamaica's hotels and villas are so enticing
that you may be loath to leave their confines. Thanks to
300 years of British rule, the tradition of service in Jamaica still holds fast, even though the country has been
independent since 1962.

To understand the layout of Jamaica, imagine the island's shape as the profile of a manatee (this endangered
species, which fed the sailor's legend of the mermaid,
actually thrives on the island's South Coast) swimming
toward the west. At the head is Negril, with the South
Coast stretching from there down to the flipper; at the top

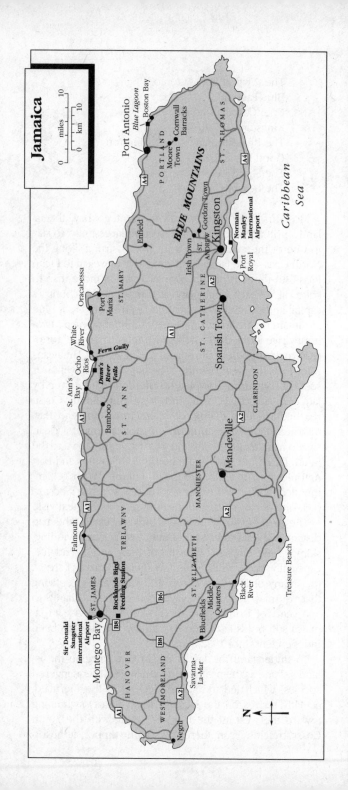

of the tail, Port Antonio. Midway between Negril and Port Antonio, on the North Coast—or cresting the spine—is Montego Bay, with Ocho Rios half again as far as Port Antonio, and Kingston on the tail's underside.

Montego Bay Area

The atmosphere at the airport in Montego Bay sets the tone of this overdeveloped resort town even before you get out of the terminal: a troupe of young women in traditional dress singing "Jamaica Farewell" flanks the immigration area, while a welcome bar dispenses lethal rum punches to throngs of eager tourists. There are few good reasons to stay in Montego Bay: you will probably push on to the (literally) greener pastures of the North Coast or head down to the South Coast, with a brief stop in Negril.

During the 1950s and 1960s, when the American rich and titled British made Montego Bay, a.k.a. Mobay, their winter place in the sun, the town peaked as the social center of the Caribbean. With jumbo jets and package deals, Montego Bay's highly exclusive status went out with the 1970s. Then, as now, the place to stay was the intimate, magical **Round Hill Hotel** (about ten miles west of town)—unless you preferred the wider open spaces of **Tryall Golf, Tennis and Beach Club**, two miles farther west, developed by Texans who felt cramped at Round Hill. (There are people who go to Jamaica just to play golf at Tryall's championship course, one of the Caribbean's best.)

Like most of Jamaica's better hotels, Tryall and Round Hill are built on the villa concept; although accommodations can be had in the main buildings, hang the cost, if you can, and go for the private, fully staffed villas, many of which have their own pool (at Tryall some of the villas have two pools). In its heyday, the loyal cadre of guests at Round Hill included the likes of Noel Coward, Oscar Hammerstein, and Jack Kennedy. While you might bump into Paul McCartney or Ralph Lauren on Round Hill's melon slice of a beach, today's typical guest is more likely to be an American or European tycoon. In February, Round Hill—like the rest of fashionable Jamaica—is deluged with the Old Guard, including die-hard colonials who've given up their major holdings on the island.

During school holidays (except summer when the hotel is partially closed), families are in abundance, yet children never intrude on the power-party atmosphere that prevails come nightfall.

Even if you don't stay in Mobay, lunch or dinner at the **Sugar Mill Restaurant**, formerly the Half Moon Club House Grill, about ten miles east of town across from the Half Moon Club Hotel, is worth a detour from anywhere in Jamaica: it's unquestionably the best table on the island. Chef Hans Schenk, a Swiss expatriate, approaches traditional Jamaican ingredients with a singularly *nouvelle* spirit, bringing forth such specialties as fettucine tossed with smoked marlin (a North Coast catch), chocho (a West Indian squash) vichyssoise, and show-stopping desserts that make the most of the fine, local Appleton rum. Everything is fresh, even the hearts of palm for which Schenk sacrifices trees from the Sugar Mill's plantation grounds, and the wine cellar is remarkable for the Caribbean. The moderately expensive restaurant caters to *soigné* but casual patrons who may linger on the candlelit terrace long after the last cup of perfect Blue Mountain coffee is poured. (Ironically, Jamaica produces the world's most expensive, exquisite coffee, but the bulk of it is shipped to Japan, making a good cup hard to find on the island.) Reservations are essential here (Tel: 953-2314). Like many fine restaurants in Jamaica, the Sugar Mill offers complimentary transportation within a radius of 15 miles or so.

While Haiti has always been considered the Caribbean hub of primitive art, Jamaica's own intuitive vision has finally come to canvas. Until recently, the art scene was confined to Kingston's hallowed museums and schools, but now galleries of all sorts (including bamboo shacks on the roadside) flourish along the North Coast. The best of these is **The Gallery of West Indian Art** opposite the Parish Church in downtown Mobay, which carries works of the leading artists of Jamaica as well as of Haiti. Often the artists are self-taught. Such is the case with Hyacinth. The gallery owner helped Hyacinth, an erstwhile laundress, parlay her sense of color and embroidery into a dazzling output of painted cedar sculptures. When enthusiasts of folk art see this Noah's Ark of whimsical creatures, they will want to buy out the lot. You might combine a visit to the gallery (which occasionally closes at lunchtime) with lunch next door at the pubby **Town House Restaurant**, a spot that is deservedly popular with locals.

Just beyond nearby Tara estate, Route B 8 (a.k.a. Long Hill Road) leads to the **Rocklands Bird Feeding Station**. In Jamaica, 252 species of birds have been recorded, 24 of them endemic. The country's national bird (Jamaica makes much ado of her many national attributes) is one of these species that has never been found elsewhere: the Doctor Bird. The most likely explanation of this hummingbird's name is that its twin streamer tail resembles a doctor's stethoscope. Normally rather shy and elusive, the Doctor Bird turns genial host in the Rocklands setting. Daily bird feeding for visitors begins afternoons at 3:30, but naturalist Lisa Salmon, who established the sanctuary 30 years ago, welcomes card-carrying bird watchers any time of day.

About two miles further inland on B 8, just after the Mt. Carey Health Clinic, **The Antique Furniture Shop Ltd.** houses not antiques but stunning reproductions in native mahogany, as well as the small factory that makes them. Paulette Jackson, matriarch of the family operation, will make anything to order ("as long as it's wood"), and will ship anywhere.

To see Montego Bay's rural environs, take the **Hilton High Day Tour** (tel: 952-3343) (named for the modest plantation house it visits) that stages a luncheon of roast suckling pig and an optional hot-air balloon ride. The tour's hosts pick up participants in a van wherever they're staying in Mobay.

Negril

The 50-mile drive west from Montego Bay to Negril is far more interesting than the town of Negril itself, which consists of little more than a ramshackle shopping mall. Just beyond Tryall, the ruins of Kenilworth Estate recall the opulent era when sugar was king and when even the mills took on the dimensions and details, among them Palladian windows, of the planters' great houses. (By mid-18th century, the island boasted some 400 sugar estates, making it then the world's largest sugar producer and England's richest colony.)

Now, every Jamaican has a stake in the tourism-based

economy, as the proliferation of one-man shops—sort of bamboo lean-tos—along the road suggests. Enterprising and persistent to a fault, the Jamaican vendor will run after your car with merchandise in hand if you happen to make eye contact with him. Works of art in themselves, many of the shanty shops are painted in contrasting neon pastels.

When the numerous fruit stands along the road give way to chockablock tee-shirt shacks, you know you're in Negril, primarily recognized for its evolution from being a haven for hippies in the 1960s to its present status as Jamaica's self-styled center of hedonism.

Unless you like nude volleyball, the most agreeable activity in Negril is walking the not quite seven-miles-long beach in the early morning while the hedonists sleep. The modest Sundowner Hotel, Negril's first guesthouse, offers a good starting point and a nice spot for breakfast on the beach. Norman Rockwell used to stay here in the 1950s, before the waves of ganja started rolling along the beach. Artists today are more apt to stay on the cliffside of Negril at the **Rockhouse**, an enchanting cluster of thatched cottages perched over a labyrinth of seaside grottoes.

Everyone goes to **Rick's Café** to see the sunset and the rare Green Flash—those atmospheric fireworks on the horizon just as the sun disappears. At Rick's you settle in around the cliff-perched alfresco bar with a banana-papaya daiquiri to watch the gaggle of divers spring from the cliffs Acapulco-style before the sun takes center stage—after which applause and an order of lobster are *de rigueur*.

The South Coast

Travelling southeast from Negril, you feel as if you are the first foreigner to encounter the strange, windswept plains here. In its southernmost reaches, the arid landscape conjures up images of East Africa.

Masses of sugarcane fields flank the inland road connecting Negril with Savanna-La-Mar, which is still a vital port for raw sugar exports. From here the main road, referred to as A 2 on the map (don't depend on infrequent road signs), follows the coast along Bluefields Bay. In the forested hills near the police station, the old Bluefields Guest House overlooks the wide bay. (Philip Gosse stayed at the Guest House in the 1840s researching his books *A Naturalist's Sojourn in Jamaica* and *The Birds of Jamaica*.) Now the only place to spend a night here is **Wilton on the Sea**, a gracious five-room guesthouse named for the wealthy woman from Wilton, Connecticut, who built it. The Jamaican social presence who now presides over Wilton, awhirl in caftans and tales of the Prime Minister, makes her guests feel as if they were personally invited rather than the paying sort. It's a fine place to turn in early and get up with the birds. However, if the idea of staying several days or more on the South Coast appeals to you, you mighty be happier at nearby **Bluefields Bay Villas**, a pair of superbly run villas with a tennis court, pool, and other diversions. For interested guests, the villas' owner will arrange tea or cocktails at the ancestral home of his eloquent neighbor, one of the vanishing breed of British colonials. A visit to this private, hilltop great house—one of few that hasn't been restored and commercialized—is in itself worth a trip to the South Coast.

Beyond Bluefields, the first town of note is Black River, with its Georgian-*cum*-gingerbread architecture that epitomizes the Jamaica of the 1920s. In fact, this entire parish, St. Elizabeth, seems to be frozen in time. Farther south in this tropical outback there's no place to stay except a rather bizarre villa in Treasure Beach—where the local people, supposedly descended from buccaneers, have blondish hair and blue eyes. Known as **Folichon**, the art-deco villa with its formal library—and with fishermen for neighbors—has been a well-kept secret among the German visitors and Kingston colonials who take its cure of utter seclusion. It sits amid a coconut grove on a barren black-sand beach from which you can see what are perhaps the most extraordinary sunsets in Jamaica. The housekeeping at Folichon is not what Jamaicans would call "up to standard," but for the ridiculously low price you can't expect the Ritz.

To return to Montego Bay, cut across the island from Black River on the A 2 road, picking up the B 6 road ten miles north at **Middle Quarters**, known as the shrimp capital of Jamaica. Middle Quarters's spindly ladies with scarved coifs sell little bags of fiery hot river shrimp that go down just fine with a bottle of Red Stripe beer and a hunk of hard dough bread. Just east of Middle Quarters lies **Bamboo Avenue**, one of the island's loveliest sights: a three-mile stretch of towering bamboo that forms an arched canopy over the little-used road.

Ocho Rios Area

Until the late 1960s, Ocho Rios was the proverbial quiet fishing village. Then developers saw the biggest fish in the sea, the tourist trickling over from crowded Montego Bay. With all its shopping arcades, parks, and endless things to do, Ocho Rios now appeals largely to day-trippers off cruise ships, to families with active children, and to those travellers who staunchly refuse to stay anywhere but their favorite hotels, Jamaica Inn and the Sans Souci. These two hostelries were in existence here before the high rises, and even now sightseeing seldom figures on their guests' agendas. The regulars are content to stay within the hotels' hermetic domains and wouldn't dream of climbing the 600-foot Dunn's River Falls—Jamaica's most highly touted attraction—in a daisy chain of tourists.

In many ways the **Jamaica Inn** *is* Jamaica as it used to be, with a staff that never dies but just gets older and still bows to every idiosyncracy of its guests. As on the old transatlantic ocean liners, an effortless elegance prevails here. On Saturday nights in season gentlemen don black tie, and ladies, long gowns (and not because they have to, either), and dine and dance under the stars to the accompaniment of civilized music. Once a private estate, the Inn comprises a main house and two wings, done in an architectural style that might be called "Jamaicanized Greek Revival" and painted in a sort of tropical Wedgwood blue, situated on the finest beach in Ocho Rios. The most favored rooms are in the west wing, where, in the White Suite, Winston Churchill used to work on his watercolors. Each room here has its own balustraded balcony jutting out over the seaside coral ledge: an idyllic spot for sunset cocktails or proper English breakfasts (with bangers and broiled tomatoes).

If the Jamaica Inn is Old Jamaica, the **Sans Souci**, just east of town, is Updated Jamaica, but still retains grace and style. The guests here tend to be a trifle younger than those at the Jamaica Inn, and more chichi, the right sort of people for Sans Souci's spring-fed mineral pool and state-of-the-art spa facilities. However, if you stray from the spa menu at the hotel's splendid **Casanova Restaurant**, whose Cipriani-trained chef trots out some of the most delectable canneloni west of Venice, a day's healthful efforts can be wiped out in a single dinner. This is the sort of place where the service is both faultless and friendly, and where the attention to detail pays off in perfection at every turn. Architecturally, Sans Souci clings to a beach-bottomed hillside in a tiered labyrinth of spacious rooms and terraces that looks like a huge candy-pink wedding cake, but the feeling is intimate. Although it's easy to get lost here at first, come nightfall all guests eventually find their way to the new Balloon Bar, where Delroy, a Sans Souci institution, presides over the piano.

Jamaicans revere their traditions with a steadfastness left over from the British. For instance, while the **Hibiscus Lodge** keeps its lobby in a cluttered, homey state, and the exceedingly plain rooms lined up along the seaside ridge recall 1950s motel decor, nobody seems to care, because the Hibiscus has always been the place for colonials who've sold their island houses to hang their old planters' hats. The price is right and, moreover, everybody—from locals to visiting celebrities—goes to the inn's **Almond Tree Bar and Restaurant.**

While ownership may have changed hands at **Moxon's,** a rather eccentric but delightful seaside restaurant, the safari-hatted old greeter, Dixie, still opens car doors and shows women guests to the "powdered" room. This pioneer among local restaurants continues to serve "hungry monk steaks" and appetizers made of ackee, the base of the national dish (ackee and saltfish) that's really a fruit but looks and tastes like scrambled eggs.

When something new opens in Jamaica the whole island goes atwitter, especially when native son Chris Blackwell has a hand in it. Blackwell, descended from a landowning Jamaican-Irish family, founded Island Records and put Bob Marley on the musical map. With **Nuccio's,** a bistro on Bower Road transplanted from Manhattan, he brings a trendy *dolce vita* to Ocho Rios. Never mind the food, such as pasta stuffed with *callaloo* (the Caribbean answer to spinach): High on a hill overlooking town, this is the fashionable but slightly pricey late-night place to dine in the area.

For daytime sightseeing, the latest entry on the local

scene is **Carinosa Gardens**, just beyond Nuccio's, 20 acres dedicated to the flora, fauna, and waterfalls of Jamaica. Prime Minister Edward Seaga fostered the ambitious, Disneyesque theme park that comes complete with guides outfitted in Banana Republic uniforms. Children love the live miniature horses (a typical touch of Jamaican whimsy), but because of the high-ticket admission, you might be happier instead to take a leisurely stroll through the old **Shaw Park Gardens**, a serene oasis of botanical grounds a mile off the road to Fern Gully.

The jitney tour of **Prospect Plantation**, a working agricultural estate just east of the White River and a mile inland, affords an excellent education in how the island's garden grows. A visit to the **Bromley Estate**, eight miles beyond Fern Gully, gives a glimpse of life as it's lived now on a small plantation. Although it's mostly a private home with the occasional room to let (but only to kindred spirits), Bromley is also in the business of making marmalade, guava jelly, fudge, and the only bottled "jerk" seasoning on the island (more on jerking in the Port Antonio section). The kindly owners of Bromley, in the noblesse-oblige tradition, also operate a woodworking shop in the nearby village of Walkers Wood that sells some of the finest carved bowls in Jamaica.

With one exception, plantation life on a grand scale exists now only in memory and in great houses that have been converted to museums (the most authentic being **Greenwood**, the ancestral home of Elizabeth Barrett Browning ten miles west of Falmouth). The exception is **Good Hope Plantation**, about ten miles inland from Falmouth, which, if the idea of staying at the island's premier treasure house appeals to you, in itself justifies a trip to Jamaica. After a 14-year hiatus, Patrick Tenison recently reopened the gates of his great house—set amidst a 2,000-acre cattle and coconut plantation—to grateful paying guests. A huge Kidd landscape in the parlor depicts Good Hope as it was 150 years ago: the quintessential West Indies plantation. Some of the outbuildings may now be in ruins, but the aura remains.

Ornithologists, historians, and culture buffs who share Tenison's interests flock to Good Hope as if it were their private sanctuary, but Good Hope also attracts the casual equestrian for its fine riding stable and superb marked trails. As in the old American South, riding expertise was essential to Jamaica's plantocracy. In addition, because of Jamaica's British heritage, polo became the planter's primary sport. Saturday afternoon polo matches, open to the public, are still played at Drax Hall near St. Ann's Bay. The international set holds tournaments at the new **Chukka Cove**, about 20 minutes west of Ocho Rios. (In fact, it's just around the bend from Seville, the site of the first Spanish capital, where archaeologists are still digging for remnants of Columbus's ships.)

The only equestrian facility of its calibre in the Caribbean, Chukka Cove offers instruction and riding holidays that include accommodation in seaside villas. Nights on the trail are spent up in the hills near the village of Bamboo, at the newly restored **Lilyfield**. When Arnold Bertram, former cultural minister under Michael Manley, decided to open a guesthouse, he came back to his native village and bought the long-deserted pimento and ginger plantation. Although Lilyfield feels more like a suburban inn than a 17th-century manor house, Bertram's enthusiastic welcome and wonderful home cooking make Lilyfield a treat.

Port Antonio Area

The trip to Port Antonio, just 60 miles east of Ocho Rios in the parish of Portland, takes a good two hours—and that's without stopping, which is almost impossible. For example, some of the island's best crafts and paintings are for sale at **Harmony Hall**, four miles east of Ocho Rios. Unless you enjoy haggling with aggressive vendors at the ubiquitous crafts markets elsewhere, shopping is much more pleasant here, and the goods (such as indigenous alabaster carvings) are of higher quality. Along with high-priced local artists, Jonathan Routh, the outrageously whimsical English painter who has become Jamaican society's somewhat offcolor darling, shows his works in the upstairs gallery. Routh's canvases, with his imaginary Queen Victoria motif (he likes to depict her in such bizarre contexts as swinging from a vine), hang in the lobbies of the island's best hotels.

James Bond fans will want to pay a moment of homage at Goldeneye, once author Ian Fleming's home in the sun. It's about seven miles beyond Harmony Hall, on the old coast road in Oracabessa—it's the only estate with neon-blue gateposts. Now occasionally rented out, the boxy white house—not officially open to the public—is nothing special, but the setting of seven untamed lush acres leading down to a private beach is (you can drive in and no one will mind). Whenever he would set to work (the character of James Bond, named after a visiting ornithologist, was created here) Fleming would close the window louvres to avoid the temptation to look at his favorite scenery.

It was after having rented Goldeneye back in the early 1950s that Noel Coward decided to build his own Jamaican retreat. He bought three seaside acres, just a few miles down the road outside of Port Maria, from the Blackwell family. In short order, the estate called Blue Harbour, a.k.a. Coward's Folly, drew a steady stream of houseguests. For his private life, Coward built another house on the hill 1,000 feet up from Blue Harbour. He left it to the people of Jamaica and it opened as a museum a few years ago. The concrete bungalow commands one of the island's most spectacular views, of the sea below and the misty Blue Mountains beyond. But what most makes it memorable are the touches of Coward's design for living: pianos, books, and clothing, all left as they were the day he died, and his artist's studio, still redolent of paints.

Ever the magnanimous mistress, Jamaica has always courted more than its share of notable suitors. Errol Flynn, for one, fell in love with Port Antonio and, while building his empire there, brought swashbuckling to the Rio Grande, the island's largest river, about six miles west of town. Flynn took the bamboo rafts traditionally used to ferry bananas down to the coast, added backbreaking seats for two, and trained his local followers to pole his pals (and, later, tourists) through the jungle-skirted rapids. Although **rafting** has turned into big business by local standards, it is nonetheless one of the most exotic interludes to be had in the Caribbean. Don't be put off by the swarm of would-be rafting escorts who swamp your car as you approach the bridge over the Rio Grande; the raftsmen are licensed by the government. At the end of the two-and-a-half-hour ride, the Jamaican-style gondoliers deposit passengers at a dock newly studded with red-and-white striped gondola-hitching posts (the restaurant here at **Rafter's Rest** serves a nice, simple alfresco lunch and tea).

The wildly incongruous Venetian effects foreshadow things to come farther down the road, in the vague atmosphere of fantasy that characterizes Port Antonio. Indeed, where else but in Portland Parish would you encounter Robbie's Jerk Stand (just beyond Ken Jones Airport, where cows lounge on the lone runway next to the one-room terminal)? Robbie is the beaming local lad in black tie and chef's hat who tends to his one-man grill on the shoulder of the road.

The seeds of Portland fantasy were planted at the century's turn when New Englander Alfred Mitchell built a 60-room version of the Parthenon on a rolling peninsula just east of Port Antonio's twin harbor. According to legend, Mitchell painted everything white and imported monkeys, dogs, horses—all white—and his Tiffany-heiress bride (who loathed the place). Known as "Folly," the structure soon started to crumble from faulty masonry. Mrs. Mitchell fled, leaving her husband and house to wither. These days graffiti-splashed gateposts lead to an eerie roofless ruin.

More follies show up a few miles down the road in the form of fallen hotels, along with a Rhine castle put up in the early 1980s by an ambitious German baroness. Left unfinished, the castle fell into the hands of its neighbor Earl Levy, Jamaica's foremost architect of whimsy, the owner of the **Hotel Trident**. This hotel annex nonpareil (affordable only to Arab sheiks) is really another monument to fantasy. Instead of lions guarding the entrance, Levy has installed two great stone alligators; in the banquet hall, a gesso frieze depicts not the usual cornucopia of grapes but local fruits such as bananas and pawpaw (papaya). But then Trident itself is pretty improbable, too, with its white-gloved service in a baronial dining room, its resident peacocks strutting about the impeccable grounds studded with gazebos. In fact, this place feels like a tropical Castle Howard, of *Brideshead Revisited* fame. It's pure theater and not the least bit stuffy, although you may find Princess Elizabeth of Yugoslavia taking high tea on the verandah. Here, even royalty goes barefoot, and the staff treats every guest as if he or she were royalty. Each room is fit for the occasional king, with luscious four-poster or canopied beds (even in the less expensive rooms in the main hotel), but the most idyllic suites are in the villas strung along the rocky seaside. By day, Trident's offerings include a small beach with water sports; a pool; tennis; and Errol Flynn's widow Pat's boutique-gallery (and perhaps a horseback tour of the Flynn plantation about 10 miles east). But come twilight in season Trident becomes a midwinter night's dream: a calypso combo plays softly on the terrace while guests enjoy cocktails before dinner by candelabra light. Afterwards the castle may host an entertainment. Or, if Trident's inimitable manager, Josef Forstmayr, decides the mood suits, he may whisk his guests off to the **Roof Club**, Port Antonio's dark and booming reggae disco in the heart of town.

For the most part the town of **Port Antonio** itself remains blissfully oblivious to the occasional tourist, who tends to think it a bit shabby anyway. The few foreigners one sees are likely to be villa owners or renters who appreciate Port Antonio for its resistance to change. Everyone—dreadlocked Rastafarians, old ladies carrying fringed umbrellas for shade, crisply uniformed schoolchildren, shoeless street urchins, sidewalk trinket vendors, somber-faced farmers balancing bananas or whatever atop their heads—gathers in the town square (pay heed to the belching buses) to talk about politics and the price of saltfish. They go to the Victorian-vintage Musgrave Market across the street (where Miss Martha, queen of Portland "higglers"—women vendors—presides over the produce stand of choice); to the rank but requisite Cheapside grocery store; to the old courthouse with its wigged judges to see who's on trial; to the Mandala, a Dutch-run quasi-art gallery for vegetarian pizza; to the Coronation bakery for the spicy meat turnovers Jamaicans call a patty (pronounced "potty"); and to the hole-in-the-wall newsstand to pick up the *Daily Gleaner.* Indeed, the beauty of Port Antonio is that you can feel you're a part of Jamaica and not just another face on a tourism brochure.

Ironically, though no evidence of it survives, Port Antonio was the island's first center of tourism. Once Yankee Captain L. D. Baker had established the town as the world's banana capital, he began filling the empty banana boats returning from Boston with well-heeled travellers who stayed at the Titchfield, the hotel he built on "The Hill" in 1905. The Titchfield burned, but just a few blocks away from The Hill at the old **DeMontevin Lodge**, a flamingo-pink gingerbread confection replete with beaded curtains, Errol Flynn's former cook dishes up curried goat or whatever West Indian specialty you request when you call ahead (Tel: 993-2604).

Food enthusiasts who want a steady diet of real Jamaican cooking would be happiest staying in a **rental villa**, where every cook is a queen of the island cuisine. Lady Sarah Churchill, who lives near Mobay, maintains that the best restaurants are in effect the villas; nowhere else can a visitor get such local delicacies as stamp'n'go (codfish fritters) or authentic pepperpot soup. At the most desirable rental villas, those situated along the "strip" between Monkey (a.k.a. Pellew) Island and the Blue Lagoon, you can dine or dive at whim off the sensational seaside terraces. (Peter O'Toole stayed in one of these villas, and the houseman now sports a black cigarette holder.) Nearby **Goblin Hill** combines a bit of the privacy and staff of villa life with such hotel-style amenities as a pool, lighted tennis courts, and a children's social director. There's no restaurant at Goblin Hill, but with its reasonable rates, a cook for each villa (guests buy their own food), and the **Blue Lagoon Restaurant** a short walk down the hill, no one seems to mind.

The supposedly bottomless **Blue Lagoon** (a.k.a. Blue Hole) ranks among the more seductive settings in Jamaica. Rudyard Kipling sang its praises, Robin Moore once owned it, and the Aga Khan kept a house near it. When Warner Brothers transformed its shore into a Robinson Crusoe-type film set, an enterprising local parlayed the place into a water-sports center along with a snappy bar and restaurant, where almost everyone orders either lobster or jerked chicken. But the best place to get jerk— not jerky but a precursor to the New Orleans invention of "blackened" foods—is in **Boston Bay**, three miles east of Blue Lagoon.

Until a few years ago, Boston Bay was the only place in Jamaica to buy the highly spiced meat, but now this regional cooking wave has flooded the island with jerk stands. Ever since Columbus discovered allspice here back in 1494 (he thought it was pepper) Jamaicans have been known for their tongue-searing cuisine. Jerking could likely be traced back to the Arawaks, but it was the Maroons, the island's early runaway slaves, who perfected the method of marinating wild pig with pimento—what Jamaicans call allspice—hot peppers, and scallions. (Descendants of the Maroons still live in the Portland hill-towns of Cornwall Barracks and Moore Town, and in the Cockpit Country south of Montego Bay.) Next to the bay in Boston, with its rolling surf, the old jerkers fire up huge smoking barbecues of green pimento sticks at dawn, and orders by the handful are ready at lunchtime. But if your tastes run to club sandwiches, head to **Frenchman's Cove**—once the Caribbean's most exclusive hotel and still the site of the best beach in Portland—where waiters in black tie spread linen tablecloths on your table in the sand.

Kingston

Despite all the bad press it gets, Kingston is nonetheless important culturally—not only to Jamaica, but to the whole Caribbean community. (After all, Jamaica is the largest English-speaking country in the West Indies.) Ignoring the capital would be like avoiding New York's Museum Mile because of its proximity to some tough spots in nearby Harlem. Granted there is crime in Kingston, but it's mostly in the rougher sections that a visitor would not encounter in the course of a stay; caution should be exercised here, as in any developing country. Not that anyone would necessarily want to spend a week-long holiday in Kingston, but to miss its considerable high points altogether would be a mistake.

Although Kingston's population is less than a million, its chaotic urban sprawl, fanning out from the enormous harbor to the foothills of the Blue Mountains, makes the city seem much bigger. Up to ten years ago the old colonials used to canter through the city's open spaces, but all available ground has been gobbled up by housing developments that seem to have deafening reggae bars on every corner. This is not a walking city.

If you want to be close to the cultural pockets, i.e., downtown, the place to stay is the sophisticated **Jamaica Pegasus Hotel**, with its V.I.P. floors, cable television, and a swimming pool the size of a cricket pitch. (The alternative is to head for the hills, to the cozy **Ivor Guest House**.) Don't come to Kingston on a weekend, when the city is dead and many of the museums close, unless it's to climb the Blue Mountain peak. This is a sublime experience, best arranged through the hospitable owners of the Pine Grove Guest House half way up the mountain.

Like much of Kingston, the **Institute of Jamaica** may surprise you. Founded in 1879 to foster cultural and scientific growth, the East Street complex serves as a sort of Smithsonian Institution. (If you're really serious about Jamaica's heritage, subscribe for a farthing to the Institute's quarterly *Jamaica Journal.*) The national schools of art and music, drama, and dance operate under its well-respected auspices, drawing students from all over the Caribbean. History scholars spend days in the stacks at the National Library, formerly known as the West Indian Reference Library, which houses the foremost research collection in the Caribbean. The **National Gallery**, a few blocks away in a new building of impressive proportions on the waterfront, exhibits the definitive collection of Jamaican artists past and present. Particularly interesting are the 19th-century scenes of plantation life (such as Belisario's), the sensitive sculpture of the late Edna Manley, who was a primary force in the development of local arts, and the work of such visionary artists as Albert Artwell, who depicts the growth of the Rastafarian movement in Jamaica. The best selection of paintings to buy is at **Bolivar Bookshop and Gallery**, on Grove Road less than a mile from the Pegasus (don't miss the West Indian room in the attic); for antique objects, such as museum-quality tortoiseshell combs dating from the 17th century, go to **The Antiquarian and Trading Co.** opposite Devon House on Hope Road.

Jamaica's reputation for excellence in the performing arts is borne out at such revered venues as the Ward Theatre (the oldest theater in the Western Hemisphere) and even in the tourist outposts of Ocho Rios and Mobay, where the off-season, weekly happenings known as "Bruckins" encapsulate the formidable array of talent. ("Bruckins," patois for "celebration," is a sort of mini-musical, staged outdoors, that celebrates the island's history.) Still, its most famous export is reggae, the rocksteady Caribbean soul music born in the slums of Kingston and spread like gospel according to Bob Marley. You don't have to be a reggae fan to enjoy the museum that was both Marley's home and the Tuff Gong recording studio; there's even a wax statue of Marley, complete with the musician's guitar and dreadlocks of silk donated by Madame Toussaud's.

Just down Hope Road from Marley's erstwhile throne is

Devon House, the 19th-century mansion of Jamaica's first black millionaire—the kind of place that Rastas and reggae regale against with egalitarian fervor. The stately museum complex showcases life as it was when Jamaica was rich—and offers one of the best spots in town for shopping (at **Things Jamaican**) and lunching.

Eating well in Kingston means leaving town, though—and calling ahead—for such enchanting spots as the **Blue Mountain Inn** (Tel: 927-7400), once the Great House of an old coffee plantation on the Gordon Town Road, 20 minutes from Kingston's hotel district; for a small fee, the restaurant provides limousine service. (Kingstonians call it their Maxim's, with the expensive fare ranging from shrimp and lobster fettucine to rich Continental-style dishes.) For a more casual meal there's **Rivers Meet** in the village of Enfield above Gordon Town square. The food's not terrific—mostly grilled meats and fish—but the setting is: tables tucked under and around a huge open cave of natural rock beside the flowing waters. **Strawberry Hill** (yet another offering from Chris Blackwell), an 18th-century hilltop country house above the village of Irish Town, is a good half hour from the city (and open only Thursday through Sunday), but is worth the drive for the dream of a view and the garden of anthuriums as well as its genuine Jamaican menu (prix fixe and surprisingly moderate) and the golden-record bar in the cellar.

From here it's all uphill: to the mysterious Blue Mountains, with their pine-crusted ridgebacks that could easily be mistaken for Tuscany. In the mountains you can stay at the old **Pine Grove Guest House**, a chalet that's short on taste and long on grace (try to overlook its tacky rooms for the warmth of the owners and its "Sound of Music" setting). Here you can only imagine the profound beat of reggae several thousand feet below.

USEFUL FACTS

What to Wear

Ascots rather than ties suit many gentlemen staying in the posher resorts, which normally require a jacket and neckwear for dinner. In Kingston, ladies are better off wearing a dress or skirt, day or night. Otherwise, casual cottons are most comfortable. For mountain climbing, bring a heavy sweater.

Getting In

Airlines serving Jamaica include American, Eastern, Air Jamaica, Air Canada, British Airways, BWIA, and in winter, the British Airways Concorde. Nonstop flights are available from many major U.S. cities including New York, Los Angeles, Atlanta, Boston, Baltimore, Washington, and Philadelphia. Trans Jamaican Airlines operates flights within Jamaica. Getting out of Kingston's Norman Manley International Airport takes much less time and hassle than Montego Bay's airport.

Entry Requirements

All visitors must supply proof of citizenship, either a passport or birth certificate.

Currency

The Jamaican dollar; banks are plagued with endless queues, so you should change money at the airport upon arrival. Save $40J for the departure tax. To change Jamaican money back to other currencies remember to save exchange receipts.

Electrical Current

In most cases, same as in the U.S. and Canada—110 volts, but 50 cycles.

Getting Around

Once out of the airport you are besieged by taxi drivers; chances are you won't need one, but if you do, look on the taxi cab door for the JUTA sticker, which signifies the most reliable transportation association. Most rates are government fixed, but determine before taking off if the price quoted is in Jamaican or U.S. dollars.

Unless your hotel has arranged your transfer, proceed immediately *before* claiming your luggage to the tourist board counter to pick up Esso's free Discover Jamaica map (you'll be helpless without it) and then proceed on to the airport car rental offices. It's wise to book a car in advance, but the process is usually such a time-consuming ordeal that you wonder why you bothered. With all the taxes, insurance, etc., the basic rate quoted back home seems to double. All of the big-name rental agencies operate franchises here, and Island Car Rental maintains a dicey reputation. Driving is on the left and gas costs a fortune (cash only). Beware of hell-bent drivers.

Business Hours

Usual business hours are from 8:30–4:30, Monday–Friday (tourist shops stay open on Saturday); banks are open Monday–Thursday from 9:00–2:00 and on Friday (try to avoid banks on Friday—it's payday) from 9:00 to noon and from 2:30 to 5:00.

Festivals

Festivals are: Reggae Sunsplash, an international festival held annually since 1977 in Mobay for five days in mid- to late August; Port Antonio International Marlin Tournament, the oldest and most prestigious fishing tournament in the Caribbean, in October; Mazda Golf Champions, the senior PGA/LPGA tournament played in mid-December at Tryall; Miami/Montego Bay Yacht Race in March.

Departure

Save enough cash to pick up some of the fine local products at the duty-free airport shops, including JABLUM Blue Mountain coffee (don't settle for any other brand), Royal Jamaican cigars, Appleton rum, Tia Maria, and Pickapeppa Sauce. Should your flight be delayed, hire a licensed taxi and head for **Port Royal**, about ten minutes from Kingston's aiport, to stroll around the ruins of what was once the "wickedest city on earth," the bastion of Caribbean pirates such as Henry Morgan—who later became governor of Jamaica.

ACCOMMODATIONS REFERENCE

The rate ranges given here are projections for fall 1988 through spring 1989. Unless otherwise indicated, rates are for double room, double occupancy. The telephone area code for Jamaica is 809.

▶ **Bluefields Bay Villas.** P.O. Box 5, Westmoreland Parish. From $90 a person a day, A.P. Tel: in U.S., (703) 549-5276.

▶ **Chukka Cove.** P.O. Box 160, Ocho Rios. Rates vary according to length of stay and type of package, e.g., $170 per person for two-day riding trek, including meals and overnight accommodation at Lilyfield. Tel: 974-2593/2239; in U.S., (800) 223-7296.

▶ **Folichon**. c/o Arthur Sutton, Marshell's Pen, P.O. Box 58, Mandeville. The villa sleeps eight and costs $80 per night, including maid service, two-night minimum. Tel: 962-2260.

▶ **Good Hope Plantation**. P.O. Box 50, Falmouth. $110 a person, double occupancy, includes meals and use of riding facilities and private beach. Tel: 954-3289.

▶ **Hibiscus Lodge Hotel**. P.O. Box 52, Ocho Rios. $52. Tel: 974-2676.

▶ **Ivor Guest House**. Jacks Hill, Ivor Dr., St. Andrew. $52. Tel: 927-1460.

▶ **Jamaica Inn**. P.O. Box 1, Ocho Rios. $275–$350, A.P. Tel: 974-2514; in U.S., (203) 438-3793 or (800) 243-9420.

▶ **The Jamaica Pegasus**. P.O. Box 333, 81 Knutsford Blvd., Kingston 5. $125–$355. Tel: 926-3691; in U.S., (800) 223-5843; in Canada, (800) 268-9761; in London, (01) 567-3444.

▶ **Lilyfield**. Without riding; see Chukka Cove for reservations.

▶ **Pine Grove Guest House**. Reservations c/o 29 Oliver Pl., Kingston, 5. From $38; M.A.P., $18 a person extra. Tel: 922-8705.

▶ **Rockhouse**. P.O. Box 24, Pristine Cove, Negril. $70–$120, E.P. Tel: 957-4373; in U.S., (312) 699-1726 or (312) 296-1894.

▶ **Round Hill**. P.O. Box 64, Montego Bay. $310–$485, M.A.P. Tel: 952-5150; in U.S., (800) 237-3237.

▶ **The Sans Souci Hotel Club & Spa**. Box 103, Ocho Rios. $240–$380. Tel: 974-2353/4; in U.S., Elegant Resorts of Jamaica, 1320 South Dixie Highway, Coral Gables, FL 33146, (800) 237-3237.

▶ **Trident Villas & Hotel**. P.O. Box 119, Port Antonio. $130–$700, depending on meal plan, size of accommodation, and season. Tel: 993-2602; in U.S., (212) 689-3048 or (800) 235-3505.

▶ **Tryall Golf, Tennis & Beach Club**. Sandy Bay Post Office, Hanover Parish, Jamaica. From $170–$360, M.A.P. Tel: 952-5110; in U.S., (212) 535-9530 or (800) 223-5581.

▶ **Wilton on the Sea**. Bluefields, Westmoreland. $60, M.A.P. Tel: 955-2852.

▶ **Villa rentals** throughout most of the island, Villas and Apartments Abroad, 444 Madison Ave., New York, NY 10017. A fully staffed, three-bedroom villa averages about $1,700 per week. Tel: (212) 759-1025 or (800) 433-3020.

HAITI

By Jessica Harris

Jessica Harris, who is fluent in French and Spanish, specializes in writing about the Caribbean, and Hispaniola in particular. She is the author of a book on Africa's contributions to New World cooking, and has written articles for Caribbean Travel and Life, Essence, Vogue, The New York Times, *and other major publications.*

Haiti, beautiful, battered, and perhaps the most controversial of the Caribbean islands, would seem today to be suffering under one of its own voodoo spells cast by a malevolent priest. Already reeling from doomsayers' incorrect reports of the island as a hotbed of AIDS, the country was then buffeted by the growing spectre of Duvalier politics and the government's numerous human-rights violations. All of this served to keep thousands away from what is one of the Caribbean's most intriguing destinations. No sooner had Bebe "Doc" Duvalier fled to a cushy exile in the South of France and hopes begun to rise, when the failure of the November 1987 elections again plunged the country into political chaos. Now only the most adept *houngan* (voodoo priest) would attempt to foresee what's in store for this country that was the second republic to be established in the Western Hemisphere and the first Black nation in the New World.

Haiti has never been a country to leave observers indifferent. Partisans praise a people whose creative force and vitality have decorated rickety buses, created masterpieces on canvas, invented a unique cuisine, and above all maintained an air of great goodwill toward visitors despite all the tricks of history. Detractors usually see only one thing—poverty. The only way to know how Haiti will affect you is to go. Those who do find that this western part of the island of Hispaniola offers no large resorts and very few important sights. Its beaches are fine, but not the primary reason for visits, either. What the country does offer is a chance to get in touch with the most African of the Caribbean islands and to spend some time in a truly fascinating place.

MAJOR INTEREST

Strong African influence
Art
Food

Port-au-Prince and Pétionville
Museum of Haitian Art
Panthéon National d'Art Haitien

Cap Haitien
Sans Souci Palace
The Citadelle La Ferriere

Elsewhere
Jacmel (beaches)

Visitors usually arrive at the international airport, a half-hour drive from Port-au-Prince. The capital city and its hillside suburb of Pétionville house most of Haiti's hotels and are the bases for most excursions. The more adventurous visitors to the country make a trip with car and driver (or on one of the infrequent flights) to the northern city of Cap Haitien to see what some have classified as one of the wonders of the world: The Citadelle La Ferrière, the fortress built by King Henri Christophe. Those determined to have their time at the beach take a southern route and head for Jacmel.

Travellers who come to Haiti in search of art find it everywhere. The many galleries in the capital sell paintings that range from the ridiculous to the sublime, priced for every budget. There are several museums and art centers in Haiti, most of them in Port-au-Prince, and it seems that hawkers selling paintings and mahogany sculpture occupy every street corner. For those for whom art extends beyond painting or sculpture to all of life, Port-au-Prince and the rest of the country provide many a

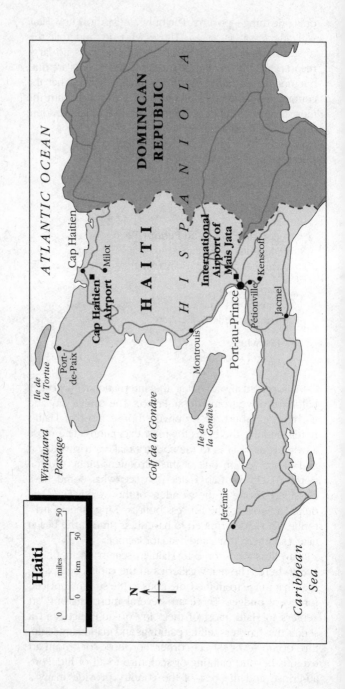

lesson in the very Haitian art of living. It is an education to watch the merger of the Haitian sense of commerce and the all-too-real need of many Haitians to earn a living. Few hands are idle in this country that could teach the rest of the Western world a great deal about recycling: old tires are transformed into sandals, orange peels are saved and used to make a liqueur, and evaporated-milk tins become oil lamps.

But this is only a part of Haiti. In the Port-au-Prince suburb of Pétionville, for example, things take a slower pace, and the French influence is more evident, especially in the elegant restaurants.

Columbus, who arrived in 1492 and set up a temporary settlement at La Navidad, named the island Hispaniola. In 1697, the Spanish granted the western part of the island to the French, and they transformed it into Saint Domingue, the "Pearl of the Antilles." The colony was so rich in tobacco, cane, and coffee that the world reeled when the shock waves of the French Revolution led first the planters, then the mulatto class, and finally the slaves to revolt in what would culminate in the declaration of 1804, which made Haiti the world's first Black republic. The revolution brought Toussaint-Louverture, Jean-Jacques Dessalines, Alexandre Pétion, and Henri Christophe to fame; their names are touchstones in the country even today.

Following the brilliance of the glory days of independence, Haiti and the Dominican Republic were one country. In 1844 the two became separate entities. Thereafter, Haiti's fortunes seesawed: rule by an emperor, occupation by U.S. Marines, and 30 years of oppressive rule by the Duvalier family—which ended in February 1986.

Voodoo

No traveller goes to Haiti without wanting to witness a bit of voodoo. Folkloric shows at all of the hotels oblige with sometimes chilling accuracy. Those in search of the real thing will probably not find it unless they are fluent in Creole and have the confidence of a Haitian friend. Until recently, a good substitute was the demonstration at the *peristyle* (voodoo temple) in Mariani, a small village on the outskirts of Port-au-Prince. This show was run by Max Beauvoir, a *houngan* and lawyer who writes scholarly articles on a computer. The complex has closed because of the recent political unrest, but you can find Beauvoir if you're diligent—and serious about your interest in voodoo.

Port-au-Prince

The Victorian gingerbread houses of Port-au-Prince lean precariously and seem to be ready to topple at the first strong wind. They are as much a testimony to the Haitian will to survive as anything. The traveller is sure to spot one or more memorable examples while passing through the city on the way to the **Musée d'Art Haitien**. The exhibition hall displays works by the masters of Haitian naïve art, among them Hector Hippolyte and Wilson Bigaud.

Works by the "old masters" can also be seen at the Episcopal Cathedral of the Holy Trinity on the corner of the rue Monseigneur Guilloux and rue Pavée; murals depict the life of Christ in Haitian Naive style.

Visitors who are intrigued by the intricacies of Haitian history should not miss the **Panthéon National**, on the Champs de Mars in front of the National Palace. Exhibits include an anchor from the *Santa Maria* and Papa Doc's physician's satchel.

Le Plaza Holiday Inn is nearby. Favored by business-people with intown activities (most leisure travellers prefer the calmer Pétionville suburbs for lodging), the hotel has a quiet garden behind its street façade.

A visit to the *Marché de Fer,* or Iron Market, takes you right into the fray of Haitian life. Currently, however, it's a case of go at your own risk, and until the political situation settles down, this area of wall-to-wall activity and bustling crowds is best avoided.

Instead, a leisurely visit to some of the capital's galleries will give the visitor a good look at Haitian art. Galleries to seek out include Galerie Monin and Galerie Nader (with a branch in Pétionville as well), and Issa's, on the rue du Chili. Claire's Gallery, in the same neighborhood, is run by Aubélin Jolicoeur, a Haitian institution himself and formerly a fixture at the airport, where—in an impeccable white suit and carrying a mahogany cane—he would greet all arrivals.

Many of the art galleries also sell original handcrafted

items such as handcarved wooden salad bowls, embroi-
dered pillows, crocheted wares, ceramics, and the like.
The best can be found at **Ambiance**, at 17 avenue M,
Gingerbread, 52 avenue Lamartinière, and **Zin d'Art**, 86
John Brown, in the Port-au-Prince/Pétionville area, and at
the **Galerie Trois Visages** in Cap Haitien. Near Claire's
Gallery and Issa's is the **Grand Hotel Oloffson**, immortal-
ized in Graham Greene's novel *The Comedians*. The
world-famous hotel was closed briefly, but reopened in
November 1987. A stop for a drink at the mahogany bar at
this Victorian gingerbread wonder is obligatory for all. The
bar has been a gathering place for the country's literati and
artistic visitors for years. Four antique-furnished guest
rooms are available, and others will be opened as tourism
on the island improves.

Haitian cuisine differs from that of the rest of the
French-speaking Caribbean; when in Port-au-Prince, try
such unique dishes as *riz au djon djon* (rice with black
mushrooms), *griots de porc* (spicy pork bits), and *soupe
au giraumon* (pumpkin soup) at restaurants like **Le Récif**
on Delmas Road or **Le Rond Point** near the Exposition
grounds, or in some of the hotel dining rooms. **Pétionville**, Port-au-Prince's hillside suburb, offers comfortable
hotels and excellent restaurants, such as Chez Gérard, La
Cascade, and La Souvenance, which could easily be in the
South of France. The Galerie Marassa and a branch of the
Galerie Monin are here, too, in adjacent buildings.

"Las Vegas goes Haitian" is the best way to describe the
El Rancho hotel in Pétionville. A nightclub and casino
keep things jumping at night, while twin pools and an
indoor/outdoor dining room are centers of activity during the day. The **Villa Creole**, a family-run property also
in Pétionville, is the favorite Haitian roost of members of
the press and businesspeople. One of the big attractions
of the moderately priced hotel is breakfasting under the
almond tree at poolside. The welcome of the owners is as
warm as the Haitian sun.

The stalwart can make a trip to the Jane Barbancourt
Castle on the road to Boutilliers and Kenscoff. This establishment, a tasting room for the Barbancourt rum distillery, offers a wide assortment of rum liqueurs flavored
with everything from coconut to hibiscus. The excursion
might continue to Boutilliers, with its panoramic view of

Port-au-Prince, and beyond to Kenscoff, a village in a pine forest high in the hills, where many wealthy Haitians have weekend homes. Kenscoff is degrees cooler than Port-au-Prince and its weekly market is a photographer's delight.

Cap Haitien

It is hard to believe that Cap Haitien was once the richest French city in the New World, known then as Cap Français. Today, for most visitors, there is really only one reason to go to the sleepy town that Cap Haitien has become: **The Citadelle La Ferrière**, a massive fortress atop a 3,000-foot-high mountain. The first stop on the way there is usually at Milot, site of the ruins of King Henri Christophe's palace, **Sans Souci**. The ascent to the fortress that the security-conscious Christophe built far above his palace is by car, on mule, and on foot, and is not for the feeble. The view from the top, however, is breathtaking. Little imagination is required to appreciate the fact that 200,000 men were needed to build it—and that 20,000 of them died. The monument to megalomania never saw battle and today is covered with moss.

Elsewhere in Haiti

Those in search of the ultimate beach resort won't find it in Haiti. Instead, they will find a family-oriented resort, Kaliko Beach, at Ouanga Bay, and Moulin sur Mer, the weekend roost of the Haitian fast set, in Montrouis. **Kaliko Beach**, its comfortable motel-style rooms strung along a curve of beach, offers one of the country's few dive centers. **Moulin sur Mer**, a more sophisticated resort, centers around a restored plantation mill and offers accommodations in two-story units near a small strip of beach. The Club Med Magic Isle, also in Montrouis, provides that company's all-inclusive type of vacation with a Haitian flair.

Jacmel, a coffee boomtown of the late 19th century, is another alternative for beach lovers. The town itself has a gray-sand beach, but secluded coves a short drive away are more enticing. Ask someone at the hotel desk to explain to your taxi driver how to get to these coves; they're quite difficult to find.

USEFUL FACTS

What To Wear

Although French chic is evident in some of Pétionville's restaurants after dark, those planning to spend any time exploring the downtown area or perhaps riding on a tap tap (a gaily decorated local jitney) should think of dressing comfortably.

Getting In

American, ALM, and Pan American have regularly scheduled flights from New York and Miami. Air Canada flies from Montreal. There are no direct flights from London.

Most visitors to Haiti arrive at Port-au-Prince's International Airport. A three-man band plays Haitian songs to help visitors pass the time as they wait in line for immigration. Then it's out into the fray. Haitian taxis include the good, the bad, and the ugly. Pick one that looks as if it has working shock absorbers and brakes, and, because taxis are not metered, negotiate the rate in advance. The driver should carry a card spelling out the rates set by the government.

Entry Requirements

U.S. and Canadian citizens must have a valid passport, birth certificate, or naturalization papers. British subjects need only a valid passport; Australian citizens need a passport and a visa issued by a Haitian consulate. An ongoing or return ticket is also required of all non-Haitians. A tourist card is issued on arrival. There is a $15 departure tax.

Currency

The basic unit of currency is the Haitian gourde. The currency has been pegged to the U.S. dollar since 1919. Five gourdes are equal to one dollar. Dollars and gourdes are interchangeable throughout the country. Canadian money and other currencies are not accepted.

Electrical Current

Same as in the U.S. and Canada—110 volts, 60 cycles.

Getting Around

Driving in Haiti is only for the initiated or the masochistic. Haitian roads, with the exception of the road to Jacmel and the road to the beaches outside of Port-au-Prince, are not well marked, not well lighted, and are patrolled by cows, donkeys, and pedestrians who tend to dart out into traffic. Haitian drivers are used to all of this and know how to use their horns to clear a path. If driving is an absolute must, a valid U.S., Canadian, or international driver's license is required.

Taxis are available at all of the hotels and can be rented by the hour or for the day.

Business Hours
They vary. Check with the hotel desk or phone ahead.

Festivals
On Sunday between Epiphany (January 6) and the beginning of Lent, the island celebrates Carnival. Dancing crowds wind their way through the streets from morning until well past dark. During the Easter Season they also celebrate rara; small bands of people parade in the streets to music and stop occasionally to perform acrobatic feats.

ACCOMMODATIONS REFERENCE
The rate ranges given here are projections for fall 1988 through spring 1989. Unless otherwise indicated, prices are for double rooms, double occupancy. The telephone area code for Haiti is 509.

▶ **El Rancho.** P.O. Box 71, Port-au-Prince, Haiti. $70–$120. Tel: 7-2080.

▶ **The Grand Hotel Oloffson.** 60 Ave. Christophe; P.O. Box 260, Port-au-Prince, Haiti. $60–$70. Tel: 3-4000/4101.

▶ **Kaliko Beach.** Pointe Paturon, La Gonâve Bay, Haiti. P.O. Box 338, Port-au-Prince, Haiti. $98–$134. Tel: 2-3742.

▶ **Moulin sur Mer.** Montrouis, Haiti. Tel: 2-1844, 2-1918, or 2-7652.

▶ **Le Plaza Holiday Inn.** 10 rue Capois, P.O. Box 1429, Port-au-Prince, Haiti. $53–$79. Tel: 2-0855 or 2-0821.

▶ **Villa Creole.** P.O. Box 126, Port-au-Prince, Haiti. $75–$105. Tel: 7-1570 or 7-1571.

OTHER ACCOMMODATIONS
▶ **Mont Joli.** P.O. Box 12, Cap Haitien, Haiti. Tel: 3-2-0300. This small, moderately priced hotel epitomizes the quiet charm of Cap Haitien, with antique furniture in the public rooms and caring attention from everyone from the owners to the chambermaids.

DOMINICAN REPUBLIC

by Jessica B. Harris

Without the Dominican Republic there might be no Caribbean vacations; it was here that Christopher Columbus, or Cristóbal Colón as he's known here, first set foot ashore in the New World. Located on the eastern portion of the island of Hispaniola—which it shares with Haiti—the Dominican Republic offers the best of two Caribbean worlds to its visitors. History lovers are sure to enjoy the majestic Spanish Renaissance buildings of Old Santo Domingo, while beach buffs will find more than enough secluded white sandy beaches and modern facilities on the southern, eastern, and northern coasts of the country to suit their fancies.

MAJOR INTEREST

Spanish influence

Santo Domingo
Colonial Santo Domingo
Plaza de la Cultura

La Romana
Casa de Campo resort
Altos de Chavon replica colonial town

Puerto Plata
The beaches of the area

Elsewhere in the Dominican Republic
Punta Caña beach resort

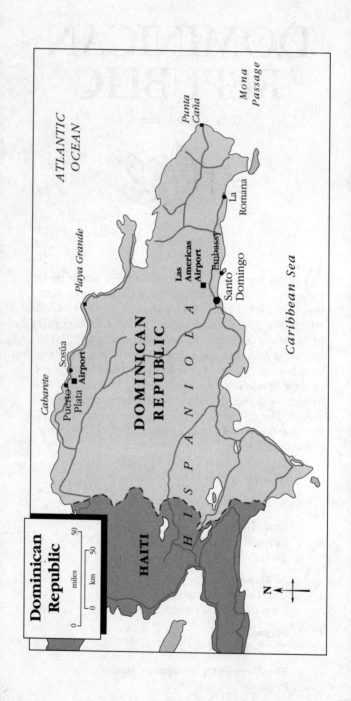

The history of the Dominican Republic reads like a précis of Caribbean history: the Spanish, British, French, and Haitians battled for it. Self-determination came in 1844, and the country has been independent—except for a brief Spanish interlude—ever since. From 1930 to 1961, the country was ruled by Generalissimo Rafael Leónidas Trujillo.

Today, the Dominican Republic greets almost a million tourists a year, welcoming them to its beaches and colonial city and entrancing them with its merengue music, its food—such as *sancocho,* a hearty stew, and *chicharrones,* fried bits of pork, chicken, or fish—and the three B's: Bermudez, Brugal, and Barcelo, locally produced rums.

Santo Domingo

Old Santo Domingo, elegant and providing glimpses into the past of the New World, can be spoken of in superlatives: It is the first permanent European settlement in the New World, for one, and its cathedral is the oldest in the Western Hemisphere. The colonial city is the soul of the capital, indeed of the country.

The best way to see the colonial city is on foot. Begin at the **Alcázar,** also known as the Casa de Colón. Built in 1510 and restored in 1957, the two-story, hewn-stone building has furnishings of the period, and it seems to be awaiting the return of Don Diego Columbus, son of Christopher and the first Spanish viceroy of the New World.

The **Atarazana,** across the plaza, was a colonial arsenal. Shops selling jewelry of amber and larimar (two Dominican specialties), art galleries, and restaurants now occupy the 16th-century buildings.

A short walk away is the **Calle Las Damas,** named for the Spanish ladies who once promenaded here in the evening. The cobbled street, lined with imposing Spanish Renaissance carved façades, still evokes images of conquistadores and their ladies. The street is lined with museums, including the **Museo de las Casas Reales,** which houses artifacts from life in colonial Santo Domingo.

Those wishing to stop for a drink or to spend a night or two in colonial splendor will enjoy the **Hostal Nicolás de Ovando,** a small, inexpensive, government-owned hotel in the restored house of a colonial governor.

It would be inconceivable to leave colonial Santo Domingo without stopping at the **Cathedral of Santa Maria la Menor** to pay homage to Columbus. The cathedral, the first in the New World and an imposing example of Spanish Renaissance architecture, is perhaps best known as one of several supposed final resting places of Columbus. (Controversy has raged for centuries as to the actual grave of the Admiral of the Americas. Some say Seville, others the cathedral in Santo Domingo, and still others Cuba. Current opinion disallows the Cuban claim and compromises on the notion that some of the bones are indeed in Spain and some in the Dominican Republic.) Remains notwithstanding, the cathedral and the tomb are impressive.

The confirmed history lover can linger for days in the colonial city visiting museums, marvelling at the façade of the Casa del Cordon, peeking into courtyards, or straining for glimpses behind half-closed doorways. Others may decide to hop into a taxi and find some local color and a few souvenirs at the **Mercado Modelo**, where bargaining is the watchword and stalls offer everything from voodoo powders to amber and gold jewelry. Those wishing to shop with a bit more tranquility will find the same items, minus the voodoo powders, at the **Plaza Criolla** on El Conde. Nearby, on the Avenida Maximo Gomez, the **Gran Hotel Lina** offers lodging and an excellent adjoining restaurant of the same name (see below).

Property belonging to Generalissimo Trujillo has been transformed into the **Plaza de la Cultura**, a complex housing the Casa de Teatro (the Dominican Republic's national theater), the public library, and several museums. Those wondering what happened before Columbus are well-served by the exhibits in the **Museo del Hombre Dominicana**. Bring a dictionary, though, because the exhibit captions are almost all in Spanish.

In the evening, diners looking for Dominican specialties head for **El Buren**, on Padre Billini, **Jai Alai**, on Avenida Independencia, or one of the capital's many other restaurants. Aside from Dominican, the favorite cuisine seems to be Spanish—such as that served at **Lina's Restaurant**. (Try the Zarzuela de Mariscos, the Dominican Republic's paella.) Lina, who was Trujillo's cook, came from Spain, and her restaurant has become famous. There are also several good Italian restaurants; **Vesuvio**, on the Malecón, is particularly good. **El Jardin de Jade**, a marvelous Chinese restaurant in El Embajador hotel, serves Peking Duck and dim sum at prices way below those of any Western capital.

Discos and nightclubs abound, particularly on the **Malecón**. The street is a sight in itself, pulsing with activity as the Dominicans parade nightly. Beer and rum is sold from containers on tailgates, mixers appear miraculously, and suddenly everyone is dancing to the merengue or whatever else is blaring from what seems to be hundreds of car radios turned up to full blast.

La Romana

First there was a sugar plantation at La Romana, a two-hour drive from Santo Domingo at the eastern end of the island. Then there were Gulf and Western and Oscar de la Renta, who together created a luxury resort called **Casa de Campo** and gave it international cachet. Today, minus Gulf and Western, the resort is a well-run complex that offers golf, tennis, polo, beaches, and general pampering to U.S. executives, international jet-setters, vacationers on special golf and tennis packages, and conventioneers.

Another attraction in the area is **Altos de Chavón**, a modern rendering of a 16th-century European city. Altos has a small Taino Indian museum, gift shops that sell sophisticated but pricey examples of local craftsmanship, and restaurants (unfortunately, the most interesting are closed at noon and not available to those taking day trips from Santo Domingo). Only 15 minutes from Casa de Campo by shuttle bus, Altos de Chavón is a good place for its guests to spend the day.

Punta Caña

The 600-bed resort village in Punta Caña is located at the extreme eastern tip of the Dominican Republic, and offers all of the inclusive vacation amenities for which Club Med is known.

Puerto Plata

The "silver port" of the Dominican Republic's north shore is rapidly becoming a tourist mecca. Its largest development, the **Playa Dorada**, is a complex of a number of hotels that offer lodging in every price range. Here the watchwords are beach, beach, and more beach. The **Dorado Naco**, with its large condominium apartments, lures families; pleasant service, golf, riding, and an excellent beach nearby are part of what makes this hotel a favorite of Americans and Canadians. The **Eurotel Playa Dorada**, which stretches down to the beach, boasts European-style luxury, while the **Jack Tar Village** has a plan that includes all meals, drinks, and sports—sort of like a budget Club Med—in the price of a room. Those in search of more secluded beaches can head for the seemingly endless strip of coconut palm-fringed strand at **Playa Grande**, a one-and-a-half hour drive from Puerto Plata. The drive takes you through the town of Sosua, where German refugees from Nazi persecution set up dairies before tourism proved more profitable; and through **Cabarete**, a sleepy village that has turned into a windsurfer's paradise and a haven for French-Canadian visitors. The road is dotted with tourist accommodations and small villages where pig farmers gather at weekly markets. There are no facilities yet at Playa Grande, only a unisex outhouse-cum-changing-room without even a door. Dominicans set up grills and cook fish and lobster and sell beer and piña coladas to the beach crowd here. However, development is on its way.

USEFUL FACTS

What to Wear

Summer and cruise-type clothing is *de rigueur*. However, the Spanish influence has imposed an air of formality on the island. Men are required to wear jackets at night in the better restaurants, and women may want to bring something with an extra bit of flair. Shorts are fine in resort areas but are frowned upon in cities.

Getting In

Eastern, American, and Dominicana fly to the Dominican Republic from New York, Miami, and San Juan. Air Canada currently offers charters, but has applied for regularly scheduled flights. Ward Air has regularly scheduled flights from Toronto. There are no direct flights from London.

Most visitors to the Dominican Republic will enter either at Santo Domingo's Las Americas Airport or, in the north, at Puerto Plata. Strangely, there are no regular flights from the capital to the north coast, and itineraries should be routed so you can visit one coast and then transfer (by convenient air-conditioned bus, car with driver, or rental car) to the other.

Tourist cards (see Entry Requirements), if necessary, should be purchased at a kiosk next to the tourism booth prior to getting in the immigration line, which moves more rapidly than expected. Baggage claim is daunting, but for a small tip someone will locate your luggage and carry it to customs, which for most travellers is perfunctory.

Entry Requirements
Citizens of the United States and Canada need only a tourist card, which costs $5 and is purchased at point of entry upon presentation of a passport (valid or expired), voter-registration card, or birth certificate. The limit of entry with a tourist card is 60 days, and the card must be presented upon departure. British subjects need a valid passport (entry visa is not necessary); entry is for 60 days.

Currency
The basic unit of currency is the Dominican peso. Its dollar sign symbol can be confusing, so travellers should always double check prices. The exchange rate fluctuates daily. Exchange establishments abound in most tourist areas, and hotels and many shops will accept foreign currency and traveller's checks—though some are reluctant to take Canadian money.

Electrical Current
Same as in the U.S. and Canada—110 volts, 60 cycles.

Getting Around
Any visitor with a valid foreign license or international driver's license may drive rental vehicles for 90 days. Driving is on the right. Roads are not well marked and a knowledge of Spanish is a must outside of cities. Taxis, unmetered, are relatively inexpensive and for most tourists are the preferred means of transportation in Santo Domingo.

Business Hours
Shops are open from 8:00–12:00 and 2:00–6:00. Most banks are open from 8:00–2:30. Other businesses are usually open from 8:00–6:00, and government offices follow a 7:30–2:30 schedule. When in doubt, call ahead.

Festivals
All of Santo Domingo is transformed into a ballroom during the latter part of July as that city celebrates Merengue Week.

ACCOMMODATIONS REFERENCE
The rate ranges given here are projections for fall 1988 through spring 1989. Unless otherwise indicated, rates are for double rooms, double occupancy. The telephone area code for the Dominican Republic is 809.

▶ **Casa de Campo.** P.O. Box 140, La Romana, Dominican Republic. $95–$210. Tel: 523-3333.

▶ **Dorado Naco.** P.O. Box 162, Puerto Plata, Dominican Republic. $100–$180. Tel: 586-2019.

▶ **Eurotel Playa Dorada.** P.O. Box 336, Puerto Plata, Dominican Republic. $55–$130. Tel: 586-3663 or 586-4333.

▶ **Gran Hotel Lina.** Avenida Maximo Gómez Squina 27 de Febrero, P.O. Box 1915, Santo Domingo, Dominican Republic. $62–$100. Tel: 689-5185.

▶ **Hostal Nicolás de Ovando.** 53 Calle Las Damas, Old Santo Domingo, Dominican Republic. $45–$55. Tel: 687-7181.

▶ **Jack Tar Village.** P.O. Box 368, Puerto Plata, Dominican Republic. $110–$170, per person. Tel: In U.S, (214) 670-9888.

OTHER ACCOMMODATIONS
▶ **El Embajador.** 65 Avenida Sarasota, Santo Domingo, Dominican Republic. $65–$75. Tel: 533-2131. The *grande dame* of Dominican hotels is still much loved by Dominicans who frequent the public rooms and the Jardin de Jade restaurant.

▶ **Jaragua.** P.O. Box 769-2 Centro De Los Heroes, Santo Domingo, Dominican Republic. $95 (garden view), $150 (superior), $170 (deluxe), $340 (suite). Tel: 686-2222. This new hotel is an expensive remake of an old hotel of the same name. The ten-story pink tower offers every amenity, from casino to European-style spa.

▶ **Santo Domingo.** P.O. Box 2112, Santo Domingo, Dominican Republic. $80 (deluxe), $85 (deluxe balcony), $100 (first floor), $300 (Presidential Suite). Tel: 532-1511. Designed by Oscar de la Renta, the hotel was one of the first to signal the new era of Dominican tourism. The expensive property caters to a flashy, mostly American crowd.

PUERTO RICO

By J. P. MacBean

J. P. MacBean's articles on travel, food, and restaurants have appeared in Travel & Leisure, Horizon, Discovery, *and* Going Places *magazines, and the* New York Daily News *and other newspapers. He is the author of a book on Puerto Rico.*

Puerto Rico has been receiving visitors for five centuries—ever since 1493, when Christopher Columbus set foot on the island's west coast.

Ponce de León established Puerto Rico's first Spanish settlement in 1508, a foothold that was to remain firm for almost 400 years. Although the English made attempts to take over the island—Sir Francis Drake failed miserably in 1595—it was not until 1897 that Luis Muñoz Rivera, the "George Washington of Puerto Rico," won from Spain the charter that gave the island autonomy. Shortly thereafter, as a result of the Spanish-American War in 1898–1899, Puerto Rico passed into U.S. hands. Today, it enjoys commonwealth status, a situation that is likely to prevail, although there are movements advocating complete independence (unlikely) or statehood (a possibility in the distant future).

From the beginning of its history (before Columbus and the Spaniards, there were the Arawak, Carib, and Taino Indians, who called the island "Borinquen"), Puerto Rico has been unique among the islands in the 2,500-mile-long Caribbean archipelago. Although it is the

70

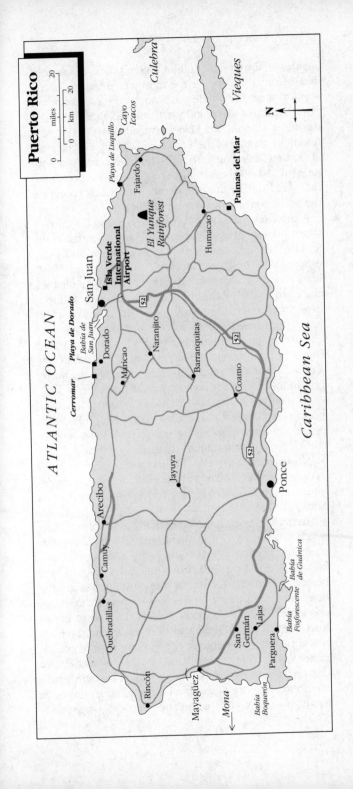

Puerto Rico

miles   20

km   20

N

ATLANTIC OCEAN

Culebra

Vieques

Caribbean Sea

Playa de Luquillo

Cayo Icacos

Fajardo

Palmas del Mar

Humacao

El Yunque Rainforest

Isla Verde International Airport

San Juan

Playa de Dorado

Bahía de San Juan

Cerromar

Dorado

Naranjito

Barranquitas

Coamo

52

52

52

Maricao

Jayuya

Ponce

Arecibo

Camuy

Quebradillas

Rincón

Mayagüez

San Germán

Lajas

Parguera

Mona

Bahía Boquerón

Bahía Fosforescente

Bahía de Guánica

smallest of the Greater Antilles (behind Cuba, Hispaniola, and Jamaica), it is by far the most affluent, diverse, and sophisticated. For all these reasons, and for a number of other reasons (social, industrial, and political), it is also the most visited. San Juan is considered the hub, the unofficial capital, of the Caribbean, and its international airport and bustling harbor are the area centers of both tourism and business traffic. Those who have not visited the island during the past decade will hardly recognize the cities, even the old historic sections.

Puerto Rico has a population of 3.5 million, a third of which lives in the San Juan area. Although Spanish is the leading language, English is widely known and used, especially in the cities. Another 2 million Puerto Ricans live in the New York City area, and since they shuttle back and forth to the mother island, visiting friends and relatives, Puerto Rico becomes more Americanized every year. Nevertheless, the roots of native culture are deep and dominant. Life on the island moves to a very definite southern rhythm, and the stress of northern urban centers will probably remain a foreign malady, no matter how industrialized the commonwealth becomes.

Manners are warm and relaxed in Puerto Rico, and human contact is effortless, even unavoidable. (Taxi drivers may become so garrulous that you will learn their life stories during a 20-minute ride.) Dignity, pride, family loyalty (especially love of children and respect for older people), proper behavior (the traditional Latin importance of the *La Bella Figura* concept)—all are virtues here.

Puerto Rico bows to no other island in the beauty of its beaches, constancy of clement weather, or embarrassment of sporting riches. Geography and nature have blessed Puerto Rico with almost 300 miles of fine, sandy beaches all around the island. The most popular are the ones on the northeast "gold coast," especially the ones connected with the Condado and Isla Verde strips in San Juan, the resorts at Dorado and Cerromar, and the magnificent Luquillo Beach east of San Juan. Yet it would be rather sad to come to this island just for the sea and sun, dazzling though they may be. As in most Latin lands, Puerto Rico's pulse picks up after the sun goes down. In San Juan—in both the old and new sections—nightlife is centered in the big hotels, with their glitzy floor shows, discos that throb till dawn, and action-packed casinos. Out on the island, nightlife is limited to the resorts at Dorado, Cerromar, Palmas del Mar, the Mayagüez Hilton, and to the *paradores* (or country inns), where some form of local entertainment may be provided on weekends.

Some other attractions: beautifully restored little Spanish towns and Indian ceremonial grounds; mountaintop inns; a tropical rain forest; an underground cave system; a space-age observatory; and phosphorescent bays—to name just a few.

MAJOR INTEREST

Old San Juan
El Morro Fortress
San José Church
La Fortaleza
San Juan Cathedral
Cristo Chapel
Shopping
Dining

New San Juan
The Condado Strip/Isla Verde (casinos, nightlife, dining, beaches, deep-sea fishing)

Out on the Island
Nature
Beaches
Resorts
Paradores (inns)

The Offshore Islands
Nature
Peace and quiet

Because no one could ever cover Puerto Rico's leading sights in one visit (as you can in, say, Barbados or Curaçao), you should probably first decide what type of vacation you wish to have, and where you would like to establish your base of operations.

OLD SAN JUAN

Ideally, one day should be spent seeing the sights of the old quarter and another shopping or browsing. Some of San Juan's most popular restaurants are located here, too. You will probably stay in the delightful **Ramada Hotel El Convento**, which has been formed from a 17th-century Carmelite convent.

El Morro. The most important historical monument in Puerto Rico, San Felipe del Morro, is a magnificent, intimidating fortress that juts into the Atlantic from a rocky promontory on the old city's northwest tip. Built in stages between 1540 and 1783, it is a formidable structure, rising 140 feet from sea level to top turret. The views of sea, bay, and city are both breathtaking and time bending—you really do feel a part of the history of another day.

Casa Blanca. This noble and heroically situated house, down a sloping field from El Morro's entrance, was built in the 16th century to be Ponce de León's residence. But he was wounded in Florida searching for the Fountain of Youth, according to legend, and died in Cuba before making it back home. Casa Blanca, tastefully restored and refurbished, is now a museum devoted to family life in 16th- and 17th-century Puerto Rico.

San José Church. A simple, spare, Spanish Gothic masterpiece, this church was begun in 1532, refurbished over the years, and restored by the Jesuits in the 19th century. Adjoining the church is the handsome Dominican Convent, where art exhibits and concerts are held today. Near the church entrance is a townhouse, the **Pablo Casals Museum,** which displays memorabilia of the master musician, including his precious cello. The Spanish-born Casals spent much of his life in Puerto Rico.

La Fortaleza. Built in the 16th century to guard the bay, this imposing structure is now the official residence of Puerto Rico's governors—the oldest executive mansion in the Western Hemisphere. The tours (weekdays except holidays) are excellent.

San Juan Cathedral. Located opposite the Ramada Hotel El Convento, this elaborate Gothic edifice dates from the 19th century, although other religious structures on the spot date back to the early 1500s. The remains of Ponce de León, which for centuries lay in San José

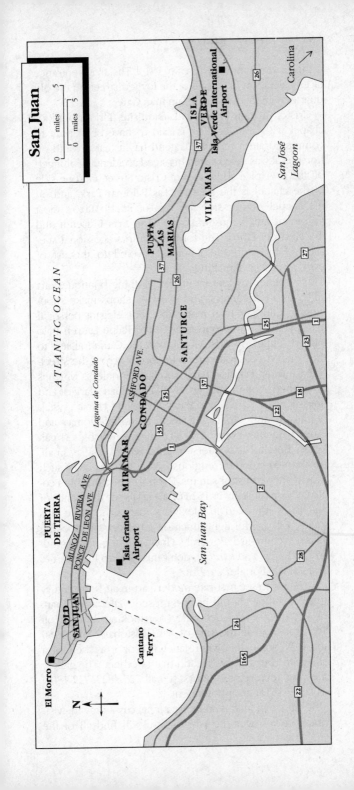

San Juan

0 miles 5

0 miles 5

N

ATLANTIC OCEAN

El Morro

OLD SAN JUAN

PUERTA DE TIERRA

MUÑOZ RIVERA AVE.

PONCE DE LEON AVE.

Laguna de Condado

ASHFORD AVE.

MIRAMAR

CONDADO

PUNTA LAS MARIAS

ISLA VERDE

VILLAMAR

Isla Verde International Airport

Carolina

SANTURCE

Isla Grande Airport

Cantano Ferry

San Juan Bay

San José Lagoon

26

37

26

37

27

25

1

23

37

25

35

1

18

22

2

28

24

165

22

Church, were moved here in 1913. The front entrance faces Caleta San Juan, one of the lovliest streets in the old quarter, which leads to the **San Juan Gate**.

Cristo Chapel. This small, exquisite, indoor-outdoor chapel with a silver altar is said to have been built to commemorate a miracle. Legend has it that a youth on horseback was saved when his steed accidentally plunged off the precipice at the end of Cristo Street. On one side of the chapel is the pleasant Las Palomas Park, and on the chapel's other side are two of Puerto Rico's most important small museums, the **Fine Arts Museum** and the **Casa del Libro**. The former features occasional special exhibits and the latter is devoted to the art of printing and bookmaking.

The numerous jewelry stores, clothing boutiques, art galleries, craft centers, and specialty shops make shopping in Old San Juan irresistible. For elegant personal and gift items, everyone goes to the Ralph Lauren Polo Factory Outlet, on Cristo just below the Cathedral, and to the London Fog boutique, catercorner across the street. N. Barquet and Gastón Bared, both on Fortaleza (which is now a pedestrian mall), are two of San Juan's largest and finest jewelry stores, and each also offers china, crystal, porcelain, and other gift items. Galeria Palomas and Galeria Botello, both on Cristo, are two notable art galleries; Botello also offers original *santos,* those small, handcarved wooden religious figures that are now such sought-after collector's items. Drop by **The Butterfly People Gallery** (upstairs at 152 Fortaleza) to see thousands of butterflies mounted in plexiglass cases. The place also serves a delightful light lunch on a balcony overlooking its inner courtyard. For crafts (including top-notch modern art works and *santos*), don't miss Puerto Rican Art & Crafts at 204 Fortaleza.

A chance to see first-rate modern art in an 18th-century Spanish setting should not be missed: **Galeria San Juan**, 204–206 Boulevard del Valle (overlooking the sea, off Norzagaray, near the fort of San Cristóbal). This 1750 house is home to owner Janet D'Esopo, as well as a gallery for her own work and that of others. The gallery does not keep regular hours, so call 725-3829, 722-1808, or 723-6515 for an appointment.

Because San Juan is an international city—drawing visitors from all over the world—you will find all of the world's major cuisines. Naturally, however, you'll want to sample local specialties, which reflect the island's four major influences: Spanish, Latin America, African, and Indian. Pork (especially succulent roast pig) and chicken are the popular meats, and fish is plentiful in coastal regions. Beans, rice, and bananas (including plantains, which are fried, baked, mashed, and worked into numerous pastries) are the ubiquitous side dishes, and fruits (pineapples, oranges, limes, grapefruit, coconuts, papayas, guavas, and avocados) are put to a thousand uses. Flan and *natilla,* a vanilla cream, are the most popular desserts, along with guava shells or guava paste and cream cheese. Puerto Rican coffee is strong and aromatic, and if you ask for Spanish coffee, you'll get it laced with liquor and topped with whipped cream.

If you are a newcomer to Puerto Rican cuisine, here are a few dishes to get you started. Roast suckling pig, as mentioned, is a must, and *asopao* (a wet rice stew, redolent with flavors and spices) can be made with seafood, chicken, beef, pork, or veal. Dried salt cod, a Friday specialty, is cooked up *en casserole* with sliced potatoes, pimentos, peas, garlic, onion, and herbs. Rice and beans (the beans—black and delicious—are spooned *over* the rice) are the perfect accompaniment to the cod. Key-lime pie (made with the local small, thin-skinned, yellow limes) and coconut pumpkin pudding are sumptuous departures from the usual *flan.* Spanish wines are excellent (they now have a world market), and they are your best bets in Puerto Rico. Local beer is also excellent; ask for Medalla, light or regular.

Among the most romantic and atmospheric restaurants in the restored area are the rather sizable **La Zaragozana**, at 356 San Francisco Street, and the small and intimate **Los Galanes**, in a townhouse near the cathedral at number 65. Both are rather formal (but certainly not stuffy), and service is attentive and unobtrusive.

El Patio de Sam, opposite San José Church at 102 San Sebastián, is the local bar/restaurant/hangout, and it looks as if it's been around forever. Bogie and Bacall would have loved this place (indeed it seems as if they just left), and you should go at least for a beer or *piña colada* at the bar. **La Mallorquina**, possibly the oldest restaurant in Puerto Rico (1848 is the date on the plaque), is a bit shabby and threadbare these days, but its authenticity is unquestioned;

try it for lunch. **The Ramada Hotel El Convento** has a lovely bar/restaurant in its cloistered patio.

A ride on the ferry across San Juan Bay (a dime each way) is essential, not only to enjoy the sweeping views and fresh sea breezes but also to watch the other passengers.

NEW SAN JUAN

For the visitor, New San Juan means the chic beach-front areas of Condado and Isla Verde, which have rows of large hotels along the sea and a number of small, modest guest houses along the side streets. The Condado Strip is lined with fashionable shops and boutiques, and a number of the city's finest restaurants are found here, and in nearby Miramar, many of them in the hotels.

As you leave Old San Juan on your way to Condado, Miramar, or Isla Verde, you will come to the large (on 17 acres) and fashionable **Caribe Hilton Hotel**, ensconced on its own spit of land—which includes old Fort San Gerónimo—in **Puerta de Tierra**. Even if you don't stay here, do tour this paradise within a paradise. Its largest restaurant, **La Rotisserie**, has long been considered Puerto Rico's finest, and its popular meeting-place bar overlooking pool and ocean is one of the putative birthplaces of the *piña colada*. There is a shopping arcade, the city's most elaborate athletic program and sports department, and a new seafood restaurant. A concrete walkway leads to a reef where you can observe fish frolicking.

The magificent, ship-shaped, Art Deco pile next to the Caribe Hilton is the old Normandie Hotel, now being restored as the new Radisson Hotel of San Juan. **Miramar**, a fashionable inland area across the Condado Lagoon, contains a few small, well-run hotels favored by business people. It is also the site of a great local favorite, the **Ali-oli** restaurant in the Excelsior Hotel. The name comes from the Catalonian words for garlic and olive oil, which the chef uses liberally in his pastas and fish dishes.

The Condado Strip

Cross the Puenta Los Dos Hermanos (Two Brothers Bridge) from Puerta de Tierra and the Caribe Hilton, and you are on Ashford Avenue—the Condado Strip, San Juan's answer to Miami Beach.

Here you'll find a world of glitz and glamour on an avenue of hotels standing like sentinels along the Atlantic Ocean shoreline. The **Condado Plaza Hotel & Casino**, the Regency, La Concha, Ramada San Juan, and Howard Johnson's—all are very modern and super-functional and all are within walking distance of the San Juan Convention Center, which brings them so much business. Only the **Condado Beach Hotel**, the great lady of San Juan hotels (built by Cornelius Vanderbilt in 1919 and lovingly preserved and restored) seems to reflect another, quieter, more graceful era. Not surprisingly, it is the Condado Beach to which Puerto Rico's 400 often come for their charity balls, anniversary celebrations, and bridal receptions.

Among and between the big hotels are some of San Juan's most notable shops and restaurants—plus a smattering of small guest houses, of which the delightful **El Canario** and **El Canario by the Sea** are the gems.

Little Switzerland, at 1055 Ashford, the handsomest shop on the Condado Strip, is actually a series of boutiques specializing in fine china, crystal, porcelain, jewelry, and gift items. Level I, at 1004 Ashford, features the best in women's fashions, and Nono Maldonado, at 1051, the latest in both men's and women's wear. Courreges, Ungaro, and Valentino designs can all be found at 1126 Ashford.

Most of Condado's finest restaurants are located in the large hotels: El Gobernador (the Condado Beach), Lotus Flower and Capriccio (the Condado Plaza), and the Greenhouse (an airy, informal, plant-filled restaurant in the Dutch Inn & Towers). But if you have time for only one Condado Strip restaurant, make it **The Chart House**, located in a magnificent old home with shaded verandas, manicured lawns, and gardens—even a treehouse section. Ceiling fans, striking art works (both modern and traditional), historic photos, and highly polished dark woodwork create an extremely pleasant atmosphere of tropical languor and modern comfort. The young service staff couldn't be more attractive and intelligent, and the aloha-shirted bartenders make what may be the best *piña coladas* in town. The menu is simple: top-quality steaks, chops, and roast beef (in giant servings), excellent salads (a Puerto Rican rarity), and perfectly grilled seafood.

Isla Verde

Isla Verde, the beach-front strip beyond Condado near the airport, has entered such a renaissance period in the past few years that it is giving the Condado Strip fierce competition. The **El San Juan Hotel & Casino** and the **Sands Hotel & Casino**—both of which have undergone top-to-bottom renovations that have turned them into posh, self-contained resorts—have joined the well-established ESJ Towers and the **Empress Oceanfront Hotel** to create a new gold coast. The long crescent beach joins all of the hotels, and the calm waters, even on breezy days, make for delightful and serious swimming. The family set, young marrieds, and jazzy singles gravitate toward the El San Juan and the Sands, while the quieter, more contemplative crowd heads for the ESJ Towers or the much smaller but enchanting Empress, with its inviting deck bar overhanging the sea.

Popular activities offered to guests of the Condado and Isla Verde hotels are deep-sea fishing trips (or you can arrange your own excursion through an outfit like Mike Benitez at the Club Náutico de San Juan at the marina in Miramar), year-round thoroughbred horse racing at **El Comandante Racetrack** in the Carolina area (tours leave all hotels), or the full spectrum of water sports, including scuba diving, snorkeling, windsurfing, waterskiing, boating, and sailing.

THE RESORTS

These are the self-contained vacation areas ideally suited for those whose main interests are sports (particularly golf and tennis) and quiet, away-from-it-all relaxation. **Hyatt Dorado Beach**, 30 minutes west of San Juan on the northern coast, is the elegant, sedate resort. **Hyatt Regency Cerromar Beach**, which adjoins the Dorado area, is a jazzier, high-rise resort that attracts large groups and conventions. **Palmas del Mar**, on the island's southeast coast, is a vast, ultramodern, multi-use resort (a hotel, an inn, and individual villas) that occupies a lush, 2,700-acre area that was once a coconut plantation. It attracts both the family trade and the young sports-minded set.

OUT ON THE ISLAND

Renting a car and driving around the island is the very best way to experience the real Puerto Rico. You can set a leisurely pace (food, drink, and rest are only minutes away no matter where you find yourself), and the Puerto Rican people couldn't be friendlier or more anxious to help. Only one word of caution: Equip yourself with good up-to-date road maps because the highways and byways, while in generally good condition, are often poorly marked. Above all, ask frequent questions, even if you speak *un poquito* Spanish—the Puerto Ricans are great communicators.

If you are a first-timer on the island, you may prefer to take a few of the guided day trips and half-day trips out of San Juan, just to get the feel of the countryside with expert guidance.

El Yunque Rainforest: You really do need a guide for this lush, dense, 28,000-acre Caribbean National Forest—otherwise you could easily miss the highlights, such as the observation tower that overlooks the remarkable preserve in its entirety. One-day trips include a visit to **Luquillo Beach**, one of the Caribbean's most perfect strands.

Ponce and the South Coast

Ponce, in the middle of the south coast, and Mayagüez, in the middle of the west coast, are Puerto Rico's second and third cities. Each is a prosperous, thriving, steadily growing commercial center. Although neither is a tourist city in itself, each place contains several notable attractions and each makes a convenient headquarters for side trips to surrounding areas.

Try to pick a day tour or route that goes south on the twisting, turning mountain road, hitting such out-of-the-way villages and towns as Naranjito and Barranquitas, then returning (when you are tired) on the infinitely faster, less taxing superhighway (Route 52). In Ponce you will have a chance to stroll through the central plaza, have lunch in a traditional restaurant—there are many good ones—and visit the estimable **Ponce Museum of Art**.

Ponce makes a perfect headquarters for explorations

along the southern coast (Phosphorescent Bay, 17th-century San Germán, Indian ceremonial centers, and spacious beaches with calm waters). Also near Ponce is Guánica, where U.S. troops first landed in 1898 during the Spanish-American War.

A Ponce stay is recommended only for second or third visits or for those who wish to concentrate on the southern attractions. First-time visitors to Puerto Rico can easily cover Ponce's principal sights on a day trip out of San Juan.

San Germán and **Phosphorescent Bay**, in the southwestern part of Puerto Rico, are best visited from a stay in either Ponce or Mayagüez. (There are no tours from San Juan for these places.) You'll want at least half a day in San Germán to stroll around the well-preserved Little Spanish Town with its 1606 Porta Coeli Church. The bay at La Parguera is ideally seen on moon*less* nights when its iridescent qualities are most evident.

Mayagüez and the West Coast

Situated in the center of the island's west coast, Mayagüez—a bustling fishing port with tuna-processing plants—is the logical stopping place for a leisurely examination of the region's unusual attractions. These include: some of Puerto Rico's most spectacular (and uncrowded) beaches, especially the one at **Boquerón**; rustic fishing villages; superb deep-sea fishing; excursions to the strange, uninhabited island of Mona; a celebrated surfing beach at **Rincón** (site of the 1988 World Surfing Championships); the lush tropical gardens of the U.S. Department of Agriculture's research station; the eerie topography of the island's southwest corner, with its bizarre limestone boulders; salt flats; and the Cabo Rojo Lighthouse, crowning the crest of a stunning promontory.

Mayagüez is also a convenient headquarters for explorations of such attractions mentioned above (under Ponce) as San Germán, Phosphorescent Bay, and Ponce itself. Unlike Ponce, Mayagüez cannot be easily negotiated in a day trip from San Juan (unless you fly), and the area is so seductive that you will want more time. The place to stay is the **Mayagüez Hilton**, which has just completed a $6-million renovation program (including a casino and the new Vista Terrace, with nightly entertainment), making it an attraction in itself.

Arecibo Observatory and the newly reopened Camuy Caves in the northwest section of the island can be taken in during a day trip from San Juan, but start early and plan carefully. (Tours from San Juan don't include these two places.) Entrance to the observatory must be arranged in advance (call 878-2612), and tours are given Tuesday through Friday at 2:00. The caves are open Wednesday through Sunday from eight to five and a weekday visit is strongly advised (call the caves' park office, 898-3100, or the San Juan number, 756-5555, for up-to-date information).

The Paradores

Some 15 small inns (ranging in size from 7 to 53 rooms) are scattered about the island and operated by Paradores Puertorriqueños, an organization sponsored by the island's tourism association. Each has its distinct personality. Coamo is located at a famous mineral springs; Vistamar is perched on a mountaintop overlooking the rugged northwest coast of Puerto Rico's Costa Brava; Hacienda Juanita and Hacienda Gripiñas are up in the mountains on old coffee plantations; Villa Esperanza and Casa del Francés (a guest house) are located on the offshore island of Vieques. They are not fancy, but they are clean and comfortable; and they are the perfect places for visitors to get next to the country and its people. Far from being exclusively tourist stops, the *paradores* are often used by the Puerto Ricans themselves as vacation spots and weekend getaways. The staffs are delightful, the food authentic and hearty, and the activities (nature walks, sightseeing excursions, and scenery appreciation) are restorative.

THE OFFSHORE ISLANDS

Once Puerto Rico has captured your heart—and you want to see and know it *all*—you are ready for an island adventure. Icacos Cay, off the northeast coast (near the fishing village of Fajardo) is a good place to start; it is a deserted natural preserve, and it makes a perfect day trip from San Juan (some of the Isla Verde hotels offer package excursions).

Both **Culebra** and the much larger **Vieques** lie off the eastern coast and are easily reached by a flight from San Juan or ferry from Fajardo; both islands offer simple and inexpensive accommodations in guest houses (five to 32 rooms) and at the Vieques *parador* (50 rooms). Island vacations and visits are not for those who feed on the glamour and the glitter of the Condado Strip's casinos, discos, and international restaurants; but if feasts of nature's wonders sustain your spirit, the offshore life is for you. The beaches on both islands are superb and beautiful, and your days will be so filled with such activities as swimming, surfing, sailing, snorkeling, and scuba diving that you probably won't even notice the absence of casinos and floor shows when night falls.

USEFUL FACTS

What To Wear

Loose-fitting, washable cotton clothing is the hard-and-fast rule: sports or athletic shirts, slacks and shorts for men; tee-shirts, tee-dresses, blouses or sports shirts, shorts, slacks or casual skirts for women; comfortable walking shoes, sneakers, or sandals for all. For dressy evenings, women may add a long skirt, and men will be fine in dark slacks, a light jacket or, to be very Puerto Rican, one of those long-sleeved, fancy dress shirts called *guayaberas*. (Casinos and leading restaurants do appreciate these touches of evening formality.)

Other necessities are sunglasses, sun hats, sunscreens, a collapsible umbrella, an extra bathing suit, U.S. stamps for letters and postcards (they can be hard to find locally), beach and pool sandals, a lightweight robe, and a small bag to carry items normally carried in suit or jacket pockets.

Getting In

Puerto Rico's San Juan International Airport, the busiest airport in the Caribbean, receives direct flights from major U.S. cities via American Airlines, Delta, Eastern, and TWA. Because there is no scheduled direct flight service from Canada to Puerto Rico, most Canadians fly to New York and then proceed directly to San Juan.

From Europe, Air France, British Airways, Iberia, and Lufthansa have recently introduced new service to the island. Virtually all Caribbean cruise ships make San Juan a principal port of call, and combination cruise in/fly out plans can be arranged.

San Juan International Airport, recently expanded, is a model of speed and efficiency. Just outside the luggage area you'll find taxis; hotel limos; inexpensive buses that make the rounds of the hotels in Isla Verde, Condado, and Old San Juan; limos that take you to the resorts of Dorado, Cerromar, and Palmas del Mar (inform these places *in advance* that you will be using their transportation); and *públicos,* the cars of the island's inexpensive car service, which take four or five passengers to cities and towns throughout the island.

Entry Requirements

No documents are required for U.S. citizens (though a passport is always the best ID). Canadian citizens need proof of citizenship (again, a passport is best but a driver's license will suffice), and British subjects need both a passport and visa.

Electrical Current

Same as elsewhere in the U.S. and Canada—110 volts, 60 cycles.

Getting Around

Transportation around Puerto Rico is easily managed via rental cars, Air Puerto Rico, or licensed *públicos* (a public taxi service that takes passengers—up to four or five—from town square to town square. You simply go to the main plaza and hop into the next available car leaving for your destination).

Culebra and Vieques islands, off the eastern coast, are easily reached by air (call Vieques AirLink, 722-3736, or Flamenco Airways, 724-7110 or 725-7707, for arrangements), or by ferry from Fajardo, which is easily reached from San Juan Airport via taxi or *público.* The ferry for Vieques (a one-hour, 20-minute trip) departs daily at 9:15 A.M. and 4:30 P.M. The ferry ride to Culebra takes two hours and leaves Tuesday–Saturday at 4:00 P.M., Saturday, Sunday, and holidays at 9:00 A.M., and Monday (via Vieques) at 9:15 A.M. Cars may be transported on the cargo ferry by calling (one week in advance) 863-0705 or 863-0852, Monday–Friday.

A lot of people fly over to Charlotte Amalie on St. Thomas for a day of duty-free shopping. There are frequent flights from San Juan International Airport; resorts such as Dorado and Cerromar can fly you over and back from their own airstrips.

Business Hours

In tourist areas, such as Old San Juan and the Condado Strip, stores and shops will often stay open late. Evening restaurant hours tend to follow the Spanish custom of late dining at around nine or ten.

Festivals

Almost every town and village in Puerto Rico has its festivals and saints days celebrations, which are listed in the free monthly guide *Qué Pasa*. San Juan's ongoing, year-round LeLoLai festival is the island's best introduction to native song and dance. Dances, music, presentations, films, cruises, and fiestas take place at different locations. The Institute of Puerto Rican Culture Theater also sponsors frequent concerts, religious festivals, and folkloric evenings. Festival Casals (held every June), the Fine Arts Center Festival Hall in new San Juan's Santurce district, and Old San Juan's historic Tapia Theater (the New World's oldest theater in continuous use) offer performances in classical and modern music, dance, and drama.

ACCOMMODATIONS REFERENCE

The rate ranges given here are projections for fall 1988 through spring 1989. Unless otherwise indicated, rates are for double rooms, double occupancy. The telephone area code for Puerto Rico is 809.

▶ **Caribe Hilton International.** P.O. Box 1872, San Juan, PR 00903. $122–$260. Tel: 721-0303 or (800) 468-8585.

▶ **Condado Beach Hotel.** 1071 Ashford Ave., San Juan, PR 00907. $150–$230. Tel: 721-6090.

▶ **Condado Plaza Hotel & Casino.** 999 Ashford Ave., San Juan, PR 00907. $185–$235. Tel: 721-1000.

▶ **El Canario** and **El Canario by the Sea.** 1317 Ashford Ave. and 4 Condado, San Juan, PR 00907. $60–$80. Tel:

724-2793 or 722-3861 (Canario) and 722-8640 (Sea). Small guest houses next to one another.

▶ **Empress Oceanfront**. 2 Amapola, Isla Verde, PR 00913. $125–$140. Tel: 791-3083.

▶ **Hilton International Mayagüez**. Route 2, Mayagüez, PR 00709. $139–$165. Tel: 834-7575 or 724-0161.

▶ **Hyatt Dorado Beach**. Route 693, Dorado, PR 00646. $275–$440. Tel: 796-1600 or (800) 228-9000.

▶ **Hyatt Regency Cerromar Beach**. Route 693, Dorado, PR 00646. $200–$275. Tel: 796-1010 or (800) 228-9000.

▶ **Palmas del Mar**. Route 906, Humacao, PR 00661. $115–$190. Tel: 852-6000.

▶ **Ramada Hotel El Convento**. 100 Cristo St., San Juan, PR 00901. $85–$125. Tel: 723-9020 or (800) 468-2779.

▶ **El San Juan Hotel & Casino**. 187 Isla Verde Rd., Isla Verde, PR 00913. $190–$390. Tel: 791-1000 or (800) 468-2818.

▶ **Sands Hotel & Casino**. Isla Verde. $175–$275. Tel: 791-6100 or (800) 443-2009.

OTHER ACCOMMODATIONS

▶ **Holiday Inn**. Route 2, Ponce, PR 00731. $95–$125. Tel: 844-1200. For those who want more modern accommodations.

▶ **Meliá Hotel**. 2 Cristina St., Ponce, PR 00731. $60–$70. Tel: 842-0260/1. A modest, long-established hotel in the heart of town, next to the historic central plaza. The hotel restaurant is a popular meeting place for locals.

THE PARADORES

The general number for information and reservations at all paradores is 721-2884 or (800) 443-0266.

▶ **Baños de Coamo Parador**. Route 546 off the superhighway running from San Juan to Ponce, Coamo, PR 00340. $58. Tel: 825-2186. Built on the ruins of the island's oldest resort. Franklin Roosevelt, Thomas Edison, and Alexander Graham Bell used to come here for the healing hot sulphur springs.

▶ **Casa del Francés**. Barrio Esperanza, Vieques Island, PR 00765. $55. Tel: 741-3751. A marvelous old white mansion turned guest house.

▶ **Hacienda Gripiñas Parador**. Route 527, Jayuya, PR 00664. $40. Tel: 828-1717. On an old coffee plantation in the mountains above Ponce. Convenient to Ponce attractions and to the Caguana Indian Ceremonial Park and other south-central attractions.

▶ **Hacienda Juanita Parador.** Route 105, Maricao, PR 00706. $40 Tel: 838-2550. On an old coffee plantation in the mountains near Mayagüez.

▶ **Oasis Parador.** Luna St., P.O. Box 144, San Germán, PR 00753. $60. Tel: 892-1175. A charming, in-town inn with a fine patio restaurant.

▶ **Villa Esperanza Parador.** Esperanza, Vieques Island, PR 00765. $50–$76. Tel: 741-8675. Puerto Rico's newest parador.

▶ **Villa Parguera Parador.** Route 304, Lajas, PR 00667. $60. Tel: 899-3975. An ideal stopping spot for visiting Phosphorescent Bay on the southwest coast.

▶ **Vistamar Parador.** Route 113, Quebradillas, PR 00742. $45–$60. Tel: 895-2065. On a hill overlooking the spectacular northwest coast.

THE UNITED STATES VIRGIN ISLANDS

By Susan Farewell

As Associate Travel Editor of Condé Nast's Bride's *magazine, Susan Farewell travels frequently throughout the Caribbean to report on honeymoon destinations.*

Film crews from around the world travel to St. Thomas, St. Croix, and St. John to shoot movies, commercials, and the pages of fashion magazines. It's easy to see why. All three islands provide that quintessential Caribbean backdrop: clear skies, unblemished white beaches, and clear blue water.

These islands are America's paradise, according to the residents' license plates, and indeed, they are very American. The United States bought this family of islands in 1917 to help guard the Panama Canal, and the islands now have fast-food restaurants, supermarkets, and even delis.

On Columbus's second voyage to the New World in 1493, he named these islands—along with the neighboring islands that are now the British Virgin Islands—after

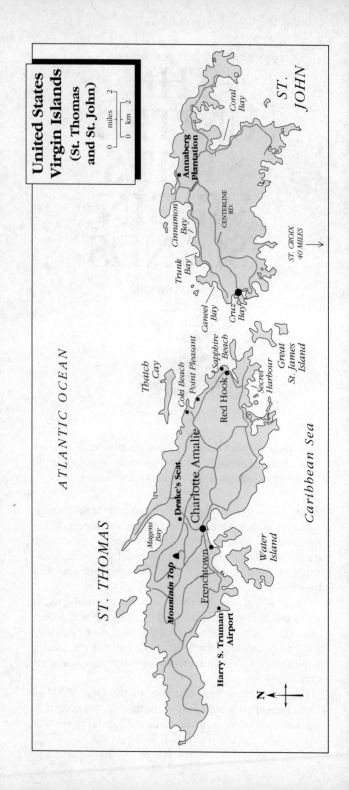

United States Virgin Islands (St. Thomas and St. John)

ATLANTIC OCEAN

Caribbean Sea

ST. THOMAS

ST. JOHN

Magens Bay

Mountain Top ▲

Drake's Seat ■

Charlotte Amalie

Frenchtown ■

Harry S. Truman Airport ■

Water Island

Thatch Cay

Coki Beach ■

Point Pleasant ■

Red Hook ■

Sapphire Beach ●

Secret Harbour

Great St. James Island

Caneel Bay

Cruz Bay ●

Trunk Bay

Cinnamon Bay

Annaberg Plantation ●

Coral Bay

CENTERLINE RD.

ST. CROIX 40 MILES →

0   miles   2
0   km   2

N

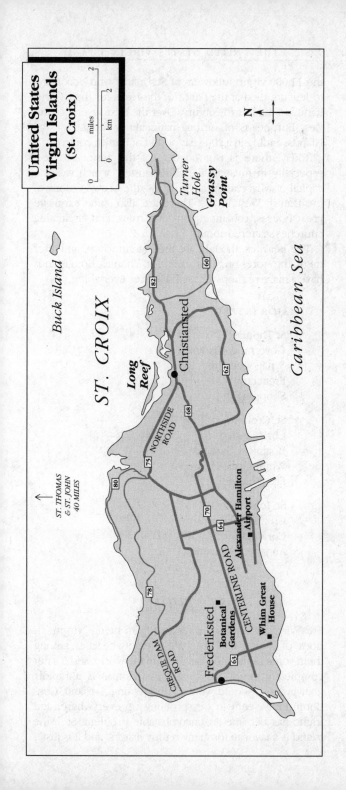

United States
Virgin Islands
(St. Croix)

miles
km

Buck Island

ST. THOMAS
& ST. JOHN
40 MILES

ST. CROIX

Long Reef

Christiansted

NORTHSIDE ROAD

Turner Hole

Grassy Point

Caribbean Sea

Alexander Hamilton Airport

CENTERLINE ROAD

Whim Great House

Botanical Gardens

Frederiksted

CREQUE DAM ROAD

the 11,000 virgin followers of St. Ursula, who, according to legend, died at the hands of the Huns for their Christianity in the fourth century. Over the next several centuries, Europeans of various nationalities fought for the islands, ending in a 200-year period of Danish control.

Today, there is a good deal of this history to see, especially in museumlike Christiansted, which was the capital of what was then—in 1733—the Crown Colony of the Danish West Indies. There are also some exquisite great houses, romantic plantation ruins, and fascinating churches scattered about.

The beaches, though, are the big attraction, and after them, the stores on St. Croix and St. Thomas. Both islands have a maze of shops that sell duty-free everything.

MAJOR INTEREST

St. Thomas
Government House
Synagogue Hill
Frenchtown
Shopping

St. Croix
Christiansted
Botanical Gardens
Whim Great House
Frederiksted

St. John
Cruz Bay area
Coral Bay
Annaberg Plantation

ST. THOMAS

This Virgin Island is the furthest from being "virgin." It does, of course, have its share of empty beaches, among them some of the most beautiful in the world, and it's not completely developed... yet. St. Thomas is a rapidly growing—or should we say "progressing"—island. Condominiums seem to be sprouting up everywhere, and traffic has become an uncombatable problem. Still, the island is a favorite for many return visitors, and it is just a boat ride away from dozens of unspoiled isles and cays, a consolation for lifelong residents.

In spite of these signs of progress, St. Thomas has managed to retain some of its original charm. Along with the fast-food places, there are open-air shacks serving West Indian dishes (some of the seediest looking joints have the best cuisine and prices). And though there are several could-be-anywhere hotels and condo communities, there are also some wonderful little hostelries, including the Hotel 1829 and Blackbeard's Castle, where guests swap sections of the Sunday *New York Times* around the pool.

Charlotte Amalie

You can see all of St. Thomas in about five hours, spending two of them weaving your way through the labyrinth of streets in Charlotte Amalie (ah-MAHL-yah). The capital of the U.S.V.I., the town has a reputation for being the biggest duty-free port in the Caribbean. One look at its main street (Dronningens Gade) and you'll understand why: One gleaming jewelry store stands next to another, interspersed with linen and leather shops. There is also a series of tunnel-like arcades that are almost always filled with cruise-ship passengers who scatter around town the minute the gangplank goes down.

Just outside the main shopping area—you can't miss it—is **Fort Christian**, a cranberry-red bastion built by the Danes in 1617. It now houses a small museum with a modest collection of Arawak and Carib Indian artifacts and a couple of displays depicting the early Danish history of the island. The **Senate Building** stands on the harbor side of the fort. Completed in the 1870s as a Danish marine barracks, today it houses the Virgin Islands legislature.

You need strong legs to venture elsewhere in Charlotte Amalie, because most of the city is built on three steep hills. The climb up the steps of Government Hill to the **Government House** on Kongens Gade is a must. Built in 1867 as a meeting place for the Danish Colonial Council, the house is now the governor's official residence. Inside there are several historical murals, as well as a collection of paintings by local artists, including the Impressionist Camille Pissarro, who was born in St. Thomas. Also on

Kongens Gade, you'll find the Hotel 1829, a European-style inn built by a French sea captain; the Street of the 99 Steps (one of the few remaining streets of the old Danish town); and **Au Bon Vivant**, where you may have a meal you rate the best on the island. It's owned by a Guadeloupe chef who creates wondrously flavorful dishes like conch ragout and grouper Creole.

The Frederik Lutheran Church, at the foot of Government Hill, was built in 1826 on the site of the island's first Lutheran church. Its 18th-century ecclesiastical silver, brought over from Denmark, is still used today. The Synagogue of Berecha V'Shalom V'Gemilath Chasidim (Blessing and Peace and Loving Deeds) is perched atop the neighboring Synagogue Hill. Built by Sephardic Jews in 1833, it is said to be the Western Hemisphere's second oldest synagogue still standing. (The oldest is in Curaçao.)

Hotel 1829 and Blackbeard's Castle are not on the water, but they make up for it with charm. The **Hotel 1829** is a St. Thomas landmark with rooms overlooking a central bougainvillaea-draped courtyard. It has antique four-poster beds, high wood ceilings, and Haitian artwork throughout. **Blackbeard's Castle** is very small (just eight rooms) and elegantly run by co-owners Bob Harrington and Henrique Konzen. The decor is simple but tasteful. Both places have terrific views of Charlotte Amalie and the harbor and an interesting roster of guests, many repeats and mostly couples.

Frenchtown

Back on the waterfront, just west of town, is Frenchtown, a small enclave settled by third- and fourth-generation descendants of refugees who fled the Swedish invasion of St. Barts in the late 18th century and who still speak a Norman-French dialect. Frenchtown is home to French fishermen and farmers, and it's also a little pocket of exceptionally good restaurants. Try **Alexander's** (hot and chilled soups, Austrian dishes, and an international clientele) and **Johnnycakes** (deliriously good kalaloo soup with blobs of chicken, seafoods with Creole sauces, and a very social atmosphere).

For the island's best local food, though, take a cab over to one of the **Eunice's** (there are two: one at the Inn at

Mandahl, the other on Smith Road). The catch of the day—broiled, boiled, sautéed, or fried—is accompanied by heaping servings of spicy rice, fungi (a mixture of cornmeal and okra), and breadfruit (an island staple).

Out on the Island

St. Thomas is not very big—just 32 square miles—so you are never far from Charlotte Amalie or from some of the island's most beautiful natural spots and beaches. Spend at least one afternoon driving over its lumpy little hills, making stops at Drake's Seat (good views), Magens Bay (an immaculate mile-long beach), and Mountain Top (the island's highest point).

Magens Bay is the island's most beautiful beach, with calm, glass-clear water and powdery white sands. **Pineapple Beach**, at the Stouffer Grand Beach Resort, has every water sport imaginable, and lessons are available there too. Other beaches worth finding include **Coki Beach** on the northeastern shore and **Sapphire** on the Eastern End. At both, you can rent snorkel gear and pollywog about in unbelievably clear water. **Hull Bay** on the northern shore has good surfing conditions. There are several dive and snorkel centers around the island, including those at Secret Harbour and Stouffers. Sportfishing and sailing (as well as snorkeling and diving) can be arranged through the Red Hook Charter Office.

There's not much in the way of terra firma sporting on St. Thomas, with the exception of a little golf and tennis. The best place for both is **Mahogany Run**, a golf/tennis/condo community on the north shore. It has an 18-hole course overlooking the Atlantic and two courts lit for night play.

At night, there are steel-band and calypso shows at many of the island's larger hotels. If you're not up for watching limbos, bottle dancing, and fire eating, though, you may want to steer clear of them. Your best bet might be to have a leisurely dinner and then settle down on chaise lounges with a couple of fruity concoctions around your hotel's pool. If you must go out, consider the **Agave Terrace** at Point Pleasant Resort: calypso Tuesdays, steel bands Thursdays, and a guitarist Saturdays and Sundays. As far as discos go, *St. Thomas This Week,* a free local publication, has the most up-to-date listings.

If you want to be on the water and out on the island, consider staying at **Point Pleasant**. Its so-called "units" (actually condos that serve as a hotel during certain times of the year) are built into a bluff and are attractively decorated with rattan and floral fabric. Each has a view of the sea. Guests are predominantly couples of all ages; many like to keep to themselves.

Right down the hill—smack dab on the beach—is the **Stouffer Grand Beach Resort**, a complex of brown-gray shingled units with motorized buggies whizzing about. It's a large, has-everything luxury resort and attracts lots of honeymooners. Over on the eastern end of the island, you'll find several condominium communities, one being **Secret Harbour**, which has spacious rental apartments (with maid service). It's set on a beach and is ideal for couples, families, and groups of friends.

ST. CROIX

"Drive past two tamarind trees, take a left at the mahogany, go up the hill, and you'll be there." Expect to hear something like this if you ask a Cruzan (a native resident of St. Croix) for directions. Although a good part of the island—like its sibling St. Thomas—has the smack of a New York City suburb, St. Croix hasn't completely lost its West Indian character either.

Christiansted

The most famous and most visited place on St. Croix is Christiansted, a warren of narrow streets lined with Easter-egg-colored buildings. The town has a Disney-esque quality about it, with sparkling paint jobs, carefully stenciled shop signs, and, overall, a very tidy look. The centerpiece is a four-square-block area of restored 18th-century Danish buildings and a small, unforbidding, squash-yellow fort. The Visitors Bureau in the Old Scalehouse building will provide you with a brochure outlining a self-guided walking tour of the area.

It seems that every visitor to St. Croix spends at least one day shopping, and cruise ships—they dock across the island in Frederiksted—send passengers over by the busload. There are bargains to be found if you are up to dealing with the throngs.

Most of St. Croix's restaurants occupy second floors above shops and hotels. The most popular breakfast spot is **Donn's**, over the Anchor Inn. You can have endless mugs of strong coffee and your choice of more than a dozen omelets while watching the action on the wharf. The dock is especially busy in the morning. Snorkel boats gear up to take amphibious types out to nearby **Buck Island** (a mesmerizingly beautiful underwater National Park), suntanned blondes scrub down sailboats, and local partygoers exchange stories about the previous night. If you're in the mood for a simple lunch, try the **Banana Bay Club** for a burger, a basket of shrimp, or a chicken salad. It, too, sits on the water.

Favorite dinner spots on the island include the **Club Comanche**—which is also a charming inn—with ceiling fans, peacock chairs, and servings big enough for two. The fish of the day cooked Cruzan style (spicy, tomatoey) is always a good choice. **Frank's**—a mainstay of the community—has a party atmosphere and specializes in Caribbean-Italian dishes. **Top Hat** is a small, elegant spot that prides itself on its Danish dishes—split pea soup, *frikadeller* (meatballs with red cabbage), and herring platters. **Tivoli Gardens**, festooned with small white lights and leafy hanging plants, has a very international menu.

Dinners can be topped off with nightcaps at a number of bars around town. The **Moonraker Lounge**, at the Lodge Hotel on Queen Cross Street, usually has some good guitar music. The **Bombay Club** on King Street features jazz seven nights a week. Try to track down where the saxophone player Jimmy Hamilton and his quartet are playing (most hotels have the information); it seems that everyone who has ever been to St. Croix knows about Jimmy.

There are several small, attractive inns in Christiansted. One of the best is **Pink Fancy**, a restored 18th-century Danish townhouse that was once a private club for wealthy planters. Each of its 13 rooms is named after one of the island's old plantations (Upper Love, Jealousy, Sweet Bottom) and is handsomely decorated in white, except for the Mexican terra-cotta tiled floors and the

Brazilian imbuia doors. Pink Fancy was popular among well-known performers, writers, and painters in the fifties, and today attracts professionals seeking peace and quiet.

The East End

The Buccaneer, just east of town, was for years considered to be the island's most prestigious resort, at least until the advent of Carambola on the northwest shore. The setting is absolutely glorious—its grounds sprawl down a hill above Christiansted Harbor. Part of the Buccaneer's now flamingo-pink main building was originally built for a Knight of Malta in 1653. Then the French bought the place and later the Danes, who turned it into a residence for the island's first governor, Baron von Prock. Guests stay in the Danish Colonial rooms in the main house or in the more modern beach-side suites and rooms. Sports include tennis and golf, and there's a spa and a private beach with scuba diving, snorkeling, swimming, sport-fishing, you name it—all are big at The Buccaneer. It's also one of St. Croix's most popular night spots, with live bands and dancing at the al fresco bar.

Just a little farther east is **Tamarind Reef Beach Club**, a collection of efficiency units with screened-in porches. It's very quiet, right next to the Green Cay Marina on a wonderfully secluded beach. Guests tend to be families. There are not many other places to stay on the eastern end of the island; one exception might be the Grapetree Beach Hotel, which—because it has recently been sold to Divi Divi with talk of ambitious plans for renovations and developments—is a bit of an uncertainty now.

Many of the island's nicest beaches are carved out of the eastern end of the island. Follow the road that clings to the coast and pull over whenever you see an appealing strand. All beaches are public. Just ten minutes outside of town is **Duggan's Reef**, one of the island's best. Those in front of hotels are open to all visitors, sometimes for a small fee. The southeast coast along Turner Hole is especially beautiful, and it's at its best at **Grassy Point**, with views of the sea stretching off in a carpet of blues and greens. And its not just the beach that will capture your attention—the lush scenery of the interior is glorious, too.

To Frederiksted

The Centerline Road, the oldest on the island, runs in a more or less straight line to connect Christiansted with Frederiksted. There are two notable stops along the way: the Botanical Gardens and Whim Great House. The gardens are built around the ruins of a 19th-century sugar-cane workers' village; the great house was built in 1794 on a sugar plantation and has been carefully restored by the Landmarks Society.

Frederiksted

Cruzans consider Frederiksted, the island's "other" town, to be the "West Indian" town of St. Croix and Christiansted to be more cosmopolitan and more Danish. Most of Frederiksted's original Danish Colonial buildings were destroyed by fire and replaced by wood Victorian ginger-bread, although some of its landmarks date back to the 1700s. Cruise ships tie up at its deepwater port, but most passengers are whisked through Frederiksted to Christiansted. As a result, Frederiksted has a marvelous, undiscovered air about it. Pick up a copy of the walking-tour guide at the Customs House and wander around to the fort, the marketplace, and other relatively untouristed places of interest.

The **Royal Dane Hotel** on Strand Street, overlooking the harbor, is a 225-year-old townhouse that has been completely renovated to become a West Indian inn. There are only about a dozen rooms, and all have high ceilings, tasteful furnishings, and prints from the owner's private collection. Guests—who tend to be young and well-heeled—can use La Grange Beach and Tennis Club, just a few minute's walk away.

The Northwest

Northside Drive follows the coastline up from Frederiksted, passing one elegant great house after another. Among them is **Sprat Hall**, the oldest continuously lived-in great house in St. Croix. It dates back to the French occupation of 1650–1690, when it was built to duplicate an original in Brittany. It is now an inn-with-dining room, run by owners Jim and Joyce Hurd, whose families have been on the island since the 1700s. The dining room occupies the original ballroom and specializes in old island recipes. Most guests come for the horseback riding; there are stables on the grounds.

To immerse yourself in some of the island's most intensely beautiful scenery, consider taking a four-wheel vehicle on nearby **Creque Dam Road**, which meanders through an Edenesque rain forest just off the Northside Drive.

The **Carambola** is the latest in a chain of the toney resorts that Laurence Rockefeller began to build in the fifties. It's set on a peach of a beach on the northwest shore at the foot of steep, green hills. Guests stay in pastel air-conditioned villas that are an architectural cross between Danish Colonial and Caribbean style and are elaborately decorated with handcarved mahogany furniture and island artwork. The guest list tends to include business people using the hotel's meeting rooms and couples of all ages, many with children in tow. Guests often come to play golf at **Fountain Valley** on the Robert Trent Jones course, which has been around since Rockefeller bought the land in the fifties.

On the north coast road leading back to Christiansted is another plantation house with overnight accommodations. **Cane Bay Plantation** is set on 22 acres at the foot of Mt. Eagle, opposite Cane Bay. The 200-year-old main house now has a lobby and restaurant. Guests (who are predominantly couples, all ages) stay in a two-story building or in one of 11 cottages that were originally slave quarters or storage areas. There are two freshwater pools on the grounds; the beach is across the street.

ST. JOHN

All too often you return to a favorite island and discover that what was once your favorite view is now the site of a mega-resort, or that a shopping mall has sprung up next to the house you've been renting for years. Thanks to Laurence Rockefeller, more than two thirds of St. John is a National Park, so there's no chance of such things happening. The Rockefeller family bought up large hunks of the island in the 1950s and turned it over to the U.S. National Parks Service for perpetual safekeeping and preservation.

Today, the whole island seems like an open-air museum. A controlled number of tourists, armed with beach bags, visors, and all sorts of cameras and lenses, ferry over daily to Cruz Bay from Red Hook on St. Thomas. Everyone comes to see the scenery and to lie on the beaches, which are lovely. Also, there are many of them, so your chances of having a strand entirely to yourself are better than on St. Thomas.

St. John is a curvaceous little island with lots of greenery and flowers that smell so sweet they are almost asphyxiating at times. It is easy to explore on your own in a rented Jeep or MiniMoke (an open-air vehicle that makes VW bugs look big), but some of the island's guided tours are exceptionally good. Most of the guides are native St. Johnians who take you to such sites as the **Annaberg Sugar Plantation**; **Trunk Bay** (the most popular beach on the island); and a number of scenic overlooks. Another standard tour follows the Danish Centerline Road to Coral Bay, the site of the first permanent Danish settlement on St. John. You have plenty of time to walk around the ruins of Fort Berg (scene of a major slave revolt in 1733–1734) and the Emmaus Moravian Church. Tours usually end in Cruz Bay, the island's hub.

For all-out beaching on St. John, head straight over to Trunk Bay or to **Cinnamon Bay**, both of which are part of the Virgin Islands National Park. Both also have chaise lounges and snorkeling gear for rent as well as changing rooms, showers, and snack bars. And both are about as beautiful as a beach can get. But you can also spread out your towels on just about any inviting little stretch of sand that happens to catch your eye as you drive around the island.

The Cruz Bay Area

Cruz Bay is a picturesque little town filled with attractive vacationers in resort attire. Everyone seems to behave "correctly." Day-tripping visitors from St. Thomas gravitate to Mongoose Junction, which is an assemblage of shops (some would call it a mall, but it's far too attractive to be given such a label). Artisans at the **Donald Schnell Studio**—you can usually watch them at work—create pottery that is quite good, especially the rough-textured coral work.

The *grande dame* of places to stay on St. John is unquestionably **Caneel Bay**, which locals refer to as "Larry's Place." Caneel Bay is the first of several resort properties Laurence Rockefeller developed in the Caribbean. Sprawling over 170 acres on a peninsula within the designated National Park area, it has an air of clubbiness, and attracts lots of affluent couples—both newlyweds and those who have been coming for 25 years. Guests have a choice of seven beaches for lounging, snorkeling, or sailing. The Rockresorts were recently sold to the CSX Corporation, a multibillion-dollar conglomerate that many fear will commercialize what have always been very select properties. Time will tell.

USEFUL FACTS

What to Wear
Dress is casual all over the U.S.V.I., but it is against the law to wear bathing suits away from the beach. The only places where you will need a tie and jacket are the Rockresorts. Nights can get a bit cool, so pack a sweater or two.

Getting In
American Airlines and Pan American fly nonstop from New York to both St. Thomas and St. Croix. American also flies direct to both from Dallas/Fort Worth. Pan American, Eastern, and Midway all have flights from Miami. Eastern offers service from a number of U.S. cities via connecting flights in San Juan.

From London, Pan American often offers special deals combining cheap transatlantic fares with Caribbean add-ons. From other parts of Europe, it's usually necessary to stay overnight in San Juan, Miami, or New York.

Passengers bound for St. John fly into St. Thomas, taxi to Red Hook, and take the 20-minute ferry over to Cruz Bay or Caneel Bay; there are also seaplane flights.

Entry Requirements
U.S. citizens need only proof of residency (a birth certificate or voter-registration card). Citizens of other nations must have passports.

Electrical Current

Same as elsewhere in the U.S. and Canada—110–120 volts, 60 cycles.

Getting Around

Seaplanes and ferries service all of the U.S. Virgins; regular flights travel between St. Croix and St. Thomas.

The best way to get around on the individual islands is by rental car. Otherwise, taxis are readily available and fairly inexpensive; they are also available for tours of the islands.

Business Hours

Shops are customarily open from 9:00–5:00 daily, except on Sunday.

Holidays

In addition to the standard American holidays, the Virgin Islands observe January 6 (Three Kings' Day); March 31 (Transfer Day, celebrating the transfer of the Danish West Virgin Islands to America); April 29 (Children's Carnival parade); April 30 (Grand Carnival parade); June 20 (Organic Act Day); July 3 (Emancipation Day, commemorating the freeing of the slaves in 1848); July 25 (Hurricane Supplication Day); October 17 (Hurricane Thanksgiving Day); November 1 (Liberty Day); and December 26 (Boxing Day).

ACCOMMODATIONS REFERENCE

The rate ranges given here are projections for fall 1988 through spring 1989. Unless otherwise indicated, rates are for double rooms, double occupancy. The telephone area code for the U.S. Virgin Islands is 809.

St. Thomas

▶ **Blackbeard's Castle.** P.O. Box 6041, Charlotte Amalie, St. Thomas, U.S.V.I. 00801. $90–$170. Tel: 776-1234.

▶ **Hotel 1829.** P.O. Box 1567, Charlotte Amalie, St. Thomas, U.S.V.I. 00801. $55–$155, E.P. Tel: 776-1829.

▶ **Point Pleasant.** Estate Smith Bay No. 4, Charlotte Amalie, St. Thomas, U.S.V.I. 00802. $150–315, E.P. Tel: 775-7200 or (800) 524-2300.

▶ **Secret Harbour Beach Hotel.** P.O. Box 7576, St.

Thomas, U.S.V.I. 00801. $135–$255. Tel: 775-6550 or (800) 524-2250.

▶ **Stouffer Grand Beach Resort.** P.O. Box 8267, St. Thomas, U.S.V.I. 00801. $155–$330, meal plans available. Tel: 775-1510 or (800) HOTELS-1.

St. Croix

▶ **The Buccaneer Hotel.** P.O. Box 218, Christiansted, St. Croix, U.S.V.I. 00820. $115–$300. Tel: 773-2100 or (800) 223-1108.

▶ **Cane Bay Plantation.** Estate Cane Bay, P.O. Box G, King's Hill Station, St. Croix, U.S.V.I. 00850. $61–$140. Tel: 778-0410.

▶ **Carambola Beach Resort & Golf Club.** P.O. Box 3031, King's Hill, St. Croix, U.S.V.I. 00850. $250–$410, E.P. Tel: 778-3800 or (800) 223-7637.

▶ **Pink Fancy.** 27 Prince St., Christiansted, St. Croix, U.S.V.I. 00820. $75–$150, C.P. Tel: 773-8460 or (800) 524-2045. (One block from the VI seaplane shuttle.)

▶ **The Royal Dane Hotel.** 13 Strand St., Frederiksted, St. Croix, U.S.V.I. 00840. $35–$110. Tel: 772-2780/2785.

▶ **Sprat Hall Plantation.** Rte. 63, P.O. Box 695, Frederiksted, St. Croix, U.S.V.I. 00840. $80–$120 (main house). Tel: 772-0305 or (800) 834-3584.

▶ **Tamarind Reef Beach Club.** Estate Southgate, Christiansted, St. Croix, U.S.V.I. 00820. $80–$195. Tel: 773-0463 or (800) 524-2036.

St. John

▶ **Caneel Bay.** Caneel Bay, St. John, U.S.V.I. 00830. $235–$575, A.P. Tel: 776-6111 or (800) 223-7637.

OTHER ACCOMMODATIONS

St. Croix

▶ **Club Comanche.** 1 Strand St., Christiansted, St. Croix, U.S.V.I. 00820. $50–$130. Tel: 773-0210. In the heart of Christiansted, a West Indian inn with some four-poster beds, old chests, and mahogany mirrors.

▶ **King Christian Hotel.** P.O. Box 3619, Christiansted, St. Croix, U.S.V.I. 00820. $60–$105. Tel: 773-2285 or (800) 524-2012. Wharfside; lots of activity. Rooms 201 and 301 have the best views and balconies facing the wharf. Many repeat guests—frequently nautical types.

THE BRITISH VIRGIN ISLANDS

By Susan Farewell

The writer Lawrence Durrell wrote about a disease not yet classified by medical science that he called "islomania," which afflicts "people who find islands somehow irresistible."

You couldn't find an archipelago that is more fitting for "islomaniacs" than the British Virgin Islands. There are about 50 islands in the B.V.I.—only 16 of them inhabited—clustered together like croutons in soup. None of them is so big you ever forget you're on an island. Water is always nearby and most often within sight.

For years, these islands have been well known among yachtsmen, who come from all over the world to explore the small bays and coves scalloped out of the shores. But the appeal of the B.V.I. extends beyond the deck of a sloop. Probably the biggest draw is the fact that the islands have not yet sprouted into a tourist mecca. They are somewhat more difficult to reach than some Caribbean islands, which means fewer people travel to them, which in turn means that there are empty beaches and undisturbed reefs. Nightlife is low-keyed, revolving around dinners and around drinks in open-air bars at the hotels.

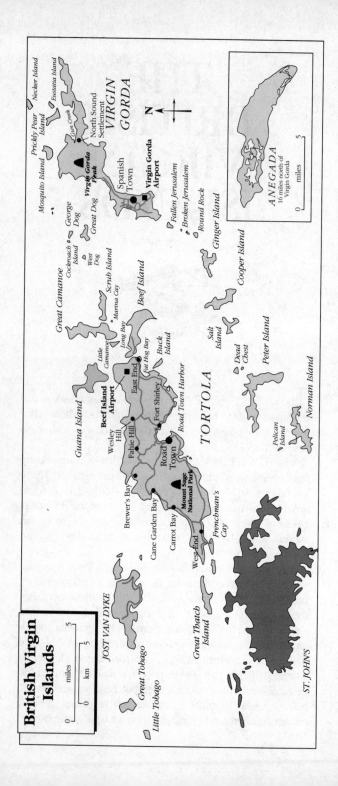

In spite of the obvious British connection, the islands make up a territory with a locally elected government, and you are more apt to find the foods, lifestyles, and people of North America as well as the West Indies. There are traces of the U.K., though, such as driving on the left, afternoon tea, and cricket.

MAJOR INTEREST

Sailing

Tortola
Road Town

Virgin Gorda
The Baths

Off Salt Island
The underwater *Wreck of the Rhone*

TORTOLA

Tortola, the hub around which the B.V.I. radiate, seems meant by nature to be a sailors' world. Perfect little coves lie scooped out of its coastline, and coral reefs segregate rough seas from smooth waters. Tortola is a small island, a mere ten square miles, which makes the scale of things reassuring. Within the span of one or two days, you can visit all its beauty spots and historic sites.

Road Town

The tiny capital of Road Town is the nucleus of all commercial and political activity in the B.V.I. Even so, it takes less than ten minutes to walk from one end of town to the other, past traditional Virgin Island houses that have been painstakingly restored. You may want to add a few minutes to the walk for a glance in the town's three-room museum, with its good collection of finds from island digs—notably some pre-Columbian artifacts—and plantation-period furniture.

A popular lunch spot is **Caribbean Casseroles** in the Old Pickering House (home of the island's first lieutenant governor, the Quaker John Pickering) on Main Street. The Canadian couple who own the place pride themselves on their interesting selection of West Indian, Mexican, and vegetarian dishes. For some exceptionally good local food, hire a taxi to take you to the impossible-to-find-on-your-own **Aries Club**. Locals crowd in, especially during weekday lunch hours, for some of the island's best fish, accompanied by ample servings of rice, potatoes, plantains, and vegetables. Try mauvy (or maube), a sweet nonalcoholic drink made from bark.

To mingle with "boaties," stay at the **Moorings Mariner Inn**, a five-minute cab ride out of town. Its open-air bar and restaurant are always packed with sailing types sporting honey-gold tans that make them look as if they were slowly roasted on a spit. The conversation is 100-percent sailing talk (winds, anchorages, the 51-foot this, the 37-foot that). Occasionally, a proud skipper dog, wearing a bandana, trots through, claws clicking on the red-tile floor. Rooms are very Caribbeana: no air conditioning, just lazy ceiling fans and tepid sea breezes wafting in with reliable consistency. Furnishings are simple—you'll never feel guilty flinging your wet towels down on them. All rooms have terraces, and some look out on the marina.

On the other end of town, the seven-room **Fort Burt** crowns a hilltop overlooking Road Town Harbour and occupies a Dutch fort that dates back to 1666. Even though the hotel is not right on the water, guests return year after year, requesting the same rooms. Service is impeccable, and the hotel's restaurant, with olde English fare served in traditional British fashion, is one of the most elegant finds in the B.V.I. Best of all, there's a view of the island that you would expect from a fort.

Out on the Island

From Road Town, a road wraps around the hills to Tortola's northern shore and Mount Sage National Park, where you can hike to the top of Mount Sage—at 1,716 feet, the highest spot for miles around—for an impressive view of the sea and the other British Virgin Islands.

From Mount Sage, continue on to Cane Garden Bay, where a century-old family distillery is still operating, largely with its original equipment. Then make your way down along the coast. Some of the island's best beaches line this shore, inviting you to try their white sands, snorkeling, and body surfing.

Mrs. Scatliffe's Restaurant in Carrot Bay is unquestionably geared to tourists, but is nonetheless an experience not to be missed. As you sit on the terrace amid a symphony of whistling tree frogs and the fruity scent of flowers, Mrs. Scatliffe and her family (kids, grandchildren, in-laws) serve artfully prepared West Indian dishes and serenade you with songs from their well-rehearsed repertoire.

If you want to stay on this coast, consider the **Sugar Mill**, owned by Jinx and Jeff Morgan, an American writing-and-cooking team. The main building is a 300-year-old sugar distillery that now houses a restaurant and an art gallery specializing in Haitian paintings. The food is unfailingly good, with such dishes as grilled boned quail with mango and papaya sauce, Caribbean bouillabaisse, and grilled scallops with red-pepper sauce. The inn's rooms are done up in soft tropical pastels and have kitchenettes and terraces. Just down the road is the **Long Bay Hotel**, a group of villas set back into a hillside along Long Beach. This beach, sweeping along for about a mile, is without question the resort's focal point. There's also tennis and a par-3 pitch-and-putt course. Guests at both the Sugar Mill and Long Bay Hotel tend to be seclusion-seeking professionals.

Stop at **Pusser's Landing** in West End for a good cold drink. Lunch (burgers, sandwiches) is nothing extraordinary, but is certainly acceptable, and as you eat you can watch sailboat crews stock up on ice and provisions.

The remarkably small Fort Recovery stands on what are now the grounds of a hotel along the southern coast road. You aren't permitted to climb up, but are welcome to admire it from sea level. The fort is about 45 feet in diameter and 30 feet high, and was built by the Dutch in 1660 to protect the island from pirates. Just a short distance away (there's no sign) is an overgrown path leading to the so-called Dungeon. This seaward battery, probably built in the mid-18th century, was dubbed the "Dungeon" because its underground cell once housed prisoners. Many of its walls and staircases still stand beneath a tangle of growth. There is another ruin nearby, on an unmarked road in Pleasant Valley—the thick, vegetation-covered stone walls of William Thornton's House. (Thornton, born in the B.V.I. in 1761, designed the U.S. Capitol.)

The East End

The eastern half of Tortola is centered on the East End Settlement, a cluster of old West Indian houses. Very scenic roads lead to Fat Hogs Bay, the site of the island's first Quaker settlement, and to Kingstown, where in 1833 a group of freed slaves built a settlement; today only the ruins of an Anglican church remain.

From Beef Island (connected to Tortola by the Queen Elizabeth Bridge) you can take a launch to **Marina Cay**, a small hotel on an island that was once home to an American couple who fled the hustle and bustle of stateside life to start anew here in the 1930s. (Robb White tells the story in his autobiographical *Two on the Isle.*) The pair eventually left the cay, and their house is now the main building of the hotel. Choose one of the new rooms, with their white stucco walls, wood-beamed ceilings, and mesmerizing views; the older ones are pea-green A-frame cottages in need of face-lifts, both inside and out. Guests are largely repeat customers, many of them couples.

VIRGIN GORDA

Any resident of Virgin Gorda is likely to tell you, with unimpeachable pride, "I put in an application to be born on Virgin Gorda." Or you may hear the it's-been-said-before-about-Greece story: "When God finished creating the heavens and the earth, he had a fist full of stones left, so he tossed them over his shoulder and made Virgin Gorda."

Virgin Gorda's northern end is dominated by lush green hills; its southern reaches are flat and desertlike, strewn with enormous cacti and whale-size boulders. Supposedly, it was Virgin Gorda's shape—from a distance, it looks like reclining pregnant woman—that inspired Christopher Columbus to name the Virgin Islands *Las Once Mil Virgines,* in memory of St. Ursula and the 11,000 martyr maidens who sacrificed their lives rather than their virginity to the Huns in 4th-century Cologne.

The origins of the gargantuan boulders on the southern end have been the topic of much geological speculation. Some say they're the result of a tempestuous storm that hurled them from the sea floor. Others say they're from a volcanic eruption. On the southwestern coast, a massive tumble of these mysterious boulders forms **the Baths**, marvelous little swimming grottoes where the water is as clear as gin. To find them, just ask any of the locals.

The Spanish Town Area

Spanish Town—also referred to as "The Valley"—is Virgin Gorda's largest settlement, spreading over the southern half of the island. Don't bother looking for a real town, because no such place exists on Virgin Gorda. The only place that comes close is the Yacht Harbour Shopping Center, a group of shops on the edge of a marina, owned by the Little Dix Bay Hotel Corporation.

Little Dix Bay, once the indisputable queen of B.V.I. hotels, was purchased by the CSX Corporation in 1987, along with most of the other Rockresorts, so it no longer has the benefit of Laurence Rockefeller's golden touch. Nor is it any longer *the* hideaway for business people and celebrities. Now you're more apt to see affluent young couples, many on their honeymoons. Little Dix Bay does, however, preserve Rockefeller's original concept of rough but refined vacationing. There are no phones, TVs, or radios in the rooms, and no outside locks on the doors.

The Olde Yard Inn is a simple, quiet accommodation most celebrated for its restaurant and library. The dining "room" is a long veranda topped by a roof of banana leaves; the kitchen specializes in local fish dishes and offers a fine selection of wines. The much-talked-about library is a pair of twin octagonal buildings that the original owners put up to house their rare-book collection. Those books have since been replaced by the current owner's collection and by numerous volumes travellers have left behind. There's no pool or beach on the grounds, but **Savannah Beach**—one of the island's best-looking strands—is just a 15-minute walk away. Rooms (just 12 of them) are simple and quite small, but comfortable.

Among locals, one of Spanish Town's most deservedly popular West Indian restaurants is **Ilma's**, a tiny red and white building (no sign outside) with plastic flowers on plastic tablecloths and a billiard table dominating the front room. To find the place, just ask any Virgin Gordian—everyone knows Ilma and can guide you there through narrow, dusty back roads.

Another local hot spot is **Thelma's**, where you can feast on boiled fish and baked chicken, and—as at Ilma's—dance on weekend nights.

The North End

Virgin Gorda narrows quite a bit in its middle, and you can see both the Atlantic and Caribbean shores from the road that meanders along the west side of Gorda Peak, past one gorgeous beach after another. Along the way, you can park and climb the North Sound Trail for an incomparable view and a look at the Nail Bay ruins, a cluster of plantation buildings.

North Sound Road connects Spanish Town with the North Sound Settlement. The road gradually ascends Gorda Peak, revealing vistas that are increasingly more beautiful the higher you get. Near the top a number of hiking trails climb from the road to the peak.

North Sound is a small settlement made up of candy-colored houses festooned in blossoms and of vacation homes that seem to hang off the hillsides. The road dips down like a water slide here and ends at Gun Creek Jetty and an aptly named bar, **The Last Stop**. Motorboats take off and charge across the bay to two marvelously remote hotels—Biras Creek and The Bitter End Yacht Club.

Biras Creek has a collection of tastefully furnished villas, many right on a wave-smashed shore. Even when the house is full (a total of 74 guests) you never feel that there are many people around—except at night, maybe, when guests convene in the hilltop bar for merrymaking and dancing. By day the guests, who are predominantly couples, many who have left the kids at home, tend to bicycle over the resort's dirt roads that pass through semiarid landscapes similar to those of East Africa.

The Bitter End Yacht Club merged with the Tradewinds next door in the fall of 1987, making it one of

Virgin Gorda's largest hotels. This is a place for serious sailors, but it attracts non-nautical types as well, including families with kids. Request one of the original Tradewind rooms (in a pyramid-roofed villa) or a Bitter End beach-front room with a wraparound terrace. (The higher it is, the better the view and the more privacy you'll have.)

OTHER ISLANDS

There are at least half a dozen other islands worth visiting in the B.V.I. However, unless you've given yourself plenty of time, hopscotching among them could defeat the whole purpose of a vacation. If time permits, consider taking the inter-island ferry from Tortola to **Jost Van Dyke**, a nice place to spend a day exploring its ruined fort, hiking its good trails, and swimming off its beaches. The ferry makes the trip twice a day. **Anegada** is the only island in this little galaxy that's flat (the highest point is a whopping 28 feet above sea level). It's encircled by doz-ens of sunken shipwrecks, a boon for serious snorkelers and divers. You can only reach Anegada by air (Air BVI flies from Beef Island) or by private boat. The **Wreck of the Rhone**—which sank in 1867—lies embedded in years of coral growth right off the coast of **Salt Island**. You can reach the wreck by private boat or by taking a guided snorkeling tour from one of the other islands. Most of the hotels offer frequent organized trips leaving from their own docks.

Peter Island is sort of a "Bermuda of the B.V.I.," a little oasis of perfection. It is almost exclusively the domain of the **Peter Island Yacht Harbor and Hotel**, a clublike resort with fabulous beaches, riding stables, and tennis courts. Its beach villas are unquestionably the better rooms: noiseless ceiling fans, huge beds piled high with pillows, wondrously comfortable bathtubs that open up to win-dow gardens, and terraces from which you can watch the moon rise. The Peter Island ferry shuttles over from Tortola's CSY Dock throughout the day.

Guana Island Club is very remote and very private, and is reached only by its own private launch (Beef Island Airport pick-ups are arranged). Guests (no more than 30 at a time) stay in lovely whitewashed cottages and have little else to do but swim, snorkel, hike, birdwatch, sail, and bask in the sun.

Necker Island, on its own 75-acre island, is a ten-bedroom villa available for private rentals. The building was originally erected in Bali, then dismantled and rebuilt in the B.V.I. All decor is Balinese, including matching batik bedspreads and bathrobes. Necker Island is surrounded by a coral reef and flanked by three white-sand beaches. There's a fleet of boats, an exercise room, tennis courts, and Jacuzzis—more than enough diversions to keep a group of friends or large family content for a week. (Guests are picked up at the Beef Island Airport by private launch.)

USEFUL FACTS

What to Wear

If you're staying at Peter Island or Little Dix Bay, men will need to pack a jacket and tie. Otherwise, dress on the B.V.I. is very casual; you'll most likely live in bathing suits, shorts, and light tops and shirts. Remember to pack the right shoes for boating, hiking, or horseback riding (you'll find stables on Peter Island and in Spanish Town on Virgin Gorda).

Getting In

There are no major airports in the B.V.I., so it is necessary to connect from San Juan, St. Croix, or St. Thomas to either Tortola's Beef Island Airport or to the airport on Virgin Gorda. Air BVI and Crown Air both fly from San Juan to Virgin Gorda and Tortola, and from St. Thomas to Tortola. Air BVI also makes daily runs between Virgin Gorda, Anegada, and St. Thomas. The Virgin Islands Seaplane Shuttle flies to and from St. Thomas and St. Croix to Tortola. From Canada, your best bet is to travel via Miami.

From London, you can take British Airways to Antigua, and connect to Air BVI or LIAT. Many of the connections are timed to meet British Airways flights, making an overnight stay on Antigua unnecessary. You can also reach the B.V.I. by taking a ferry from various locations on St. Croix, St. Thomas, and St. John in the U.S.V.I. to Tortola, Virgin Gorda, Anegada, and Jost Van Dyke.

Entry Requirements
All visitors must have a current passport. There is a $5 departure tax.

Currency
The U.S. dollar is the official currency. Many hotels and restaurants don't take credit cards, but most accept travellers' checks.

Electrical Current
Same as in the U.S. and Canada—110–120 volts, 60 cycles.

Getting Around
Think twice about renting a car in the B.V.I.: The rollercoaster-like roads are quite treacherous. There are no rental agencies at the airport; it's necessary to taxi into Road Town on Tortola or Spanish Town on Virgin Gorda, or see if your hotel can make the arrangements. You may want to rent a MiniMoke, a Land Rover, or a Jeep so you can forge ahead on roads that might be considered bridal paths back home. You need a valid driver's license and must also buy a temporary B.V.I. license, good for 30 days, for $5 at the rental agency. Taxis are plentiful, and especially on the smaller islands should be used instead of a rental. For short distances do as the locals do: walk.

Business Hours
Shops and museums are generally open from 8:30–4:30 Monday–Saturday; banks, 9:00–2:00 Monday–Thursday, 9:00–6:00 Friday.

Festivals
August is carnival time. On the first Sunday, Monday, Tuesday, and Wednesday of that month everything closes as residents commemorate the 1834 slave Emancipation with singing, dancing, and parades. In addition, Virgin Gorda has a three-day Easter Festival. The islands recognize British bank holidays, Territory Day (July 1), and Saint Ursula's Day (October 21).

ACCOMMODATIONS REFERENCE
The rate ranges given here are projections for fall 1988 through spring 1989. Unless otherwise indicated, rates

are for double rooms, double occupancy. The telephone area code for the B.V.I. is 809.

▶ **Biras Creek**. P.O. Box 54, Virgin Gorda, B.V.I. $280–$570, A.P. Tel: 494-3555/6; in U.S., (800) 223-1108.

▶ **The Bitter End Yacht Club**. Box 46, Virgin Gorda, B.V.I. $220–$300, A.P. Tel: 494-2746.

▶ **Fort Burt**. P.O. Box 187, Road Town, Tortola, B.V.I. $55–$90, E.P. Tel: 494-2587; in U.S., (800) 526-7489.

▶ **Guana Island Club**. P.O. Box 32, Road Town, Tortola, B.V.I. $235–$345, A.P. Tel: 494-2354; in U.S., (914) 967-6050. A boat meets guests at Beef Island Airport.

▶ **Little Dix Bay**. P.O. Box 70, Virgin Gorda, B.V.I. $345–$525, A.P. Tel: 495-5555; in U.S., (212) 765-5950 or (800) 223-7637.

▶ **Long Bay Hotel**. P.O. Box 433, Road Town, Tortola, B.V.I. $60–$150, E.P. Tel: 495-4252 or (800) 223-5695.

▶ **Marina Cay Hotel**. P.O. Box 76, Tortola, B.V.I. $160–$360, E.P. Tel: 494-2174.

▶ **Moorings Mariner Inn**. P.O. Box 139, Road Town, Tortola, B.V.I. $65–$135, E.P. Tel 494-2332.

▶ **Necker Island**. P.O. Box 315, Road Town, Tortola, B.V.I. $7,500 per day (11–20 people) or $5,500 (one–ten people). Includes three meals, all drinks (open bar, extensive wine cellar), all sports, transfers from Beef Island Airport. Tel: 494-2757; in U.S., (212) 696-4566 or (800) 225-4255.

▶ **Olde Yard Inn**. P.O. Box 26, Virgin Gorda, B.V.I. $120–$215, M.A.P. Tel: 495-5544 or (800) 633-7411.

▶ **Peter Island Yacht Harbor and Hotel**. P.O. Box 211, Road Town, Tortola, B.V.I. $245–$425, M.A.P. Higher-priced villas also available. Tel: 494-2561; in U.S., (800) 346-4451.

▶ **The Sugar Mill**. Box 425, Tortola, B.V.I. $95–$140, E.P. Tel: 495-4355.

OTHER ACCOMMODATIONS

▶ **Frenchman's Cay** P.O. Box 1054, West End, Tortola, B.V.I. $80–$130 (one-bedroom villa). Tel: 495-4844; in U.S., (212) 599-8280 or (800) 223-9832. A collection of co-op villas, each with one or two bedrooms, a sitting room, a fully equipped kitchen-cum-dining room, and a terrace. Caters to a professional crowd.

▶ **Guavaberry-Spring Bay Vacation Homes**. P.O. Box

20, Virgin Gorda, B.V.I. $65–$100 (one-bedroom house). 495-5227. A cluster of homes built around boulders and cacti; very attractive, very quiet.

▶ **Rockview Holiday Homes**. P.O. Box 263, Road Town, Tortola, B.V.I. Weekly: $900 (two-bedroom hillside villa)– $3,500 (three-bedroom villa with pool). Tel: 495-4220 or 494-2550. These 25 homes on the northwest coast are tastefully decorated, meticulously maintained, and magnificently situated.

ST. MAARTEN/ ST. MARTIN

By Julie Wilson

Half Dutch and half French, this 37-square-mile island is the Caribbean's supreme playground. It's cocky, sensual, and exciting; quiet, greedy, and sophisticated; earthy, glamorous, and sleazy—whatever the moment requires. But it's no longer a noticeably two-nation island. The once-distinct personalities of the Dutch and French sides have merged, and the border between the two is more or less ceremonial.

St. Maarten/St. Martin's natural assets include dark green hills, three dozen or so beaches, and the largest inland body of water in the Caribbean (salty, calm Simpson Bay Lagoon). With resources like these, it couldn't miss. It also has two manmade attractions: duty-free status and Princess Juliana Airport. The latter, which processes some 500,000 visitors a year, allows easy access from different parts of the world, and is a base for small planes flying to nearby islands. For a minor dot on the map the island has a surprisingly impressive traffic pattern.

Among its polyglot residents are French and Americans who settled here 30 years ago in the wide-eyed frontier days; Dutch, Italians, Arubans, Chinese, Indians, Scandinavians, and some whose passports change according to circumstances; and, of course, the original inhabitants of the island. These are divided between an old guard, who remember the sleepy days and wonder where they've gone, and a young generation who came of age during a tourist boom and know nothing else. The real border on this island is not between Dutch and French, but between past and present.

These two harmonious worlds give the hundreds of tourists who pop off planes daily an enviable choice. You can hole up in the quiet island of the past, or swing into the constant carnival of the present. Or both. St. Maarten/ St. Martin has some of the best sporting facilities anywhere: tennis, golf, great snorkeling, great sailing, good diving, and every manner of water-borne contraption known to man. There's no getting around the fact, however, that dining constitutes the island's major preoccupation. From Creole to "country French," and back through Chinese and *nuova cucina*—the island lays out a fabulous international spread that covers nearly every base but sauerbraten and sauerkraut. Keeping up with what's new is as difficult as it is in a major city, for no sooner does an innovative restaurant appear than a half dozen imitators sweep in on its coattails.

MAJOR INTEREST

  Dining
  Shopping
  Sailing excursions
  Casinos (St. Maarten)

No one tours St. Maarten/St. Martin simply by setting out on the road that circles the island. Instead, people decide what they want to do (or where they want to eat) and sightsee along the way. But don't expect many historical sights. On this today-and-tomorrow island, the sights consist mainly of hotels, water-sports centers, duty-free shops, restaurants, and more restaurants.

Philipsburg

The Dutch capital does have one historic monument: a nearly 200-year-old colonial-style courthouse smack in the middle of town. Some people who have been coming to the island for years have never noticed it. Philipsburg has other distractions.

Set on a sand bar between a salt pond and Great Bay Harbour (where cruise ships haul themselves over the horizon regularly), Philipsburg is essentially one big duty-free shopping street broken by places to eat, places to sleep, and places to gamble away whatever money you have left. Bring your Christmas list to **Front Street** for French sportswear, tee-shirts, crystal, Italian shoes, perfume, china, cameras, gems, Gucci, gewgaws—whatever the whim demands and the credit card allows.

Old Street represents this Caribbean Bloomingdale's latest effort to provide top-of-the-line merchandise. Looking more like Disney's Magic Kingdom than the old Dutch village it's supposed to resemble, this squeaky-clean, colorfully painted street runs between Front and Back Streets. It's a "walking street," so pedestrians are safe from the high-spirited vehicular mayhem found elsewhere.

In a town where accommodations range from big hotels to beachfront apartments, **Pasanggrahan** stands out— in a manner of speaking—from the rest. Set off of Front Street in the beach sand, it can hardly be seen at all. It is, however, the island's original guest house, built back in the days when a tourist boom consisted of the Dutch Royal Family making a ceremonial visit. It's a quirky, maybe even a little seedy, survivor of the old days.

Picking Philipsburg's best restaurant is really a matter of tuning in to the local grapevine and waiting for a good tip. Three establishments, however, are on nearly everyone's short list. The high-priced **Le Bec Fin**, at the bottom of Front Street, consistently delivers top-quality French food. Close by, **Wajang Doll** serves the only Indonesian rijsttafel on the island—a strange state of affairs when you consider that the Dutch Trading Companies put the island on the map. The **West Indian Tavern**, at the top of Front Street, staked its claim as the island's premier place to meet a long time ago. This ever-expanding restaurant, its ambitions masked by a deceptively goofy air, serves flamboyantly tropical drinks and local fish and langouste. Local fish and langouste aren't cheap.

Philipsburg is also the island's seagoing center, with two neighboring marinas (Bobby's and Great Bay), and the centrally located Little Pier, where cruise-ship tenders tie up. A score of boats leave from the marina for picnic sails, snorkeling sails, sunset sails, and day trips to neighboring islands. (These can easily be arranged through any hotel, or at the kiosk on Little Pier.) The marinas also accommodate private yachts, and their piers swarm with

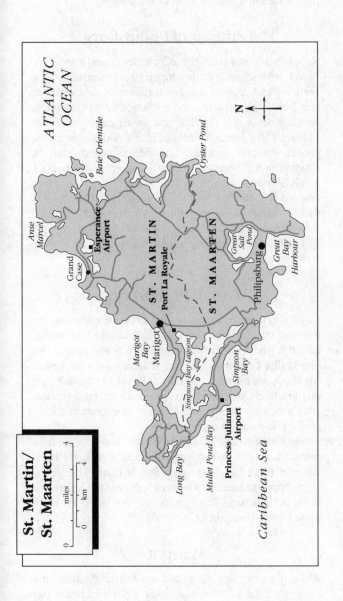

St. Martin/St. Maarten

ATLANTIC OCEAN

Anse Marcel

Baie Orientale

Grand Case

Esperance Airport

ST. MARTIN
Port La Royale

Oyster Pond

Great Salt Pond

Philipsburg

Great Bay Harbour

ST. MAARTEN

Marigot Bay

Marigot

Simpson Bay Lagoon

Simpson Bay

Long Bay

Mullet Pond Bay

Princess Juliana Airport

Caribbean Sea

N

miles

km

0   4

0   4

jaunty, sunburned people whose idea of duty-free shopping is having someone else buy their jeans.

Northeast of Philipsburg

St. Maarten's east coast is the least developed part of the island, with some least developed roads to match. At the French-Dutch border there is a cluster of development: one big hotel, a marina, some ominously mushrooming developments, and **Oyster Pond**, an expensive, exclusive hideaway. Set like a fortress at land's end, the romantic Oyster Pond is secluded and self-contained, with 20 rooms ringing a center courtyard and a brand-new pool. Meals here are among the island's best, and always draw a few savvy outsiders willing to make the trip. Mostly, though, hotel guests are left to enjoy the beach and each other's company. This isn't the sort of place for a couple whose idea of an evening together is watching the seven o'clock news.

West of Philipsburg

Skimming over the mountain top and skirting the Lagoon, the road passes the airport and continues through **Mullet Bay**, the island's only full-scale resort. Some people dislike Mullet because it's so big. Others love it because it has shopping plazas, an 18-hole golf course (the only one on the island), a grocery store, tennis courts, eight restaurants, a beach, water-sports facilities (the best on the island), a disco, and a casino.

Surprisingly, discos and late-night jazz places have never taken hold on this carnival island, so casinos dominate the night life. There are eight of them. The best is glitzy **Treasure Island at Cupecoy**, next to Mullet Bay. The stone-faced dealers dress up like pirates, but don't seem to be a swashbuckling lot.

Marigot

While the Dutch capital is laid out in straight lines, the French capital is an unruly maze onto which the city fathers have been unable to impose order. Sprawling from the harbor back to Port La Royale on the Lagoon,

Marigot still speaks with a French accent. The business here is selling: of sports clothes (also French accented), meals, baguettes, and baubles. The intense competition drives many small boutiques and cafés out of business, but their replacements are always fresh and hopeful.

From Marigot harbor, high-speed commuter launches make regular runs to Anguilla. Right on the harbor, St. Martin's best outdoor market is at its best on Saturday mornings, when boats from neighboring islands putter in loaded with produce, and local fishermen spill out their colorful cargo.

Marigot conversations, like those elsewhere on the island, tend to revolve around restaurants. **Poisson d'Or** captures the essence of local dining spots. Its menu is French (of the *nouvelle* persuasion), its dining porch overhangs the beach, its thick stone walls are decorated with local art, and its prices are high (figure on spending $150 for two, not including artwork). If Poisson d'Or is booked, head back to the harbor, where a string of long-established restaurants with similar menus and similar prices (and in some cases, the same owners) deliver good value for good money, with a harborside atmosphere in the bargain.

West of Marigot

Past rows of new condos, halfway to the sunset, stands **La Belle Creole**, St. Martin's "historic sight." A hotel designed along the lines of Xanadu, it nearly opened 20 years ago. But cash flow problems caused the workmen to throw down their tools along with their empty pay envelopes. Conrad International bought it and, after a few false starts, has opened it to guests. It's worth staying here just to be part of a legend.

Farther down the road lies the legendary **La Samanna**, a survivor of the glory days when St. Martin was as exclusive as it is expensive. Celebrities, jet setters, and the just plain rich tuck into two-story, whitewashed units hidden along a very private beach. Some flaunt their celebrity status, but most appreciate the quiet luxury afforded by this private hotel, so private that the owners have all but dug a moat and pulled up the drawbridge. It's worth swimming the moat for one of La Samanna's meals.

Grand Case

In this case, discovering the "flavor" of the town is easy, for one-street, beachfront Grand Case is devoted to gastronomy. French, Italian, Vietnamese, Creole, and American restaurants elbow each other for a place in the sun. The ever-useful island grapevine keeps tabs on which is this year's best, new find, fairest priced, and rip-off. The dubious award for the latter recently went to the Ritz Café, where menu prices look reasonable but specials carry unannounced price tags approximating the GNP of an emerging nation.

In an unobtrusive house along Grand Case Boulevard, Marty and Gloria Lynn run an informal gallery in their home (that is, pictures and sculptures are strewn around the living room). The Lynns and their two talented sons represent an esthetic side of St. Maarten/St. Martin. Artists, home-grown and transplanted (including Jasper Johns, the late Romare Bearden, and Roland Richardson), have always flourished here. Their work is sometimes primitive, sometimes romantic, sometimes glib, sometimes sensual, and always colorful—an accurate depiction of this remarkable island.

USEFUL FACTS

What to Wear

Anything or nothing (there are a couple of nudist beaches above Oyster Pond at Baie Orientale) goes. Sports jackets and shorts coexist in even the finest restaurants. Women dress up more than men do.

Getting In

There are direct flights from New York to St. Maarten on American, Pan Am, and ALM; from Miami on Pan Am and Eastern; from Los Angeles and Dallas/Fort Worth on American; from Toronto on American; and from Paris on Air France. There are also many flights from San Juan, and good connections to nearly everywhere in the Caribbean.

Entry Requirements

Passport; U.S. and Canadian citizens however need only proof of identity—e.g., a birth certificate or voter-registration card. There is a departure tax of $5.

Currency
French francs and Netherlands Antilles guilders are in use, although U.S. dollars are universally accepted.

Electrical Current
110 AC, 60 cycles on the Dutch side; 220 AC, 60 cycles on the French side.

Getting Around
Rental cars are plentiful and most roads are fine. Driving is on the right. Watch out for traffic jams in the three towns day and night, and on access roads during rush hours.

Business Hours
In St. Maarten, 8:00–6:00, with a one-hour lunch break; in St. Martin, 9:00–noon and 2:00–6:00.

Festivals
St. Maarten's Carnival is at the end of April, St. Martin's in February.

ACCOMMODATIONS REFERENCE
The rate ranges given here are projections for fall 1988 through spring 1989. Unless otherwise indicated, prices are for double rooms, double occupancy. The telephone area code for St. Maarten is 599; for St. Martin, 590.

St. Maarten
▶ **Mullet Bay Resort and Casino.** P.O. Box 309, Philipsburg, St. Maarten, N.A. $155–$335, E.P. Tel: 5-42-801; in U.S., (212) 840-6636 or (800) 223-9815.

▶ **Oyster Pond Yacht Club.** P.O. Box 239, St. Maarten, N.A. $180–$360, E.P. Tel: 5-22-206; in U.S., (212) 696-1323.

▶ **Pasanggrahan Royal Guesthouse.** P.O. Box 151, Philipsburg, St. Maarten, N.A. $57–105, E.P. Tel: 5-23-588; in U.S. (203) 847-9445 or (800) 622-7836.

St. Martin
▶ **La Belle Creole.** B.P. 118, Pointe des Pierres à Chaux, Marigot, 97150, St. Martin, F.W.I., $225–$515, C.P. Tel: 87-58-66; in U.S. 800-HILTONS.

▶ **La Samanna.** B.P. 159, Baie Longue, St. Martin, F.W.I., $600–$1,342, M.A.P. Tel: 87-51-22; in U.S. (212) 696-1323.

OTHER ACCOMMODATIONS

St. Maarten

▶ **Caravanserai.** P.O. Box 113, Philipsburg, St. Maarten, N.A. $115–$360, E.P. Tel: 5-42-510; in U.S. (212) 840-6636 or (800) 223-9815. Conveniently located at the end of the airport runway, it was, in pre-jet days, the island's finest hotel, and still has the most attractively situated dining room—at the end of a rocky promontory.

▶ **Treasure Island Hotel and Casino at Cupecoy.** P.O. Box 14, Philipsburg, St. Maarten, N.A. $150–$275, E.P. Tel: 5-44-297. A big, sprawling complex; the best rooms overlook the water and interior gardens.

▶ **La Vista.** P.O. Box 40, Pelican Key Estate, St. Maarten, N.A. $80–$215, E.P. Tel: 5-43-005; in U.S., (212) 849-2039 or (800) 223-9815. High on a hill looking down on Simpson Bay. Big rooms, kitchen facilities, casual atmosphere.

St. Martin

▶ **Grand Case Beach Club.** Grand Case, 97150, St. Martin, F.W.I. $175–$215, C.P. Tel: 87-51-87; in U.S., (212) 661-4540 or (800) 223-1588. American-owned, American-oriented, and a short walk from all those Grand Case restaurants.

▶ **L'Habitation.** P.O. Box 230, Marcel Cave, 97150, St. Martin, F.W.I. $250–$280, E.P. Tel: 87-33-33; in U.S., (212) 757-0225 or (800) 847-4249. New, big, colorful, and isolated up on the north coast. There's a health club and disco just up the hill.

▶ **La Résidence.** Rue du Général-de-Gaulle, Marigot, 97150, St. Martin, F.W.I. $110–$200, C.P. Tel: 87-70-37; in U.S., (401) 849-8012 or (800) 932-3222. A "city hotel" in the middle of Marigot, it's worth a mention for its exceptional charm and its second-floor dining terrace.

ST. BARTS
(ST. BARTHELEMY)

By Julie Wilson

Many call it the Caribbean St. Tropez. As stylishly—sometimes determinedly—French as its Mediterranean sister, this small island known to cartographers as St. Barthélemy is a bastion of Gallic joie de vivre. A quiet island, there is little nightlife, few tennis courts, and no golf course. Long lunches in beachside cafés, gourmet dinners beneath the stars, French balladeers, and magnums of fine wine are the order of the day here.

Rockefellers and Rothschilds were the first to adopt St. Barts as a vacation spot. The island is currently a favorite of celebrities and jet-setters, many of whom eschew the fine hotels in favor of the rental villas scattered around the island.

MAJOR INTEREST

Small, intimate accommodations
Dining, mostly French
Casual but chic atmosphere

St. Barts consists of a mere eight square miles of rugged hillsides that sweep down to the sea. The island has always been different from the rest of the Caribbean. Because the terrain is unsuitable for growing sugar cane, the island never developed a slave economy. Instead, St. Barts was settled by fishermen and farmers from Normandy and Brittany, who over the centuries have remained fishermen and farmers and adhered to the culture of their homeland. An old French patois is still

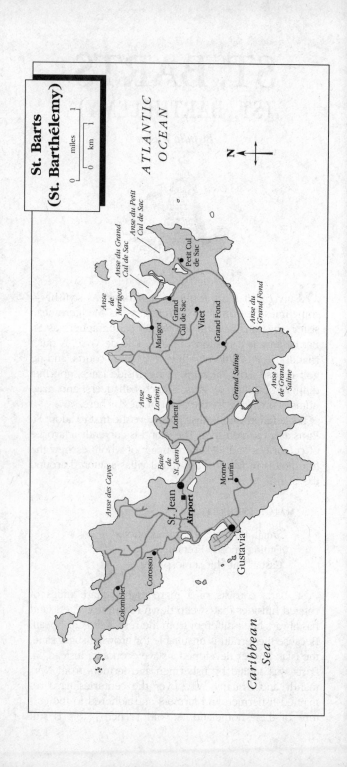

spoken in the villages and some older women continue to wear the traditional French *calèche,* a pleated, white cotton sunbonnet. The present population of 3,500 is predominantly white.

In 1784, islanders were shocked to learn that one of Louis XVI's scheming ministers had given St. Barts to Sweden in return for some warehouses in Goteburg. To them, it was like trading a professional sports star for a school champion. The new owners named the capital Gustavia for King Gustav III and declared it a free port, ushering in a wave of commercial prosperity for St. Barts. Trading had waned by the time France regained the island a century later, though its duty-free status was yet another attraction when tourists began to discover St. Barts. Today, St. Barts is a Sous-Prefecture of Guadeloupe, which itself is an Overseas Department of France. While the predominant language is French, English is spoken almost everywhere—though sometimes reluctantly.

St. Jean

St. Barts's best swimming beaches lie along its sheltered northern coast. The wide, sandy arc on the bay at St. Jean, roughly in the center, is one of the island's most popular, backed by a cluster of shops, hotels, and beach restaurants. On an island where fine French restaurants are the norm, the perennially popular **St. Jean Beach Club** has made its mark with simplicity. While chefs prepare your salad, pommes frites, grilled chicken, or lobster, you can nip down the steps for a quick swim. That's simple.

A detour uphill from St. Jean leads to Eden Rock, the island's first hotel. It's a bit rundown now, but the view and the memories (Greta Garbo was one of the hotel's first guests, in 1955) are worth the drive. **Manapany**, one of the newer hotels, is nearby on a hill above a secluded cove at **Anse des Cayes**. Small and private, it has just 20 cottages that climb up the hillside and 12 club suites on the beach. It has a tennis court (rare on St. Barts) and—this being an island of gastronomic inclinations—it also has two restaurants. The privacy-seeking clientele has included Mick Jagger, Peter Allen, and the less well-known wealthy.

Just west of St. Jean, arriving planes soar over a small mountain, then do a kamikaze dive to the alarmingly short runway (just 2,626 feet long) at the Gustav III airport (appropriately nicknamed "La Tourmente"). This runway, suitable only for small planes and specially trained pilots, is one of the reasons St. Barts is so quiet.

Colombier and Corossol

Driving the routes west and east of St. Jean, you will see the island's steep hills, windswept shoreline, and cove beaches. The scene is not unlike the rocky coast of France.

In remote Colombier, near the western end, is the atelier and salesroom of artist **Jean-Yves Froment**. Monsieur Froment is famed for his hand-blocked print fabrics, inspired by local flora, fauna, and colors. He has marked a path to his door by placing blue bird signs (a special shade of blue, his trademark) all over the island.

The brand-new terrace restaurant at **François Plantation** sits on a hill with a distant view of the bay. It's beautiful; it's "classic French"; it's expensive.

More than the inhabitants of any other part of the island, residents of the fishing village of Corossol retain the character of St. Barts's French settlers. Men tend their colorful skiffs, while barefoot, bonneted women sell wide-brimmed Panama hats, purses, and other items woven from dried strips of latania palm fronds. (The women don't like to be photographed, but the fishermen don't mind.)

The Eastern Route

A succession of beaches—Lorient, Marigot, Grand Cul de Sac, and Petit Cul de Sac—stretch to the east of St. Jean. Beyond the surf-pounded shores of the Grand Fond district are the hills of Southern Vitet, a pastoral region of stone-fenced meadows and tile-roofed farm houses. Except for the profusion of tropical flowers, this could easily be Brittany.

Guanahani, the newest of St. Barts's luxury hotels, is out at Grand Cul de Sac, on the banks of a bay so shallow that even diminutive swimmers can wade out hundreds of yards before submerging completely. Guanahani is the largest of the island's hotels, though it has a mere 80 rooms, some of which have private pools and all of which have decks or patios with a view of the sea. It, too, has two restaurants—a poolside café/bar, and the formal, indoor, highly-respected **Bartolomeo**. Don't look for glitz here. This place has dignity, and attracts a sophisticated, conservative crowd.

Restaurants out here are among the island's best, and most expensive—figure on $150 for dinner for two, maybe more. **La Toque Lyonnaise**, at **El Sereno Beach**, has successfully transplanted the cuisine of Lyons to the beaches of St. Barts. And **Club Lafayette**—open for lunch only—is quintessentially St. Barts. The guest book is signed by Raquel Welch, Steve Martin, and their starry ilk, and gorgeous young models parade around in fashions from the restaurant's boutique. The food is unapologetically pricey (lobster salad goes for $30, hot entrées start at $50), but the food is so beautifully presented that it vies with the models for attention.

Gustavia

The capital of St. Barts is three-blocks deep and runs along a sheltered, yacht-filled harbor. It is doll-house pretty, a mix of island gingerbread and a Swedish clock tower. Chic boutiques stock French and Italian designer fashions, and duty-free shops sell the usual range of perfume, jewelry, watches, china, and crystal.

Castelets, a regally private hotel on a peak high above town, has long been a favorite hotel among the chic set. No one seems to mind that it has no beach; its ten antique-filled rooms, the dependably fine food, and the views of St. Jean from its tiny pool are the draw.

Down by the old anchor at the public dock, local fishermen bring in their catch about ten in the morning. After viewing this colorful mid-morning ritual, visitors frequently repair to the **Bar de l'Oubli** for a late-morning omelette, or amble over to the internationally known **Le Select**, where the nighttime-type action starts early in the day, for a beer.

Gustavia's "in" restaurant these days is **Aux Trois Gourmands**, on the far side of the harbor. Behind its floor-to-ceiling windows, Bocuse-trained chef Christophe Gasnier serves up such winning dishes as salmon cutlets in tomato fondue, sliced lobster in chive cream, and an outrageous chocolate truffle. It's a little less expensive than the other "in" restaurants; figure on $100 for two.

Not *all* food on the island is expensive. Stop at a Gustavia patisserie for fresh-baked croissants, made from a local recipe that keeps them flaky in the sultry St. Barts air. They are unmistakeably French, with an island inflection—much like St. Barts itself.

USEFUL FACTS

What to Wear
Dress is casual chic, but what you wear is important. By day, bikinis, tight jeans, status tee-shirts, pareos (cotton sarongs), and loose cotton shirts are *de rigueur*. By night, island cottons, dressy pants, or caftans for women, and sports shirts for men are the uniform. Ties and jackets are not required.

Getting In
The best connections are from St. Maarten. Flights from there to Gustav III Airport take ten minutes. Sailing and motor catamarans run between Philipsburg (on St. Maarten) and Gustavia; the trip takes 1½ hours, depending on the weather. Seas can be rough. (Most people take the boat trip only once.) Both air and boat fares run about $50 round trip. There is also air service to St. Barts from San Juan, St. Thomas, Antigua, and Guadeloupe. You must pay a 10-franc departure tax when leaving St. Barts for French St. Martin and Guadeloupe; the tax is 15 francs for other destinations.

Entry Requirements
A passport or other proof of citizenship (such as a notarized birth certificate with a raised seal or a voter-registration card accompanied by a government-authorized identification with photo) is required.

Currency
The legal tender is the French franc. Dollars are accepted nearly everywhere.

Electrical Current
220 AC, 50 cycles. American- and Canadian-made appliances require converters, plugs, and transformers.

Getting Around
Small cars such as VW Beetles and MiniMokes are most practical for navigating the narrow, hilly island roads, but be sure you are comfortable using a stick shift. Motor bikes may also be rented (driver's license required), and there is ample taxi service.

Business Hours
Shops are open 8:00–noon, and 2:00–6:00. Shops are closed on Sunday.

Festivals
The Festival of St. Barthélemy, the feast day of the island's patron saint, is celebrated on the weekends preceding and following August 24. The festivities may remind you of a country fair. The Pre-Lenten Carnival ends with a Mardi Gras.

ACCOMMODATIONS REFERENCE
The rate ranges given here are projections for fall 1988 through spring 1989. Unless otherwise indicated, prices are for double rooms, double occupancy. The telephone area code for St. Barts is 590.

▶ **Castelets.** Morne Lurin, St. Barthélemy, F.W.I. 97133. $140–$285 C.P.; suites, $450 C.P. Tel: 27-61-73; in U.S., (212) 319-7488.

▶ **Guanahani.** Anse de Grand Cul de Sac, St. Barthélemy, F.W.I. 97133. $250–$330, E.P.; suites, $400–$665, E.P. Tel: 27-66-60; in U.S., (212) 308-3330 or (800) 235-3505.

▶ **Manapany Cottages.** Anse des Cayes, St. Barthélemy, F.W.I. 97133. Double $270–$370, E.P.; suites, $400–$780, E.P. Tel: 27-66-55; in U.S. (212) 757-0225 or (800) 847-4249.

OTHER ACCOMMODATIONS
▶ **El Sereno Beach.** Grand Cul de Sac, St. Barthélemy, F.W.I. 97133. $120–$267, C.P. Tel: 27-64-80; in U.S., (212) 477-1600 or (800) 223-1510. 20 rooms facing patios or private gardens.

▶ **Emeraude Plage**. Baie de St. Jean, St. Barthélemy, F.W.I. 97133. $145–273, C.P. Tel: 27-64-78; in U.S., (401) 849-8012 or (800) 932-3222. 30 bungalows built around a garden facing the beach.

▶ **Filao Beach Hotel**. Baie de St. Jean, St. Barthélemy, F.W.I. 97133. $170, E.P. Tel: 27-64-84. A 30-room beach-front hotel with lovely interior gardens and a pool.

▶ **Hostellerie des Trois Forces**. Vitet, St. Barthélemy, F.W.I. 97133. $140–$170, C.P. Tel: 27-61-25; in U.S., (401) 849-8012 or (800) 932-3222. 8 bungalows, each named after a zodiac sign. In the hills, with a fine restaurant and pool.

▶ **Marigot Bay Club**. Marigot, St. Barthélemy, F.W.I. 97133. $180, E.P. Tel: 27-75-45; telex 919897 GL. 6 studios with sea views.

▶ **Village St. Jean**. Baie de St. Jean, St. Barthélemy, F.W.I. 97133. $88, C.P; studio, $100. Tel: 27-61-39; in U.S., (803) 785-7411 or (800) 633-7411. 26 rooms, all simple and pleasant.

▶ For **villa rentals**, contact WIMCO, (401) 849-8012 or (800) 932-3222.

ANGUILLA

By Julie Wilson

Refusing to accept independence in 1967, Anguilla (An-GWIL-a) earned some amused notoriety as the British "eel that squealed." (Anguilla is Spanish for eel, and it is easy to see why the Spaniards who discovered the island thought of an eel when they sighted it—long and slender, it is 17 miles long and three miles across at its widest point.

Point made, secure as a Crown Colony, the island settled back into amiable somnolence—until recently. Anguilla is now the scene of considerable development, spearheaded by an ambitious collection of luxury hotels.

What attracted the hotels were Anguilla's 33 **white-sand beaches**, generally acknowledged to be the best in the Caribbean. A ring of offshore reefs ensures calm waters and snorkeling that is as good as snorkeling can get. The island itself isn't particularly lush; what even-handed Nature lavished on the beaches, she stinted on the flora.

With a lifestyle that is a mixture of island traditions and gilt-edged sophistication, Anguilla can be divided unofficially between the West End (development) and the East End (still traditional).

MAJOR INTEREST

White-sand beaches
Offshore reefs for snorkeling
New luxury hotels

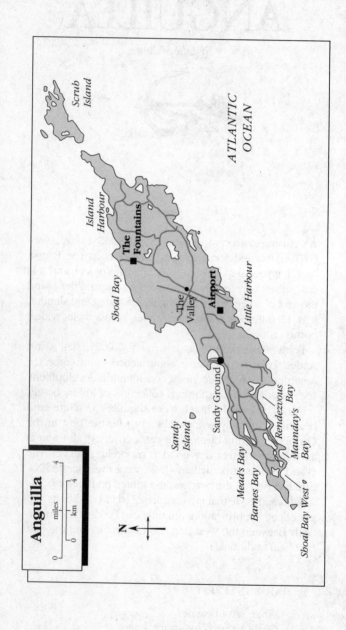

West End

The main road runs straight from the roundabout above Sandy Ground to Blolly Ham Bay, with a few spurs leading to the new shoreline hotels. **Malliouhana**, on splendid Mead's (MAID's) Bay, started the boom just four years ago. Jet-setters and the otherwise well-heeled lounge around its pools, while French chefs stir things up in the kitchen.

Malliouhana is the Arawak name for Anguilla, and *coccoloba* is the Arawak name for sea grape. **Coccoloba Plantation** is the new name given to the hotel that was once called La Santé. Unveiled last winter after thorough renovations, Coccoloba inherited an A-frame lobby, which looks like a ski lodge gone south, from the previous owners. The management, under David Brewer, who has skippered some of the best hotels in the Caribbean, has painted the lobby a soft yellow and white, so it sort of fades away discreetly. With two beaches (on Mead's Bay and Barnes Bay), the hotel draws a well-bred crowd—many of whom came initially simply because David Brewer was there.

Cap Juluca (*Juluca* is the Arawak name for the local rainbow god) also opened last winter. This Moorish fantasy is on the dazzling, near-deserted beach at Maunday's Bay, and it owns the 179 acres behind and in front of it. It was built by Robin and Sue Ricketts, the attractive couple who codeveloped Malliouhana, so you know what sort of clientele to expect.

Sandy Ground

Anguilla's deepwater port, Sandy Ground, is lined by a beach, behind which is one of those salt ponds that were so important in the days before refrigeration. There are a couple of water-sports centers here, and small restaurants line Sandy Ground's beachfront. Anguillian cuisine is pretty basic—simple West Indian fare with the occasional stab at *nouvelle* something. Restaurant staples include fresh fish, conch, and langoustes, along with stews made of less elegant animals and their less elegant parts. For local authenticity, try **Lucy's Harbour View** (up the hill a piece). Lucy's is pretty basic, too.

From Sandy Ground, boats speed out to **Sandy Isle**, a tiny coral island covered with palm trees. Snorkelers snorkel off Sandy Isle, and the lazy lounge on the sand, enjoying the delicious isolation. The new **Mariners**, built in old West Indian style, occupies one end of the beach. It's less expensive than the West End blockbusters and is a favorite among old Anguilla hands, who swap the latest gossip in the bar.

The Valley

Driving east from Sandy Ground, you will soon come to Anguilla's capital, The Valley. Stop in at the Department of Tourism (in the Secretariat) and ask about the schedule for two of Anguilla's most endearing attractions. One, the **Mayoumba Folkloric Troupe**, is a select group culled from the ranks of the Anguilla Choral Circle that sings West Indian folk songs and plays and dances up a storm. The other is the Anguilla Archeological and Historical Society's walking tours that meander through The Valley. The tours include St. Gerard's Roman Catholic Church, with its elaborate triptych front, and Wallblake House (an 18th-century great house "where the priest lives").

East End

Driving along the eastern half of the island, you'll see the more traditional side of Anguilla: cement-block houses with fretwork overlays, chickens in the road, old ovens in side yards, banana trees, undernourished flamboyants, and trees no taller than a man.

Island Harbour, the fishing center up on the north shore, is a small settlement with an expensive roadside restaurant (The Fish Trap), a cheap beachfront restaurant (Smitty's Seaside Saloon), and scores of fishing skiffs whose design is unique to the island. Long before they started building hotels, the Anguillians were great boat builders.

Shoal Bay, just down the coast, ranks first among Anguilla's beaches. Long the favorite spot for secluded picnics and snorkeling, it has recently become more civilized, with villa complexes and a trio of simple restaurants.

Heading back inland, you will come to **The Fountains**, underground springs where the ancient Indians painted petroglyphs on the cave walls. The Anguillian government is constructing an entrance tunnel to replace the rickety ladder that now provides the only access and is mapping out a four-acre park around The Fountains. Preservation of history and nature is as typically Anguillian as the new hotels.

USEFUL FACTS

What to Wear
Dress code is conservatively casual, and no nude bathing is allowed. "Elegantly casual" is standard during the evening at the fancy resorts.

Getting In
There are several daily flights to Wallblake Airport from San Juan (American Eagle), St. Maarten (WINAIR), and St. Thomas, and several weekly flights from Antigua and St. Kitts. Ferries from St. Martin's Marigot to Anguilla's Blowing Point Pier run frequently. A one-way ticket costs $6– $8. The journey takes only 11 minutes in a flat, calm sea.

Entry Requirements
Passport; U.S. and Canadian citizens, however, can use another form of official identification that has a photograph, such as a driver's license or voters-registration card. A departure tax of $5 is levied at the airport, $1.15 at Blowing Point Pier.

Currency
Eastern Caribbean Dollar; U.S. dollars are accepted nearly everywhere.

Electrical Current
Same as in the U.S. and Canada—110 AC.

Getting Around
To rent a car, you must have a valid license and obtain a three month permit ($6). Driving is on the left.

Business Hours
8:00–4:00; some businesses close between noon and 1:00.

Festivals

Carnival is the first week in August; boat racing is the highlight.

ACCOMMODATIONS REFERENCE

The rate ranges given here are projections for fall 1988 through spring 1989. Unless otherwise indicated, prices are for double rooms, double occupancy. The telephone area code for Anguilla is 809.

▶ **Cap Juluca.** P.O. Box 240, Maunday's Bay, Anguilla, B.W.I. $225–$250, C.P. Tel: 497-6779; in U.S., (212) 308-3330 or (800) 235-3505.

▶ **Coccoloba Plantation.** P.O. Box 332, Barnes Bay, Anguilla, B.W.I. $100–$480, A.P. Tel: 497-6871; in U.S., (212) 840-6636 or (800) 351-5656; in Canada, (800) 468-0023; in U.K., 01-730-7144.

▶ **Malliouhana.** P.O. Box 173, Anguilla, B.W.I. $260–$650, E. P. Tel: 497-6111; in U.S. (212) 696-1323.

▶ **Mariners.** P.O. Box 139, Sandy Ground, Anguilla, B.W.I. $130–$285, E.P. Tel: 497-2671; in U.S. (212) 840-6636 or (800) 223-9815; in Canada, (800) 468-0023.

OTHER ACCOMMODATIONS

▶ **Cinnamon Reef Beach Club.** P.O. Box 141, Little Harbour, Anguilla, B.W.I. $200–$250, E.P. Tel: 497-2727; in U.S., (212) 840-6636 or (800) 223-9815; in Canada, (800) 468-0023. A small hotel on the south shore with a small beach, big rooms, and a big pool.

▶ **Cove Castles.** Shoal Bay West, Anguilla, B.W.I. $350–$600. Tel: 497-6801; in U.S., (212) 840-6636 or (800) 223-9815; in Canada, (800) 468-0023. A group of luxurious housekeeping villas.

▶ **Rendezvous Bay Hotel.** P.O. Box 31, Rendezvous Bay, Anguilla, B.W.I. $55–$85. Tel: 497-6549; in U.S., (201) 738-0246, (212) 840-6636, or (800) 223-9815; in Canada, (800) 468-0023. Family-owned, family-managed, idiosyncratic, old-time Caribbean on a prize beach.

SABA

By Julie Wilson

Twenty-eight miles southwest of St. Maarten, the five-square-mile rock that is Saba (SAY-ba) rises improbably from the sea. Because of the rain cloud that is hooked permanently on the top of its highest peak, Saba is a very green, flower-bedecked rock. With its teensy red-roofed cottages, built next to tropical gardens in which the residents' ancestors are buried, Saba elicts such adjectives as "storybook," "quaint," and "picturesque." Visitors frequently dub it "Shangri-la." Sabans call it "The Unspoiled Queen."

A darker side rescues Saba from cloying sweetness. Seen close up from the water, Saba is jagged, forbidding, brooding. The bare rock of its cliff-rimmed shoreline, gouged by deep gulleys, disappears into the sea. There's no place to take a handhold here, no place to go but away. Seen from this angle, Saba is so unhospitable it seems to repel even the rain. This sweet/savage contrast makes Saba a very interesting island.

MAJOR INTEREST

Scuba diving
Small-town peace and quiet (no beaches)

Scuba divers have long known about Saba's dramatic underwater pinnacles and caves, its fathoms-deep undersea mountain valleys. Experienced divers cannot help but bring along an underwater camera to record their "you-won't-believe-this" dives; Saba is one of a handful of the best diving sites in the Caribbean. There are no beaches and precious few protecting reefs. So, aside from divers,

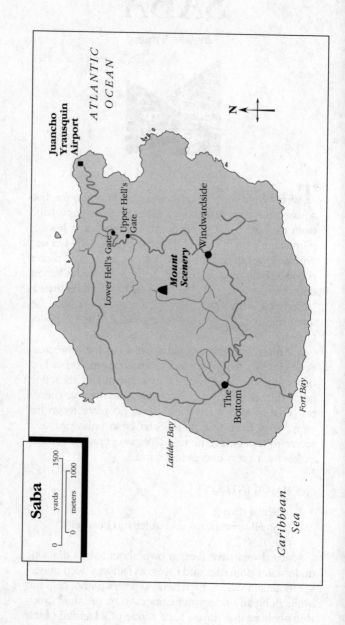

Saba

yards 0 1500

meters 0 1000

ATLANTIC OCEAN

Juancho Yrausquin Airport

Upper Hell's Gate

Lower Hell's Gate

Mount Scenery

Windwardside

The Bottom

Ladder Bay

Fort Bay

Caribbean Sea

N

the vacationers who come to Saba are those who like quiet and more quiet.

Though Saba is a self-governing part of the Netherlands Antilles, most of its 1,100 inhabitants have Irish/Scottish backgrounds (going back to Elizabethan days). And most of them—white and black—are named Hassell or Johnson—except for those who are named Simmons. Rumor has it that Saba consumes more Heineken beer per capita than any other nation on earth. Sabans don't confirm the rumor, nor do they deny it.

Saba begins and ends with the Road, a well-maintained, two-lane highway built by hand in the 1940s when the Sabans discovered Detroit. Hugging the mountainsides, the Road climbs steeply, drops alarmingly, snakes wildly, looks like the Great Wall of China, and offers views that are both beautiful and terrifying—that ever-present Saban dichotomy. Walls on one side keep the Road clear of falling rocks; walls on the other side (presumably) keep the Road from sliding into the ravines. The Road begins at Fort Bay and ends at the tarmac runway of Juancho E. Yrausquin Airport, or the other way around.

Fort Bay

For most people, Fort Bay is just a place to arrive or leave by boat, though local residents use the concrete ramp as a beach. Divers regard Fort Bay as a launch pad, because **Sea Saba** (whose headquarters are in Windwardside) and **Surfside Saba Deep** keep their boats and equipment here. Though these waters are heaven for serious divers, both operations offer courses for beginners. Otherwise, it's off to the Road, past tangles of flowers the Sabans call "love weed" and which the rest of the world calls coralita.

The Bottom

Plopped down in a hollow spot among the hills, Saba's capital gets its name from the Dutch *de botte,* which means "the bowl" but which Saba has chosen to translate as "The Bottom." (The town's real name is Leverock.) Along lanes hemmed in by knee-high, waist-high, and shoulder-high walls, the few government buildings are of little interest to anyone outside the government. The Bottom's best attraction is **Saba Artisan's Foundation,** a local industry producing some very attractive fabrics, resort wear, and tee-shirts at moderate prices.

Although Saban meals tend toward home cooking on the simple side, **Queenie Simmons's Serving Spoon** is an exception. Queenie has no menu, offering instead a ridiculously inexpensive "plate of food" for those who care to make a reservation. Some plate. Onion chicken or curried goat, flanked by rice and beans, french fries, fritters, vegetables, and salads add up to more food than the average mortal could eat in a week. There's no service charge, but if you care to leave a tip, "God will surely bless you."

One of The Bottom's progressively narrow roads—ask directions—culminates in the old "step road" to Ladder Bay. The strong of limb can climb down and up, gaining with each step increased respect for the Sabans who once carried every imported essential (from flour to cement) up on their backs.

Windwardside

From the Bottom, the Road climbs upward, and at an altitude of about 1,500 feet reaches Windwardside, a town that slides up and down a few steep alleys, against which the Tourist Office and Sea Saba's Dive Shop gather.

The **Saba Museum** occupies a sea captain's cottage built around the time of the American Revolution, and displays old (no one knows how old) family (but everyone knows which family) heirlooms.

A few shops in town sell postcards and souvenirs, as well as Saba's major products: Saba Lace and Saba Spice. Intricate, hand-drawn threadwork, the lace is embroidered onto shirts, aprons, napkins, and other items. Saba Spice, home-brewed and rum-based, has a fragrant bouquet and a mulelike kick.

From Windwardside, 1,064 slippery steps, overhung by vines and crowded in by jungle and dark imaginings, climb another 1,500 feet to the top of Mount Scenery. The moderately able can manage the climb, though even if the greenery doesn't swallow you up, the cloud at the top may carry you off.

Windwardside has most of Saba's hotels. **Scout's Place** and **Captains' Quarters** (with a couple of dozen rooms between them) are the hangouts for divers, day-trippers, locals, and retired Americans who live on the island. In short, everyone. Much Heineken is consumed in the course of a day. Simple but well-prepared lunches and dinners have the air of a family gathering. Just above Captain's Quarters's pool, **Juliana's Apartments** are owned by Juliana Johnson, whose brother, Steve Hassell, manages Captain's Quarters. That's typically Saban. Juliana's modern rooms are most comfortable, her hibiscuses the size of Frisbees, and you can use her brother's pool. At **Guido's Disco** (Guido's real name is Rob), young Sabans in Benetton shirts seem as interested in the dart board as the dance floor.

Road's End

From Windwardside, the remarkable Road slashes through Hell's Gate, a town where neighborhood ladies sell more Saba Lace and Saba Spice in the Community Center behind the Holy Rosary Church. The Road drops through Lower Hell's Gate, then down a series of switchbacks to the airport—a bandaid slapped down on a flat part of a cliff. WINAIR's crack pilots negotiate the short runway as though it were three miles long, but for a newcomer to Saba, takeoffs and landings are both beautiful and terrifying. It's that old Saban combination once again.

USEFUL FACTS

What to Wear
Casual sports clothes of a conservative nature (i.e., no tank tops). Bring a sweater; cool winds blow across Windwardside in the evening.

Getting In
Windward Islands Airways (WINAIR) makes the 15-minute flight from St. Maarten's Juliana Airport three times a day. The "Style," a high-speed boat, makes the run from Philipsburg in St. Maarten to Fort Bay five times a week; $45 round trip.

Entry Requirements
Passports are required, but U.S. and Canadian citizens can substitute other proof of citizenship, such as a birth

certificate or a voter-registration card. There is a $1 departure tax.

Currency
The Netherlands Antilles guilder; U.S. dollars are accepted everywhere.

Electrical Current
Same as in the U.S. and Canada—110 volts AC, 60 cycles.

Getting Around
Depend on taxi drivers. The Road is picturesque but no fun to drive.

Business Hours
8:00–12:00, 1:00 to 5:00.

Festivals
Carnival is in July.

ACCOMMODATIONS REFERENCE
The rate ranges given here are projections for fall 1988 through spring 1989. Unless otherwise indicated, rates are for double rooms, double occupancy. The telephone area code for Saba is 599.

▶ **Captains' Quarters.** Windwardside, Saba, N.A. $75–$95, E.P. Tel: 42201; in U.S., (212) 840-6636 or (800) 223-9815; in Canada, (800) 468-0023.

▶ **Juliana's Apartments.** Windwardside, Saba, N.A. $45–$75, E.P. Tel: 42269.

▶ **Scout's Place.** Windwardside, Saba, N.A. $85, with full breakfast. Tel: 42205.

STATIA
(ST. EUSTATIUS)
By Julie Wilson

Exactly what St. Eustatius is, is hard to say. "An eight-square-mile island in the Netherlands Antilles Windwards," while accurate, hardly describes the special charms of this relatively undiscovered dot of green.

Friendliness may be what distinguishes Statia (STAY-sha) from her more developed neighbors. Statians seem genuinely delighted to welcome visitors (whom they prefer to call guests). In this, Statia is the perfect choice for self-sufficient travellers seeking the Caribbean as it was.

MAJOR INTEREST

The feeling of a friendly small town
Peace and quiet
No mass tourism

A 20-minute flight from St. Maarten will deposit you at St. Eustatius's Franklin Delano Roosevelt Airport. From here, it's only a mile or two by taxi to Oranjestad, the island's capital and, it must be admitted, its only town. **Oranjestad** is a gallimaufry of yellow-brick buildings dating from the island's heyday in the 18th century when it was mercantile center of the Caribbean; shingled "zinc"-roofed 19th-century townhouses; and a smattering of newer cement-block structures, vibrantly painted in pink, lavender, and sky-blue. "Good-days" sound from just about every doorway and a visitor's appearance in the morning is almost certain to be discussed avidly over lunch. Arrival on St. Eustatius guarantees instant celebrity.

The island hasn't always been so serene. "Statia" has a history far out of proportion to its size. During the American War of Independence European allies transshipped supplies through Statia to General George Washington's beleaguered troops. The warehouses, the ruins of which huddle now at the base of the cliffs in Oranjestad's Lower Town, were crammed with gunpowder, muskets, and bolts of woolen cloth destined for America.

It was probably with an eye on this lucrative trade that Statia's Governor, Johannes de Graaff, ordered the guns of Fort Oranje to salute the colors of the newly proclaimed republic flying from the mast of the American brig-of-war, *Andrew Doria,* on November 16, 1776. His salute was the first official foreign recognition of the United States of America, and it proved to be disastrous for Statia. In February 1781, British Admiral George Bridges Rodney attacked and plundered the island long called "the Golden Rock" and which Rodney now dubbed "a nest of vipers."

Today, Statia's colorful history is also celebrated in the St. Eustatius **Historical Foundation Museum,** located in the Doncker-de Graaff House. The 18th-century structure stands, tall and dignified, in the center of town. Coins minted on the island, glistening examples of delftware and Chinese export porcelain, and other artifacts attest to Statia's wealth two centuries ago. The island's pre-Columbian history is encapsulated in displays that include the 1,500-year-old skeleton of an Arawak Indian and examples of astonishingly elegant Indian pottery.

Statia's other diversions are generally of the very low-keyed do-it-yourself variety: exploring the graveyard of the 18th-century Dutch Reformed Church; visiting Honen Dalim, the second-oldest synagogue in the New World; prowling the ramparts of Fort Oranje; or descending to the rain forest that flourishes in the crater of The Quill, the extinct volcano whose symmetrical silhouette dominates the island.

Divers can investigate the wreck of a man-of-war that capsized in the 1700s, or snorkel over the walls of buildings that sank beneath Gallows Bay at about the same time. For tennis buffs there's a night-lighted cement court

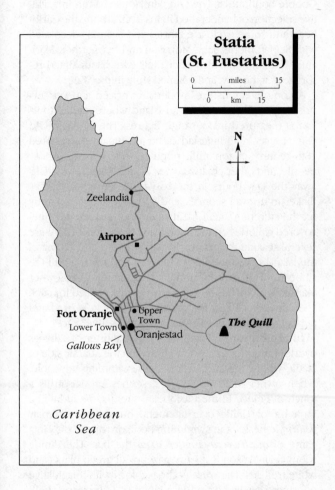

**Statia
(St. Eustatius)**

0   miles   15

0   km   15

N

Zeelandia

Airport

Fort Oranje
Lower Town
Gallows Bay

Upper
Town
Oranjestad

The Quill

*Caribbean
Sea*

at the Community Center off Rosemarielaan. (Bring your own racquet and balls.)

While duty-free shopping on Statia is fairly limited—cigarettes and liquor are good buys—**The Sign of the Goobie** boutique at The Old Gin House has an imaginative selection of handcrafted items from around the Caribbean and some exclusive fabrics and fashions decorated with Statian motifs. Jana Morrison and her partner, Marianne Fitzsimmons, also offer their own handpainted resortwear at the tiny, aptly-named **Hole in the Wall**.

Accommodations are moderately priced and yet surprisingly sophisticated for an island where annual tourism is measured in four-digit figures. The 20-room **Old Gin House** in Oranjestad is an imaginatively restored 18th-century cotton mill, popular with writers, theater people, and other creative types. A rare Bristol clock ticks away the lazy hours in the rosy-brick taproom, candles flicker in tin wall sconces, and a Vivaldi suite plays softly on the stereo. A small freshwater pool reflects the vine-covered galleries on the inland side of the inn. (There are several seaside rooms overlooking the most appealing of the island's pewter-colored beaches and the tranquil Caribbean.) The kitchen, under the direction of co-owner Martin Scofield, has been internationally praised for such specialties as chilled melon soup, lobster in Pernod and peppers, and paté of snapper with mousseline sauce.

La Maison sur la Plage is actually a cluster of cabanas overlooking a long crescent of sand on the Atlantic side of Statia, where the surf makes pool-swimming advisable. When owner Michelle Greca describes La Maison as a touch of France in the Caribbean, she may be indulging in a bit of Gallic overstatement, but guests can play *pétanque* beside the swimming pool, or roll the dice in a game of *quatre-cent-vingt-et-un* at the bar. The dining room at La Maison is an airy gazebo, all green plants and white trellises. The *carte* is chockablock with imaginative offerings—snails nestled in a cloud of puff pastry, shellfish in an anise-scented sauce, and a traditional beef filet with *sauce moutarde*.

Relaxed and inexpensive restaurants featuring many West Indian dishes include **Talk of the Town** on the Airport Road leading from Oranjestad, and **The Stone Oven** in town. For the latest news about island events, stop by **Cool Corner** on Van Tonningenweg for a Heineken (called "a greenie"). Close to the Government Offices in Fort Oranje and at the crossroads of town, this friendly rum shop seems to be, at one time or another, the gathering spot for just about everyone on the island.

USEFUL FACTS

Getting In
There are several flights daily to Franklin Delano Roosevelt Airport on Windward Islands Airways (WINAIR) from St. Maarten.

Entry Requirements
U.S. and Canadian citizens arriving for stays of up to three months must have a valid passport or one that has expired only within the past five years; a notarized birth certificate; or a voter-registration card. Others require a valid passport or Alien Registration Card. A return or onward ticket is also necessary for all visitors. No departure tax need be paid if you are returning to St. Maarten or Saba. For other destinations, the tax is U.S. $3.

Currency
The legal tender is the Netherlands Antilles guilder. U.S. and Canadian dollars are accepted everywhere. The exchange rate is subject to currency fluctuations, but the N.A. guilder has been pegged to the U.S. dollar for many years. Hotels and banks will exchange currency.

Electrical Current
Same as in the U.S. and Canada—110 AC, 60 cycles.

Getting Around
Several local car rental agencies operate on the island. A valid driver's license is required.

Business Hours
Banking hours: Monday–Thursday, 8:30–1:00; Friday, 8:30–1:00 and 4:00–5:00.

ACCOMMODATIONS REFERENCE
The rate ranges given here are projections for fall 1988 through spring 1989. Unless otherwise indicated, rates

are for double rooms, double occupancy. The telephone area code for St. Eustatius is 599.

▶ **La Maison sur la Plage**. Box 157, Zeelandia, St. Eustatius, N.A. $55–$75, C.P. Tel: 3-2256.

▶ **Old Gin House**. Lower Town, St. Eustatius, N.A. $100–$130, E.P. Tel: 3-2319.

ST. KITTS AND NEVIS

By Julie Wilson

A sometimes treacherous two-mile strait called The Narrows separates the two-island federation of little (36 square miles) Nevis and big (65 square miles) St. Kitts. An even bigger gulf separates them temperamentally. Petite, sophisticated Nevis (NEE-vis) long ago turned its plantation great houses into inns and capitalized on its romantic history. Ungainly St. Kitts, doggedly growing sugar cane long after anyone wanted to pay much for it, let its great houses crumble into ruins, playgrounds for marauding goats. A few years ago, St. Kitts built a new airport and deepwater port, and waited—and the tourists are finally coming. This pleases the Kittitians enormously, but worries those tourists who loved the island for its simple air.

MAJOR INTEREST

St. Kitts
Golf
Water sports at Frigate Bay

Nevis
Inn-hopping

ST. KITTS

Shaped like a primitive cricket bat, St. Kitts has a fat end that is dominated by rainforests, mountain ranges, and

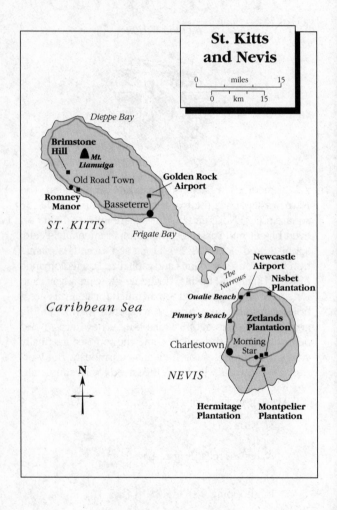

St. Kitts and Nevis

| 0 | miles | 15 |
| 0 | km | 15 |

Dieppe Bay

Brimstone Hill ▲ *Mt. Liamuiga*

Old Road Town

Golden Rock Airport

Romney Manor

Basseterre

ST. KITTS

Frigate Bay

Newcastle Airport

Nisbet Plantation

The Narrows

Oualie Beach

Caribbean Sea

Pinney's Beach

Zetlands Plantation

Charlestown

Morning Star

NEVIS

N

Hermitage Plantation

Montpelier Plantation

above all the nearly 4,000-foot-high peak of Mt. Liamuiga. (*Liamuiga* is a Carib word meaning "fertile isle"; until recently, the mountain was called "Misery," but that didn't square with the new tourist image.) The other end, the skinny southeast peninsula, is scrubbier and, for the most part, is left to wild cattle and scampering vervet monkeys. The best beach is where the two ends meet.

Basseterre

The capital's French name and British face are a tip-off to just who fought over St. Kitts in colonial days. In case anyone should mistake its allegiance, Basseterre's terribly British treasury building on the waterfront, its statue of Queen Victoria, and its tidy, formally laid out Independence Square make things perfectly clear. The British-style Circus comprises a four-sided clock tower that few pedestrians bother to look at, preoccupied as they are with dodging Kittitian taxis. At the same time, two-story, pastel-colored Basseterre, located next to Golden Rock Airport, is unmistakably Caribbean. Chickens share pathways with pedestrians, and on occasional Saturday nights the entire town turns out for wing-ding block parties, a must for anyone with a taste for gay abandon.

While there are few restaurants on this West Indian (chicken and rice, chicken and fries) island, Basseterre claims two of the best. Surrounded by thick stone walls, **Georgian House**, on Independence Square, has the formal air of a Georgian house. Lunches are served in a shady walled garden under a mango tree. The second-floor balcony of bright new **Ballahoo** looks down on the Circus (parrot fish and garlic conch are on the menu). The **Spencer Cameron Art Gallery** occupies the harbor end of the balcony.

The ever expanding **Ocean Terrace Inn** spills down a hillside on the edge of town, past condos, pool, bars, and gardens to "Fishermen's Village," a condo/restaurant/marina complex. Admirers compare the place to Singapore's Raffle's; detractors complain about OTI's all-too-obvious eye toward profit and its sometimes disappointing food. No matter. Sooner or later everyone shows up here for a meal, a drink, a boat trip, or just to meet someone else.

The Road

St. Kitts's main road follows the shoreline around the island, running parallel to and sometimes crossing a narrow-gauge cane railroad. The Atlantic (windward) side of the island is still in the thrall of cane and is notable mainly for its small hamlets, which vie annually for the "Best-Kept Village" award.

Running up the leeward coast, the road slips through Old Road Town, where Sir Thomas Warner established the first settlement and supposedly where Columbus landed. The oldest (1623) house on St. Kitts is Sir Thomas's former residence. It still stands, in ruin, on Road Town's waterfront.

Romney Manor

Caribelle Batiks set up shop and showroom some 15 years ago in Romney Manor, an old estate house that is surrounded by rainforest and formal gardens. (A 350-year-old saman tree looms over the other foliage.) Unfazed by onlookers, local girls with steady hands use old hot-wax techniques to batik cotton destined to become sports shirts, skirts, and sundresses. The tropical designs incorporate local flora and copies of Indian petroglyphs that have been discovered on the island. You can see some of these ancient markings down by the main road near the manor, inscribed on a pile of otherwise undistinguished lava rocks. One of the images looks like the symbolic monkey of St. Kitts, but in fact represents a pregnant woman praying to the sun god to save her baby.

Brimstone Hill

A couple of miles beyond Romney Manor looms one of the Caribbean's most startling sights: **Brimstone Hill**, 32 acres of a no-nonsense British fort, capable of defending a small continent. Wedged between mountains and sea and looking toward half a dozen neighboring islands, the "Gibraltar of the Caribbean" took a century to build and changed hands twice—once by battle, once by treaty. In both cases, ceremony took precedence over bloodshed.

The contrast of massive black walls and the peaceful green landscape surrounding them exaggerate the enormity of Brimstone Hill. The fort is far from completely restored, but you may climb, on extremely steep steps, to the topmost part of the citadel, which contains a few interesting rooms. Skip the museum shop; there's nothing for sale that you can't find elsewhere, and the store doesn't even accept local currency.

The Inns

Two exceptionally fine inns coexist harmoniously up where the road swings over the top of St. Kitts. **Rawlins Plantation**, reached by narrow tracks through cane fields, has been home to the Walwyn family for a couple of centuries. Philip Walwyn and his parents turned the estate into a hotel some years ago. Isolated amid acres of vegetable and flower gardens, Rawlins's eight rooms are divided between small cottages and a restored sugar mill. The inn draws self-sufficient people who can afford the price and who appreciate the privacy and the good meals.

More accessible, on the black-sand beach of Dieppe Bay, Arthur Leamon's **Golden Lemon** has long been recognized as a Caribbean legend among those who don't bestow legend status lightly. The hotel is a very personal combination of colonial antiques, comfortable beds, Caribbean colors bright enough to make sunglasses advisable, unobtrusive service, and island food elevated to the rank of food for the deities. The Golden Lemon is quiet, except for those days when knowledgeable passengers from cruise ships head up the coast for lunch here.

Frigate Bay

The government has earmarked the Frigate Bay Development area, near Basseterre on the Atlantic side of the island, for tourist facilities. So far, there is the island's 18-hole golf course, a casual casino, a good beach with bar/restaurant/water-sports operations, and a number of unfinished hotel/condos. Frigate Bay is also the site of the hard-to-overlook **Jack Tar Village/Royal St. Kitts**. A prepaid, all-inclusive resort, massive Jack Tar supplies just about any sport imaginable, along with all the booze its basically young clientele can drink. Jack Tar guests can be recognized by the required photo I.D. they wear around their necks.

Southeast Peninsula

St. Kitts is now extending the stone road down the nearly uninhabited peninsula that forms the southeastern part of the island—the project being the major topic of conversation on St. Kitts these days. Long ago, two small inns entrenched themselves at the far end of the peninsula, just across from Nevis and accessible only by boat. Ocean Terrace Inn recently bought the two, connected them, refurbished them, and reopened them as **Banana Bay**. Until The Road is finished and people can drive up to the back door, Banana Bay will remain a sublime escape, a place of quiet and beauty. That quiet is shattered a bit when OTI's launch brings out day-trippers for lunch, or when the occasional Windjammer cruise ship flings about 100 passengers onto the usually deserted beach.

NEVIS

Young Alexander Hamilton; sad-eyed Fanny Nisbet; the evil, slave-flogging planter Edward Huggins—on Nevis these historic figures are as much a part of the present-day scene as the fellow tourists at the next dinner table. On a clear day, it is entirely possible to believe that a speck on the horizon is the H.M.S. *Boreas,* bringing Horatio Nelson back again.

Charlestown

The ferry from Basseterre on St. Kitts docks on Nevis at Charlestown, the island's capital and the only town on Nevis of any consequence. Charlestown has some government buildings, a few banks and a few bar/grocery stores, and neighborhood shops that sell local handicrafts and hot sauce. The waterfront birthplace of Alexander Hamilton, not far from the pier, is now a small museum, with Hamilton mementoes and Indian artifacts.

Out on the Island

From Charlestown, the road runs parallel to the island's best beaches, starting at palm-backed **Pinney's** and going straight along the coast to **Oualie Beach**, home of Nevis Watersports.

Some 200 years ago, young Captain Nelson was watering his boats at the freshwater springs near Jamestown when he first saw Fanny Nisbet. Or so one story goes; another has them meeting at a dinner party on the other side of the island. An earthquake and tidal wave wiped out Jamestown, Nevis's first capital, in 1680, and a few cannons along a wall are all that remains. Only a jailed convict survived the disaster. He may have wondered if answering his prayers for freedom with total destruction was a bit excessive. Typical of the Nevisian penchant for capitalizing on history, the site is now the Fort Ashby bar and restaurant.

At the top of the island, not far from Newcastle Airport's short runway, history of a different sort surfaces. At **Newcastle Pottery**, Almena Cornelius and her acolytes use Amerindian techniques, passed down through generation after generation, to produce primitive, red-clay pottery, firing the finished works in open fires fueled by coconut husks.

Nisbet Plantation, across the road, has become a well-known inn, with a stately path running between coconut palms—one of the Caribbean's most photographed sights. There are other assets, too: a calm beach, cottages that are widely spaced among the trees, a main house retaining reserved 18th-century charm, and a fine dining room.

A Gothic tale, worthy of the Brontë sisters, surrounds Eden Brown Estate, now in romantic ruin farther down the east coast. After a pre-wedding party here the groom and his best man killed each other in an ill-timed duel. The bride, it is said, screamed until she died, and her ghost can still be heard moaning in the moonlight.

A pocket of historic-homes-turned-inns is nestled up in the hills above the east coast. Beaches are a ways below, but these places all have pools, and each has its champions who claim it serves the best food on the island. And those hospitable little inns do serve good food—imaginative without being fancy, with lots of fresh fish, vegetables, and fruits. Golden-haired Pam Barry owns **Golden Rock**, which occupies an estate that has been in her family (she is a Huggins) for generations.

The pleasantly cool public rooms are in the old estate buildings, with their thick stone walls, and the bedroom units are scattered across the hillside. Honeymooners favor the suite called the "Sugar Mill," with the oldest mahogany four-poster bed on Nevis. "Paradise" comes in a close second, with bamboo four-poster beds and a private porch screened by plantings. Golden Rock has its own patch of sand at Pinney's Beach for lunches, drinks, and water sports. Golden Rock also has David Freeman, its head gardener who moonlights as leader of "The Honey Bees," a Nevisian string band of considerable charm and enthusiasm. The band plays at most of the island's inns.

Zetland Plantation also has its patch of Pinney's and a sugar-mill suite, as well as some suites with private pools. (Though Pinney's Beach is across the island, nothing is far away in Nevis; and both hotels offer free transportation.) **Croney's Old Manor Estate** rambles around yet another estate, this one from the 18th century. Bedrooms are the size of ballrooms. The place isn't completely restored, but they're working on it, and the restaurant, oddly enough, resembles an Adirondack summer-camp dining hall.

Hermitage Plantation's great house, complete with its original wood shingles, is the oldest house in the Antilles. Seen from the front, it appears to be a strong wind away from oblivion, but don't be deceived; those planters usually built things to last forever. Cottages climb up the hill, and each room has its own hammock on a porch facing the sea. Wonderful meals are served at the antique-filled main house, and Hermitage is so easygoing that more than one guest has gone into the kitchen to ask for a recipe.

Fanny Nisbet and Horatio Nelson were married at **Montpelier Plantation**. Neither the original house nor the marriage survived the test of time, but the stone inn built in the 1960s looks as though it's been there for years. Owners James and Celia Gaskell are English, as are many of the guests.

The Nisbet-Nelson marriage is recorded nearby, in the sturdy stone Fig Tree Church. The small Nelson Museum, at Morning Star, houses a remarkably interesting collection devoted to the hero of Trafalgar.

As you near Charlestown on your way back along the

shore road, you'll come to the **Bath Hotel**, a relic from the days when Nevis was Queen of the Caribbees and the fashionable of the known world sailed here to take the waters. Long-deserted, this place by all rights should have crumbled years ago, had it not been well-built enough to withstand earthquakes, floods, and every force nature could throw at it. The floors have been shored up, so you can walk through the old rooms and listen for echoes of long-forgotten waltzes and flirtatious whispers. **Hot-spring streams** still flow below the hotel's balconied façade, affording curative baths to those who have a desire to plunge into the past.

USEFUL FACTS

What to Wear
Attire is casual, sometimes elegantly so. A sweater or jacket is advisable for cool evenings in the hills.

Getting In
BWIA has direct flights to Golden Rock Airport from New York on Sundays and from Toronto on Saturdays. There are connecting flights from San Juan, St. Maarten, Antigua, St. Thomas, St. Croix, and Guadeloupe.

Entry Requirements
Passports; U.S. and Canadian nationals may, however, substitute another proof of identity, such as a birth certificate or voter-registration card. The departure tax is $5.

Currency
The Eastern Caribbean dollar; U.S. dollars are universally accepted.

Electrical Current
220 volts, 60 cycles, AC. Some hotels have converted to 110 volts, AC.

Getting Around
Driving is on the left. Roads are good on both islands. A temporary local license costs $12.

Getting Across
A ferry runs between Basseterre and Charlestown twice a day (no crossings on Thursday and Sunday). The crossing takes 40–45 minutes and costs $4 each way.

Business Hours
Monday–Saturday, 8:00–12:00, 1:00–4:00. Some businesses close Thursday afternoons.

Festivals
Carnival is in late December.

ACCOMMODATIONS REFERENCE
The rate ranges given here are projections for fall 1988 through spring 1989. Unless otherwise indicated, rates are for double rooms, double occupancy. The telephone area code for St. Kitts and Nevis is 809.

St. Kitts
▶ **Banana Bay**. Same address and telephone as Ocean Terrace Inn. $150–$220, M.A.P.

▶ **The Golden Lemon**. Dieppe Bay, St. Kitts, W.I. $215–$330, M.A.P. Tel: 465-7260; in U.S., (803) 785-7411 or (800) 223-5581.

▶ **Jack Tar Village/Royal St. Kitts**. P.O. Box 406, Frigate Bay, St. Kitts, W.I. $130–$145 a person, per day. Tel: 465-8651; in U.S. (800) 527-9299.

▶ **Ocean Terrace Inn**. P.O. Box 65, Basseterre, St. Kitts, W.I. $134–$224 M.A.P. Tel: 465-4121/4122; in U.S., (800) 223-5695; in Canada, (800) 387-8031; in U.K., 01-367-5175.

▶ **Rawlins Plantation**. P.O. Box 340, Basseterre, St. Kitts, W.I. $230–$330, M.A.P. Tel: 425-6221/2098; in U.S., (617) 367-8959; in Canada, (416) 622-8813.

Nevis
▶ **Croney's Old Manor Estate**. P.O. Box 70, Nevis, W.I. $125, E.P.; $185, M.A.P. Tel: 469-5445; in U.S., (800) 223-9815; in Canada, (800) 468-0024.

▶ **Golden Rock Estates**. Box 493, Nevis, W.I. $150, E.P., $200, M.A.P. Tel: 469-5346; in U.S., (212) 840-6636.

▶ **Hermitage Plantation**. St. John Fig Tree Parish, Nevis, W.I. $135–$190, M.A.P. Tel: 469-5477; in U.S., (800) 223-9815; in Canada, (800) 468-0023; in U.K., 01-730-7144 or 01-602-7181.

▶ **Montpelier Plantation Inn.** P.O. Box 474, Nevis, W.I. $126–$280, M.A.P. Tel: 469-5462; in U.S., (800) 243-9420; in Canada, (800) 268-0424; in U.K., 01-367-5175.

▶ **Nisbet Plantation Inn.** Nevis, W.I. $240–$300, M.A.P. Tel: 465-5325; in U.S. and Canada, (218) 722-5659; in U.K., 01-580-8313/8314.

▶ **Zetland Plantation.** Nevis, W.I. $150–$210, M.A.P. Tel: 465-5454; in U.S., (203) 965-0260 or (800) 243-2654.

ANTIGUA
AND
BARBUDA

By Julie Wilson

It is odd that Antigua (An-TEE-ga), rich in British naval history and a place where prehistoric megaliths keep their secrets up in inaccessible hills, somehow seems to have sprung from the sea around 1960. That year marked the beginning of Antigua's ascent as a serious sailing center, the beginning of big-time tourism on the island, and the opening of the first of the beachfront luxury hotels. Nevertheless, whether it is the British influence on this former colony or the influence of the wealthy professionals from America's Northeast, who were among Antigua's first regulars, the island still has a conservative air to it. At times, Antigua seems as much a club as it does a vacation spot. And that is a great part of the island's charm. You have the feeling that no matter how much mass tourism touches it, it will remain—like Bermuda—essentially unchanged. And the Antiguans themselves are chatty and friendly, given to instant discussions of theology, political reality, agriculture, and the world beyond their island.

MAJOR INTEREST

Antigua
Very good beaches
Redcliffe Quay for shopping

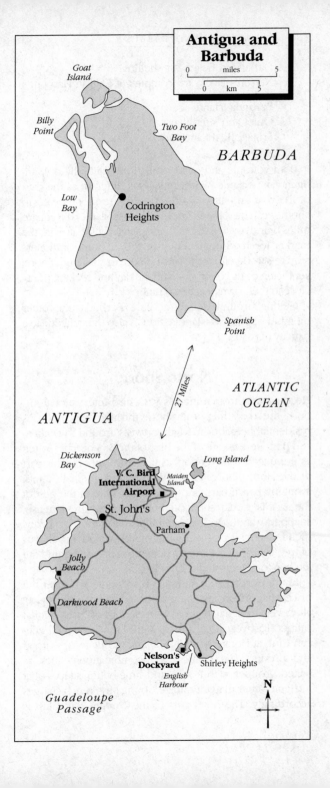

Antigua and Barbuda

miles		
0		5
0	km	5

Goat Island

Billy Point

Two Foot Bay

BARBUDA

Low Bay

Codrington Heights

Spanish Point

ATLANTIC OCEAN

27 Miles

ANTIGUA

Dickenson Bay

V. C. Bird International Airport

Long Island

Maiden Island

St. John's

Parham

Jolly Beach

Darkwood Beach

Nelson's Dockyard

Shirley Heights

English Harbour

Guadeloupe Passage

N

Darkwood Beach for shelling
Nelson's Dockyard complex at English Harbour

Barbuda Island
Quiet and simplicity
Frigate Bird Sanctuary

Both volcanic and coral, sometimes painfully dry, Antigua claims some 365 beaches—as different as the days of the year and all beautiful. Getting from one beach to another can be difficult, for this is a big island (108 square miles), and the roads that cross its center are in the market for road engineers. For this reason, vacationers tend to stay on either the North Shore or the South Shore, venturing cross country during the day and sticking pretty close to their own beaches at night.

Getting around delightful little Barbuda, the other member of this two-island nation, is also difficult, due to a paucity of roads.

North Shore

Heading west from Antigua's V. C. Bird International Airport, the road hugs the shore through a prosperous residential neighborhood, then twists around to **Dickenson Bay**. Here is one of the best of the 365 beaches, often as populated with vendors as it is with bathers. This part of the North Shore has a concentration of small hotels, swinging beach bars, and restaurants. One of the best of the last is **Cockleshell** on Fort Road, where kingfish, snapper, wahoo, and barracuda headline the blackboard menu. Dining is on the porch—accompanied by a chorus of tree frogs—and there's a pottery workshop behind the kitchen for post-prandial browsing.

In the past, most of Antigua's restaurants, whatever the price and pretension, have been good but little more. However, Antigua now has a restaurant of international caliber. Last year, Englishman Mark French opened **Pelican Club** at Hodges Bay Club. Using mostly local seafood and produce, he creates new combinations—such as baked grouper with a rum and lime-butter sauce—that intrigue rather than intimidate. Young Mr. French charges accordingly. The hotel part of the **Hodges Bay Club** is equally stylish, for Jane French is as skilled at the hostelry end of the business as her husband is in the kitchen.

A couple of beaches away, the recently refurbished and expanded **Blue Waters** attracts what the hotel calls a "traditional West Indian clientele" (which means about 75 percent British). The hotel is discreet and lovely, with plumbago around the pool, hammocks on the lawn, and rooms that face the sea.

St. John's

The streets of the capital, hilly and traffic-jammed, call for stout walking shoes. St. John's does have a few attractions, but it is not a town in which you'll want to spend much time—especially when there are 365 beaches out there. You will, however, want to take a look at the enormous **Cathedral of St. John the Divine**, atop one of the town's highest hills. The history of Christian Antigua is etched on the church's polished brass plaques and carved in the stones of its graveyard—where you may have to push aside a snoozing goat to read who lies beneath a marker. In any city the Cathedral would be impressive; in St. John's it is astounding.

The **Museum of Antigua and Barbuda** is housed in the 240-year-old Neoclassic Old Court House halfway between the Cathedral and the harbor. It is remarkable for the coherent and thoughtful manner in which the displays of Amerindian culture and the island's later history are presented, and is one of the Caribbean's best sources of information about Arawak and Carib cultures.

Down on the waterfront the shops and restaurants of **Redcliffe Quay** occupy the buildings that once housed slaves prior to their auction. Among the discos and pizza parlors you'll find an old island tradition, Antiguan pottery. Rough, primitive, and functional, much of the pottery is made in the backyards of homes in Seaview Farms, an inland village where mothers have handed down pottery techniques to their daughters for generations.

Parham

Parham, Antigua's original capital—east of St. John's on the North Shore—makes no attempt to prettify its history.

Aged stone foundations still support wooden second floors, unless the last inhabitants were termites, in which case the foundations support vines. The exception may be St. Peter's Anglican Church, which stands in a wind-swept field looking like the setting for a Sir Walter Scott wedding scene. The church is totally out of proportion to the little town; massive and six-sided, with coral walls, it is also said to be the prettiest church in the West Indies. Like all of Parham, it combines past and present with a refreshing lack of sentimentality.

Jumby Bay owns the 300-acre Long Island, off the northeast shore. This, the newest of Antigua's conservative expensive resorts, reached only by a private launch arranged by the hotel from a mainland marina, has a style of its own. Dinners are served in the courtyard of an old great house. There is a resident naturalist and a resident horticulturist, and archaeologist Desmond Nicholson (director of the museum in St. John's) leads walks. Even though the rooms in the Pond House have Roman bath-tubs, the original, two-unit rondevals are more private, and privacy is what Jumby Bay is all about.

West Coast

Darkwood Beach is Antigua's best shelling beach. (It is just below **Jolly Beach,** the big, brash, beachfront resort that is popular among the younger set.) The early bird catches the keyhole limpet here, and by the time the **Darkwood Beach Bar** opens for breakfast, the prize shells may be in someone else's sandy pocket. Never mind; stay around for a beach-bar lunch of hamburgers, chicken and chips, or lobster.

South Shore

In the days of the Royal Georges, **Nelson's Dockyard** at English Harbour was the headquarters of the British Fleet—one of whose captains was the eager 26-year-old Horatio Nelson. These days, Nelson's Dockyard crosses its Maritime Museum with a yachting center, hotels, restaurants, and other facilities of modern commerce. Plan on spending a day here, breaking for a salad, omelette, or grilled fish on the shady terrace at **Admiral's Inn,** then going back to watch the activity on the charter yachts.

Always a busy place, English Harbour really swings during Sailing Week in the spring. Sailing Week is a time for some serious racing and some serious partying. The ubiquitous Desmond Nicholson (whose family's yacht-broker/charter-service business is headquartered at English Harbour), and Howard Hulford, the dashing owner of the Curtain Bluff hotel, originated the event some 20 years ago with the vague intention of extending the winter season a bit.

The road on the other side of the Harbour leads up to Shirley Heights, the site of the ruins of an old fort and remarkable mainly for its photographic possibilities. Part way up is **Clarence House**, built in 1787 as a home away from home for the 23-year-old Duke of Clarence (later King William IV) when he was stationed here. It is now the Governor General's Official Country Residence and is open to the public for short tours. There is no fee, but you should tip the caretaker.

Not far from English Harbour—although it seems far when you are negotiating the rough roads through the rain forest—is **Curtain Bluff**. The hotel has made the "Ten Best" list of knowledgeable travellers for about 25 years now. Nicely situated between breezes and two beaches, Curtain Bluff is as nearly perfect as a Caribbean hotel can be—perfect enough to be Antigua's only Relais & Châteaux property and perfect enough for gentlemen to comply uncomplainingly with the jacket-and-tie dress code at dinner. Genuine hospitality, beautiful rooms, superb meals, and an improbably fine wine cellar are a small price to pay for a tight collar.

BARBUDA

Sixty-two square miles of scrub and pink sand, Barbuda gives new meaning to the word flat. Its one hill would be dwarfed by a four-story building, and Martello Tower, from which defenders could scan the horizon, isn't all that much bigger than a fire hydrant. But this matzo on the waters possesses an inordinate amount of charm. Just fifteen minutes by small plane from Antigua's airport, it is the quietest place imaginable, where time has no relevance and simplicity comes stripped down. In **Codrington**—the town in which most of Barbuda's 1,200

residents live—a petrol-filled drum and siphon constitutes the gas station, and the very rumor of paving a
street causes much excitement. Visitors to Barbuda find
themselves doing such long-forgotten things as noticing
the sound of the wind over grass.

The **Frigate Bird Sanctuary**, just two miles by boat from
Codrington's pier, is reason enough to go to Barbuda.
From a small skiff puttering in and out of the mangrove
bushes, you will see male frigate birds—their scarlet neck
pouches puffed up like bright balloons—swoop, soar,
and court possibly amorous females. What with thousands of birds flying just overhead, the scene has a certain
Hitchcockian menace.

Though Barbuda is basically a day trip from Antigua,
there are a few small places to stay and one proper resort,
Coco Point Lodge. Built in the 1960s, Coco Point makes a
fetish out of its remote location. Remote the hotel is, but
$750 a day seems a bit steep for small rooms and the
privilege of having no telephone.

USEFUL FACTS

What to Wear
Dress is casual but conservative; some restaurants require
a jacket at dinner.

Getting In
From New York, American Airlines has daily flights and
BWIA has five flights a week; from Miami, BWIA has daily
flights; from Toronto, BWIA has two flights a week; from
London, British Air has four flights a week; from Frankfurt, Lufthansa has two flights a week. There are easy
connections from San Juan, St. Martin, and other Caribbean airports.

Entry Requirements
Passport is required, but U.S., Canadian, and U.K. citizens
may substitute another proof of citizenship, such as a
birth certificate. There is a $6 departure tax.

Currency
Eastern Caribbean dollar; U.S. dollars are accepted
widely.

Electrical Current
220 volts, but most hotels have 110 volts, 60 cycles.

Getting Around
A local driving permit costs $15 and isn't worth it: Roads
are unmarked and pocked with craters; other hazards
include goats, sheep, cows, and maniacal drivers. Car
rental companies charge as though avoiding these hazards is a privilege. Driving is on the left. Taxis are also
expensive, but rates are government-fixed. Best bet: Find
a driver who seems to be attached to your hotel; use him
exclusively and negotiate.

Business Hours
Monday–Saturday, 8:00–1:00, 2:00–4:00. Most stores close
at noon on Thursday; some close at 1:00 on Saturday.

Festivals
Carnival begins in late July; Sailing Week begins in late
April.

ACCOMMODATIONS REFERENCE
*The rate ranges given here are projections for fall 1988
through spring 1989. Unless otherwise indicated, rates
are for double rooms, double occupancy. The telephone
area code for Antigua and Barbuda is 809.*

▶ **Blue Waters.** P.O. Box 256, St. John's, Antigua, W.I.
$250–$340, M.A.P. Tel: 462-0290/0292; in U.S., (212) 725-
5880 or (800) 223-5695.

▶ **Coco Point Lodge.** Barbuda, W.I. $400–$750, A.P. Tel:
462-3816; in U.S., (212) 646-4750.

▶ **Curtain Bluff.** P.O. Box 288, Antigua, W.I. $365–$595,
A.P. Tel: 463-1115/6/7; in U.S., (212) 289-8888.

▶ **Hodges Bay Club.** P.O. Box 1237, St. John's, Antigua,
W.I. $150–$300, 1-bedroom apartment, E.P. Tel: 462-2300;
in U.S., (212) 535-9530 or (800) 223-5581.

▶ **Jolly Beach Hotel.** P.O. Box 744, St. John's, Antigua,
W.I. Rates start at $110, M.A.P. Tel: 462-0061; in U.S., (800)
321-1055; in Canada, (800) 368-3669.

▶ **Jumby Bay Resort.** P.O. Box 243, St, John's, Antigua,
W.I. $525–$675, F.A.P. Tel: 462-6000; in U.S., (516) 626-
0600 or (800) 437-0049.

OTHER ACCOMMODATIONS

▸ **Admiral's Inn.** P.O. Box 713, St. John's, Antigua, W.I. $80–$94, E.P. Tel: 463-1027; in U.S. (212) 725-5880 or (800) 223-5695; in Canada, (416) 447-2335 or (800) 387-8031. A small, pubby, clubby, and historical accommodation in Nelson's Dockyard. The best room is #1.

▸ **Copper and Lumber Store.** P.O. Box 184, St. John's, Antigua, W.I. $90–$225, E.P. Tel: 463-1058; in U.S., (800) 633-7411; in U.K., (01) 731-7144. A renovated 18th-century building in Nelson's Dockyard. The corner suites are decorated in Regency style; the English pub in the courtyard serves Scotch eggs and other authenticities.

▸ **Half Moon Bay Hotel.** P.O. Box 144, St. John's, Antigua, W.I. $160–$305, M.A.P. Tel: 463-2101/2; in U.S., (212) 832-2277 or (800) 223-6510; in Canada, (416) 622-8813; in U.K., (01) 948-7488. A fine small resort hotel on the southeast coast, known for tennis, water sports, and its half a golf course. The lively crowd here will be speaking a half dozen different languages.

▸ **The Royal Antiguan.** P.O. Box 1322, St. John's, Antigua, W.I. $200–$350, E.P. Tel: 462-3733; in U.S., (212) 983-3560; in Canada, (800) 531-6767. Brand new on the West Coast, this is Antigua's first high-rise (nine stories) hotel; water sports, casino, conference facilities, and a hair salon.

▸ **St. James's Club.** P.O. Box 63, St. John's, Antigua, W.I. $195–$500, M.A.P. Tel: 463-1430; in U.S., (212) 486-2575 or (800) 274-0008; in Canada, (416) 598-2693 or (800) 268-9051; in U.K., (01) 236-1038/4311; in France, (47) 04-2929. This Brit-glitz, jet-set property on the South Shore is trying to take off, but it still looks like a Holiday Inn.

MONTSERRAT

By Julie Wilson

From various points on the British Crown Colony of Montserrat, the neighboring islands of Guadeloupe, Antigua, Nevis, and St. Kitts can be seen on the horizon. This is a nice neighborhood. Few people come to Montserrat on business—aside from rock musicians, who, unlikely as it may seem, record here. Nobody comes looking for jet-skis or jet sets. Rather, people come to enjoy the neighborhood and to be neighborly.

"Neighborly" defines Montserrat. Because there are only a handful of small hotels on the 39-square-mile island, most visitors rent homes or apartments. So, no artificial barriers—lobbies, room service, valet parking—separate visitors from the locals. Everyone shares the same street, the same market aisle.

MAJOR INTEREST

Getting away in a quiet way

Blessed with a lushness that makes most other Caribbean islands look like sand traps; mountainous Montserrat is as green as the Irish shamrock on its passport stamp. Islanders have even been known to call their home the "Emerald Isle." This bit of whimsy, and the shamrock, go back to 1632, when Irish settlers from English St. Kitts came to Montserrat. Even today the phone book reads as though it could have been lifted straight from County Cork.

There aren't too many brogues left on Montserrat today, nor much sailing, fishing, or snorkeling off the black-sand beaches. However, farmers do lead donkeys laden

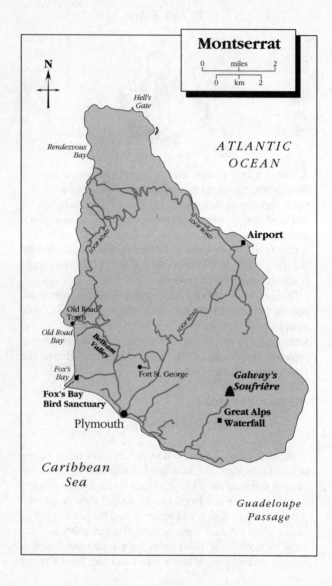

MONTSERRAT

Montserrat

miles 0 — 2
km 0 — 2

N

Hell's Gate

Rendezvous Bay

ATLANTIC OCEAN

Airport

LOOP ROAD

LOOP ROAD

LOOP ROAD

Old Road Town

Old Road Bay

Belham Valley

Fort St. George

Fox's Bay

Fox's Bay Bird Sanctuary

Galway's Soufrière

Great Alps Waterfall

Plymouth

Caribbean Sea

Guadeloupe Passage

with produce—including potatoes—down from their hillside farms. (Only an Irish island would grow potatoes in the Caribbean.) In other words, Montserrat offers a slow-paced lifestyle and a chance to get to know the neighbors. If you're looking for an easy-going, picturesque vacation place, Montserrat is it.

Montserrat's main road loops from Plymouth, the capital, over the top of the island, past Blackburne Airport, and down through a vibrant green, fertile valley that often inspires taxi drivers to say immodestly, "This may be the only Paradise you see before you die, so enjoy it."

Plymouth

The heart of this, the capital, is the town square and the clock-faced War Memorial. A few cannons—taxi drivers stuff empty soft-drink bottles into the barrels—point listlessly toward the sea. Post-office boxes are stuck into the outer walls of the robin's-egg-blue Treasury Building. Just about everybody in town knows everybody else.

Whatever is worth buying on Montserrat can be bought in Plymouth: rough, creamy cotton products at Sea Island Cotton and whimsical tee-shirts at the T-Shirt Shop. In Plymouth, also, are the island's few bars (rock musicians hang out at **The Plantation**) and a couple of discos, but they're usually open only on weekends. And it's on weekends that restaurants rustle up batches of "goatwater" stew and curried mutton. The island's best-known dish is "mountain" chicken, which is not chicken at all, but leg of the frog. Mountain chicken comes dear because, well, there just aren't that many good-sized frogs to go around.

Galway's Soufrière

From Plymouth, a spur road leads down the southwest coast then cuts inland to Galway's Soufrière, a 3,000-foot-high "inactive" volcano. You can walk to the hot sulphur springs that bubble up from its restless innards. The trail shifts frequently due to washouts and periodic collapses, but it's worth persevering on the 15-minute scrabble through a bleak, merciless, foul-smelling landscape to get to the source, from which boiling water trickles over bare lava and rock. Galway's Soufrière was named after David

Galway, whose nearby 18th-century sugar plantation is being restored.

South of the volcanic scar on the way back toward the coast, Great Alps Waterfall pushes through a narrow spot in the rocks and gushes down some 70 feet. To see it requires a stiff hike from car park to falls—not to be attempted wearing sandals.

Loop Road

From Plymouth, the main road goes north to **Fort St. George**, built in 1782 as a defense against the French and now a popular place for church picnics beneath the tamarind trees. Looking at the little that remains of the fort, including its cannons, you can see just what a strategic view it affords of Plymouth's harbor, a good two and a half miles away.

Egrets, herons, kingfishers, coots, and their feathered relatives live near the fort at **Fox's Bay Bird Sanctuary**. Unfortunately, the more popular the sanctuary becomes with sightseers, the fewer the number of birds that take refuge here. You can have a good walk over dim, damp trails that meander among sweet lime and manchineel trees and are laced with crab holes so big a Honda could disappear in one. As you step over fallen cherry trees thick with termite nests, you'll see why Montserratians build their houses of stone.

Belham Valley

Up by Old Road Town, Belham Valley is known locally as "Beverly Heights." Wealthy foreigners have built some impressive villas here, and the well-manicured gardens are a testament to the skills of the gardeners who beat back an ever encroaching jungle. The 11-hole Montserrat Golf Course (where one of the hazards is likely to be a flock of sheep moving briskly down the edge of the fairway) is in the neighborhood, as is the excellent **Belham Valley Restaurant** (dinner only).

The island's best hotel—**Vue Pointe**, a "cottage colony" (with a new conference center)—is up here. Right next to the golf course, Vue Pointe has a couple of tennis courts, two small beaches on Old Road Bay, a nice pool—and the sort of easy-going clientele who won't mind loaning you a book if you've run out of things to read. Up here, too, is record-producer George Martin's Air Studios, and you may see the likes of Eric Clapton and Elton John in the neighborhood.

From Belham Valley, the road loops up into fairly deserted territory—over bridges crossing deep gorges, and past high, windy plains where goats graze—and back to the airport.

USEFUL FACTS

What to Wear
Conservatively casual clothes are in order. Bring sturdy shoes for climbing.

Getting In
Montserrat Aviation Services flies from Antigua to Black-burne Airpoint several times a day; there are also flights from St. Kitts and Guadeloupe.

Entry Requirements
U.S. citizens need only a driver's license, voter-registration card, or birth certificate. Others must have passports. There is a departure tax of $7.50.

Currency
Eastern Caribbean dollar. The U.S. dollar is widely accepted.

Electrical Current
220 volts; American- and Canadian-made appliances require converters.

Getting Around
For an extended stay, you will probably want to rent a car. Driving is on the left, and roads are good. A permit that is valid for six months costs $7.50. The Tourist Office in Plymouth has a list of taxi drivers and government-fixed prices.

Business Hours
8:00–12:00 and 1:00–4:00.

ACCOMMODATIONS REFERENCE
The rate ranges given here are projections for fall 1988 through spring 1989. Unless otherwise indicated, rates are for double rooms, double occupancy. The telephone area code for Montserrat is 809.

▶ **Vue Pointe Hotel.** P.O. Box 65, Plymouth, Montserrat, W.I. $135–$185, M.A.P. Tel: 491-5210; in U.S., (617) 533-4426.

OTHER ACCOMMODATIONS
▶ **Montserrat Springs Hotel.** P.O. Box 259, Montserrat, W.I. $90–$135, E.P. Tel: 491-2481; in Canada, (416) 928-4016. This "businessman's hotel" just outside Plymouth and above Emerald Isle Beach has air-conditioned rooms, a pool with a view, and an open-air dining room.

▶ For **rentals** of homes or apartments, contact the Montserrat Tourist Board, P.O. Box 7, Plymouth, Montserrat, W.I. Tel: 491-2230.

GUADELOUPE

By Robert Grodé

Robert J. Grodé, a journalist, reviewer, and longtime resident of the Caribbean now based in New York City, has written travel and cultural articles for magazines in the U.S. and abroad. He is the author of a book on the gravestones of St. Eustatius.

Half-way down the archipelago that stretches from the coast of South America to the Florida Keys is an island that is spread out on the sea like a butterfly. Guadeloupe, the *papillon* of the French West Indies, is in fact a pair of islands, joined with airy grace by a thin isthmus of land. The eastern "wing," Grande-Terre, is a rolling, beach-ringed coral atoll; its western counterpart, Basse-Terre, is volcanic, mountainous, and lushly beautiful. Together they form an island that offers a blend of French, East Indian, and African cultures. Such surprising pleasures as curry-scented stew served on a Sevres china plate and music with Creole patois lyrics and a pulse-quickening beat testify to the island's mixed heritage and make Guadeloupe an intoxicating place to visit.

MAJOR INTEREST

Exploring Pointe-à-Pitre (markets, restaurants)
French and Creole dining
The Parc Naturel

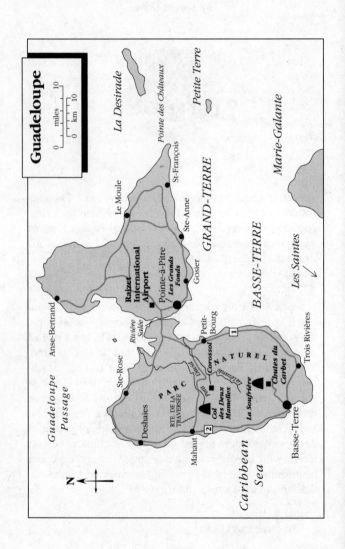

Guadeloupe

0	miles 10
0	km 10

Guadeloupe Passage

Anse-Bertrand

Ste-Rose

Rivière Salée

PARC

Deshaies

RTE. DE LA TRAVERSÉE

Mahaut

Col des Deux Mamelles

NATUREL

La Soufrière

Chutes du Carbet

Basse-Terre

Trois Rivières

Caribbean Sea

Petit-Bourg

Corossol

Raizet International Airport

Pointe-à-Pitre

Les Grands Fonds

Gosier

Le Moule

St-François

Ste-Anne

GRAND-TERRE

BASSE-TERRE

Les Saintes

Marie-Galante

La Désirade

Pointe des Châteaux

Petite Terre

N

GRANDE-TERRE

Much of the resort activity takes place in Grande-Terre. **Gosier**, six miles from the international Raizet Airport and four miles from Guadeloupe's capital, Pointe-à-Pitre, is the location of what might somewhat overstatedly be called the hotel strip. The shoreline, scalloped with sandy coves, actually *is* edged by several large hotels, as well as one of the island's two casinos. The most inviting of the hotels is the moderately priced **Auberge de la Vieille Tour**, which is more than a quarter of a century old. The 80-room Vieille Tour, while offering a resortlike roster of activities, has managed to maintain an intimate atmosphere, thanks to a friendly staff and to public rooms and recreation areas that have been kept to a manageable size. It's popular with families; bare-bottomed toddlers and their sharp-eyed grandmothers gather around the pool or on the small beach to while away the afternoons, while more energetic family members are off playing tennis or volleyball, and pedal boating, windsurfing, or sailing. The dining room has an island-wide reputation for the excellence of its classic French cuisine, an unexpected bonus often not found in larger hostelries.

Pointe-à-Pitre

Pointe-à-Pitre is one of the most captivating cities in the Caribbean, and you should set aside a morning to explore it. The bustling marketplace, a good starting point, is liveliest in the early hours. The market stalls, covered with a vast cast-iron shed, spread over a full city block near the center of town.

Inside the market *aerosols de benedicion* (spray-on blessings!) with names like "High John the Conqueror" and "Double Fast Luck" are spread out on broad marble-topped counters, along with mysterious bundles wrapped in banana leaves and tied with lemon grass. On closer inspection, these prove to contain live land crabs fresh from the rain forests and ready for the pot. Aisles are piled with straw mats, palm-frond brooms, and stacks of broad-brimmed fishermen's hats, called "salakos." Half sombrero and half coolie hat, salakos make perfect sunshades for the beach.

Coffee bars dot the neighborhood around the Market,

and you might want to take a break at one. Inside, elderly gentlemen, each sipping a morning *decollage* (literally, "takeoff") tot of rum, study their copies of *Le Figaro* or *Le Monde*. Order a *café au lait* and join in that time-hallowed Gallic pastime: watching passersby. On Guadeloupe, they're likely to be even more animated than their Parisian cousins on the Boulevard St. Germain.

The recently dedicated **Musée Saint-John Perse** is just a few blocks south of the outdoor market at the corner of rue de Nozieres and rue Achille René-Boisneuf. The 19th-century *folie,* with pale yellow walls and turquoise-painted cast-iron galleries, contains a splendid upstairs collection of memorabilia of the poet, diplomat, and Nobel-Prize winner, who was born in Guadeloupe in 1887. On the main floor of the magnificently restored colonial townhouse, furnishings, costumes, and artifacts recapture the atmosphere of a late 19th-century Guadeloupean home.

Guadeloupe is regarded by many as the culinary capital of the Caribbean. More than 200 restaurants—from elegant hotel dining rooms to "front porch" establishments where a few tables are set up on the cook's breezy verandah—dot the island. Pointe-à-Pitre itself is chocka-block with restaurants. One of the most popular is **La Canne à Sucre**, located in a small building on rue Henri IV/Jean Jaures (the name of the street was changed a few years ago, but both versions are still used). The cool, high-ceilinged room is decorated in gentle pastels, and a silk-fringed lamp casts a pink glow over the tiny bar. La Canne à Sucre serves what owner/chef Gerard Virginius describes as *nouvelle* Creole cuisine; his grilled lamb chops with chicken livers and ginger are excellent.

Another lunch or dinner possibility is **La Plantation**, a short distance out of town at the Marina Bas-du-Fort. The restaurant's banal exterior is deceptive; just through the front door is a pair of small coralita pink dining rooms. The lamps hanging over each table are draped in *broderie anglaise;* the china is sprigged with flowers; and the crystal sparkles as brightly as the mirrored walls. In charge of the kitchen is Francis Delage, whose *Encyclopedia of Creole Cuisine* is regarded hereabouts as a culinary classic.

Diners at La Plantation might want to explore **A la Recherche du Passé**, a tiny shop a few steps away from the restaurant. Here, owner Laurent Chassaniol and his wife have assembled a collection of delightful bibelots. Children will find the brightly painted whirligigs downright lovable. There are also handsome old hand-colored maps and antique volumes of Antillean lore, many illustrated with fine engravings.

Out on Grande-Terre

For a pleasant morning excursion, head across Grande-Terre to its easternmost tip at Pointe des Châteaux. Driving on Guadeloupe can provide its own pleasures—and distractions. *"Attention!"* is the byword along the highways, and almost every crossroads is dominated by an ex-voto shrine. Rusting tin cans brimming with sunflowers and oleander huddle around the foot of the cross or the hem of the Virgin's mantle.

About halfway between Pointe-à-Pitre and Pointe des Châteaux, the village of Sainte Anne, site of **Caravelle**, Guadeloupe's Club Med complex, curves along the island's most inviting beach. Looking down on the reef-bracketed bay is a cozy, decently priced caravanserai called **La Toubana**. Its housekeeping cottages crown a landscaped hillside and cluster about a breezy pale-peach dining area ringed with tanks of tropical fish. A small swimming pool just outside seems to be suspended in space above the shimmering sea.

Shortly before Pointe des Châteaux, the road passes through another seaside village, **Saint-François**. Daylong excursions to the tranquil, unspoiled island of **La Desirade** aboard the motor launches *La Kikalie* and *La Fregate* leave from Saint-François's Marina de la Grande Saline. The service offers other island-bound excursions: from Pointe-à-Pitre to **Marie Galante**, and from Trois-Rivières in Basse-Terre to **Les Saintes**. For those who feel uncomfortable on the water, there is regular air service to all the islands. (Contact the Guadeloupe Tourist Office in Pointe-à-Pitre for schedules and rates.)

A large East Indian population, descendants of workers brought here from India in the mid-1800s, lend colorful touches to Saint-François, particularly during the *Fête Annuelle* each October. For one long weekend, the waterfront is transformed into a lively street fair. Booths are draped in cotton printed with traditional red-and-white

Indian designs; the air is filled with the sounds of sitars and steel "pans"; and the scent of sandalwood incense mingles with that of curry. Any time of year, however, Saint-François offers travellers on their way to Pointe des Châteaux a chance to sample one of Guadeloupe's innumerable ti-lolo's. These tiny rum shops are especially inviting in Saint-François because many have a view of the busy waterfront. Life seems to center about the ti-lolo. Everyone from the local fishermen to the gendarmes in their *kepis,* it seems, stops by for a bit of gossip over a "ti-punch," the potent mix of rum, lime juice, and sugar syrup that is something of a national drink.

Outside Saint-François is one of Guadeloupe's most comfortable and highly praised hotels, **Le Hamak.** This cluster of bungalows is set amid manicured gardens at the edge of a tranquil 800-acre lagoon and next to the island's largest hotel, **Le Meridien.** Le Hamak has three small private beaches and offers golf at the nearby Robert Trent Jones-designed 18-hole course (the only one on Guadeloupe); gambling at a nearby casino; and windsurfing, water-skiing, and sailing.

Pointe des Châteaux itself provides a dramatic view of foaming breakers and stunted windswept trees. The limestone cliffs and sea-sculpted rocks reminded early settlers of the ruined walls of some great country house, and gave the place its name. A tall cross crowns the heights; visitors who climb the winding path to it are treated to a sweeping view of sea and sky, with the islands of La Desirade and Petite Terre floating between. The climb is more demanding than it seems from below and should be undertaken only by the sound of wind and stout of heart. Nor is swimming recommended for the faint-hearted, as the surf can be rough along this Atlantic shoreline.

A winning luncheon spot a few minutes down the road from Pointe des Châteaux is **Au Coin du Port**, an airy thatched pavilion with a good view of the sea. *Burgaux* (whelks served in a court bouillon of eye-watering fieriness) and crispy *accras,* the traditional deep-fried codfish fritters of the Antilles, as well as snapper, langouste, and chicken *colombo,* a curried stew, are on the Creole-accented bill-of-fare.

From Saint-François, the road veers north through rolling countryside to the village of **Le Moule**. Here, the Atlantic breakers roll in and the sea is dotted with surfers, drawn to the village by what is possibly the finest surfing in the Caribbean. Just north of Le Moule, the road swings inland again through a region of hilly farmland known as Les Grands Fonds. The settlers here were originally Bretons, and their descendants, a self-sufficient lot, have retained many of the traditions of their forebears. Long-skirted women in flaring sunbonnets stride along the roads and families eye passersby from shadowed front porches with a reserve not found elsewhere on the island.

BASSE-TERRE

Another five- or six-hour excursion explores one of the Caribbean's most impressive nature reserves. A few years ago, in what must have been one of the ecological breakthroughs of the century, the government of Guadeloupe set aside nearly one fifth of its entire area as a natural park. Today it's possible to explore this vast area by car or hike its well-marked trails, picnic in its sun-dappled glades, inspect its several small *maisons* with their exhibits about volcanoes, the forest, coffee, sugarcane, and rum.

Parc Naturel

To get to the Parc Naturel take Route 1 west from Pointe-à-Pitre across the Rivière Salée and then south to Petit-Bourg, where a delightful inn, the **Auberge de la Distillerie**, might have been the setting for an early film by Jean Renoir. Wrapped around with grape arbors and decorated in a style best described as eclectic—antimacassars, a jaunty plastic parrot, and framed samplers—the inn offers such simple pleasures as picnicking in meadows, boating, and bathing in La Lezarde River. There is also a freshwater pool a few steps from the shady dining verandah.

From Petit-Bourg, go west again, following the Route de la Traversée through the mountains to the village of Mahaut. You should stop at the Cascade aux Ecrevisses, named for the freshwater crayfish that are a staple of Guadeloupean cuisine. The waterfall is an easy ten-minute walk along the banks of the Corossol River. A mile or two farther, at Bras David, nature trails of various distances and difficulty have been set up. Next to the parking lot is a small exhibition hall that displays the various flora and fauna you may encounter during your hike. There is also a new Parc Zoologique nearby. The Col des Deux Mamelles is about halfway along the Traversée; the view back to Pointe-à-Pitre 2,000 feet below is spectacular, and a rustic restaurant, the **Gîte des Deux Mamelles**, offers light lunches.

More ambitious nature lovers may prefer to explore the southern portion of the Parc Naturel, dominated by La Soufrière. This nearly 5,000-foot-high volcano still spews forth sulphurous fumes and jets of steam from its fumeroles. Since a minor eruption in 1976, Soufrière's vents and fissures have lost a great deal of their drama. Instead, you may wish to sign up for a guided nature hike to the Chutes du Carbet, a series of three spectacular waterfalls, each plunging hundreds of feet down the mountainside. Arrangements can be made on the island by telephoning Monsieur Berry of the Organisation des Guides de Montagne de la Caraibe at 81-45-79.

At the west coast of Basse-Terre, the Traversée joins Route 2. If you drive north to the village of Deshaies, you'll be rewarded with a dip in the calm sea and lunch at the edge of a beach the color of raw sugar. At **Restaurant Karacoli**, owner Madame Lucienne Salcede greets her guests at the door and seats them either indoors or in the palm-shaded garden. The hum of conversation around the oilcloth-covered tables mingles with the sound of the surf a few feet away. Creole dishes, as well as continental entrées, are splendidly prepared and served by a smiling staff who seem genuinely eager to make lunch at this out-of-the-way spot memorable.

From Deshaies, Route 2 continues across the northern coast of Basse-Terre, through pineapple plantations and banana groves, to the hamlets of Sainte-Rose and the aptly named Monplaisir. In Sainte-Rose, **Chez Clara**, on the porch of chef Clara Lesueur's home, is another good spot to have lunch; its menu is imaginative and its atmosphere casual.

USEFUL FACTS
See Martinique. For *Getting In:* Air Guadeloupe serves the Guadeloupe archipelago—St. Martin, St. Barts, La Desirade, Les Saintes, and Marie Galante—daily.

ACCOMMODATIONS REFERENCE
The rate ranges given here are projections for fall 1988 through spring 1989. Prices are for double rooms, double occupancy, unless otherwise noted. The telephone area code for Guadeloupe is 590. All addresses are in Guadeloupe, F.W.I.

▶ **Auberge de la Distillerie.** Tabanon, Petit-Bourg 97170. $100–$120, C.P. Tel: 94-25-91; in U.S., (212) 840-6636 or (800) 223-9815.

▶ **Auberge de la Vieille Tour.** Gosier 97190. $160–$222, E.P. Tel: 84-23-23; in U.S., (212) 757-6500 or (800) 223-9862.

▶ **Caravelle/Club Med.** Sainte-Anne 97180. Weekly rates per person, $580–$1,250, A.P., depending on week; Tel: 88-21-00; in U.S., (800) 528-3100.

▶ **Le Hamak.** Saint-François 97118. $280–$430, E.P. Tel: 88-59-99; in U.S., (212) 477-1600, (212) 832-2277, (803) 785-7411, (800) 223-1510, (800) 223-6510, or (800) 633-7411.

▶ **Le Meridien.** Saint-François 97118. $130–$150, E.P. Tel: 88-51-00; in U.S., (212) 265-4494 or (800) 223-9918.

▶ **La Toubana.** Sainte-Anne 97180. $100–$174, C.P. Tel: 88-25-78; in U.S., (212) 840-6636, (212) 477-1600, (800) 223-9815, or (800) 223-1510.

OTHER ACCOMMODATIONS
▶ **Gîtes Ruraux de Guadeloupe** are intimate, frequently family-run guest houses scattered along the coast and in the countryside. They are unpretentious and perfect for getting to know your Guadeloupean hosts and their friends. At least a passing familiarity with French will prove helpful. Contact Office Departmental du Tourisme, Boîte Postale 1099, Angle des Rues Schoelcher et Delgres, 97110 Pointe-à-Pitre, Guadeloupe, F.W.I. Tel: 82-09-30.

DOMINICA

By Robert Grodé

The Dominican landscape is a constantly shifting kaleidoscope of emeralds, viridians, celadons, and jade greens, splashed here and there with chartreuse and absinthe. Perhaps nowhere else in the Caribbean is nature so unstinting in its bounty. The highlands in the center of the island receive approximately 300 inches of rain each year. Vegetation runs riot, and streams and rivulets, cascades and waterfalls streak the landscape.

MAJOR INTEREST

> Lush vegetation and natural beauty
> Freshwater swimming
> Nature hiking
> Creole dining
> Unspoiled and tranquil atmosphere

However, on Sunday, November 3, 1493, Christopher Columbus was apparently not inspired by all this beauty. Rather than naming the mountainous, mist-shrouded island that loomed before him after a saint or a religious shrine, he decided to call his latest discovery "Sunday"—*Dominica* in Spanish, and pronounced Do-mi-NEE-kah. Of course, his lack of inspiration might have been due to his brief acquaintance with the island: threatened by spear-wielding Carib Indians, Columbus stopped only long enough to put a few goats ashore in hopes of establishing a herd that would provision future expeditions, then sailed north in search of more hospitable lands.

The Caribs's unwelcoming ways discouraged European settlement of the 290-square-mile island for more

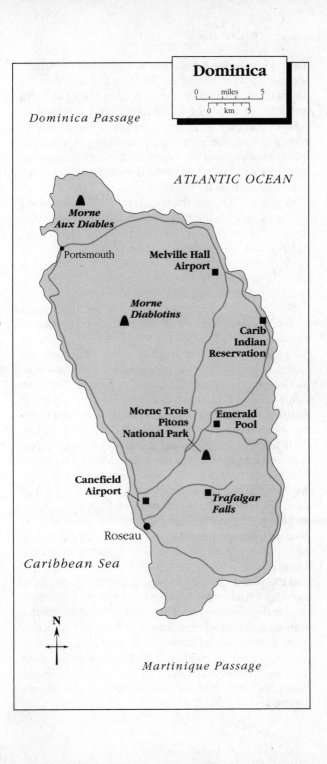

than two centuries. Even as late as 1748, when the French and British were slicing up the West Indian pie at the Treaty of Aix-la-Chapelle, they agreed to leave Dominica well enough alone; the Indians were just too difficult to subdue. Naturally, this arrangement didn't last. The Europeans, armed with greed, guile, and guns, soon established footholds on the island, and bloody battles between the two major Old World rivals began to break out with disconcerting frequency.

Finally, in 1795, after the French had torched the island capital of Roseau, the exhausted British paid what they termed "a ransom" of 12,000 pounds to the French and, in 1805, took sole possession of the island. It remained a British Crown Colony until it gained independence in 1978. As a result of this mixed heritage, Dominicans speak both English and a French-Creole patois.

Now, after several years of national unrest, Dominica is serene. Its approximately 80,000 people seem eager to welcome visitors. Dominicans, who ordinarily are among the most dedicated individualists in the Caribbean, are joining together these days in dozens of projects—from producing prefabricated houses to restoring a massive fortification in Portsmouth that dates from the heyday of British power. At Canefield Airport, a new terminal building with a soaring gull's-wing roof has replaced the hot, dusty wooden shed that used to make arrivals and departures something of a trial. Happily, the immigration officials in their crisply starched white jackets are even more accommodating in their new surroundings than they were before. Roseau's **Fort Young Hotel**, long popular for its "Sadie Thompson" atmosphere but destroyed by pounding seas a decade ago, has been rebuilt and is accepting reservations. Dominica, it seems, is on the move.

Is the island, then, on its way to becoming another of the Caribbean's mini-Miamis? Far from it. Dominica's very real pleasures are of the simpler sort: freshwater swimming in lakes and rivers (Dominica's beaches, while swimmable, fall somewhat short of dazzling), birdwatching, hiking, sampling such local dishes as *ti-ti-ri* (tiny fresh-water fish) and *crapaud* (immense island frogs), and, best of all, getting to know the Dominicans themselves.

Roseau

Most of these delights are to be discovered outside of Roseau. During his 1859 visit, Anthony Trollope felt that everything in Roseau "seems to speak of desolation," and today's visitors usually agree. Though the explanation most commonly given for Roseau's general air of dilapidation is *David,* the devastating hurricane that ravaged the island in 1979, neglect, not nature, must take a large share of the blame. The reason for the neglect is not hard to discover. With an annual per-capita income only slightly higher than that of Haiti, Dominica is one of the poorest of the West Indian nations.

The best of the little shopping available in Roseau is at the restored **Old Market** at the southern edge of town on a cobblestone square bright with oleanders and hibiscus. Here tiny craft shops offer exquisite baskets made by the Carib Indians, whose reservation, the only one in the world, is on the Atlantic side of the island. The Market also offers dolls dressed in the madras skirts and bandanas that are the Dominican national costume, and a selection of locally crafted jewelry and hand carved figurines.

The Roman Catholic Cathedral is located, appropriately enough, on Virgin Lane, on a hill overlooking the road. If nothing else, you'll enjoy the chance to catch the cool breezes that seem to sweep constantly through the church's open windows. There is also a charmingly naïve mural adorning the Mary altar. In depicting the flight into Egypt, the artist has filled the sky with cherubs strewing roses in the path of a Holy Family whose members seem to be suffering from a bad case of "donkey-lag."

Another Roseau establishment worth visiting is **Tropicrafts**, the island's largest producer of the straw rugs that, over the years, have decorated nearly every inn and private home in the West Indies. In a factory tucked away on Turkey Lane, owner Mrs. R.E.A. Volney oversees a staff of about eight who, hunkered down on the cement floor, plait dried palm fronds into rugs, handbags, valises, and hats. Tropicrafts offers a behind-the-scenes glimpse of a continuing island tradition.

Local well-heeled diners regard the air-conditioned **La Robe Creole** near the Old Market as Roseau's best restaurant. Attractively done up in madras cloths and slowly revolving ceiling fans, it features a well-thought-out, subtly seasoned Creole/Continental menu. Unfortunately, its charm is a sometime thing. At some meals, the radio blares and the service gives new meaning to the term "lackadaisical." On other occasions, however, everything seems shipshape.

Around Roseau

Outside the capital, Trollope's mood of desolation vanishes and all is well, from places to stay to places to see. Accommodations on the island are, as might be expected, small and unpretentious. The 17-room **Reigate Hall**, two miles outside Roseau, is a restored estate house, all whitewashed walls and mahogany planter's chairs. It also boasts a swimming pool, tennis court, sauna, gym, and the slightly formal air of a British colonial club.

The **Evergreen Hotel**, about a mile from town, is a bit more relaxed. This recently opened, reasonably priced guest house has spotless rooms and a staff as smiling and helpful as can be found anywhere. Dining is family-style, and such superbly prepared Dominican specialties as mountain chicken (frogs' legs) and stuffed crab back are often on the menu. Another plus: an atmosphere that encourages an easygoing camaraderie among the guests. Most are Americans and Europeans assigned to one or another of the development programs that are transforming Dominica, and after-dinner talk on the broad, breezy, second-story veranda generally concerns one project or another. A new guest with a sharp ear can become an instant authority on the latest happenings around the island.

Undoubtedly the most unusual accommodations on the island are at **Papillote Wilderness Retreat**, a straight-out-of-Edgar-Rice-Burroughs aerie nestled near the foot of the stunningly beautiful Trafalgar Falls. Former New Yorker Anne Baptiste and her island-born husband have put together a birdwatcher/hiker/nature lover's Eden: a half-dozen cozy, comfortable rooms, decked out with handmade quilts (nights can be chilly here in the foothills) and colorful wall paintings, and a rustic, covered dining terrace that looks out over a tangle of breadfruit and mahogany trees, lobster claw ginger, and trailing lianas. In one corner, a hot tub, bubbling with water from a natural hot spring, invites diners to take a pre- (or post-) prandial dip. The tranquility is occasionally shattered by the raucous cry of the Baptistes' pet peacock, but this merely adds to the jungle atmosphere.

Touring the Island

A network of excellent roads links almost all parts of the island, thanks largely to aid provided by several foreign governments. The roads make a circuit of the northern half of the island a pleasant and varied four- to five-hour excursion. Visitors who are a bit nervous about left-hand driving may want to hire a car and driver.

An early morning start is best; beginning your circuit on the western (Caribbean) coastline is also a good idea because the western coast tends to be warmer than the eastern side in midday. The highway threads through several fishing villages—each with a dazzling view of the sea and, on clear days, a vista that stretches as far as Guadeloupe—to **Portsmouth**, Dominica's second largest town.

This village set along the edge of a curving, palm-fringed harbor was slated to be the island capital in the 18th century. Unfortunately, frequent outbreaks of malaria and yellow fever in this then-swampy area soon put paid to these plans. Today, the diseases have long since been eradicated, but Portsmouth remains a sleepy spot, now favored by visiting yachtsmen because it offers the most protected anchorage in these parts.

Cabrits is an 18th-century fort that crowns the heights at the mouth of the harbor. Restoration is far from complete and the climb up a rock-strewn path can be tricky. The fort's battlements are impressive, however, and a few small gun emplacements have been outfitted with historical displays.

From Portsmouth, the highway swings east into country that would have sent Le Douanier Rousseau scurrying for his paintbox: banana plantations glow in the tenderest of blue-greens on terraced hillsides and African tulip trees tilt their scarlet blooms toward the sky. At the Atlantic coast, the road sweeps past Melville Hall, the island's "second" airport.

About midway down the Atlantic flank of the island is the **Carib Indian Reservation**. Visitors expecting exotic ethnicity are bound to be disappointed—no quaint thatch-roofed longhouses or colorfully costumed villagers here. The Caribs have adopted the West Indian style, and their homes, yards ablaze with canna blossoms, are all but indistinguishable from their neighbors'. Several small shops line the road, and prices for the Carib crafts—fine basketwork, irresistible model boats, carved calabash bowls, straw cassava strainers—are temptingly low.

Morne Trois Pitons National Park is reputedly the oldest in the English-speaking Caribbean. The Park's **Emerald Pool**, about a 20-minute hike from the highway, is one of its loveliest sights. Wear rubber-soled shoes for the excursion because the sun-dappled path, though not difficult, can be slippery. It descends in a series of doglegs, with benches at convenient intervals, to Emerald Pool itself, a swirling body of water at the base of a 50-foot cascade that tumbles over fern-hung grottoes.

Trafalgar Falls cascades down the hills just above Roseau. This billowing veil of water plunging 100-feet down a sheer cliff captures, in one heart-stopping image, just what it is that has made Dominica a favorite for travellers in search of the unspoiled beauty of the tropics. Its beauty is still unspoiled and, with its tranquility restored, Dominica is once again a place of delight for any true island lover.

USEFUL FACTS

Getting In
LIAT has daily flights to Canefield or Melville Hall Airports from Antigua, St. Lucia, Guadeloupe, Martinique, Barbados, Trinidad, and Puerto Rico. From Guadeloupe, there are flights daily except Sunday on Air Guadeloupe or Air Martinique.

Entry Requirements
U.S. and Canadian citizens arriving for stays of up to three months must have a valid passport, a notarized birth certificate with raised seal, or a voter-registration card, as well as a return or onward ticket. There is a departure tax of $6.

Currency
The legal tender is the Eastern Caribbean dollar, but U.S. and Canadian dollars are accepted almost everywhere. The exchange rate is subject to currency fluctuations. Most hotels and all banks will exchange currency.

Electrical Current
Voltage is 220 AC, 50 cycles. American- and Canadian-made appliances require converters.

Getting Around
The island has several local rental-car agencies. A valid driver's license is required, as is a Visitor's Driver Permit (about $12), obtainable at airports and at the Police Traffic Department in Roseau.

Banking Hours
Monday–Thursday, 8:00–1:00; Friday, 8:00–1:00, 3:00–5:00.

Festivals
The island celebrates Korné Korn-La (which means "blow the conch shell") on the second Saturday of every month at Soufrière or Scotts Head. Usually, there's much other music, too, and delicious food sold from stalls on the beach.

ACCOMMODATIONS REFERENCE
The rate ranges given here are projections for fall 1988 through spring 1989. Unless otherwise indicated, rates are for double rooms, double occupancy. The telephone area code for Dominica is 809.

▶ **Evergreen Hotel**. Castle Comfort, Box 309, Commonwealth of Dominica, W.I. $70, M.A.P. Tel: 448-3288/3276.
▶ **Papillote Wilderness Retreat**. Trafalgar, Box 67, Roseau, Commonwealth of Dominica, W.I. $100, M.A.P. Tel: 448-2287.
▶ **Reigate Hall**. Reigate, Commonwealth of Dominica, W.I. $70–$100, C.P. Tel: 448-4031.

OTHER ACCOMMODATIONS
▶ **Fort Young Hotel**. P.O. Box 462, Roseau, Commonwealth of Dominica, W.I. $75, C.P. Tel: 448-8501/3908. 33 rooms, a disco, and a swimming pool.

MARTINIQUE

By Robert Grodé

Martinique is the scent of frangipani mixed with a trace of Gauloise smoke; the strains of "Island in the Sun" sung *en français;* an haute couture gown accented with hibiscus blossom. Arriving on the island, there is no mistaking you are in the tropics, but these are tropics that have been refined and enlivened by a French sensibility. There is a flirtatiousness, subtle as perfume, in the glances of women, and a Gallic insouciance in men's strides as they swing along the streets of Fort-de-France.

Martinique has always inspired superlatives. Before the arrival of the French in 1635, Christopher Columbus called the island he discovered the "best, richest, sweetest, most charming country in the world." In 1859, Anthony Trollope, taking a break from his duties as a Postal Inspector on the English islands, cast aside his British reserve and praised Martinique's "rich green . . . beauties." A few years later, Paul Gauguin confessed he "could live here as happy as could be." Today's visitors will almost certainly agree with all of the above. From the mountainous north, with its towering green peaks and dew-spangled banana plantations, to the shimmering coral beaches and rustling cane fields of the south; from the sophistication of Fort-de-France to the simple appeal of such villages as Sainte-Luce and Trinité, Martinique offers a variety and charm equalled on few, if any, West Indian islands.

MAJOR INTEREST

> The blend of French and West Indian influences
> Shopping and dining in Fort-de-France
> Excellent small museums

196

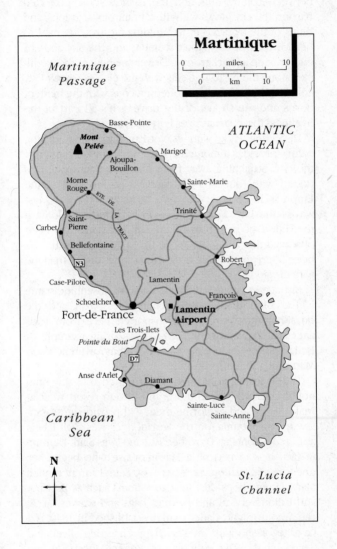

Martinique

Martinique
Passage

ATLANTIC
OCEAN

Basse-Pointe

*Mont
Pelée*

Marigot

Ajoupa-
Bouillon

Morne
Rouge

Sainte-Marie

RTE. DE

LA TRACE

Trinité

Saint-
Pierre

Carbet

Bellefontaine

N3

Robert

Case-Pilote

Lamentin

Schoelcher

François

Fort-de-France

■ **Lamentin
Airport**

Les Trois-Ilets

Pointe du Bout

D7

Anse d'Arlet

Diamant

Caribbean
Sea

Sainte-Luce

Sainte-Anne

N

St. Lucia
Channel

Fort-de-France Area

Martinique's capital and major city is Fort-de-France. Set between rolling hills and the island's most protected harbor, the city glows with the vibrant pinks, greens, and blues of the tropics—in its building façades, the madras headdresses of its market women, and the sky and sea that provide its background. Drivers maneuver their vehicles along the narrow streets with the élan of *Grand Prix* contenders, and the air is often raucous with the blare of horns and the shouts of the drivers. It's all part of the liveliness that characterizes Fort-de-France.

La Savane Park, with its verdant lawns and arching palms, provides a momentary respite from the clamor of the city. Stretching away from the busy waterfront, it is dotted with fountains and statues, notably one of the Empress Josephine, who was born at Trois Ilets, just across the bay. She stands atop a pedestal, holding a medallion of her husband in her left hand. It's been observed that she looks more like a housewife who has been interrupted while drying the dinner dishes than the wife of Napoléon.

Just across rue de la Liberté from the Josephine statue is the **Bibliothèque Schoelcher**, a cast-iron and tile quasi-Byzantine structure transported here from Paris after the Exposition of 1889. This soaring example of Belle-Epoque exoticism houses exhibits of French and Martiniquais culture.

The streets of Fort-de-France are lined with tiny boutiques offering Paris couture and Riviera resort wear at real savings, and exploring them will provide a pleasant few hours. **Mounia**, on rue Perrinon, carries such labels as Claude Montana, Dorothée Bis, and Yves Saint-Laurent; in fact, it is owned by a Martiniquaise who began her phenomenal fashion career as a top Saint-Laurent model. Many larger shops deal in luxury items such as Baccarat and Lalique crystal and Hermès bags and scarves. At 72 rue Antoine Siger, **Cadet-Daniel**, established in 1840, is a favorite of shoppers in search of Christofle silver and Sèvres china. The counters of **Roger Albert**, on rue Victor Hugo, glitter with bottles of French perfumes, often sold at one-half U.S. and European prices. (Many stores give a 20-percent discount on luxury items purchased with travellers' checks or certain credit cards; be sure to ask.) Traditional Creole bracelets and necklaces, made on the island in 18-karat gold, are particularly evocative of Martinique, especially the *colliers choux,* or "darlings' necklaces," which for centuries have been treasured heirlooms for the island's women. **Montaclair, L'Or et L'Argent,** and **Thomas de Rogatis** are three shops that have outstanding collections of Creole jewelry.

An equally traditional island product is fine rum, first produced here in the 17th century by French friars. It's both light and dark, reasonably priced, and will prove to be, as Ernest Hemingway said, the "perfect antidote to a rainy day."

The Gallic emphasis on fine dining is evident in the many superb restaurants in Fort-de-France. Martiniquais take their gourmandizing seriously, and the island chefs are constantly coming up with imaginative (and delicious) adaptations of classic dishes. Gerard Padra of **La Biguine,** for example, has a real genius for working subtle variations on such Creole staples as *crabes farcis,* land crab mixed with herbs, spices, and bread crumbs and baked in the shell; and *blaff,* the West Indian version of bouillabaisse. Located in a time-mellowed Creole house on the Route de la Folie, La Biguine offers a choice of the Provençal dining room upstairs or the more informal grill downstairs.

There are many other excellent restaurants in Fort-de-France. A good choice for lunch, both because of its menu—including an unusual sea-urchin quiche—and its sweeping view of La Savane and the busy harbor, is **Le d'Esnambuc.** On the third floor of a building at the foot of the rue de la Liberté, the light-filled dining room provides a view of the statue of its namesake, Belain d'Esnambuc, the first settler of the island. Next door, on the second floor of the **Lafayette Hotel,** chef Henri Charvet prepares classic French-Creole dishes with an island twist, such as grilled saddle of lamb with paté of avocado, aubergine, and plantain. And just out of town, in Lamentin, **Le Verger,** set on a breeze-cooled covered terrace, combines French-Creole specialties with the regional dishes of Perigord.

Fort-de-France offers a few compelling reasons to stray from your hotel after dark: A number of clubs feature local groups such as Kassav and Malavoi, which perform hot new *zouk* hits (*zouk* is a kind of West Indian jazz).

Just on the outskirts of Fort-de-France is **La Bateliere**, set amid poinciana-shaded gardens on low cliffs overlooking a small sandy cove. Smaller than Le Meridien at Pointe du Bout, it has comfortable, air-conditioned rooms, a pool, a discotheque, and indoor and outdoor restaurants that offer everything from pizza to filet mignon. A piano bar overlooks the sea, and guests eager to improve their French arithmetic might do well to take part in the Bingo games—"B—sept," "O—soixante-huit"—that take place here every evening except Sunday at six. If Bingo is too tame for your tastes, La Bateliere also has a casino, where the action is also in French.

Grands Ballets de la Martinique, a folkloric group that performs such traditional island dances as the Calenda, the Biguine (yes, Cole Porter heard it first on Martinique), and the Ting Bang, appears at various hotels on different evenings during the week. Performances are generally preceded by eye-popping (and belt-stretching) buffets. (Check with the Martinique Tourist Office in Fort-de-France or at your hotel for schedules.) Though unlikely to cause Alvin Ailey any sleepless nights, Grands Ballets makes up in charm and enthusiasm for any slight lack of sophistication and polish.

Jardin de Balata

It is outside Fort-de-France that many of Martinique's special charms become apparent. Because the island is relatively small (just 50 miles long and 22 miles wide), excursions into the countryside are easy. They may range from a morning's tour to a day-long exploration. One of the best destinations is the Jardin de Balata, just north of Fort-de-France on the Route de la Trace. Here, Jean-Philippe Thoze and his wife, Marie-Claude, have created a picture-perfect tropical Eden that even those who don't know a bougainvillaea from a breadfruit will find enchanting.

Only an acre in area, the gardens are so superbly laid out that they seem much larger. Gently graded gravel paths ramble beneath arbors festooned with orchids through groves of palms and past trees hung with salmon-pink bromeliads.

The tour of the garden begins and ends at a charmingly restored West Indian cottage, the former country home of

Monsieur Thoze's family. The sparkling white house, laced with gingerbread-trimmed verandahs, is furnished with antiques and reproductions of Martinique armoires and side chairs, crystal lamps, and sepia photographs. The louvered windows look out onto a vista of mist-shrouded peaks.

On the half-hour journey to the gardens, you will pass the **Sacré Coeur de Balata**, a scaled-down version of the church in the Montmartre section of Paris. Pilgrims, seeking favors or acknowledging an answered prayer, light candles in the amber glow of stained glass windows that capture in Matisse-like forms Martinique's lush tropical foliage—croton and breadfruit leaves—a fitting prelude to a visit to the Balata Gardens.

The Island's North

Martinique's ten small museums rank as some of the Caribbean's most delightful surprises. Commemorating everyone and everything from Empress Josephine to one of this century's most cataclysmic volcanic eruptions (that of Mont Pelée in 1902), and celebrating dolls, dugout canoes, and the "demon rum," these intriguing collections offer insights into Martinique's history and culture.

Four of the most fascinating museums can be seen during one daylong excursion around the northern section of the island. Set off from Fort-de-France on Route N 3, then head north along the Caribbean coast through a series of drowsy seaside villages. At Case Pilote is the island's oldest church, a specimen of Colonial Baroque exuberance that's all bonbon-colored garlands and dimpled cherubs. In Bellefontaine there is a house set on a hillside that is shaped like a ship, the creation of a retired sea captain.

At the village of Carbet, its stone walls draped with golden-trumpet vines, keep an eye peeled for the sign on the right announcing the **Centre d'Art Paul Gauguin**. This museum commemorates the four months in 1887 that this Post-Impressionist artist spent on Martinique. Family photographs and copies of letters the painter wrote during his island stay are on display, as are reproductions of the 12 paintings Gauguin completed in a nearby hut. Downstairs, a display of antique Creole costumes evokes the days when the ever-susceptible Gauguin praised the beauty of the island women and found them "gay and affable."

Next stop is the village of **Saint-Pierre**. At the turn of the century a visitor described the then-thriving city as having "a population of the Arabian Nights." On May 8, 1902, the fairy tale ended. A massive cloud of white-hot dust and gas burst from the side of nearby Mont Pelée, wiping out in a single blinding flash the town and all but one of its 30,000 inhabitants. Today, a small museum tells the story of the catastrophe in haunting displays. Some potent reminders of the disaster still stand in the town: the sweeping double staircase of the opera house, the shattered façade of the cathedral, and the underground cell in which the only survivor, a prisoner named Cyparis, was, ironically, protected from the destruction.

From Saint-Pierre head inland into the lush mountains, passing through Morne Rouge and the village of Ajoupa-Bouillon, where a floral *bienvenue* planted at the roadside marks the city limits. Continue north a short distance along the Atlantic coast, then continue to Basse-Pointe. A mile or so out of town is **Plantation Leyritz**. At the superbly restored 18th-century estate, now a nearly irresistible combination resort/spa, visitors can eat lunch in what was formerly the plantation granary, then examine the delightful creations of Will Fenton. This talented young artist has fashioned a gallery of what he calls *poupées vegetales,* sophisticated doll-size mannequins that he makes from more than 600 kinds of fronds, leaves, and other plant parts.

Leyritz also offers accommodations that recall gentler days. Of its 50 rooms, the most gracious are the four guest chambers on the second floor of the main house, furnished with four-poster canopy beds, cane rocking chairs, and toile hangings. The salon downstairs is a shadowy retreat decorated with island antiques, family portraits, and an ancient phonograph with a flaring morning-glory horn. Other rooms are located in the former guard house, the family cookhouse, workers' cottages, and a six-room annex. Leyritz's new spa facilities include herbal baths, massage, loofah treatments, and the usual exercise and gymnastic equipment.

Return to Basse-Pointe, then swing south along the coast through Marigot to Sainte-Marie. In Sainte-Marie, the **Musée de Rhum**, operated by the St. James Distillery, is set in a restored estate house. Its displays outline the long, colorful history of rum production in Martinique with implements and rare old prints. Information about the exhibits is available in English.

The road winds on to Trinité and Robert, a pair of villages overlooking the island-studded sea. The **Saint Aubin**, atop a low hill outside Trinité, is a splendidly reconstructed colonial manor house ringed with broad cast-iron galleries. Now a small hotel, it has 15 rooms. The graceful exterior and the manicured grounds promise more than the slightly spartan accommodations inside, but the rooms are clean, comfortable, and air-conditioned. Just pulling up under the soaring porte-cochère or lolling beside the pool in the immaculately tended gardens will inspire reveries of a more gracious age. Turn west again and drive through cane fields to Lamentin, the site of Martinique's international airport, then back to Fort-de-France.

The Island's South

Southern Martinique was the birthplace of the Empress Josephine, and **La Pagerie**, just outside the village of Les Trois-Ilets, was her childhood home. Set among verdant hills, it now houses a tiny museum in what was once the kitchen of the estate. Perhaps the most unusual item on display is a passionate letter from the Emperor enclosing *"mille baisers amoureux, partout, partout"* for the woman he called "incomparable, completely divine." Nearby is the island golf course, which was designed by Robert Trent Jones.

After Trois-Ilets, the **Pointe du Bout** curves protectively about the entrance to the harbor at Fort-de-France, and several fine hotels, including the Bakoua and the PLM Azur Carayou, stretch along the shore. The **Bakoua**, recently enlarged, is a well-run commercial-style hotel with many balcony rooms. The **Carayou**'s 200 air-conditioned rooms are set around a tropical courtyard; the hotel also boasts three restaurants, a discotheque, a pool, tennis courts, and a private beach.

Perched like a seabird at the farthermost tip of the point is the 303-room **Le Meridien**, Martinique's premier four-star hotel. With its spacious, airy lobby—glittering with mirrors and brightly decorated with island-inspired murals—its well-appointed rooms, its pool and beach, two restaurants, shops, casino, lounge, nightclub, and water-sports marina, Le Meridien has been designed for those seeking an "everything-within-easy-reach" vacation.

From Trois-Ilets or Pointe du Bout, drive south along Route D 7 to Anses d'Arlets, a village that might have been inspired by a van Gogh seascape. Fishing boats painted in reds and yellows are beached under spreading sea grapes hung with bright blue nets. Diamant is a vast rock two-and-a-half miles offshore, which during the French and British skirmishes of the Napoléonic Wars was defended by English tars for 18 months. It was later designated a man-of-war by the Royal Navy, and is still known in English naval records as H.M.S. *Diamond Rock*. Every passing British warship gives it a 12-gun salute.

One of the island's most spectacular (and most popular) beaches, the **Plage des Salines**, is flung like a silk scarf along the coast south of **Sainte-Anne**. Palms cast flickering shadows along the edge of the coral sand and across the topless torsos of *les jeunes filles*. Weekdays are the best time to visit Sainte-Anne; on weekends, it seems that the entire population of Fort-de-France has converged in campers, on mopeds, and on racing bikes to bask on the two-mile strand.

The cool, shadowy public rooms at the nearby **Manoir de Beauregard** provide a pleasant lunchtime respite from the dazzle of sea and sky. The 18th-century stone walls of the Manoir are hung with faded tapestries, and its gleaming tile floors reflect wrought-iron screens and polished mahogany. The dining area to the rear is a bit less traditional; it's decorated in the familiar bamboo-and-thatch tropical style. The bill of fare combines Continental and Creole offerings; special salads, often made with chicken, shellfish, and local fruits and vegetables are especially welcome on an island where the midday meal can take on gargantuan proportions.

From Sainte-Anne, follow winding country roads north to the town of François. In the center of the village, a massive Corbusier-style church, all soaring concrete walls and abstract stained glass, contrasts with a fretwork-trimmed Victorian City Hall in a silent confrontation of past and present. Between the two a memorial to the dead of World War I is strung incongruously with Christmas tree lights. From François, it's a short drive back to Fort-de-France.

USEFUL FACTS

Getting In

There are regular flights to Lamentin Airport on Martinique (or to Raizet Airport on Guadeloupe) on American Airlines from New York, and from other U.S. cities via San Juan; on Eastern Airlines from New York, and other U.S. cities via San Juan or direct from Miami or Atlanta; on Air Canada from Montreal and Toronto; on Air France from Miami and San Juan; on LIAT (from neighboring islands); and on Air Martinique to and from St. Maarten, Dominica, Barbados, St. Lucia, St. Vincent, Mustique, Union Island, and Trinidad.

Entry Requirements

For stays up to three months, U.S. and Canadian citizens must have a valid passport or one that has expired within the past five years. A notarized birth certificate with raised seal or a voter-registration card are also accepted if accompanied by another authorized government I.D. with photo. The above documents qualify a visitor for a temporary visa issued upon arrival at no charge. Citizens of most other countries must have a passport, as well as a return or onward ticket.

Currency

The legal tender is the French franc, but U.S. and Canadian dollars are accepted almost everywhere. The exchange rate is subject to currency fluctuations.

Electrical Currrent

Voltage is 220 AC, 50 cycles. American- and Canadian-made appliances require converters.

Getting Around

Major U.S. car rental companies, including Avis, Budget, Hertz, and National, have offices on Martinique and Guadeloupe, as do several local agencies. A valid driver's license is required to rent a vehicle for up to 20 days; for longer periods an International Driver's Permit is required.

Banking Hours
Monday–Friday, 7:30–noon and 2:30–4:00. Banks close on the afternoons preceding public holidays.

Festivals
Martinique's Vaval, as Carnival is called on the island, erupts every weekend between New Year's and the beginning of Lent.

ACCOMMODATIONS REFERENCE
The rate ranges given here are projections for fall 1988 through spring 1989. Unless otherwise indicated, prices are for double rooms, double occupancy. The telephone area code for Martinique is 596. Martinique is part of the French West Indies (F.W.I.), and letters should be so addressed.

▶ **Bakoua Beach**. Pointe du Bout, Martinique 97229. $205–$275, C.P. Tel: 66-02-02; in U.S., (914) 472-0370 or (800) 221-4542.

▶ **La Bateliere**. Schoelcher, Fort-de-France, Martinique 97233. $138–$209, E.P. Tel: 61-49-49; in U.S., (201) 488-7788, (800) 221-1831, or (800) 221-1832.

▶ **Manoir de Beauregard**. Sainte-Anne, Martinique 97227. $79–$104, C.P. Tel: 76-73-40; in U.S., (212) 832-2277 or (800) 223-6510.

▶ **Le Meridien–Trois-Ilets**. Pointe du Bout, Martinique 97229. $130–$150, E.P. Tel: 66-00-00; in U.S., (212) 265-4494 or (800) 223-9918.

▶ **Plantation Leyritz**. Basse-Pointe, Martinique 97218. $95–$150, C.P. Tel: 75-53-92; in U.S., (212) 840-6636, (212) 477-1600, (800) 223-9815, or (800) 223-1510.

▶ **PLM Azur Carayou**. Pointe du Bout, Martinique 97229. $84–$146, E.P. Tel: 66-04-04; in U.S., (212) 757-6500 or (800) 223-9862.

▶ **Saint Aubin**. Trinité, Martinique 97220. $82, C.P. Tel: 69-34-77; in U.S., (212) 840-6636 or (800) 223-9815.

OTHER ACCOMMODATIONS
▶ **Relais Creoles**. These small, often family-operated guest houses located throughout the island are good places to meet local people and sample island life. Some knowledge of French will increase the pleasures to be found in these friendly, personal hostelries. (Contact the Tourist Office in Fort-de-France; Tel: 63-79-60.)

ST. LUCIA

By Jennifer Quale

It's said that St. Lucia has always been on the verge of being discovered (even Columbus passed it by). This is precisely why you should go, and soon, before any more commercial development takes hold. This lush, mountainous island in the Windward chain retains the elsewhere-vanishing vestiges of West Indian culture. Little, in fact, has changed since Somerset Maugham and Alec Waugh discovered its charms a generation or so ago.

After being tossed back and forth like a tennis ball between the British and the French for two centuries, St. Lucia finally landed on the English side of the court during King George III's reign in 1803. Although political independence within the Commonwealth was achieved in 1979, the island still exudes both a Gallic flair and English comities; while English is the official language, patois is the native tongue.

Mostly, though, St. Lucia exists for and of itself. Bananas, not tourists, bring in the bulk of its foreign income, which is to say the St. Lucians don't quite know what to do with the other assets they've got. These begin with the Pitons, the most magnificent pair of mountains in the Caribbean, that rise half a mile above the sea like woolly green pyramids. The island's rugged interior rain forest conjures visions of *Green Mansions,* and its drive-in volcano and sulphur springs could save Hollywood a fortune in special effects. St. Lucia's plucky capital of Castries teems with hotels and restaurants, while the soporific town of Soufrière in the south hasn't budged from the 19th century. And the beaches are sufficiently inviting to make you want to forget about all the things to see and

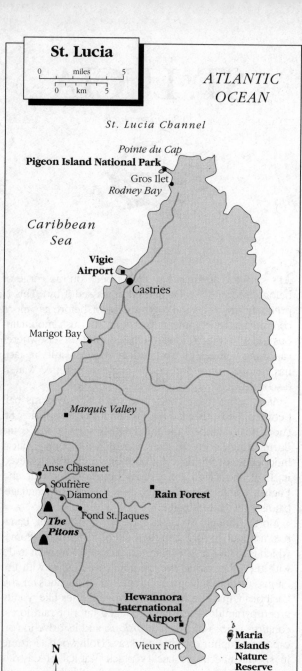

St. Lucia

0 miles 5

0 km 5

ATLANTIC
OCEAN

St. Lucia Channel

Pointe du Cap

Pigeon Island National Park

Gros Ilet

Rodney Bay

Caribbean
Sea

Vigie
Airport ■

● Castries

Marigot Bay ●

■ *Marquis Valley*

Anse Chastanet ●

Soufrière ●

Diamond ●

■ **Rain Forest**

● Fond St. Jaques

The
Pitons

Hewannora
International
Airport ■

Vieux Fort ●

Maria
Islands
Nature
Reserve

N

St. Vincent Passage

do. Luckily, the island is relatively small (14 miles wide, 27 miles long), so the compulsive visitor who wants to do it all can manage comfortably in a week's stay.

Overall, St. Lucia offers a sense of discovery; natural wonders, especially the Pitons; and a rich and unfettered West Indian culture.

MAJOR INTEREST

Castries
The Pitons' natural beauty
A drive-in volcano and the Sulphur Springs
Diamond Baths
The rainforest
Maria Islands Nature Reserve

Picture St. Lucia in the shape of your right hand signaling "stop." At the tip of the index finger is Cap Estate, primarily a villa community of 1,500 manicured but arid acres, replete with golf course and riding stables, squash courts and beaches. Castries lies between the forefinger and thumb on the Caribbean side (almost everything of interest is on the Caribbean, or leeward, side—which is fortunate, because the roads on the windward side of the island make the lunar surface look smooth). Soufrière, home of the Pitons and the volcano, sits on the base of the thumb. Hewannora Airport, which serves international carriers, is at the bottom of the hand, at St. Lucia's southern tip. (Vigie Airport, wedged between a beach and a cemetery outside Castries, accommodates only inter-island flights.) Most first-time visitors, lured by the (relatively) more aggressive marketing of the northwest, make the mistake of spending their entire vacation in and around Castries. But a day trip to Soufrière just isn't long enough. You will be much happier if you spend a few days in the north and the same—or more—in the south.

Castries

The town of Castries, laid out in grid style along its huge, almost landlocked harbor, looks neither old nor quaint, having burned to the ground several times. Despite the 1950's replacement architecture, Castries carries on by the spunk of its people. With its bustle and patois and *je-*

ne-sais-quoi, it's more French than English, more fren-
zied than languid.

For the savvy traveller, Castries is **Rain**. This winsome
bar and restaurant on Columbus Square, set like a stage
for the Maugham story with its paddle fans, ferns, and
gingerbread trim, occupies one of the few colonial buildings that survived the last fire. When New Yorker Al
Haman, Rain's creator and master of nostalgic ceremo-
nies, came to St. Lucia nearly 20 years ago, he revived a
certain style that had long lain dormant (19th-century
Castries was quite a cultural scene, with its fancy dress
balls and performances of the latest Paris comedies).
Every night Haman re-creates the historic Champagne
banquet of 1885 as served to members of the Castries
Philharmonic Society. Indeed, Rain is a sort of salon for
local and visiting intelligentsia; if native son Derek Wal-
cott were in town, you would expect to find him lunching
on the balcony, perhaps with resident poet Robert Lee.
Although no one goes to Rain for the food, it's really quite
good (especially the stuffed crab backs and hand-cranked
ice creams); be sure to book a table on the balcony, so
you can watch the town go by on the square below.

In the heart of town, **Columbus Square** contains a
sprawling, ancient saman tree. From here you can walk
about in search of the town's nooks and crannies (such as
the iron market, stamp shop, and West Indian Sea Island
Cotton shop). On the square, the massive Cathedral of the
Immaculate Conception is worth seeing for its painted
interior, particularly the unusual flying buttresses; on the
occasion of the Pope's visit in 1986, the island's leading
artist, Dunstan St. Aumer, got carried away with his colors
and patterns upon patterns—but it all somehow works.

Because of its spectacular landscapes, St. Lucia has
always attracted foreign artists. Recently, however, expatri-
ates and local artists have joined together to stimulate and
recognize local talent, which is prodigious considering
the island's small population. The **St. Lucia Artists Association** shows at La Galerie de la Porte Noire on Jeremie
Street. It's tucked on the second floor of the gingerbready
Alliance Française building, and a bit hard to find; hours
are Wednesdays and Fridays from 10:30 A.M. to 2:00 P.M.
The new **Artsibit**, as au courant as the gallery's name
implies, exhibits a wider range of works in its well-lit
space at Brazil and Mongiraud Streets. About 15 minutes

south of town at Eudovic's studio, you can sometimes watch the master carver working on a huge tree stump, absently tweaking two long gray strands of hair from his beard. The highly polished, fluid forms of Eudovic's sculpture and furniture all start with the right root or tree, which he finds on foraging trips in the forest.

Back toward Castries, just over the hill—St. Lucia seems entirely hilly, even the beaches—lies **Bagshaw's**, the renowned shop that turns silk-screening and batiking into a local art form. Bagshaw's draws most of its free-spending customers from the neighboring Hotel La Toc and its swish sister property, **La Toc Suites**. Until this year the main hotel and the villa suites strung along the ridge behind it were operated as one large complex: to stay at the Cunard resort was like being on the QE2, with the suites comparable to first class and the hotel rooms akin to below decks. Recognizing the difference, Cunard officially split the properties, thus making the Suites by far the best place to stay in the Castries area. Where else can you leap from your bedroom into a private plunge pool (feet-first, and forget about the length for laps: it's about six by ten), turn on a VCR in your living room when it rains, and call for room service from one of the island's finer restaurants? (In general, service here is exceptional, owing to tight-ship training of the genial St. Lucian staff.) On the 110 acres of Cunard grounds, guests have free access to the better of the island's two 9-hole golf courses, a professionally managed tennis club, and a superb beach with the usual array of water sports with instructors. The unusual pool has its own palm tree-studded island. During the day, the top local steel band may play (such incongruous tunes as "In the Mood") for visiting cruise-ship passengers on the hotel terrace, but come nightfall all is quiet on the blissful suite-side beach front. Suite guests (an eye surgeon there, a money broker here) mingle at the natty Les Pitons piano lounge, which, like most St. Lucian bars, offers a wildly inspired "cocktail of the day," along with the most addictive, homemade plantain chips in the Windwards. Next door, or actually outdoors, the surf almost rolls in to the elegant Les Pitons Restaurant, where the lobster comes fresh from the hotel's own traps (unfortunately many local restaurants serve lobster that has been frozen).

Most of the restaurants within easy reach of Castries are

on the water, along the harbors, or in Rodney Bay—
which makes sense considering St. Lucia is quite a yachting center. Creole cuisine reigns supreme, with a few
aberrations (such as the Italian menu at Capone's, a tropical art deco-styled entry from Al Haman). You would have
to stay in Castries a month to try all its funky spots, but
among the more intriguing are **Jimmy's**, the **Coal Pot**,
and the **Charthouse**. For the big night out, only **San
Antoine** will do. This wonderful restaurant on the historic
Morne ("hill") makes you yearn for the days of its colonial
splendor, when Maugham and Waugh stayed here. Once
a private great house, San Antoine was converted into St.
Lucia's first hotel in the 1920s and became the domain of
English portrait painter Aubrey Davidson-Houston. Although San Antoine burned in 1970, an expatriate couple
has recently parlayed the stone shell and archways that
were left into one of the most romantic spots in the
Caribbean. All this and heavenly food, too (particularly
the crayfish specialty, sautéed in lemon garlic butter, a
rare treat anywhere in the islands). Book a table in the
front room to see through an arch darkly the sparkling
lights of the harbor below.

Nightlife in Castries consists mostly of predictable discos, but on Friday nights everyone seems to turn out at
Gros Islet (by day a small, picturesque fishing village) for
its street festival. With a Creole-cum-Latin beat, it's a little
like Mardi Gras in New Orleans: by ten the streets are so
packed you can hardly squeeze past the impromptu jam
sessions, coalpot cook stands and rum carts, and "roll and
tumble" gambling tables. For a bird's-eye view, head to
Scott's Café, where everyone hangs off the balcony in a
merry stupor.

Beyond Castries

Although much ado is made of Morne Fortune ("Hill of
Good Luck"—whose, nobody knows) as the stronghold
of the ever-changing colonial powers, the more significant outpost was **Pigeon Island** a few miles north of
Castries. It was from here that Admiral Rodney sailed in
pursuit of Count de Grasse, routing the French in the
crucial Battle of the Saints and giving the British the final
edge in the West Indies. Legend has it that the island was
named for the carrier pigeons Rodney bred. Now a na-

tional park, with the old naval barracks housing a rather dusty museum, it's connected to the mainland by a causeway. There is a splendid view of St. Lucia—and Martinique 20 miles to the north—from the fort ruins atop the hill.

Martinique likes to claim Josephine Tascher de la Pagerie as its native daughter, but St. Lucia insists Napoléon's empress was born on her family's plantation at Morne Paix Bouche northeast of Castries. Although the house overlooking Marquis Valley has fallen into ruin, plans are afoot to establish a museum honoring Josephine in Soufrière, where the Taschers kept their second estate, Malmaison.

Soufrière

Getting to Soufrière can either be a sublime experience or a tribulation, depending on how you go. Avoid the tortuous roads and spend the extra money on boat passage from Castries harbor (one hour by speedboat, three by sail), which your hotel can arrange. For a cheaper—but less serene—alternative to a private boat charter, book a one-way trip on the tall ship *Brig Unicorn,* which makes a day out of cruising the coast, sightseeing in Soufrière, and lunch and punch on board, complete with steel band.

Seen from the sea, St. Lucia's immense natural beauty is almost overwhelming. When the producers of "Dr. Doolittle" were scouting Caribbean locations for Everyman's vision of a tropical paradise (but one that few had seen) they chose **Marigot Bay**, about ten miles south of Castries. The film crew left behind their commissary, now a popular restaurant called "Doolittle's." Long a favored anchorage among discerning yachtsmen, Marigot harbor once provided safe haven for a British fleet hiding from the French; by lashing coconut fronds to their masts, the British fooled the French into thinking their ships were just another thicket of palm trees. If you want to charter a boat—for a day or a week—**The Moorings** operation here is the place to do it.

The farther south you sail, the more exotic the coast becomes, with empty, tempting beaches giving way to tiny fishing villages where children play in the surf right off the town's doorstep. Then, suddenly, the boat rounds the headland off Anse Chastanet Hotel and you realize what you came for: **The Pitons**. These volcanic spires are the most compelling sight in the Caribbean. In fact, travellers have been known to sit and stare at them for hours, so entrancing is their stark beauty. One of the best vantage points is the hilltop cluster of bungalows—actually octagonal gazebos—at **Anse Chastanet Hotel**, currently the only place to stay in the Soufrière area (unless you rent a villa). But a wonderful place it is, especially for those who revel in seclusion and unpretentious but seductive surroundings. Except for the new beach-side suites (some with plunge pools), most of the bungalows cling—along with bougainvillaea—to the hillside. The 125-step climb is a killer, but the view makes it worthwhile. There are no phones, TVs, or room service, but that's the way the hotel's guests want it (indeed, many repeat clientele would prefer that the road to Anse Chastanet remain in a state of disrepair to keep it that much more remote). Here you bow to nature, especially on the hotel's half-mile-long beach of fine gray sand. With plenty of thatched bohios (sort of a thatch-roofed, open-sided structure for shade), a highly touted diving operation (with instructors for beginners and experts, and even underwater camera equipment) among other water-sports facilities, an open-air bar and restaurant, and one of the best shops on St. Lucia, some guests never leave the beach until sunset (except possibly for a game on the nearby tennis courts). The more adventurous walk down the beach and over the rocks to the neighboring coconut plantation, where the stone buildings lie in ruin but the old overseer commands the place as if it were still thriving as it was in the 19th century.

This anachronistic mode of life spills over from **Soufrière** two miles distant. Soufrière is the oldest settlement on St. Lucia. A guillotine once dominated the central square on the wharf, which now serves as a lackadaisical gathering spot for Rastafarians, suitcase vendors, and young boys who greet incoming yachts. The fishermen who give the town its raison d'être live in squalor just beyond the wharf, in the shadow of the Pitons, but if the town fathers have their way the waterfront will soon undergo a facelift—with care not to sacrifice its aura. The wooden colonial buildings, some painted in vibrant colors that could only be concocted in the Caribbean, contribute to that aura, along with the courtly ways of the

townspeople, who know their big attraction is the volcano. But don't miss the little things here—like the
church and Archie's purple grocery, or the rum bars and
hole-in-the-wall craft shops. If you don't mind eating
lunch above the gas station, **Charlo's** serves a good roti
(meat and potatoes rolled, West Indian style, in a pan-
cake). And, if you can stand the seediness, head for **Captain Hook's Hideaway** on the road to Anse Chastanet for
fresh tuna sandwiches made by one of Soufrière's most
respected cooks (there aren't many).

The **drive-in volcano**, over the ridge behind town, is
actually a seven-acre, smoking crater: you drive up to the
rim and proceed on foot with a guide (ask for Ricardo).
Negotiating the sulphur beds and springs, bubbling like
so many pots of pea soup, requires not only a nimble foot
but a sturdy snout to withstand the rotten-egg odor. Occasionally one of the guides will bring along an egg or
potato to demonstrate the volcano's cooking capacity.

The **Sulphur Springs** feed the mineral baths on the
adjacent **Diamond Estate**. St. Lucians make an annual
ritual of soaking in the hot tubs, claiming the waters take
off ten years and ten pounds. This rejuvenating experience was discovered in 1784, when the French found that
the water contained the same medicinal minerals as those
at Aix les Bains. Forthwith, Louis XVI ordered construc-
tion of the baths to keep his troops fit. Although largely
destroyed after the French Revolution, the baths were
resurrected in 1966 and now, for a small fee, anyone may
use them. This is definitely the place to go if you've stayed
up half the night at the Hummingbird or Coco-Bef at
Jalousie Plantation, Soufrière's night spots of choice.
(They're just as good for lunch, too.)

On the waterfront, just off the road to Anse Chastanet,
the **Hummingbird** feels like a cozy cave with its stone
walls. It opens onto a pool set in a garden, but no one
comes here to swim; rather they come for the rum-
inspired camaraderie, ceviche, and curry (and during the
day to shop at the nifty adjacent boutique).

You can get to **Jalousie Plantation**, nestled on a
coconut-studded strip between the Pitons, most easily by
boat (hire an ersatz water taxi at Anse Chastanet). Such a
glorious entrance is just what lord of the manor Colin
Tennant intended. Known primarily as the British magus
of Mustique in the nearby Grenadines, Tennant (a.k.a.

Lord Glenconner) has initiated here another facet of his fantasies: If they all come true, soon a great house hotel will be put up smack between the Pitons, and villas à la Mustique will grace the lushly quilted slopes above his newly built **Coco-Bef Restaurant**. For now, on the beach beside Petit Piton, Coco-Bef, with its whimsical mango motif decor, brings mainstream pizazz as well as toney travellers to Soufrière. Most of the simple food is to Tennant's liking—local seafood and chicken along with plenty of fresh vegetables (such as *christophène au gratin*) and fruit grown right on the back 450 acres. Tennant's local agent, who happens to be Soufrière's dashing mayor, runs the place with a Maxim's aplomb. And, of course, Bupa, Tennant's smiling elephant, is always on hand to eat your camera if you didn't bring her a banana.

Special-Interest Excursions

The road to the **rain forest**, from Soufrière toward Fond St. Jacques in the interior, is often impassable due to rain. In dry weather, the half-day trip stuns the senses with a riot of tree ferns and orchids cloaking the sounds of the rare St. Lucia parrot (*Amazona versicolor*)—but don't expect to see one.

The **Maria Islands Nature Reserve**, on the Atlantic side, off the southern tip of St. Lucia, has an abundant variety of sea birds and endemic species of reptiles. Before you go, check with your hotel to make certain the reserve is open.

USEFUL FACTS

What to Wear
This is one island where ties look silly, although jackets at Les Pitons Restaurant aren't out of place. Cottons are most comfortable, but shorts are frowned upon in town.

Getting In
With a swift change of planes in San Juan, American Airlines makes the trip from New York a breeze. Other carriers serving the island include BWIA, Eastern, British Airways, and Pan Am. If you're island hopping, say from

Barbados or Mustique, inter-island planes put down at Vigie Airport, just outside Castries.

Save about $7 for departure tax and enough time to have lunch at **The Cloud's Nest Hotel** in Vieux Fort (St. Lucia's second largest town), just ten minutes from Hewannora airport. With its whirling fans and photos of the Royal Family, breadfruit balls and blazing curries, the Cloud's Nest captures all that's West Indian under its red tin roof.

Entry Requirements
British, Canadian, and U.S. citizens must present a passport, voter-registration card, or other valid form of identification, as well as a return or ongoing ticket. Citizens of other countries must present a passport.

Currency
Legal tender is the Eastern Caribbean Dollar. U.S. currency is also accepted.

Electrical Current
220–230 volts, 50 cycles. American- and Canadian-made appliances require converters.

Getting Around
This dilemma of whether or not to rent a car is best solved by hiring a taxi at the airport (unless your hotel arranges the transfer; for example, a representative from La Toc Suites meets guests at their flights) and deciding after your first bout with the local roads whether or not you want to tackle them yourself. It's a standard joke that while driving is on the left, there is usually no left or right, and barely a middle. The taxi drivers, among the Caribbean's most knowledgeable and polite, not only know every pothole in the road but even apologize for each one. Some drivers double as guides, but despite government-set rates taxis don't come cheaply. If you rent a car (get a Jeep), plan to buy a local driver's license (about $5) and let your hotel assist in the arrangements.

ACCOMMODATIONS REFERENCE
Unless otherwise indicated, rates are for double rooms, double occupancy. The telephone area code for St. Lucia is 809. All addresses are on St. Lucia, W.I.

▶ **Anse Chastanet Hotel**. (They also manage some villas in the area.) P.O. Box 216, Soufrière. Rates start at $49 a person a day. Tel: 454-7354; in U.S., (212) 535-9530 or (800) 223-5581; in Canada, (514) 848-9245 (collect). (Ask about their dive packages.)

▶ **Cunard La Toc Suites**. P.O. Box 399, Castries. $115–$210. Tel: 452-3081; in U.S., (800) 222-0939; in U.K., (01) 930-4321; in Canada, (416) 924-1711; in Australia, (02) 264-6486. (The suites on the Point are worth the higher rate for the greater privacy and dramatic setting.)

▶ **Villa rentals**. Tropical Villas, Box 1189, Cap Estate, Castries. Tel: 452-8240; in U.S., (212) 759-1025 or (800) 433-3020.

BARBADOS

By Susan Farewell

Rarely does a visitor return from Barbados without mentioning the people. More than the beaches, more than the scenery, more than anything else, the Bajans— short for native-born Barbadians—are what one remembers most. Very simply, they're people people. So much so that they choose to build their houses facing the road rather than the sea, so they can watch passersby. They don't look at you, they look into you. Unlike some islands, you're not whisked away from the airport to some walled-in tourist fortress (though you could be, if that's what you want). The Bajans are a wonderfully welcoming people, and by their very nature invite visitors to join their society temporarily.

Britain was considered the mother country for almost 350 years until 1966, when the umbilical cord was cut and independence declared. Today Barbados is an independent state within the Commonwealth, structured with an elected representative assembly. There are signs of England everywhere: place names like Windsor, Yorkshire, and Trafalgar Square; afternoon tea served at many hotels; and cricket as the national sport. But the island's West Indian culture is—without question—dominant.

Barbados has all of the Caribbean island requisites, among them seemingly endless stretches of sloping white-sand beaches, all sorts of water sports, and tepid breezes off the sea. There are small, classic hotels hidden under clusters of palm trees and a handful of reliably good restaurants that serve spicy island dishes, fish just minutes out of the water, and frosty rum punches. And yes, there's duty-free shopping.

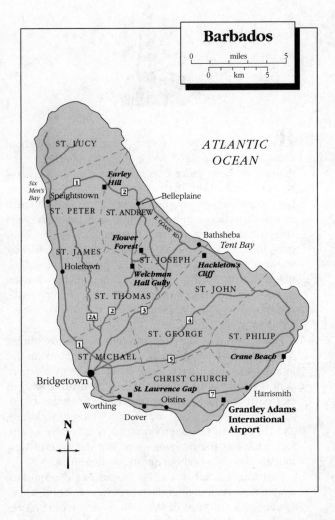

Barbados

0 — miles — 5

0 — km — 5

ST. LUCY

Six Men's Bay

Speightstown

ST. PETER

ST. ANDREW

Farley Hill

1

2

Belleplaine

ATLANTIC OCEAN

E COAST RD

Bathsheba

Tent Bay

ST. JAMES

Holetown

Flower Forest

ST. JOSEPH

Welchman Hall Gully

Hackleton's Cliff

ST. JOHN

ST. THOMAS

2

3

2A

4

ST. GEORGE

ST. PHILIP

1

ST. MICHAEL

5

Crane Beach

Bridgetown

CHRIST CHURCH

St. Lawrence Gap

Oistins

7

Harrismith

Worthing

Dover

Grantley Adams International Airport

N

What may come as an unwelcome surprise for those wanting to plop down on a beach for a week is the multitude of attractions on Barbados. You could easily fill seven days touring its old Indian cave dwellings, gracious plantation houses, and other sights in between.

MAJOR INTEREST

British colonial atmosphere

Bridgetown
Barbados National Trust
Barbados Museum
Baxter's Road nightlife

Around the Island
Speightstown fishing village
Six Men's Bay (boat-building)
St. Nicholas Abbey
Andromeda Gardens
Sunbury House

Bridgetown

The greatest appeal of Bridgetown, the island's capital, is what isn't there. Though much visited by tourists, it doesn't have a generic any-port-in-the-Caribbean feel about it. Streets aren't chockablock with duty-free shops (though there are enough). You are not constantly bothered by hawkers pushing their wares. Rather, Bridgetown is a thriving little metropolis where life goes on as usual and tourists aren't everything.

You can see all of the town in about an hour. Start in the general area of the Careenage on the harbor-side promenade where a reincarnated warehouse now houses a couple of restaurants and shops that are popular among locals and tourists alike. For lunch, try the second-floor **Fisherman's Wharf**. On Fridays and Sundays, they spread out an exceptionally good Bajan buffet. With its huddle of sidewalk tables, the **Waterfront Café** downstairs has become a magnet for passersby. The place provides a fine perch from which to watch the activity in the busy harbor while sipping a cold Banks beer or a glass of iced tea; the service, though, is lamentable. (Most of Barbados' finer restaurants—and hotels—are outside town, along the west and south coasts.)

Trafalgar Square, across the bridge, is all the more British for its bronze statue of Lord Nelson—unveiled in 1815, it predates London's by several decades. (Nelson is a local of sorts, as for many years he was stationed in the West Indies.) The square is surrounded by Victorian Gothic government buildings, including the House of Assembly, with its stained-glass windows representing English monarchs from James I to Victoria. A block or so south is **St. Michael's Cathedral**, noted for its arched roof, which used to be the widest in the world. Amen Alley to its side was so named because slaves—forbidden entry into the church—listened outside, exclaiming "Amen" at the end of services.

Though Barbados is not known for its exceptional shopping, you will find duty-free stores (including large department stores that sell everything from plastic sandals to Hilda of Iceland sweaters) crowding around Broad Street. At the **Best of Barbados** shop, tucked away in Mall 34, you can pick up fine-quality island crafts and silk-screen prints. If you're strongly interested in local crafts, poke around the Temple Yard District, where a group of Rastafarians have set up shop. Steps away stands the geared-for-tourists complex called Pelican Village. Its collection of shops are worth a look, especially Karl Broodhagen's painting and sculpture gallery.

Just on the edge of town, in historic Belleville (the island's most posh district, distinguished by its columnar royal palms), is the **Barbados National Trust**, modeled after the National Trusts of England and Wales. The Trust is a Victorian Barbadian house, the Ronald Tree House, furnished to look as it would have in 1893. It also has a riveting photographic display of old Barbados and churches around the island.

The Garrison Savannah, farther out of town, was in the 1600s the training ground for British soldiers stationed in Barbados. It is now the site of major sporting and ceremonial events, and the home of the **Barbados Museum**. (To one side stands the Savannah Club, a historical regimental building crowned by a four-faced clock. The coat of arms of King William IV on its façade is the only one outside the U.K.) The Barbados Museum, occupying what was a British military prison back in the early 1800s, displays Arawak Indian artifacts, plantation furnishings, and an impressive collection of old maps.

After dark, Bridgetown lights up like a Christmas tree, and all-night revelers emerge from their daytime slumbers. Tanned beachgoers too show up, clad in crisp whites. There are a couple of discos and clubs worth a visit, including the always-packed **Warehouse**, the undisputable favorite, right on the Careenage. Even if you're not up for the loud, pulsating sounds and strobe lights, you can't help but find yourself mesmerized watching the Barbadians dance. You can also hear some outstanding jazz on the island, especially at **Bajan**, a dimly lit, smoke-filled bar on Bay Street.

Perhaps the most fascinating after-dark attraction in town is **Baxter's Road**, a little strip of inextinguishable vitality. Sometime after midnight and before dawn, all strata of society make their way to this row of rum shacks. At the northern end, a quartet of feisty women vie for your attention as they prepare the catch of the day, usually dolphin*fish* (not dolphins), over wood fires.

The West Coast

The **St. James Coast**—also known as the Platinum Coast—is lined with one hotel after another, all set within feet of the water. This is the playground of the island, with every kind of water sport imaginable, as well as every kind of bathing suit imaginable.

The **Treasure Beach Hotel**, right on the beach a couple of miles south of Holetown, is one of the island's smallest and most personally run hostelries. Owners Mary and Charles Ward (she's American; he's Bajan) have indeed created a little treasure. A collection of suites surrounds a central courtyard verdant with lush greens and tropical blossoms. Almost all of the suites have cathedral ceilings, kitchenettes, and living rooms that open onto enormous balconies. The open-air dining room has become one of the island's most esteemed restaurants, with house specialties such as Supreme de Volaille Treasure Beach (breast of chicken stuffed with cream cheese, herbs, spinach, and a touch of garlic), and a variety of creamy pâtés. It's necessary to reserve rooms well in advance because there are many repeat guests (mostly couples from Europe and families with older children).

Just about halfway up the coast is **Holetown**, where the British landed in 1627 on the *Olive Blossom*. An obelisk commemorates the event, but its plaque says they landed in 1605. No matter; it's not uncommon to hear conflicting dates and facts about the colorful history of the island. Settlers built the island's first church in Holetown. Unfortunately, it and later its replacement were washed away in hurricanes. The **St. James Church** that now stands on the site dates to 1875 and houses a bell from 1696, predating the American Liberty Bell by 54 years.

A little farther up the coast is the **Coral Reef Club**, with cottagelike buildings that spill over 12½ acres fronting on the water. Guests can also stay in the main building, once a private house. All rooms are air conditioned and have private patios or terraces. Service is impeccable, with the owners—the O'Hara family—tending to all the details. Guests here are all ages, mostly couples who want peace and quiet.

Cobblers Cove is one of the most exclusive hotels on the island. Its main building, a beach house that once belonged to a planter, is now encircled by buildings that house suites with living rooms, bedrooms, baths, and kitchens that are well stocked with British teas and Bajan rums. Dining in the open-air, gable-roofed restaurant on water's edge is first rate. During winter months, the clientele is predominantly English; the rest of the year, it's mixed, with many repeat guests. The most coveted rooms are the ones with sea views.

Speightstown, the island's second-largest town, is a fishing port of old two-story wood buildings; many housing shops are in the process of being renovated. Just to the north is **Six Men's Bay**, one of the last places on the island where old-style wooden fishing boats are still made. Boat-building is one of the oldest livelihoods on Barbados, and painting these boats—in bright crayon colors—is an island art.

Whether you settle on the west coast or not, you'll undoubtedly head here for a meal in one of its restaurants. There are several commendable ones, all on the expensive side. Top on the list these days is **Raffles**, just west of Holetown, where the menu includes such island-style dishes as blackened fish, curried shrimp, and baked chicken with mango chutney. The **Bagatelle Great House** is a longtime favorite on Highway 2 A in St. Thomas, with elegant five-course meals served amid antique furnishings. **Reid's** on Highway 1 south of Holetown specializes in fresh fish and lobster. The **Carambola**, poised on a cliff over the sea, is the island's prettiest restaurant, but the food needs some work (it's also on Highway 1, north of Bridgetown).

The Scotland District

One look at the view from **Farley Hill** and you'll know why the northeast part of Barbados is known as the Scotland District. Rugged green hills spread out before you. The thrashing Atlantic crashes against jagged shores.

Farley Hill is the shell of an old mansion whose late 19th-century gentleman owner, Thomas Graham Briggs, entertained royalty and neighboring gentry in lavish style. You'll see the house's exquisite furnishings in buildings all over the island, including the Ronald Tree House and the Barbados Museum—they were auctioned off after a devastating fire. The government now owns and maintains the grounds and what remains of the structure.

Nearby **St. Nicholas Abbey** is one of the two 17th-century Jacobean-style plantation houses on the island. The house is furnished with a fine collection of 18th- and 19th-century antiques, but the real attraction is the film that tells the story of a honeymoon trip that the owner's grandfather made on a ship from Dover to Barbados in 1934.

Highway 1 climbs over the spine of the island through a canopy of mahogany trees to Cherry Tree Hill, where Bajan boys will try to sell you cuts of sugarcane for a coin or two.

The East Coast Road follows the path of the old railroad that ran between Bridgetown and Belleplaine from 1881–1938, slicing through some of the island's most beautiful scenery. The surf rushes in on one side, and black-bellied sheep crowd over soft green hills on the other. Though you may pull over for a rest along the seemingly endless wide beach here, don't try to swim; the undertow is dangerous.

About midway down the coast is the small fishing village of **Bathsheba**. Expert surfers from around the world come here for the gigantic waves. The attraction for landlubbers is the cliff-clinging **Andromeda Gardens**, named after the Greek maiden who was chained to a rock. The gardens are filled with exotic blossoms, lovingly maintained by owners Iris and John Bannochie.

The noonday buffet at the **Atlantis Hotel** (overlooking Tent Bay near Bathsheba) always attracts a knowing local crowd. Here you can watch the waves roll in while you sample all sorts of Bajan specialties—pumpkin fritters, fried eggplant and plantains, eddoes, breadfruit, flying fish, dolphinfish, and turtle steak. Be careful with the seemingly innocent yellow sauce in small jars on the tables—Bajan hot sauces are wondrously flavorful but hot as lava.

The South

The parish of St. John is richly cultivated country covered with banana and sugar plantations. Its church stands at the southern edge of Hackelton's Cliff, which offers more beautiful views of the Scotland District. The crowded little churchyard has an intriguing gravestone proclaiming "here lyeth ye body of Ferdinando Paleologus, lyne of the last Christian Emperors of Greece, Churchwarden of this parish, died Oct. 1678." Villa Nova is a magnificently preserved house that sugar baron Edmund Haynes built in 1834. In the garden are two portlandias that Her Majesty Queen Elizabeth II and Prince Philip planted in 1966, when they were luncheon guests of the Earl and Countess of Avon. Codrington Theological College, at the end of a long drive lined with royal palms, is a seminary of the Anglican community that was opened in 1745.

The coastline of St. Philip's parish has some of the island's most beautiful and least-discovered beaches. The one at **Harrismith** (at the end of a long, bumpy dirt road) is carved out of the base of limestone cliffs and book-ended by large boulders, sheltering it from ferocious waves and winds.

Perhaps the best-known attraction on the island is **Sam Lord's Castle**, an opulent, mahogany-furnished mansion in the center of what are now the grounds of a Marriott resort. Sam Lord was a despicable character known for luring ships onto the nearby reefs and looting them. He was also said to have locked his wife in the cellar to collect an inheritance meant for her.

If you stay any place other than the west coast, consider

Crane Beach in the parish of St. Philip, an elegant hotel overlooking an astoundingly beautiful pink-sand beach. It was originally built in the 18th century as a retreat for travellers seeking the medicinal effects of the Barbadian air. Rooms have high ceilings, canopy beds, antiques, and fabulous views. Its out-of-the-way location is ideal if you really want to get away and relax.

If you are going to visit just one great house on Barbados, make it **Sunbury**, a bit inland in the parish of St. Philip. Well-versed history buffs lead you through every room, not just two or three that have been roped off for visitors. The original part of the house is a stately Georgian box, built in 1660. Owners Sally and Nick Thomas have added a delightful restaurant in the back courtyard for coffee, a light lunch, or afternoon tea.

Christ Church stands on a ridge overlooking Oistins, the island's fishing center. This is the scene of the "Great Coffin Mystery" of 1820, in which coffins in a crypt began to rearrange themselves. Some Barbadians brush off the strange events as earthquakes, but most believe it was a divine act. If the churchyard attendant is about, ask him to take you into the Chase Vault, now empty since the coffins were ordered removed.

In St. Lawrence Gap, a little pocket between Worthing and Dover, you'll find a wonderful local art gallery (**Coffee and Cream**) and three of the island's best restaurants. **Josef's** is the one you hear the most about. Chef/owner Josef Schwaiger, an Austrian, offers a Continental menu with Austrian accents. **Witch Doctor** is known for its spicy Bajan specialties and ice cream smothered with homemade rum-raisin topping. **Pisces** serves delicious seafood.

Inland Barbados

One of the island's greatest treasures hangs above the altar of St. George Parish Church—a painting of "The Resurrection" by the American artist Benjamin West. (Take Highway 4 from Bridgetown.) Two other masterpieces, the works of nature, are nearby: the Flower Forest, 50 acres of well-nurtured blossoms in the parish of St. Joseph, and Welchman Hall Gully, a botanical garden filled with indigenous plants and trees on Highway 2 in St. Thomas.

USEFUL FACTS

What to Wear

Barbados dress leans toward the conservative, a result of the island's lingering Britishness. For touring, shorts or slacks for men and shorts or skirts for women are appropriate. Bathing suits are appropriate only on the beaches; there's no topless—let alone nude—sunbathing. A few hotels require jackets on Saturday nights and during the winter holiday season. It's a good idea to take along a sweater or windbreaker for cool evenings and boat rides.

Getting In

American Airlines, Pan American, and B.W.I.A. fly direct from New York (about four-and-a-half hours). Air Canada flies from Toronto and Montreal. Eastern Airlines flies from Miami, Boston, Chicago, Atlanta, New York, and Washington, as well as Puerto Rico and some other Caribbean islands. Caribbean Airways has direct flights from Luxembourg and London. Leeward Islands Air Transport (L.I.A.T.) connects Barbados with other Caribbean islands.

Barbados' Grantley Adams International Airport, opened in 1979, is modern by Caribbean standards, and entry is usually relatively uneventful. The terminal was built by the Canadians and supposedly can stand five feet of snow! The only inconvenience you should anticipate is long lines for immigration when the big planes arrive. Airport taxis are abundant, right outside the door once you pass through customs. A dispatcher will usually set you up with a driver, but be sure to ask the fare.

Entry Requirements

U.S. and Canadian citizens must have either a valid passport or birth certificate with a photo I.D. British, Australian, and New Zealand citizens need passports. All visitors must have a return or ongoing ticket. There is a departure tax of $8.

Currency

The Barbadian dollar—the official currency—is pegged to the U.S. dollar and valued at approximately half the amount. Most shops, hotels, and restaurants accept U.S. and Canadian bills as well as travellers checks.

Electrical Current
Same as in the U.S. and Canada—110 volts, 50 cycles.

Getting Around
By car. Though the roads are well kept and reasonably well marked, driving can be a bit nightmarish at times. Many roads are narrow and windy and are frequently clogged.

You can rent a MiniMoke from one of the major hotels or at rental agencies in Bridgetown. These open-air vehicles are easy to drive (all standard) and one of the island's most economical buys. Drivers must register at a local police station and pay $15 for a permit.

By taxi. All are unmetered, so prices must be settled in advance. There are some good fares for island tours, though keep in mind that some drivers have great imaginations. Those displaying the Barbados Board of Tourism (B.B.O.T.) badge have attended a two-week-long tourism seminar. (See "Special Tours.")

By bus. There are two types of buses on Barbados, state-owned (big and blue) and privately run (yellow with blue stripe). You can pick up either at any of the red-and-white bus stop markers alongside roads all around the island; the fare is 75 Barbados cents. Avoid the buses on Saturdays when everyone piles in with their week's worth of groceries from the market.

Special Tours
Custom Tours offers fabulous tours of the island customized to your liking, with elegant picnic lunches in some of the island's most beautiful settings. Cost for two persons is $150 (which includes lunch and admission fees). Contact Margaret Leacock; (809) 425-0099. **The Outdoor Club of Barbados** leads walking tours in various areas around the island, taking breaks to swim and eat. Cost for two persons is $70 (which includes three meals). Contact Julian Hunte; (809) 436-5328 or 426-0024.

Business Hours
Shops are normally open from 8:00–4:00 weekdays, 8:00–noon Saturdays. Bank hours are 8:00–1:00 Monday–Thursday; 8:00–1:00 and 3:00–5:30 Friday. Museum hours are 9:00–6:00, Monday–Saturday.

ACCOMMODATIONS REFERENCE

The rate ranges given here are projections for fall 1988 through spring 1989. Unless otherwise indicated, rates are for double rooms, double occupancy. The telephone area code for Barbados is 809.

▶ **Cobblers Cove.** Barbados, W.I. $270 (room only)–$450 (breakfast and dinner daily, holiday season). Tel: 422-2291; in U.S., (212) 832-2277 or (800) 223-6510; in U.K., (01) 730-7144.

▶ **Coral Reef Club.** St. James Beach, Barbados, W.I. $180–$357, M.A.P. Tel: 422-2372; in U.S., (800) 223-1108.

▶ **Crane Beach.** St. Philip, Barbados, W.I. $70–$250, E.P. Tel: 423-6220.

▶ **Treasure Beach.** St. James, Barbados, W.I. $95–$270. Tel: 432-1346; in U.S., (212) 832-2272 or (800) 223-6510.

OTHER ACCOMMODATIONS

▶ **The Colony Club.** St. James, Barbados, W.I. $165–$280, M.A.P. Tel: 422-2335; reservations, 422-2741. A classic Barbados hotel: wonderful low-key elegance and a British air.

▶ **Royal Pavilion.** St. James, Barbados, W.I. Winter rates, $222–$575. Tel: 422-4444; in U.S., Robert Reid Associates, (800) 223-6510. Opened December 1987. The plan is to make this the most luxurious hotel on the island. All the rooms—actually one-, two-, and three-bedroom suites, villas, or penthouses—are waterfront.

▶ **Sandpiper Inn.** Holetown, St. James, Barbados, W.I. $115–$300, M.A.P. Tel: 422-2251; in U.S., (800) 223-1108. This inn has a marvelous South Seas atmosphere. Stucco one- and two-story cottages are clustered around a garden and pool. There are cottages on the beach, too. A quiet spot; many couples of all ages.

ST. VINCENT AND THE GRENADINES

By Jennifer Quale

If Gauguin's search for the unfamiliar hadn't taken him to Tahiti, he might have been equally content in the Grenadines, easily the most exotic cluster of islands in the Caribbean. That they are also the least accessible, being the southernmost of the Windward island chain, protects them from the incursion of high-rise tourism. For these are islands mostly without cars, where even the dogs have character, and the characters are the stuff of Conrad novels.

Here you can do nothing at all and not feel guilty about it. While there are a few compelling "sights," the history of this archipelago can be grasped in a wink, and its culture absorbed by merely adapting to the uncomplicated way of life. In the Grenadines, Mother Nature provides the luxuries—such as incomparable waters for sailing and diving, truly deserted beaches, and sunsets that weaken the knees.

Getting to these secluded, spectacular islands, however, is rarely even a fraction of the fun. The journey normally involves changing planes in Barbados for St. Vincent, which, 100 miles to the west of Barbados, is the gateway and government seat of the Grenadines. Or you might choose to charter a sailing vessel, perhaps the best way to see all the Grenadines, in which case you would fly to St. Lucia, 22 miles north of St. Vincent, to pick up the boat. Although it's possible to island hop, spending a few days each at different resorts, most visitors usually stay in one place and make day trips, if they wish, to nearby islands.

MAJOR INTEREST

St. Vincent
Little North American-style development
Kingstown
Botanic Gardens
The coastal drives

The Grenadines
(in order south from St. Vincent)

Young Island
Bequia
Mustique
Mayreau
Tobago Cays
Palm (a.k.a. Prune) Island
Petit St. Vincent

Imagine these 40-odd tiny islands as a stream of teardrops falling from the eye of St. Vincent—known locally as the mainland—with Grenada at the puddle 50 miles to the south.

The 133 square miles of St. Vincent, a volcanic cone with volatile Mt. Soufrière dominating its northern reaches, make few demands on visitors, except those with a botanical bent. You would not go to St. Vincent for its beaches, which, on the windward side, are rough and rocky, and on the leeward side are mostly integral parts of the coastal villages. (The beaches of the Grenadines more than compensate.) The handful of historical venues is concentrated in the south, around the capital of Kingstown. Most first-time visitors bypass St. Vincent (unless they are obliged to overnight en route to the Grenadines). This is unfortunate, because St. Vincent could well be the last sizable island in the Caribbean untouched, as yet, by North American-style development.

About a dozen of the Grenadines are inhabited. A few are privately owned, some comprising a single resort. Each hotel reflects the personality of its creator, an effect

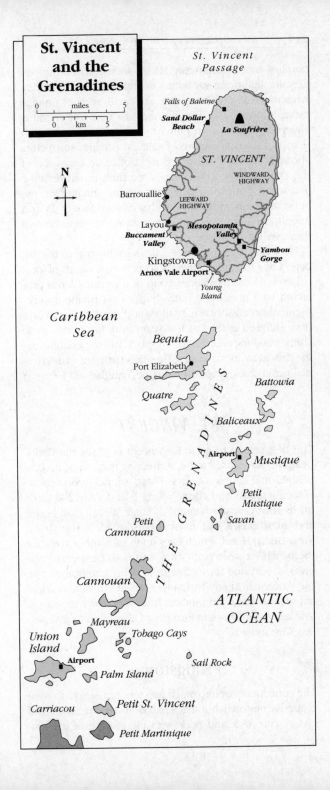

St. Vincent
and the
Grenadines

miles
0   5

km
0   5

N

*St. Vincent
Passage*

Falls of Baleine
**Sand Dollar
Beach**
La Soufrière

ST. VINCENT

WINDWARD
HIGHWAY

Barrouallie

LEEWARD
HIGHWAY

Layou
**Buccament
Valley**

*Mesopotamia
Valley*

**Yambou
Gorge**

Kingstown

Arnos Vale Airport

*Young
Island*

*Caribbean
Sea*

Bequia

Port Elizabeth

Quatre

Battowia

Baliceaux

Airport

Mustique

*Petit
Mustique*

Savan

*Petit
Cannouan*

T H E   G R E N A D I N E S

*ATLANTIC
OCEAN*

Cannouan

Mayreau

Tobago Cays

*Union
Island*

Airport

Palm Island

Sail Rock

Carriacou

Petit St. Vincent

Petit Martinique

perhaps more profoundly felt in such isolated milieus. Despite significant variations in atmosphere, the resorts have much in common: they are small, with 24 units at most; informal and friendly (the first order of arrival is always a ruthless rum punch); and well equipped with tennis and water-sports facilities (diving instructors abound). The architecture is most often an extension of the environment, and cottages are built in native stone and wood. Simple furnishings combine paddle fans, rattan chairs, and rush mats—with a blessed lack of TV and telephone. Here you can throw away the room key (if they even give you one).

Most resorts can arrange a day's sailing trip to the **Tobago Cays**, the uninhabited (except for the camps of local fishermen), once-pristine group of four tiny islands protected by a horseshoe reef—but not yet by the government. Almost a shrine for sailors and snorkelers, the cays have suffered in the last few years from too many cruise ships, vendors, and fishermen; plans call for establishing the cays as a national park. (These cays are part of the Grenadines and not, despite their name, Trinidad and Tobago.)

ST. VINCENT

The best reason to go to St. Vincent is to see the Caribbean the way it used to be, something that can be accomplished in a couple of days. There are no resorts on St. Vincent (unless you count Young Island, only 200 yards off its shore), just a handful of small West Indian hotels and guesthouses. The most sophisticated is **The Grand View Beach Hotel**, which lives up to its name (except for the beach—a steep walk away and nothing special) and gives good value for its low tariff. Once the home of an old Vincentian family, this quiet hotel in a hillside residential section about ten minutes from Kingstown appeals to low-key Americans and Europeans, as well as to prosperous West Indians.

Kingstown

The concept of zoning, much less tourism, seems to have eluded Kingstown, but that's part of its charm. Grace and civility run neck and neck with the naïveté of the Vin-

centians: even at the market—the town's heartbeat—
vendors approach visitors with a Tiffany's aplomb, switch-
ing from patois to the King's English in a flash of deference.
Capturing the town's flavor is best done by ambling along
Bay Street, ducking into the Cobblestone Inn arcade for
lunch at **Basil's Bar and Restaurant** (where the West Indian
cuisine gives buffets a good name). Except for the St.
Vincent Philatelic Society, which produces some of the
world's most impressive stamps, and the Craftsmen's Centre, housed in the old Sea Island Cotton ginnery, shopping
should be saved for the smaller islands.

About a mile west of town, the **Botanic Gardens** are the
oldest in the Western Hemisphere, having been established in 1765 as a quarantine for medical plants bound
for England's Kew Gardens. The variety of tropical species here is stunning. Be sure to hire one of the guides,
who will point out such oddities as the mimosa plant
(light a match near its leaves and they fold up like an
army closing ranks), as well as the Gardens' most renowned tree, a spur of Captain Bligh's original breadfruit
plant. The story goes that when Bligh first tried to bring
breadfruit to the Caribbean on board the *Bounty,* he gave
more water to the plants than he did to his crew, thus
instigating the mutiny. His second voyage was more suc-
cessful, and ever since the starchy stuff has been a delicious staple in the West Indian diet. (Combined with
jackfish, it supplies the national Grenadine dish.)

Set among these 20 parklike acres is the last curator's
home, which now houses the small, rather informal, but
remarkable **Archaeological Museum**. The museum's artifacts are the legacy of Dr. Earle Kirby, St. Vincent's most
respected historian and a great raconteur who leaves no
stone unturned. Among his prize specimens is a bat effigy
stand carved out of stone, an early Indian icon dating
from the 7th century, found in a fossil swamp near the
airport some 15 years ago. Since the museum opens only
on Saturday mornings and Wednesday afternoons, an
appointment with Dr. Kirby is well worth arranging
(through your hotel) if you have a serious interest.

The Black Caribs

Like most of the Caribbean, these islands were originally
settled by the Arawaks, or Amerindians, who came from

South America in their dugout canoes—the likes of which still ply the Grenadine waters. A few centuries later, the stronger Caribs followed. What differentiated St. Vincent and the Grenadines was their evolution of the Black Carib tribe, so fiercely independent that the British (who ultimately added the islands to their empire) could never organize a sugar industry there. In 1675, when a slave vessel sank off Bequia, the Africans who swam ashore joined forces with the Caribs. For the next two hundred years, the Black Caribs fought the French and English to maintain possession of St. Vincent with a determination unparalleled in the Caribbean. A series of paintings poignantly depicts their struggle: ironically, these paintings, the Lindsay Prescott collection, hang in the erstwhile officer's quarters of Fort Charlotte, the last British stronghold, on a ridge above Kingstown. Today, descendants of the Black Caribs live quietly in the villages of Owia and Sandy Bay at the northern tip of the island.

Out on the Island

The coastal drives along the leeward and windward sides of St. Vincent yield stunning and often unexpected scenery. The Leeward Highway hugs steep cliffs that dip down into tiny fishing villages on the shore, among them Barrouallie, where whalers still go out in search of blackfish and small pilot whales. Near the quaint town of Layou, a huge pre-Columbian petroglyph on a riverbank attracts intrepid visitors; you would expect such a significant rock carving to be treated as a national monument, but here it's private property and the owner can be less than hospitable.

The wide-open, windswept expanse of the windward side brings to mind the wilder reaches of Scotland's Argyle, for which part of this area is named. Indeed, the village of Escape, where cattle frolic by the sea beneath the old stone church on a grassy knoll, makes for a perfect Turner landscape.

Turning inland along the Yambou Gorge brings another surprise: the **Mesopotamia Valley**, a great, fertile bowl with a froth of mist. The valley is cool enough to grow grapes along with bananas, cocoa, nutmeg, and the like.

Special-Interest Excursions

At **Buccament Valley**, marked nature trails lead through a tropical rain forest, providing an opportunity to see the protected St. Vincent parrot (*Amazona guildingii*) and whistling warbler, both endemic to the island. Plan to spend the day, with a picnic and a swim at Table Rock.

The Falls of Baleine, on the leeward side almost at the northern tip of the island, compare dramatically with Dunn's River Falls in Jamaica (minus the hordes of tourists); however, they are accessible only by boat (easily arranged through your hotel) and well-shod foot. **Sand Dollar Beach**, where the boat anchors, proves a happy exception to the St. Vincent beach rule.

Because of the sudorific climate, the three-plus-mile hike up to the crater of La Soufrière should only be tackled by the fit. Start early in the morning.

Visitors, along with savvy locals, usually end their day at **The French Restaurant** on "the Strip" at the southern shore. The open-air seaside setting, combined with genial service and the best *pommes frites* south of St. Barts, make this the most endearing restaurant in St. Vincent and the Grenadines. But on weekends, along with your *gateau,* you get disco blasts from the neighboring Aquatic Club.

THE GRENADINES
Young Island

Although Young Island is just a few minutes' boat ride from St. Vincent (boarded across from the French Restaurant on the Strip), it's in a world by itself. The feeling here is playful, as if the staff and guests were all suiting up for some TV sitcom about life on a resort-contained island. It all starts with the chug-chug ride on a diesel-powered vessel reminiscent of the *African Queen.* Greetings at the dock include the customary rum punch, proper fortification for hiking up to one of the fetching, Tahitian-style cottages (beach-side accommodations suit the weary, but the extra privacy and better views of the hilltop aeries are worth the hike). While every water sport imaginable is available here, most guests seem content to loll in a hammock or wade out to the Coconut Bar, a thatched bamboo hut secured to a raft off the beach. By twilight, entertainment starts in the bar, a most convivial place where patrons occasionally initiate their own jump-ups, those moveable musical feasts that are so contagious in the Grenadines. On Friday nights all the stops are pulled out when Vidal Browne, Young Island's sleek owner-cum-manager, ferries his guests over to the nearby islet of Fort Duvernette for a torch-lit cocktail party.

Bequia

With its amusing cafés and boutiques, and a harbor full of foreign sailboats, Bequia (BEK-wee) casts a certain spell over its visitors, some of whom have never left. The only way to get here is by boat, either on the cargo schooner that makes a round trip daily from St. Vincent or the supply boat that services the islands (both leave from the main harbor in Kingstown); the nine-mile trip, an adventure in itself, takes about an hour and a half. If you come on your own yacht (or charter), Admiralty Bay makes a lovely anchorage. The sailor never forgets his first night here, enchanted by Bequians who row out to the yachts to serenade them with songs of the islands.

Of all the Grenadines, Bequia has the most local color—there's even a boutique by that name. Its history is nautical, with Yankee whalers setting its course from the 1870s. They came to hunt the humpback whale, and the generations of local fishermen that followed them are now the world's last hand harpooners, sailing out in open wooden boats as they did a century ago. The annual catch of one or two whales keeps the island's economy going—as well as its spirit.

Boat-building, too, is part of the Bequian tradition, from little fishing boats to major schooners, such as Bob Dylan's 68-foot *Water Pearl*. When a new boat is launched, the town of Port Elizabeth, true to its jolly nature, turns out at water's edge with sufficient rum to celebrate. In the hands of Lawson Sargeant, model boat-building achieves the Grenadines' most notable art form; his replicas of some of the world's finest yachts, built from blueprints to scale, include H.M.Y. *Brittania,* commissioned for Queen Elizabeth on the occasion of her recent visit. Sargeant's workshop, with models in progress as well as for sale, ranks as a museum in itself.

The shoreline of **Port Elizabeth** is almost wall-to-wall

cafés and boutiques—the most gratifying in the Grenadines, even though you have to walk along the beach to get to many of them, often through the water and up and down jetty walls. Among the better-known shops are the **Crab Hole**, specializing in brilliant batiks and silk screens, and the Bequia Bookshop, with its outstanding selection of books about the Caribbean. Unfortunately, the best shops close for the weekend. The **Harpoon Saloon**, built on stilts, draws Bequian devotees at sunset, while nobody goes to Bequia without stopping at **Mac's Pizzeria**, lauded for its lobster pizza. Next door, the venerable **Frangipani Hotel** serves as the island's social hub, where visiting literati and other creative types mingle with local characters and the yachting crowd. Memorable moments come from sipping drinks on the Frangi's terrace, gazing at the sea of boats in Admiralty Bay and chatting with knowledgeable strangers who are kindred spirits. Politics often dominate the conversation, particularly since Bequian James "Son" Mitchell came into power as the country's Prime Minister and Queen Elizabeth's only Privy Counselor in the Caribbean: The Frangi was formerly the Mitchell family home, and has been operated by Son and his wife, Pat, as a hotel for 22 years. Despite a lack of creature comforts, it has always been the place to stay or eat on Bequia (unless you're on a boat), and it's a bargain to boot. The resorts on the island's other side may offer more space and tranquility, but staying there would be missing the point of Bequia, which is to be part of a beguiling island scene. Even the most reluctant visitor can't resist joining in the jump-ups. One of the best is at the **Sunny Caribee Hotel**, where, by the way, the new French chef performs wonders with local ingredients.

To see the other side of Bequia, hire a taxi (ask for "Nobleman" or Curtis); a tour of the island, complete with folklore and visits to the whaling village of Paget Farms and deserted beaches, takes a couple of hours, depending on how long you linger. If you are sailing out of Bequia to the south, keep an eye peeled for Moonhole, an extraordinary group of homes carved out of a rocky headland.

Mustique

The mystique of Mustique can be explained rather simply: It's the only privately owned island in the world where royalty and rock stars gather regularly, hiding out from the press and entertaining one another with parties that nonetheless ooze their way into the more enviable social columns. Ah, the bliss of finding a place where one's bodyguard can take the day off! Along with peace and privacy, such are the lures that bond Mustique's imposing band of homeowners.

Thirty years ago Mustique was nothing but a barren spit of 1,350 acres. Then along came Colin Tennant, the Scottish aristocrat (now Lord Glenconner), who could afford to parlay his eccentric fantasies into a utopian verity. He planted the rolling hills with a lush green carpet, brought in set designer Oliver Messel to fashion some exquisite villas, and turned the old **Cotton House** into one of the Caribbean's prettiest hotels. Its main salon, with verandahs that go on forever, is done up with treasures from Tennant's ancestral castle in Scotland, while each of the 22 guest rooms is a cozy mix of English country style and West Indian touches. The beach is just a short walk away—though many guests prefer the pool, framed in Romanesque columns like some operatic stage set.

As a wedding present, Tennant gave Princess Margaret a piece of Mustique (on which her uncle Oliver built a neo-Georgian villa), thus setting the precedent for membership in his unofficial club. There's no roster per se, just a natty six-page telephone book with listings like "Jagger, Mick," and "Lichfield, Lord".

Things have changed recently: Tennant sold his interest in the Mustique Company to Venezuelan capitalists, and anyone can stay, for a price, at Princess Margaret's Les Jolies Eaux, one of three-dozen rentable villas. Still, although references are no longer required, the unheralded visitor might feel a bit on the outs in season. The best time to stay at the Cotton House is actually off season, when it allows a flexible meal plan. And you want to be flexible because the place to eat on Mustique—indeed, the rendezvous of choice in the Grenadines—is **Basil's Bar and Raft Restaurant**. Basil Charles, the flamboyant Vincentian, brings together Mustique's regulars and the uninitiated under his thatched roof for barracuda sandwiches, barbecued whatever, and inimitable jump-ups. Ever the entrepreneur, Basil also offers all manner of water sports, island tours, and even a boutique (which, along with Anita's Affair and the Cotton House boutique, makes shopping on Mustique a pleasant diversion).

Mayreau

At first blush Mayreau appears to be a humble island with a church on its goat-nibbled hilltop, a ho-hum village on one side, and a magnificent horseshoe beach on the other. Then you discover the **Saltwhistle Bay Club**, a magical enclave set in a sea-grape grove fringing the beach. Like extra-virgin olive oil, this tiny inn captures that first pure essence of the Grenadines, enhancing nature's stage with its deceptively simple aura. (For instance, the absence of tennis is by the owner's design, because the *pong-whap* of balls would disturb the ineffable peace.) That it may prove too rustic for some yields a Robinson Crusoe dream for others—it's the sort of place where you wonder why you brought any luggage, where the nearest phone is an island away. The dream begins from the moment Roland, the club's Swiss nautical chauffeur, fetches guests from the airstrip on nearby Union Island and sails literally into the sunset to Mayreau. At night, most of the guests—often burned-out executives—thank the stars there's nothing to do but make their way through the wooded garden to the beachside bar and the intimate dining tables, made of stone and roofed with thatch, that could serve in a tropical Camelot.

Palm Island (a.k.a. Prune Island)

Ten years ago, Palm Island had a barefoot, carefree atmosphere much like that of Mayreau. And then came the mammoth cruise ships, making Palm a regular port of call. Since then, the island resort that the legendary Coconut Johnny built from scratch has changed, its once homey feeling giving way to a camplike bustle. The chief attraction is John Caldwell himself, who (if you haven't read his book, *Desperate Voyage*) will recount how he sailed round the world until he landed here, planting thousands of palms and leasing the island for 99 years. Last year Johnny started a health club, added TV/video to the games room, and took on a partner—whose yen to renovate Palm will hopefully prune it of cruise-ship day-trippers.

Petit St. Vincent

PSV, as this island resort is known, ranks among the Caribbean's top resorts (with prices to match) because its owner, Haze Richardson, keeps an eye on every detail. Even getting there is relatively worry-free since the reservationist also books connecting flights and alerts PSV's cruiser to pick up guests at Union Island, 20 minutes away. Run with the efficiency of a big-city hotel and the grace of West Indian hospitality, **Petit St. Vincent Resort** puts Herman Wouk's *Don't Stop the Carnival* to shame: indeed, where else in the tropics can you order, at the hoist of a room-service flag, an egg boiled to the minute of choice, and see it delivered to your suite as fast as the MiniMoke can ferry it? Perfection such as PSV's brand rarely prevails in such remote ends of the earth. Which is what PSV feels like except for all the improbable amenities (for instance, Julia Child's Cambridge, Massachusetts, butcher provides the meat for PSV's outstanding table). The older, repeat clientele like to think of PSV as their country club in the sun, while the younger cosmopolitan set mostly work on their tans and bar bills. What they all have in common is a desire to get away from everything but pampering. PSV is so private that a guest could easily pass the day without seeing anyone, either in the seclusion of a hilltop or beach-side cottage, or at one of the hammock-studded beaches for two that rim the island—or on Petit St. Richardson, the whimsically named islet in the middle of nowhere, a saucer of sand with nothing but a beckoning shade of thatch. At night most of the 40-odd guests, along with a few chic yachtsmen, gather at the main, cliffside pavilion. Once a week Richardson, a Boston-born maverick, gives in to romance, with dinner served on the beach, to the accompaniment of Brahms played on the piano that's stuck in the sand.

USEFUL FACTS

What to Wear
Bug repellant.

Getting In

International airlines that serve Barbados include American, BWIA, British Airways, Eastern, Air Canada, and Pan Am. The most reliable, hassle-free way then to get to St. Vincent, Mustique, or Union from Barbados is on Mustique Airways, which operates daily flights in and out of Barbados and is available for charter. Tel: (809) 458-4818; in U.S., (800) 526-4729. As a rule hotels will arrange the air charter and meet their guests at one of these airports. As a way station, Union Island is sort of fun—full of Europeans in eternal transit, boats, a café where you can get cappuccino—but you wouldn't want to stay there.

Entry Requirements

Valid passports required by all except nationals of Canada, the U.K., and the U.S. holding proof of identity, and whose stay does not exceed six months.

Currency

Eastern Caribbean, or E.C., dollars depict a windsurfer in one corner. U.S. dollars are generally accepted, although you'll get a better rate if you pay in E.C.

Electrical Current

Mostly 220 volts; American- and Canadian-made appliances require converters.

Getting Around

Except for St. Vincent and Bequia (the latter has a few taxis) there are no cars. Renting one on St. Vincent, along with buying a local driver's license, is hardly worth the trouble for a short period; taxis, with government-set rates, are plentiful and the drivers are courteous (they open doors and wish you "all the best").

Sailing the Islands

In some Caribbean waters, sailing has become so popular that it's more like playing bumper boats; not so here, where you can often find an anchorage all to yourself. Although charter companies operate out of St. Vincent, the best is on St. Lucia: The Moorings in Marigot Bay. Contact The Moorings, USA, Inc., 1305 U.S. 19 South, Suite 402, Clearwater, FL 33546; Tel: (800) 535-7289; in

Florida, (813) 535-1446. Day trips to the Tobago Cays or other islands can be easily arranged through your hotel.

Business Hours
Lunch is strictly observed between noon and 1:00. Everything shuts down at 4:00 Monday–Friday and at noon on Saturday (except for some hotel boutiques).

Festivals
Carnival lasts for ten days in late June and early July; it was changed from the traditional winter Mardi Gras date.

ACCOMMODATIONS REFERENCE
The rate ranges given here are projections for fall 1988 through spring 1989. Unless otherwise indicated, rates are for double rooms, double occupancy. The telephone area code for St. Vincent and The Grenadines is 809.

▶ **Cotton House**. Box 349, Mustique, St. Vincent and the Grenadines, W.I. $242–$400. Tel: 456-4777; in U.S., (212) 696-1323 or (800) 372-1323.

▶ **The Frangipani Hotel**. Bequia, St. Vincent, W.I. $40–$80. Tel: 458-3255.

▶ **Grand View Beach Hotel**. St. Vincent, W.I. $72–$103. Tel: 458-4811; in U.S., (212) 832-2277 or (800) 223-6510; in Canada, (416) 622-8813 or (800) 268-0424.

▶ **Palm Island Beach Club**. St. Vincent and the Grenadines, W.I. $195–$290, A.P. Tel: 458-4804; in U.S., (800) 223-5581 or (212) 535-9530.

▶ **Petit St. Vincent Resort**. Grenadines, St. Vincent, W.I. $300, A.P. Tel: 458-4801; in U.S., (800) 654-9326; in Ohio, (513) 242-1333 (collect).

▶ **Saltwhistle Bay Club**. Mayreau, St. Vincent and the Grenadines, W.I. $190–$320, M.A.P. Tel: (800) 387-1752; in Canada, (416) 366-8559 (collect).

▶ **Young Island**. P.O. Box 211, St. Vincent, W.I. $200–$400, M.A.P. Tel: 458-4826; in U.S., (800) 223-1108.

▶ For **villa rentals** on Mustique (each comes with a Jeep): The Mustique Co., Ltd. Tel: 458-4621; in U.S., (212) 696-4566.

OTHER ACCOMMODATIONS
▶ **Firefly House**. Mustique. $65–$75. Tel: 458-4621. A comfortable guest house that's a new, reasonable alternative to the above.

GRENADA

By Julie Wilson

Grenada, just 100 miles off the Venezuelan Coast, is one of the lushest of the Caribbean islands. It is the "Isle of Spice," and of fruits, vegetables, flowers—anything that grows. Throw a seed on the ground, say the Grenadians, and it sprouts. Instantly, it seems. The mountains are covered with a tropical green so intense it can almost be felt. The scent of spice rides on the merest breeze, and clings to the skin like perfume.

In addition to this fecundity, Grenada (Grah-NAY-dah) has the allure of a dramatic past that was once a painful present. In this case, it's the "past" of October, 1983, when the U.S. 82nd Airborne swarmed onto the 120-square-mile island after the assassination of Prime Minister Maurice Bishop. Whatever the rest of the world thinks about "The Intervention," the Grenadians consider it a blessing, pointing out rusting remains of Cuban trucks and planes with a combination of pride and reflection.

Despite its recent troubles and the slow rebuilding of its economy, Grenada is neither dispirited nor depressing. The Grenadians are optimistic, gutsy, polite, warm, and generous. They are also independent. Don't expect big resorts with international staffs or branches of duty-free department stores. Nearly all hotels and businesses are locally owned, small, and personal—in an unmistakably Grenadian way.

The combination of sensibility, past, and sensuality makes Grenada a pleasantly unsettling island—conducive to sudden romance or a previously unsuspected interest in poetry. Or maybe it's just all that spice in the air.

Grenada is actually a three-island nation. The other

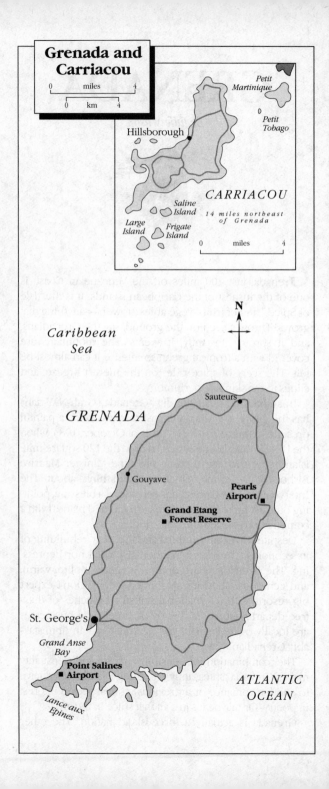

Grenada and Carriacou

0   miles   4

0   km   4

Petit Martinique

Petit Tobago

Hillsborough

CARRIACOU

14 miles northeast of Grenada

0   miles   4

Saline Island

Large Island

Frigate Island

Caribbean Sea

N

GRENADA

Sauteurs

Gouyave

Pearls Airport

Grand Etang Forest Reserve

St. George's

Grand Anse Bay

Point Salines Airport

Lance aux Epines

ATLANTIC OCEAN

members are Carriacou and Petit Martinique. The major occupation on Carriacou is boat-building. On roadless Petit Martinique it is reputed to be smuggling; this is a wealthy island.

MAJOR INTEREST

> Lush greenery
> Relatively undeveloped for tourism
> Port Salines Airport
> Lance aux Epines hotels
> Grand Anse Beach
> St. George's Harbour
> Carriacou Island (even more undeveloped than
>   Grenada)

The Southwest Corner

Grenada begins at new Point Salines Airport, a focus of The Intervention and, consequently, one of the few airports in the world that constitutes a tourist attraction. But long before the airport was built, this corner of Grenada was the tourist center. It still is. The Spice Island Marine Services (well known to yachtsmen cruising the Grenadines) is here, and so are the casually elegant hotels of **Lance aux Epines**, such as **Calabash**—where flowering thunbergia vines shade the dining terrace and high-walled pool suites are the ultimate in privacy. Here, too, is the blinding-white two-mile **Grand Anse Beach**. Students from the St. George's School of Medicine jog daily along the beach, in front of the excellent hotels that seem to have been dropped like coconuts behind the strand.

On the breezy dining terrace at **Spice Island Inn**, an international clutch of guests watch the joggers over cups of breakfast coffee, then walk a few steps from their cottage to the beach, or retire to the seclusion of a pool suite. A few palm trees up the beach, Grenada's only "big" hotel (all two stories of it) is now the **Ramada Renaissance**. Despite its international affiliation, this Ramada is perfectly Grenadian in atmosphere. Newest of the Grand Anse hotels, **Coyaba** (the Arawak word for "heaven") is locally built, owned, and operated. Engagingly enthusiastic, it draws an active crowd who willingly sacrifice luxurious rooms for tennis, water sports, volleyball—and that heavenly beach.

Mama's, a laughably underpriced restaurant that epitomizes Grenadian cooking, is on the road to St. George's from the southwest corner, not far from Grenada Yacht Services. The decor—best described as "clean"—isn't much, but the food is unadulterated West Indian, and this is one of the only places in the West Indies to find it. Mama cooks the same things as any other Grenadian housewife; she just cooks more of them. Count on about 24 dishes, including callaloo soup (made from the dark green leaves of the dasheen plant), stewed armadillo, baked turtle, breadfruit salad, curried chicken, and soursop ice cream.

St. George's

St. George's is so intent on being functional that it has remained ingenuously unaware that it is one of the prettiest harbor towns in the world. Steep hills and narrow roads (where wide drainage ditches make street-crossing a vaulting experience) climb from the curved lagoon; in the harbor inter-island vessels, working skiffs, and a few transport ships engage in man-powered loading and unloading. A few cruise ships and moored yachts add photogenic sophistication. The Carenage, the promenade that skirts the harbor, accommodates as many pedestrians as cars—and nothing moves very fast.

An oddly urban vehicular tunnel—built in the 1800s—connects the Carenage side of St. George's to the market side. On Saturday mornings every farmer, fruit grower, maker of straw hats, and spice dryer in the area comes to market and spreads his or her wares across wooden stalls or on the courtyard cobblestones. One vendor makes rotis, another stirs a fragrant oil-down (a local stew), and the smell of cinnamon and clove hangs in the air. Whatever nonedibles aren't at the market can be found a block away at **Grencraft**, the government-owned cooperative for cottage industries. Don't look for sophistication at Grencraft; look instead for masks made of calabash wood, black coral jewelry, packaged spices, and lots of baskets.

Grenada's **National Museum**, behind the thick walls of a onetime prison, is what one might call a "hands-on museum"—that is, it contains anything the curators could get their hands on. On display is stuff as varied as farm implements, early telephones, and Empress Josephine's bathtub. The most popular section is the one that describes, through yellowed news clippings and 8-by-10 glossies, the Bishop Years and The Intervention.

West Coast

The sleepy pose of the town of Gouyave (pronounced Guave), just north of St. George's, masks furious activity in the Nutmeg Station cooperative. Amid the drying, crushing, and grading, women sort nutmegs with lightning-fast skill. Nutmegs—along with the mace that clings to the shells—are Grenada's major exports; 15 minutes in the station will go a long way toward explaining what makes the island tick. At Dougalston Estates, a banana and spice plantation up in the nearby hills, women scrape mace off nutmeg shells in a low-ceilinged barn. They will pause willingly from this task to describe the bay leaves, nutmeg fruits, cinnamon, allspice, and cocoa beans— other Grenadian export items—laid out on a display table.

Two of Grenada's new bootstrap-economy industries are also up in the hills above the west coast. Grenada Wine Coolers, a cellar full of light fruit wines, is the joint venture of a Persian-American and a burly Grenadian named Sancho. Sancho's grandmother supplied the recipes. And Spice Island Cosmetics mixes local cocoa butter and nutmeg oil into all manner of body lotions, shampoos, and pomades. In both cases the products are as good as anything produced in the "outside world," and their secret ingredients are distilled charm and a lot of love.

North Coast

In the 17th century a number of Indians threw themselves off the cliff at Sauteurs rather than surrender to the invading French. Today Carib's Leap is overgrown and apparently not as high.

Morne Fendue, a well-maintained plantation house set among well-maintained gardens inland from Sauteurs, is a uniquely personal visitor attraction. Owner Betty Mascoll's living room is cluttered with family photographs and framed press clippings, and her buffet lunches (by reservation only; Tel: 440-9330) are memorable. Her specialties include callaloo soup, pepper pot, and island-vegetable casseroles. The bartender makes a bold, nutmeg-flavored rum punch.

Grand Etang Forest Reserve

The mountain range in Grenada's center virtually explodes with tactile-green lushness and fertility. On a hill overlooking Grand Etang Lake (the crater of an extinct volcano), the new National Park Unit has established a Visitor Center/Interpretive Building. The park has cut trails and opened up a wilderness that was formerly accessible only to serious hikers equipped with machetes, pitons, crampons, croutons, and who knows what else.

West of Grand Etang Lake, the pretty 40-foot waterfall at **Annandale** (not exactly Iguassu, but pretty) is surrounded by exotic plants, thickly foliaged trees, and elephant ears that Dumbo would covet. Guides from the Welcome Center will tell you all there is to know about the medicinal uses of these leaves and roots. (A sign at the Welcome Center warns that "Jumping from the cliff is prohibited.") At **Bay Gardens** (about 20 minutes away), trails wend through three acres dense with every fruit, flower, tree, and bush that grows in Grenada. Most are labeled, and knowledgeable guides will identify the rest. Accustomed to nature's lavishness, Grenadians may wonder why visitors are so astounded by it all; but they're pleased by the astonishment and delighted to share it all.

Carriacou

Surrounded by tiny islands, 13-square-mile Carriacou (CAR-ee-a-koo) is the largest of the Grenadines. This hilly island, a 17-minute plane ride from Point Salines Airport, is like Grenada but much drier. It is so undeveloped that the sound of a car horn heralds a plane's arrival, warning drivers off the airstrip/road.

Hillsborough, where 18th-century stone-and-shingle buildings hug the narrow roads, is the only town of any consequence on the island—the only town at all, in fact. The settlement of Windward (across the island) harbors aspirations of town status. Right now, Windward is the boat-building center, and local craftsmen construct wooden schooners, scratching the plans in beach sand as they go along.

Up in the cooler inland hills, Americans Lee and Ann Katzenbach have recently opened **Prospect Lodge**, a comfortable collection of cottages, mainhouse rooms, and sunset views. Ann Katzenbach will—by prior arrangement— serve a lunch of fish chowder, just-baked bread, salads, and ice cream. (For reservations, call from Grenada; 443-7380). Guests staying at Prospect Lodge usually picnic on a beach at lunchtime, or wander into the kitchen to find some leftovers.

To escape the fervor of mainland Carriacou, take a red-and-yellow motor boat leaving from Hillsborough for **Sandy Island**. No more than two clumps of palms and sea grapes connected by a sandbar, this private paradise has reefs for snorkeling, a sand beach for swimming, and shade for napping.

USEFUL FACTS

What to Wear
Conservative sportswear. No jackets required.

Getting In
BWIA flies direct daily from Miami, and three times a week nonstop from New York. British Air flies nonstop once a week from London. The best connection is through Barbados via LIAT, which has several flights a day to Point Salines.

Entry Requirements
Passports required. U.S. and Canadian citizens can substitute two proofs of citizenship (birth certificate, expired passport, driver's license), one with a photograph. There is a departure tax of $10.

Currency
Eastern Caribbean dollar; U.S. currency is widely accepted.

Electrical Current
220/240 volts, 50 cycles; American- and Canadian-made appliances require converters.

Getting Around

Don't rent a car. The new roads are good, but most roads you'll encounter are twisting, unmarked, paved goat paths. Depend on taxis or tour services. If you do rent a car, you will need a valid license and $6 for a local permit. Driving is on the left.

Business Hours

Monday–Friday, 8:00–11:45 and 1:00–3:45; Saturday, 8:00–10:45 A.M.

Festivals

Carnival begins the second Tuesday in August.

ACCOMMODATIONS REFERENCE

The rate ranges given here are projections for fall 1988 through spring 1989. Unless otherwise indicated, rates are for double rooms, double occupancy. The telephone area code for Grenada is 809.

▶ **Calabash.** P.O. Box 382, St. George's, Grenada, W.I. $100–$200, M.A.P.; pool suites, $180–$350, M.A.P. Tel: 444-4234/4334; in U.S., (212) 840-6636 or (800) CALL-GND; in Canada, (800) 468-0023; in U.K., (01) 387-1555.

▶ **Coyaba.** P.O. Box 336, St. George's, Grenada, W.I. $65–$85, E.P. Tel: 444-4129; in U.S., (212) 840-6636 or (800) CALL-GND; in Canada, (800) 468-0023.

▶ **Prospect Lodge.** Carriacou, Grenada, W.I. $24–$45, plus $14 a person for M.A.P. Tel: 443-7380.

▶ **Ramada Renaissance.** P.O. Box 441, St. George's, Grenada, W.I. $95–$180, E.P. Tel: 444-4371; in U.S., (800) 2-RAMADA; in U.K., (01) 493-0621.

▶ **Spice Island Inn.** P.O. Box 6, St. George's, Grenada, W.I. $135–$190, M.A.P.; pool suites, $155–$230, M.A.P. Tel: 444-4258/4423; in U.S., (212) 840-6636 or (800) CALL-GND; in Canada, (800) 468-0023.

OTHER ACCOMMODATIONS

▶ **Blue Horizons.** P.O. Box 41, St. George's, Grenada, W.I. $60–$100, E.P. Tel: 444-4316/4592; in U.S., (212) 840-6636 or (800) CALL-GND; in Canada, (800) 468-0023. Serviceable cottages on a hillside near Grand Anse Beach. Highlight: the food at Blue Horizons' restaurant, **La Belle Creole**.

▶ **Horse Shoe Beach**. P.O. Box 174, St. George's, Grenada, W.I. Rates start at $95, E.P. Tel: 444-4410/4244; in U.S., (212) 840-6636 or (800) CALL-GND; in Canada, (800) 468-0023. On the beach at Lance aux Epines. Cottages with stucco walls and mahogony four-poster beds; a romantic dining room.

▶ **Secret Harbour**. P.O. Box 11, St. George's, Grenada, W.I. All-inclusive, $1,177 per person, seven nights. Tel: 444-4548; in U.S., (212) 840-6636 or (800) CALL-GND; in Canada, (800) 468-0023. Known for its mahogany four-posters and sybaritic bathtubs with a view of Mount Hartman Bay or Lance aux Epines; there is a small beach down steep steps.

▶ **12 Degrees North**. P.O. Box 241, St. George's, Grenada, W.I. One-bedroom apartment, $75–$100, E.P. Tel: 444-4580; in U.S., (212) 840-6636 or (800) CALL-GND; in Canada, (800) 468-0023. Very small (eight apartments) and individualistic, this is a real getaway. It's a short hike down to the pool and to Lance aux Epines Beach, and a short stroll to the tennis courts. No restaurant, but every apartment has a cook.

TRINIDAD AND TOBAGO

By Jeanne Westphal

Jeanne Westphal, a trustee of the Society of American Travel Writers Foundation based in Miami, has been a consultant to the World Tourism Organization, Organization of American States, and a number of Caribbean islands.

For the holiday traveller searching for some still-unspoiled and still-undiscovered islands in the Caribbean, Trinidad and Tobago may just be the answer.

On Trinidad, there is the bustling capital city of Port of Spain, where traders and merchants from all over the world conduct their business in the usual hurried fashion. The real allure of Trinidad, however, is outside Port of Spain, in the lush valleys, on green mountainsides ablaze with tropical flowers, and along nature trails with brilliantly colored birds.

On Tobago, the atmosphere is tranquil and unhurried. The island is a place to unwind. Finding your own private cove, your own special fishing ground, or your own underwater cave are all part of a day's normal routine—usually ending with a spectacular sunset. Tobago weaves a special magic that makes you want to share its pleasures with a very special person.

MAJOR INTEREST

Trinidad
Asa Wright Nature Center
Caroni Wildlife Sanctuary
Queen's Park Savannah in Port of Spain
Carnival

Tobago
Tranquillity
Resorts for beaches and sports activities
Little Tobago

The Amerindians who were the first settlers of Trinidad called it "Iere" (Land of the Humming Bird). When Columbus landed in 1498 and took possession on behalf of the Crown of Spain, he renamed the island Trinidad, for a trinity of mountain peaks dominating the southeast coast.

In 1523 the Spanish created their first settlement, which was destroyed by Sir Walter Raleigh in 1595. The Dutch and French raided during the 17th century, and finally in 1802 the island was ceded to the British Crown by the Spanish in the Treaty of Amiens. Columbus also discovered Tobago in 1498, but the island was left undisturbed until 1641, when James, the Duke of Courland, arrived with a number of Courlanders to settle on the north side. During the 16th and 17th centuries Tobago changed hands among the Dutch, British, and the French, who in 1763 finally ceded it to Britain under the Treaty of Paris. In 1888 Tobago was affiliated with Trinidad politically. The islands achieved their independence from Great Britain in 1962 and became a republic of the Commonwealth in 1976.

Today, Trinidad and Tobago's personality reflects a rich ethnic mix. The African heritage is strong, as is the East Indian. Many of these settlers came in the 1800s when Britain, then the ruling power, adopted a free-trade policy that resulted in major social changes. There is a blending of French, Spanish, Creole, Portuguese, Chinese, British, and Middle Eastern cultures.

As could be expected from a culture of such diverse people, the cuisine of Trinidad and Tobago is exciting and varied. While you can easily find Indian, Chinese, French, and other cosmopolitan menus, you'd be remiss not to sample some of the typical island fare.

The local culinary offerings include callaloo soup, rich in crabmeat and okra; crab backs, a crab-meat mixture served in the shell; corned fish with cassava; and, for the adventurous, armadillo or possum stew. There is also a bounty of tropical fruits available for the tasting, including mangoes, paw-paws, hog plum, and sour cherry.

For many, the drink of choice is the brewed-in-Trinidad Carib beer. Stag is another local brand. Angostura Bitters are also produced in Trinidad, and they are used in a variety of powerful drinks.

Beaches are usually synonymous with Caribbean Islands, but in the case of Trinidad you may wish to put a day on the beach at the end of your list of things to do. The closest to Port of Spain are Maracas Bay and Las Cuevas, located on the northern coast approximately ten miles from the city. Accommodations there are limited, and you would be better off waiting until you get to Tobago, where beaches should have top priority.

TRINIDAD
Out on the Island

Trinidad is the more commercial of the two islands. If the prevalent notion among travellers is that the Caribbean is a place for lazing on sunny stretches of beaches, then Trinidad is indeed an anomaly. The island's energetic (but not too frenetic) pace quickly captivates visitors, prodding the senses day and night in its own hospitable way. There is, however, another side to Trinidad: the unexpected plenitude and beauty of its tropical flora and fauna. Some of this wealth, unique to Trinidad, can be seen in bird sanctuaries, botanic gardens, and nature centers, or just by looking out of your hotel window.

A drive through a rain forest only one hour outside Port of Spain ends at the mountaintop **Asa Wright Nature Center and Lodge**, on Spring Hill Estate. The center, at 1,200 feet above sea level, can accommodate up to 25 guests in simple but tastefully decorated rooms of the former Wright home. Operated as part of a nonprofit organization, the Center's nature-trail tours are led by experienced guides. The highlight on the tours is a visit to Dunston Cave, the breeding place of the almost-extinct nocturnal "oilbird," found only in Trinidad.

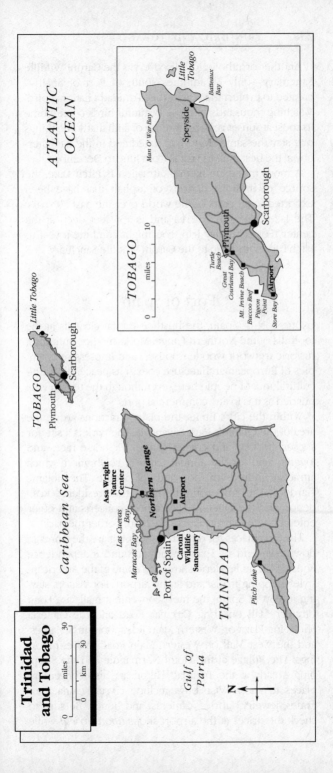

Trinidad and Tobago

CARIBBEAN SEA

ATLANTIC OCEAN

TRINIDAD

Gulf of Paria

Port of Spain
Maracas Bay
Las Cuevas Bay
Asa Wright Nature Center
Northern Range
Airport
Caroni Wildlife Sanctuary
Pitch Lake

TOBAGO
Plymouth
Scarborough
Little Tobago

TOBAGO

Man O' War Bay
Speyside
Little Tobago
Batteaux Bay
Plymouth
Turtle Beach
Great Courland Bay
Mt. Irvine Beach
Buccoo Reef
Pigeon Point
Store Bay
Airport
Scarborough

N

Another ornithological discovery is the **Caroni Wildlife Sanctuary**—only 30 minutes south of Port of Spain—created to protect the scarlet ibis, Trinidad's national bird. Watching thousands of these beautiful birds come home to roost at sunset restores a sense of faith that some things *can* stay the same. Tours are scheduled in the late afternoon; the best time to visit is from June to December.

A more mundane natural attraction is **Pitch Lake**, the source of millions of tons of asphalt that have been exported to all parts of the world over the past 70 years. The lake covers 115 acres and is 135 feet deep at the center. For a full-day trip, you might combine a visit to Pitch Lake with a trip to the Caroni Wildlife Sanctuary.

Port of Spain

Exotic Port of Spain, the bustling capital city, sits at the foothills of the Northern Range. Modern office buildings, historic fretwork wooden houses, and impressive examples of European architecture coexist as peacefully as the cultural mix of people here, even though the tempo is as hurried as it is in any commercial port.

Within the city's limits, the main attractions are in the area of the **Queen's Park Savannah**. The park is a site for soccer, hockey, and cricket games, for horse races and jogging, and for the annual Carnival celebration, which attracts hundreds of thousands of people. The Botanic Gardens, The Emperor Valley Zoo, the President's Residence, and the Queen's Hall, where concerts and other entertainment performances are held, border the park.

The best places for duty-free shopping are the stores in downtown Port of Spain, mainly around Independence Square and on Frederick Street, in some of the American-style shopping malls, and at the airport. For visitors staying in Port of Spain, the most convenient malls are Long Circular Mall on Long Circular Road and the Galleria Shopping Plaza on Western Main Road, both in St. James, and the West Mall on Western Main Road in Westmoorings. The Village at the Hotel Normandie and the Shopping Arcade at the Trinidad Hilton are also convenient places to shop. Wise buys include crystal, china, perfumes, jewelry, fabrics, cameras, and liquor. Be sure to check the prices at the airport shops *upon arrival* while waiting for your baggage (no other island offers this opportunity to shop before clearing customs). There is no duty-free shopping on Tobago, so plan to make your purchases in Port of Spain or upon arrival at or departure from Piarco International Airport on Trinidad.

If you want to stay in downtown Port of Spain, the only hotel is the **Holiday Inn**, recently refurbished with all the amenities of a top, first-class business hotel. The rooftop restaurant offers spectacular views of the city. However, because of its location in the business district there is not too much activity of interest to the visitor at night here.

Most hotels and restaurants are in the neighborhood of the Queen's Park Savannah. The largest hotel on the island is the expense-account oriented **Trinidad Hilton**, which overlooks the Savannah. It offers all of the trappings of a deluxe hotel—a pool, tennis courts, a health club, convention facilities, and so on. More of a find in this area, however, is the redecorated and expanded **Hotel Normandie**. With some new loft-type rooms opening to a courtyard swimming pool, the atmosphere is charming and relaxing. The guests are a combination of international visitors and residents from other parts of Trinidad and Tobago visiting the capital city. The adjoining Market contains shops and restaurants and a gallery that exhibits local artists. Another possibility for accommodations in Port of Spain is a bed and breakfast. The local association has 24 members, all of which have been approved by the Trinidad and Tobago Tourist Board; some are in private homes conveniently located in the Queen's Park area.

The majority of Port of Spain's restaurants are either in the hotels or in the Queen's Park area. There is more choice of cuisine than time will allow the visitor to sample in one trip. Restaurants worth considering, and easily accessible, are La Boucan (Continental), in the Hilton Hotel; La Fantasie (Creole *nouvelle*) and Il Giardino (Italian) near the Hotel Normandie; Mangals (East Indian) on Queen's Park East; and Tiki Village (Polynesian) and Café Savanna (Continental) at the Kapok Hotel. Be sure to check to see which credit cards the restaurant of your choice accepts.

Nightlife here is rather limited. Check local papers for performances at Queen's Hall that feature steel bands—which originated in Trinidad.

TOBAGO

Tobago is a paradise for the active person whose interests include golf, tennis, biking, fishing, swimming, surfing, and diving, as well as for the passivist who might prefer bird-watching or beachcombing, exploring nature trails, relaxing around the pool, watching a beautiful sunset, or doing nothing at all. In short, there is something for everyone on Tobago.

There is snorkeling at **Buccoo Reef**, a wonderland of exotic undersea coral gardens and multicolored fish, not far from Pigeon Point, and at nearby **Nylon Pool**, where the water is so clear it seems invisible; deep-sea fishing for marlin, barracuda, dolphinfish, and wahoo, just to name a few of the catches; windsurfing and body surfing at **Pigeon Point**; and diving among the spectacular reefs on the northeast coast around **Man O' War Bay**. There is tennis at the major hotels and outstanding golf at the 18-hole championship course at the Mt. Irvine Bay Hotel.

The list of beaches on Tobago is long—Turtle Beach, Mt. Irvine Beach, Pigeon Point, and Store Bay are the most popular and the most accessible to the major hotels. However, the northeast coast also has miles of beaches, most of them deserted. From Speyside, you can sail off to discover the beaches on **Little Tobago**, also known as "Bird of Paradise Island," which has a 258-acre bird sanctuary that is home to the feathered residents of the same name.

Scarborough

Tobago's capital city of Scarborough, ten miles from the airport, is perched on a hill overlooking the sea. The House of Assembly, where local government operates, occupies the restored chamber of the 19th-century assembly that was opened in 1985 by Queen Elizabeth. For islanders, the city is the center of action; for visitors, there is much local color, including a native market and crowded, winding streets. The highest point is at **Fort King George**, 430 feet above sea level. On a clear day, you can see Trinidad from this fort built by the British in the late 1770s to protect Tobago from the French. (In spite of the efforts, the French seized the island anyway.) The

Botanical Gardens and St. Andrew's Church are also worth a visit.

While there aren't many good restaurants outside of the hotels, there are two exceptions in Scarborough. The **Old Donkey Cart**, in a former French colonial house on Bacolot Street, is a wine bistro with a lovely garden overlooking the bay. Known for its excellent selection of German wines, the restaurant serves a selection of salads, open-faced sandwiches on homemade bread, and imported cheeses, as well as gourmet cuisine. At the **Blue Crab**, on the corner of Main and Robinson streets, locals and visitors enjoy a variety of freshly caught fish prepared the Caribbean way. All of the hotel dining rooms on the island are open to the public, and for native cuisine don't miss the Kariwak Village on Store Bay Road and the **Cocrico Inn** in Plymouth.

Out on the Island

The majority of the hotels and resorts on Tobago are located on the Caribbean side of the island, only a short taxi ride from Crown Point Airport. The most deluxe resort is **Mt. Irvine Bay Hotel**, with views of the sea and the fairways of the 18-hole championship golf course of the Tobago Golf Club. It has tennis courts, a swimming pool, its own private beach, a choice of accommodations in cottages or the main building, and a restaurant in a converted sugar mill. Its guests are an international mix of Americans, Canadians, Europeans, and residents of the Far East.

Arnos Vale, another deluxe but smaller hotel, has undergone complete renovation by its new management, which is concentrating on attracting European travellers, especially Italians. It is off the beaten path, on a hill overlooking the sea, and has a freshwater pool, walking trails, and snorkeling just a few yards offshore. **Turtle Beach Hotel**, undergoing expansion, is situated right on the beach overlooking Great Courland Bay. Facilities include a pool, tennis courts, shuffleboard, a water-sports center, and facilities for children. Turtle Beach is a popular choice for groups of British, Canadians, and Germans.

For a completely different atmosphere, there is **Kariwak Village**, near Store Bay and only minutes from the airport. The cottages, surrounding the pool amidst lush foliage, are easily accessible to the beach. Kariwak's open-air restaurant provides some of the best Caribbean cuisine on the island. For the vacationer who primarily wants privacy and seclusion—yet still wants to be close to excellent diving and fishing, as well as nature trails—**Blue Waters Inn**, located on the northeast coast of the island at Speyside, is the spot. Situated on Batteaux Bay, it is a 90-minute drive from the airport up and down mountain roads that offer picturesque views of hidden coves, virgin white sand beaches, and vibrant tropical flowers and trees. The Blue Waters' cottages face Little Tobago.

While touring the island, visit some of the estates, or "great houses," of former plantation owners. Some of these are now being restored as guest houses. In the direction of the Blue Waters Inn, there is **Richmond House**, at Belle Garden. Built 200 years ago, it has five guest rooms and commands a spectacular view of Richmond Bay and the verdant valley below. Overlooking Scarborough is **Arcadia House**, with a restaurant open to the public for lunch and dinner; don't miss it.

USEFUL FACTS

What to Wear
Lightweight, casual, resort-type clothes—preferably cotton—are recommended.

Getting In
Piarco International Airport in Port of Spain is the major arrival point for both islands. BWIA provides regular daily service for the 20-minute flight to Crown Point Airport in Tobago and also operates a nonstop flight from Barbados to Tobago. The major airlines that serve Trinidad are BWIA, from Miami, New York, Toronto, Boston, Baltimore, San Juan, Frankfurt, and London; Air Canada, from Toronto, and from Montreal via Toronto; Eastern Airlines, from Miami; Pan American and World Airways, from New York and Miami; American Airlines, from New York; British Airways, from London via Antigua or Barbados; KLM, from Amsterdam–Caracas–Port of Spain (connection in Caracas); and ALM (all connections are through Curaçao from the following gateways: Aruba, New York, San Juan,

St. Martin, Bonaire, Miami, Port au Prince, and Santo Domingo).

Ground transport from Piarco Airport and Crown Point Airport is provided by approved taxi services supervised by a dispatcher. Standard fares to hotels and other principal destinations are available on request from the dispatcher, or from a tariff board displayed at each terminal. Taxis at Crown Point Airport are operated by the Tobago Taxicab Coop Society (Tel: 639-2707/2659) and other appointed operators. PTSC Bus service is available from Piarco Airport to Port of Spain, and from Crown Point Airport to Scarborough. The average cost from Piarco to, say, the Hilton Hotel is $14 one way. From Crown Point to Mt. Irvine Bay Hotel is about $10.

Entry Requirements
Passports must be valid for a minimum of six months beyond date of entry; Commonwealth and U.S. citizens must possess an ongoing ticket. There is a departure tax of about $6.

Currency
The monetary unit is the Trinidad and Tobago dollar, made up of 100 cents. Traveller's Checks are accepted almost everywhere. The larger hotels will generally honor all credit cards. Expect to have to use local currency in smaller establishments, though U.S. dollars are widely accepted.

Electrical Current
115 or 230 volts, 60 cycles AC. American- and Canadian-made appliances require converters.

Getting Around
Visitors from the U.S., Canada, and the U.K. who have a valid driver's license may drive a car on the islands for as long as 3 months. For most other nationalities, an international driver's license is required. Driving is on the left. For touring, a taxi carrying a maximum of 4 people charges $10–$15 a person for 4 hours.

Business Hours
Shops are open from 8:00–4:00, Monday–Friday, and close at noon on Saturday. Malls are open late on Friday and

Saturday. Banks are open 9:00–2:00, Monday–Thursday, and 9:00–2:00 and 3:00–5:00, Friday.

Festivals

While **Carnival**, usually in February or March, is the best-known festival on Trinidad, other annual events are worth noting. In the fall, *Hosein* (pronounced ho-SAY), a three-day-long Moslem celebration, includes music, colorful costumes, and parades. The Hindu Festival of Lights (*Divali*), which honors the goddess Lasshni, occurs in late October or November. It is followed by *Parang*, which features Spanish songs that celebrate the birth and joys of the Nativity.

The major festival on Tobago, of course, is Carnival, a mini-version of Port of Spain's nonstop party, with Scarborough as the focal point. On Easter Tuesday, don't miss the traditional goat- and crab-racing festival, now a 60-year-old tradition, that takes place at Buccoo Village. However, throughout the year there are many village festivals and events where visitors are warmly welcomed.

Other annual events include the Johnny Walker Pro-Am Golf Tournament every January and the Tobago Open in May; the National/Petroleum/Carib International Game Fishing Classic in March; and the powerboat Great Race from Trinidad to Tobago in August.

ACCOMMODATIONS REFERENCE

The rate ranges given here are projections for fall 1988 through spring 1989. Unless otherwise indicated, rates are for double rooms, double occupancy. The telephone area code for Trinidad and Tobago is 809.

Trinidad

▶ **Asa Wright Nature Center and Lodge.** P.O. Box 10, Port of Spain, Trinidad. $50–$65, A.P. Tel: in U.S., (914) 273-6333 or (800) 327-2753.

▶ **Bed & Breakfast Association.** P.O. Box 3231, Port of Spain, Trinidad. With 24 members, all private homes.

▶ **Holiday Inn.** P.O. Box 1017, Wrightson Road, Port of Spain, Trinidad. $92–$103, E.P. Tel: 625-3361; Telex: 387-22456, in U.S., and Canada, (800) HOLIDAY; in U.K., (01) 722-7755.

▶ **Hotel Normandie.** 10 Nook Avenue, St. Ann's, Port of

Spain, Trinidad. $70–$80, E.P. Tel: 624-1181; Telex: 387-22639; in U.S., (212) 840-6636 or (800) 223-9815; in Canada, (800) 468-0023.

▶ **Trinidad Hilton.** P.O. Box 442, Port of Spain, Trinidad. $120–165, E.P. Tel: 624-3211; Telex: 3319 (WUI); 319 (RCA ITT); in U.S., (800) HILTONS; in Canada, (800) 268-9275; in U.K., (01) 631-1767.

Tobago

▶ **Arnos Vale Hotel.** P.O. Box 208, Scarborough, Tobago. $120–$170, M.A.P. Rates in season, $115–$130, E.P. Tel: 639-2881.

▶ **Blue Waters Inn.** Batteaux Bay, Speyside, Tobago. $34–$64, E.P. Tel: 660-4341.

▶ **Kariwak Village.** Crown Point, P.O. Box 27, Scarborough, Tobago. $76–$110, M.A.P. Tel: 639-8545; Telex: 38323-CROWN-WG.

▶ **Mt. Irvine Bay Hotel.** P.O. Box 222, Scarborough, Tobago. $195–$400, M.A.P. Tel: 639-8871; Telex: 294-38463 Goftel; in U.S., (212) 725-5880 or (800) 223-5695; in Canada, (416) 447-2335 or (800) 387-8031.

▶ **Richmond Great House.** Belle Garden, Tobago. $75–$105, M.A.P. Tel: 660-4467.

▶ **Turtle Beach Hotel.** P.O. Box 201, Scarborough, Tobago. Tel: 639-2851; Telex: 387-38324; in U.S., (212) 832-2277 or (800) 223-6510; in Canada, (416) 622-8813.

BONAIRE

By Jeanne Westphal

Most travellers journey to Bonaire to explore the phenomenal undersea life just offshore; the island is one of the top places in the world for scuba diving and snorkeling.

MAJOR INTEREST

Scuba diving and snorkeling
Washington/Slagbaai National Park
Bird-watching around salt ponds

In fact, most photos from the tiny island are of its underwater vistas, complete with dramatically colorful coral and fish. Above the waterline, however, the island is a desert landscape of cactus and succulents.

The Arawak Indians inhabited Bonaire for many centuries, and the island took its name from the Arawak word *bo-nah,* meaning "low country." Amerigo Vespucci landed here in 1499, and in the late 16th and early 17th centuries Spain sought to colonize the island. In 1634, the Dutch took over and developed salt production and some agriculture. The British occupied Bonaire for a brief time in the early 1800s, but the Dutch soon regained control. The late 1800s and early 1900s were bad years for the economy of Bonaire, but by the mid-20th century the salt pans—and tourism—contributed to a solid recovery.

If it weren't for the underwater attractions of this reef-protected island, though, Bonaire even today would hardly be more than the deserted salt ponds that are a nesting ground for thousands of long-legged pink flamingos. But, as chance would have it, the placid waters just

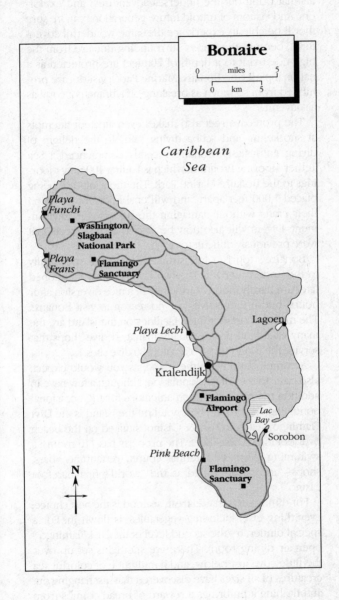

Bonaire

miles   0 — 5

km   0 — 5

*Caribbean
Sea*

■ *Playa
Funchi*

■ **Washington/
Slagbaai
National Park**

■ *Playa
Frans*

■ **Flamingo
Sanctuary**

● *Lagoen*

Playa Lechi ■

Kralendijk ●

■ **Flamingo
Airport**

*Lac
Bay*

● **Sorobon**

Pink Beach ■

**Flamingo
Sanctuary** ■

N

offshore abound with the magnificent creatures and cor-als that bring out the undersea adventurers and explor-ers. And visitors of untold future generations can be sure they'll be able to experience the same wonderful adven-tures, because the waters surrounding Bonaire from the high-tide mark to a depth of 200 feet are protected as a national park (the **Bonaire Marine Park**); visitors are pro-hibited from so much as breaking off a branch of coral as a souvenir.

The protective reef also makes even amateur attempts at snorkeling and scuba diving safe. To the delight of diving enthusiasts, Bonaire recently commenced a Sea Tether Mooring Program, which is adding 100 new moor-ings to the Bonaire Marine Park. The moorings are being placed 1,000 feet apart, and will enable divers to station their crafts without damaging the underwater environ-ment. Divers will also now be able to explore reefs that were previously difficult to reach.

Bonaire's tourism infrastructure is geared specifically to the underwater set. The two hotel-casinos mentioned later are hardly Monte Carlo; they're a nice diversion after hours, but in themselves are no reason to visit Bonaire. The most important tourist facilities on the island are the many excellent, professionally managed dive shops that service the island's approximately 80 dive sites.

Accommodations on the island, as you would expect, also cater to the "dive" population, although a few have in addition the more common amenities for the occasional nondiving visitor. The best hotel on the island is the **Divi Flamingo Beach Resort & Casino**, situated on the beach overlooking Calabas Reef. The property has 110 rooms, a swimming pool, two tennis courts, restaurants, bars, shops—and what's billed as the "world's first barefoot casino."

For dining on Bonaire, fresh seafood is the best choice; everything else, including vegetables, is flown in. For a special dinner, try the second level of the Divi Flamingo's open-air dining room. There are spotlights set up over the little cove just below, and a multitude of colorful sea creatures of all sizes have discovered that just hanging out and flashing a fin brings a reward of bread crumbs from fascinated diners above. Adjacent to the Divi Flamingo is the 40-room Club Flamingo, which has a complete diving operation.

The **Bonaire Beach Hotel & Casino** is the island's other large (145-room) full-service hotel. The Bonaire Beach Hotel, on the Playa Lechi beach, is the site of Bonaire Scuba Center. Adjacent to the Bonaire Beach Hotel is the **Den Laman Seafood Restaurant and Aquarium**, where you can pick your own lobster from the tank.

Smaller hotels and rental condominiums are available to those who really just want to dive and don't require additional services and facilities. Among these is **Cap'n Don's Habitat & Hamlet**, a casual, rustic dive resort with a conglomeration of 46 cottages and villas.

The 16-room **Sorobon Beach Naturist Resort**, on a peninsula in Lac Bay on the Caribbean side of the island, is a choice for those who appreciate a clothes-optional policy. The property includes rustic chalets, a casual restaurant, and a private beach; guests staying at other hotels who want to spend some beach time *au naturel* can utilize the Sorobon's beach for a small daily fee.

Kralendijk

Kralendijk, the capital city of Bonaire, is a sedate little village without the hustle and bustle of other Caribbean cities. The city and its suburbs are home to 1,500 Bonaireans; what little activity there is is primarily geared to residents rather than visitors.

Most of Kralendijk's action is centered on the two main streets, Kaya Grandi and Kaya C.E.B. Hellmund, and revolves around the retail stores, the government buildings, and Plaza Reina Wilhelmina (Queen Wilhelmina Plaza).

The shopping area here is picturesque, with quaint, colorful architecture. Shops of interest to visitors include the **Arie Boutique**, which carries Dutch china and some souvenir-type items, and **Littman Jewelers** and **Spritzer & Furman**, both known for their selections of jewelry, crystal, and fine china. Dynamite Discobar carries records and tapes featuring local music.

The diving on Bonaire is so good that the island attracts aficionados of all kinds. Black-tie formals and gourmet dining are foreign to Bonaire, and the moneyed set that comes here doesn't turn up its nose at dining with dive enthusiasts who think "formal" means the pair of jeans that hasn't yet been cut off.

Most of the island's handful of restaurants are located

in Kralendijk. Continental dining is offered at the **Bistro Des Amis**, and the **China Garden** serves up lunch and dinner in a restored Bonairean mansion. One of the newest restaurants is **Le Chic**, with a French kitchen turning out full-course dinners as well as "grazing" types of snacks. Seafood is the order at the **Zeezicht Bar and Restaurant**, overlooking the harbor from its pleasant waterfront location.

Out on the Island

Other than diving and just lazing in the sun, there is little other activity on Bonaire, unless you insist on a half-day tour that takes in the **salt ponds**, which are a good source of income for the island and also serve as a haven for flamingos (which are here protected as a natural resource). Nearby the salt ponds there are a few historic slave cottages, now open to visitors.

The best beaches on Bonaire include the public **Playa Lechi**, which is slated for some commercial development; the white-sand beach at the Bonaire Beach Hotel, next to the Playa Lechi; and pristine, secluded **Pink Beach**, located a couple of miles south of the airport. You may also want to tour the **Washington/Slagbaai National Park**, a protected haven for the fragile plant and animal life of the island. Bonaireans have long been sensitive to environmental preservation, recognizing that conservation is beneficial to the overall welfare of the island. The park's 15,000 acres, with desertlike topography, were the first official wildlife sanctuary in the Netherlands Antilles.

Birders will delight in seeking out the 130 species to be found within the park's boundaries, including great numbers of flamingos. Lizards, goats, donkeys, and sea turtles also roam the area. Two well-marked driving routes meander through the park, although the roads are a bit rugged.

Nondivers can also water-ski, using the facilities at the Dive Inn, one of the island's top water-sports' operators; sail, either on a sunfish rented through the Bonaire Scuba Center or the Dive Inn, or on a crewed day trip, which can be arranged through most of the hotels; wind-surf, with instructions, at the Bonaire Scuba Center; and go deep-sea fishing on a boat chartered through the Divi

Flamingo Beach Resort. Arrangements can also be made through the Bonaire Scuba Center (Tel: 8448). Chris Morkos at the Piscatur Fishing Store (Tel: 8774) runs half- and full-day trips, at prices that include gear, bait, and refreshments. Dive Bonaire (Tel: 8285) also offers complete outfitting with charters. The Bonaire Beach Hotel has two tennis courts, and it also rents bicycles, as does the Flamingo Beach Hotel.

USEFUL FACTS

Getting In
Most travellers connect to Bonaire via ALM from Aruba or Curaçao; several major carriers, including Eastern and American, provide frequent service to Aruba and Curaçao. ALM also has direct, nonstop flights to Bonaire twice a week from Miami and once a week from New York. American has direct service from San Juan. From New York, Avensa has one flight a week with a connection in Caracas.

Bonaire has no public buses, so you'll have to rely on taxis or a rental car to reach your hotel. Taxicabs are unmetered, but typical fares from the airport are $5 to Kralendjik; $4 to the Flamingo Beach Hotel; and $8 to the Bonaire Beach Hotel.

Entry Requirements
U.S. and Canadian citizens must have a passport or other proof of citizenship, such as a birth certificate or voter's registration card. British subjects must have a "British Visitors" passport. Passports are required for all other travellers. All visitors must have a confirmed room reservation and a return or continuing ticket. There is a departure tax of $5.75.

Getting Around
Major car rental firms operating in Bonaire include Budget and Avis. You'll also find several local companies, including AB Car Rental, Flamingo, Sunray, and Tropical. Drivers licenses from all other countries are valid; driving is on the right. Taxis can be identified on the street by a "TX" designation on the license plate. Stores and restaurants will order taxis for you.

Language
Papiamento (a local dialect endemic to the Netherlands Antilles) and Dutch; English and Spanish are also widely spoken.

Currency
The Netherlands Antilles florin (also called guilder) is tied to the U.S. dollar, and fluctuates in relation to other currencies according to that current value. U.S. dollars are widely accepted.

Electrical Current
127/220 volts; 50 cycles AC. American- and Canadian-made appliances should work, albeit slowly.

Business Hours
Stores are generally open from 8:00–noon and 2:00–6:00, Monday–Saturday. Stores may be open for a few hours on Sundays when cruise ships are in port. Banks are open from 8:30–noon and 2:00–4:00, Monday–Friday.

Festivals
The biggest annual events in Bonaire are Carnival (with festivities taking place over the two weekends prior to Ash Wednesday); and the week-long Annual Sailing Regatta, with top-class sailing and windsurfing races in October. For a week in mid-June the focus is on underwater photography, with the Nikonos Shoot-Out competition (sponsored by Nikon Camera), which offers a variety of prizes.

ACCOMMODATIONS REFERENCE
The rate ranges given here are projections for fall 1988 through spring 1989. Unless otherwise indicated, rates are for double rooms, double occupancy. The telephone area code for Bonaire is 599-7.

▶ **Bonaire Beach Hotel & Casino.** P.O. Box 34, Bonaire, N.A. $110–$120, winter; $70–$90, summer, C.P. Tel: 8448; in U.S., (212) 840-6636 or (800) 223-9815.

▶ **Cap'n Don's Habitat & Hamlet.** P.O. Box 88, Bonaire, N.A. Rates start at $512 a week. Tel: 8290; Telex: 1280BON; in U.S., (305) 373-3331 or (800) 327-6709; in The Netherlands, (70) 644-938.

▶ **Divi Flamingo Beach Resort & Casino.** Kralendijk, Bonaire, N.A. $90–$180, winter; $60–$90, summer. Tel: 8285; Telex: 4442016; in U.S. and Canada, (800) 367-3484; in the U.K., (452) 813-551.

▶ **Sorobon Beach Naturist Resort.** P.O. Box 14, Bonaire, N.A. $85 for a studio–$120, for a one-bedroom chalet, winter; $55–$75, summer. Tel: 8080; Telex: 1280.

▶ **Condominium rentals** are available on Bonaire. For information, contact the Bonaire Government Tourist Office, 275 7th Ave., New York, NY 10001; (212) 242-7707; the Bonaire Tourist Information Office, 815-A Queen St., Toronto, Ontario M4M 1H8; (416) 465-2958; or the Bonaire Government Tourist Bureau in Bonaire on Kaya Grandi in Kralendjik, 8322 or 8649.

CURACAO

By Jeanne Westphal

Curaçao has all of the ingredients for a relaxing holiday in the sun—fine beaches, good food and accommodations, shopping bargains, pleasant climate (80 degrees all year—and no hurricane season), and friendly people. However, it does have something special that sets it apart from other Caribbean islands—a European flavor that reflects its Dutch heritage. It is everywhere: in the architecture, which tends toward Dutch gable buildings colorfully painted in bright pastel colors; in rijsttafel and Amstel beer; in the sense of order and cleanliness; and in the language. The cosmopolitan population is a melting pot of Dutch, British, Spanish, Portuguese, French, West and East Indians, Hindus, and Chinese.

Curaçao also has a strategic location in the Caribbean. The island's proximity to its Latin American neighbors has made it an important trading center for transshipment of products from all parts of the world, as well as a haven for offshore companies. Its port is the seventh largest in the world and handles a steady flow of cruise and cargo ships, especially the large supertankers that carry oil from the refinery outside of Willemstad, the capital. Tourism, however, is now sharing the limelight with trade. Both the government and private sectors are spending millions of dollars on improvements to existing hotels and beaches, development of new attractions, and new resort hotels, not only in Willemstad but on the completely undeveloped northwestern end of the island as well. This rugged countryside (*cunucu*) has a charm all its own: cactus 20 feet high; the unbelievable divi-divi tree, with its branches always at right angles to its trunk;

thatched huts; wild goats; and the handsome *land-huizen,* old plantation houses, many of which are being restored. It has an "old west" flavor not found on any other island in the Caribbean.

Now that its house is in order, Curaçao is emerging cautiously from its cocoon into the world of international tourism.

MAJOR INTEREST

Dutch food and atmosphere
Historic Willemstad
Christoffel Park
Curaçao Underwater Park
Curaçao Seaquarium

Discovered by Alonso de Ojeda in 1499, Curaçao was occupied by the Dutch in 1634. It subsequently became a haven for Spanish and Portuguese immigrants, especially Jews fleeing the Inquisition. Peter Stuyvesant governed the island in 1642, before becoming governor of New Amsterdam (later renamed New York). Despite several brief interludes, the Dutch ruled the island until 1954, when it achieved autonomy.

Only 35 miles north of the coast of Venezuela, Curaçao has a total area of 180 square miles (about eight times the size of Manhattan). It is the seat of government of the Netherlands Antilles (the other island members of which are Aruba, Bonaire, St. Eustatius, and Saba). While the islands are autonomous, the Kingdom of the Netherlands assumes responsibility for their defense, foreign affairs, and observance of human rights.

Willemstad

The capital of the island of Curaçao and of the Netherlands Antilles, Willemstad is a city of charm and color. It is a painting come to life with its pastel-painted 17th-century Dutch-style buildings facing the busy harbor and the harbor's floating market of schooners from Venezuela, Colombia, and other islands selling produce and fish. St. Anna Bay, at the entrance to the Port of Curaçao, divides Willemstad into two parts. The eastern side, called Punda, is where the majority of tourism and business activities take

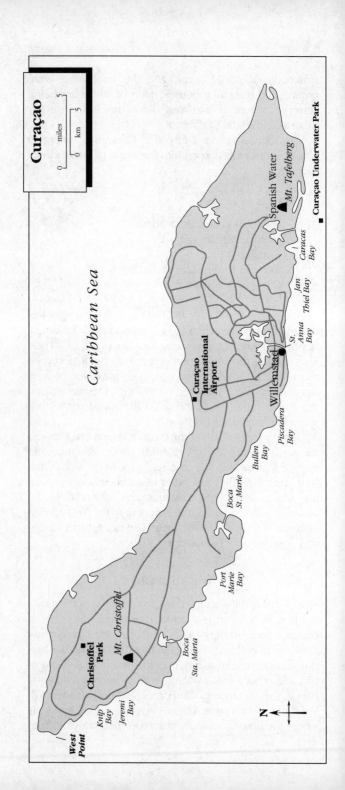

place, and in Otrabanda, on the western side, a number of historic buildings dating back to the 1600s have been restored for offices and shops. The two sides are connected by the Queen Emma pontoon bridge, which swings open at least 30 times a day to allow cruise and cargo ships enroute to the port to pass. If the bridge is open, you can cross the bay on the free pedestrian ferry anchored at the waterfront, next to the floating market on the Punda side.

The majority of Willemstad's shops are located in a six-block area on the Punda side. Some front the harbor, and all are within walking distance of the Curaçao Plaza Hotel. The hotel is built on the site of an old fortification, Waterfort, at the entrance to the harbor. The boutiques and restaurants of an adjacent new shopping complex, **Waterfort Arches**, occupy the prison cells of the old fort. The **Curaçao Plaza Hotel and Casino**, the tallest building in town, has views of both the bay and the Caribbean. It is one of the few hotels in the world that, because of its location, carries marine collision insurance. The 254-room hotel has all the amenities to attract both tourists and business travellers: a swimming pool, meeting facilities, a casino, shops, and a fine rooftop restaurant, the **Penthouse**, with spectacular views of the city and harbor. Guests at the hotel can make arrangements to swim or dive at one of the nearby beaches.

The **Mikve Israel-Emanuel Synagogue**, located in the shopping area at 29 Hanchi Snoa, near Columbusstraat, is the oldest synagogue in the Western Hemisphere in continual use. It was dedicated in 1732. Visitors are welcome to attend services, and the synagogue's courtyard museum houses replicas of the oldest and most elaborate gravestones from the island's Bet Chayim Cemetery, which dates from 1659.

Curaçao has its share of the forts the Dutch built to protect their harbors. Some eventually became office buildings of the government, as was the case with **Fort Amsterdam**, just to the north of the Curaçao Plaza Hotel. This was the most important of Curaçao's eight forts, and when it was completed in 1637 it became the seat of government of the Netherlands Antilles, which it continues to be. If Parliament is in session, you can watch island government in action.

On the Otrabanda side, the Riffort, built in 1828, served as a lodging for U.S. noncommissioned officers during World War II. The **Bistro Le Clochard** restaurant is located in the vaults of the fort, and one of its rooms looks out on the harbor. Also in the Otrabanda area is the **Curaçao Museum**, with interesting artifacts of the Caiquetios Indians, who were the first settlers on the island.

The **Avila Beach Hotel**, only five minutes from the Punda side of Willemstad and the Curaçao Plaza Hotel, is located in a lovely residential area, and is popular with visitors who want to be close to town and still be on a beach. Formerly the country home of one of the island's governors, the hotel retains the atmosphere of a private home. Its 45 rooms are comfortably furnished, and some have views of the sea. The outdoor restaurant, overlooking the beach, is one of the best in town. Next door is the **Octagon House Museum**, originally owned by the sisters of Simon Bolivar and filled with memorabilia from the time of his visit in 1812.

The cuisine of Curaçao can be characterized as a truly international blend of flavors, reflective of the various cultural backgrounds of the people who now call the island home—Creole, Dutch, Indonesian, Chinese, French, Swiss, and South American. The various dishes all make good use of fish and fresh produce, much of it imported from nearby Venezuela.

One of the most popular and exciting dining experiences to be had on Curaçao is an authentic Indonesian rijsttafel (rice table), featuring a variety of numerous side dishes of meat, fish, chicken, pork, and more. The **Garuda Restaurant** at the Seaquarium on the southeastern coast and the **Restaurant Indonesia** at Mercuriusstraat 13, in the Salina residential area of Willemstad, are the best places to try rijsttafel. Both are located only ten minutes from downtown and 15 minutes from hotels in the Piscadera Bay area.

Local specialties include *erwtensoep,* a hearty pea soup flavored with meat, and *keshi yena,* an Edam cheese stuffed with meat or fish and baked. Beer is the most popular drink on the island, and the locally brewed Amstel should be your choice. For after dinner there is, of course, the world-famous, locally produced Curaçao liqueur, made from the skins of local oranges. (There are free tours of the local liqueur plants.)

Other dining experiences not to be missed on Curaçao are: the **Wine Cellar**, an intimate (only eight tables) hideaway a few minutes from the Curaçao Plaza. The menu and wine list are extensive. **Fort Nassau**, which occupies the ruins of an old fort perched high above Willemstad, affords a view of the entire city and harbor. The dining choices here include Dutch, local, and international specialties. A disco, **Infinity**, is part of the Fort Nassau complex. The elegant **La Bistroelle**, in the Promenade Shopping Plaza about 15 minutes northeast of downtown, has French selections, such as bouillabaisse, escargots, and crepes suzette. **De Taveerne**, near La Bistroelle at Landhuis Groot Davelaar, is a historic spot on a former estate, decorated with antiques that belonged to the original owners. De Taveerne features continental cuisine and is easily accessible from anywhere around Willemstad.

While the number of hotels on Curaçao is limited, there is enough variety to satisfy the wishes of a visitor looking either for a lot of activity or none at all. All of the hotels outside of downtown Willemstad are located on the south shore of the island facing the Caribbean and are easily accessible to the city center (approximately ten minutes) and the airport (20 minutes).

For the true resort atmosphere, **Curaçao Caribbean Hotel-Casino**, with 200 rooms, is the best choice. The hotel has a private beach on Piscadera Bay, a pool, tennis courts, water sports, a shopping arcade, an open-air dining room, a gourmet restaurant, and a casino. Special activities and entertainment for the guests are also provided, and there is a free shuttle bus to Willemstad throughout the day. Next door to the Curaçao Caribbean is **Las Palmas Hotel and Vacation Village**, a combination of 100 hotel rooms and 84 two-bedroom villas with fully equipped kitchens. The beach on Piscadera Bay is only a five-minute walk away. There is a complete program of water sports, plus tennis courts and two swimming pools—one for adults and a smaller one for children. There is a snack bar at the beach, and a restaurant, casino, coffee shop, mini-market, and bar with nighttime entertainment in the hotel. Both hotels are adjacent to the new International Trade Center, used for major conventions and special events.

Another good choice for a beach hotel is the 204-room

Princess Beach Hotel and Casino. Located five minutes from Willemstad on the beach at Jan Thiel, it is a diver's paradise because of its proximity to the Seaquarium and the Curaçao Underwater Park. It is also the headquarters for the annual International Windsurfing Competition, held in late May. In addition to its own beach, it has a swimming pool, tennis courts, a sauna, a dive shop, a new nightclub with local and international entertainment, and a casino and lounge area.

Out on the Island

There are two sides to the island of Curaçao. As you drive toward the northwestern end, there is a feeling of openness and wide vistas of rugged coastline and desertlike landscapes. Along the route, you will see a number of old estate houses that have been restored and are open to the public. One of particular interest is the **Landhuis Ascension**, in the town of the same name, used by the Dutch Navy as a rest-and-relaxation center. The sailors host an "open house" on the first Sunday of every month. At the Landhuis Savonet, a few miles farther west, is the entrance to **Christoffel Park**, originally three private plantations and now totalling 4,500 acres.

Opened to the public in 1978, the park provides a choice of three driving tours and one walking tour, on each of which visitors can enjoy the breathtaking views of the countryside and sea. The hearty can try the three-hour climb to the top of Mt. Christoffel. Flora and fauna abound everywhere, including two species of rare orchids, the ever-present divi-divi tree, and the sabal palm. The protected wildlife here includes the shy Curaçao deer and a variety of birds, among them the Curaçao barn owl.

The return trip takes you through the picturesque fishing village of West Point and continues along the southern coast past the beach coves of Jeremi, Boca Sta. Marta, Port Marie Bay, Boca Sint Marie, and the Curaçao Oil Terminal at Bullen Bay. (There is certain to be at least one supertanker at dockside.) Of the 38 beaches on the island, the best are along the western, or Caribbean, side. On the northern end, about 45 minutes from Willemstad, the most popular public beaches are West Point (with a nice outdoor restaurant), Knip, and Klein Knip. Due to the volcanic nature of this part of the island (Mount Christoffel in the western part of the island rises 1,239 feet) the beaches are generally dark gray, but the swimming and diving are very good. Changing facilities are limited. In the south, where most of the hotels are located, there is excellent swimming at Piscadera Bay and Jan Thiel.

As you approach Willemstad, end your day with a visit to either the Amstel Brewery, to sample the only beer in the world made from distilled seawater, or to the Curaçao Liqueur Distillery.

Curaçao is a new name in diving circles with the opening, in December 1983, of the **Curaçao Underwater Park**. Some 12½ miles of coral reefs stretch along the park's watery acreage off the southeastern end of the island, only ten minutes from the capital city of Willemstad and the major hotels. An underwater nature trail has been charted for snorkelers and, for more experienced divers, there are more than 20 marked dive sites. The general visibility is 60 to 80 feet, and sometimes up to 150 feet. No harpooning, spear fishing, or breaking or removing of coral is permitted. Wrecks of ships have been added to the underwater landscape to add adventure to discovery.

The nearby Curaçao **Seaquarium** was opened in 1985 and is considered to be one of the world's most natural habitats for sea life outside of the ocean itself. The exhibition area has 75 aquariums that range in capacity from 750 to 2,500 gallons, creating a natural environment for exotic tropical fish and colorful coral. There is a shark channel and natural holding "pools" for dolphins, seals, and sea turtles, as well as facilities for swimming and wind surfing and a complete dive center for trips to the Curaçao Underwater Park. For nondivers, there are glass-bottom boat excursions to the park.

Caracas Bay, also on the southern end of the island, is where the large cruise ships tie up. Nearby is the site of Fort Beekenburg, with its perfectly preserved battle tower, and Mt. Tafelberg, a mountain of phosphate overlooking **Spanish Water**, a lagoon east of Willemstad that is the island's headquarters for the boating community.

USEFUL FACTS

What to Wear

Light, casual clothing is acceptable almost everywhere on the island; visitors who are conducting business or plan to frequent some of the more elegant restaurants and nightspots will want to bring along somewhat more formal clothing.

Getting In

The major airlines serving Curaçao include: ALM, from Miami, New York, and San Juan; American, from New York; Eastern, from Miami; KLM, from Amsterdam.

Taxicabs provide the easiest means of getting from the airport to most of Curaçao's hotels; the cost usually ranges from $10 to $15. The central phone number for taxis is 84-574/5.

Entry Requirements

U.S. and Canadian citizens need proof of citizenship (passport, birth certificate, or voter-registration card). British subjects need a British Visitor's passport (available at any post office), but not a regular passport. Visas are not necessary for stays of less than three months. There is a departure tax of $5.75.

Currency

The Netherlands Antilles florin (or guilder) is tied to the U.S. dollar.

Electrical Current

Same as in the U.S. and Canada—110–130 volts AC, 50 cycles.

Getting Around

Public buses are inexpensive, convenient, and can be boarded at specially marked bus stops. Taxis are unmetered, so you should come to an agreement with the driver before embarking on a trip. Most hotels offer complimentary shuttle buses into central Willemstad.

Business Hours

Banks are open 8:30–noon and 1:30–4:30 on weekdays. Stores are generally open Monday–Saturday, 8:00–noon and 2:00–6:00. When cruise ships are in port, some shops also open on Sunday.

Festivals

The **Curaçao Jewish Festival**, held in January, highlights the origins of the island's Jewish heritage with events organized by members of the local Jewish community; Curaçao's version of Carnival, at the beginning of Lent, is the largest and most raucous festival on the island, with a parade and much music and revelry; in late May there is a windsurfing tournament; the Simon Bolivar Regatta between Venezuela and Curaçao is held in August; and the Sunfish sailing championships are in September.

ACCOMMODATIONS REFERENCE

The rate ranges given here are projections for fall 1988 through spring 1989. Unless otherwise indicated, rates are for double rooms, double occupancy. The telephone area code for Curaçao is 599-9. All addresses for Curaçao are in the Netherlands Antilles (N.A.).

▶ **Avila Beach Hotel.** 130-134 Penstraat, Willemstad, Curaçao. $78–$98. Tel: 61-4377; in U.S., (402) 498-4300 or (800) 448-8355 (except Nebraska).

▶ **Curaçao Caribbean Hotel-Casino.** J.F.K. Blvd., P.O. Box 2133, Willemstad, Curaçao. $130–$170. Tel: 62-5000; in U.S., (312) 452-4333 or (800) 444-1010.

▶ **Curaçao Plaza Hotel and Casino.** Plaza Piar 229, Willemstad, Curaçao. $70–$145. Tel: 961-2500; in U.S., (212) 661-4540 or (800) 223-1558 (except New York State); in Canada, (800) 531-6767.

▶ **Las Palmas Hotel and Vacation Village.** Piscadera Bay, P.O. Box 2179, Willemstad, Curaçao. $98–$115; villas, $115–$135. Tel: 62-5200; in U.S., (203) 849-1470 or (800) 622-7836; in Canada, (416) 366-9041; in U.K., (01) 568-9144.

▶ **Princess Beach Hotel and Casino.** Dr. Martin Luther King Blvd. 8, Willemstad, Curaçao. $80–$140. Tel: 61-4944.

ARUBA

By Jeanne Westphal

In a part of the world that is known for its spectacular beaches, Aruba has some of the best. For the most part, it is the beaches that draw travellers to this Dutch Caribbean island off the coast of Venezuela, but visitors also enjoy varied nightlife, shopping, dining, and water sports. Add to that a pleasant and hospitable populace with origins from around the globe and a willingness to make visitors feel comfortable in their own language, whether it's English, Spanish, Dutch, or even French and Portuguese.

MAJOR INTEREST

Palm Beach
Smaller secluded beaches
Dutch influence, especially food

The Spanish first came to Aruba in 1499, and the colonial years that followed brought an array of visitors, including a fair share of pirates. In the mid-17th century the Dutch took control of the island, relinquishing their influence—to the English—only for a short time in the early 19th century.

On January 1, 1986, Aruba separated itself from the Netherlands Antilles and became a quasi-independent entity within the Kingdom of the Netherlands. The island is presently governed under a democratic system, with a Governor who is appointed by the Queen of the Kingdom to act as her representative. Today, tourism accounts for the bulk of the Aruban economy (the notorious oil refinery near San Nicolas was shut down in 1985), and the infrastructure is gradually changing as a result. By the end

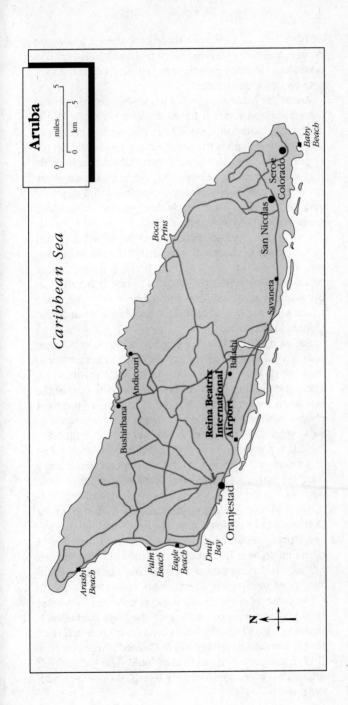

of 1989 the island will have three new casinos, a new golf course, and new hotels managed by Hyatt and Ramada. In addition to tourism growth, new business enterprises are actively being encouraged.

Aruba has made the most of her assets, and has created a sophisticated vacation haven out of a landscape that is otherwise rather unremarkable. The undisputed topographical highlight is the breathtaking seven-mile stretch of pure white powdery sand known as **Palm Beach** on the leeward side of the island. The calm, clear seas there provide exceptional visibility, sometimes to a depth of almost 100 feet. Vistas on Aruba's northeast coast are more rugged and sweeping. Inland, the island is mostly dry, with cacti, rock formations, and the eerie but picturesque beauty of the windblown divi-divi trees. Many visitors to Aruba are surprised to find persistent, strong winds blowing across the island. On one hand, this can occasionally make life uncomfortable; on the other, the winds keep the humidity at a comfortable level, and tend to keep insects away.

Set along Palm Beach are many of the hotels, some with a relaxed atmosphere, others more in keeping with the casinos they house—and the high rollers those attract. The **Golden Tulip Aruba Caribbean** is one of the best-liked resorts on the island and has one of the most elegant casinos, but with 400 rooms it's best suited to those who don't mind being one among the multitudes, including conventioneers. The hotel offers a wide range of services and amenities, including a sports center and a comprehensive fitness center. A couple of other large hotel/casino complexes here are the glitzy Aruba Concorde and the Americana Aruba. The high-rise **Aruba Concorde** faces a pretty stretch of beach and has a swimming pool, restaurants, a casino, tennis courts, and a shopping arcade. The **Americana Aruba** also has its own spacious beach, as well as a casino and nightclub, swimming pool, tennis courts, restaurants, and more.

For those who appreciate the conveniences of a suite, including an equipped kitchenette, the **Playa Linda Beach Resort** is a good choice. It's located on Palm Beach right next to the **Aruba Holiday Inn & Casino**, a large complex (390 rooms) that is well appointed with all of the amenities—water sports, beach, tennis, shopping arcade, and more.

The **Divi Divi Beach Hotel**, on Druif Bay just south of Palm Beach, is pleasant and friendly, and a good choice if you're seeking service and an atmosphere that is more low key than you'll find at larger complexes. The beach views are inspiring, and management is keen on such special touches as fresh flowers and unobtrusive room service. You might also consider the 150-room **Bushiri Beach Hotel**, also on Druif Bay; it serves as a training site for young Arubans entering the hospitality industry. As a result, a stay may require a bit of patience, but the experience can be rewarding and the staff is genuinely eager to please. It recently became the first all-inclusive (everything included) family resort hotel on the island, with special rates for children.

Aruba is known as having some of the best nightlife in the Caribbean, and most of the activity is clustered in and around the island's six casinos. Most of the gaming parlors are located in the hotels. The **Alhambra Casino and Bazaar**, near the Divi Divi, is an exception, a complete entertainment complex.

Oranjestad

The picturesque town of Oranjestad is Aruba's business and shopping hub. It bustles with activity, and is an interesting place to wander on foot and drink in the whimsical Dutch architecture. Most of the shops are located on one street, **Nassaustraad**, with an abundance of Delft china, watches, perfumes, linens, and resort wear at duty-free prices. The enclosed Boulevard Shopping Mall on the harbor has more than 60 shops. In the morning you can stroll along the wharf here and watch fresh fish and produce being unloaded from the boats, or walk down Lloyd G. Smith Boulevard to the waterfront Wilhelmina Park, a showcase for exotic flora.

The gastronomy of Aruba is of top quality and quite diverse, thanks to the peripatetic Dutch. In Aruba's independent restaurants—many here in central Oranjestad—and in the hotel dining rooms you'll find traditional Dutch dishes, Indonesian fare, Latin American-style specialties, Continental cuisine, and Caribbean food. Try some of the local specialties including *pastechis,* small pies filled with shrimp, lamb or beef; *cala,* bean fritters; *sopit,* a hearty fish chowder made with coconut milk; and *keshi yena,* stuffed Edam cheese. Many restaurants also offer a traditional Indonesian rijsttafel (rice table), a meal composed around mountainous portions of rice served with scores of side dishes—meats, vegetables, pickled accompaniments, and more.

One of the most famous of Aruba's restaurants, **The Talk of the Town**, in the Best Western Talk of the Town resort, is deserving of its fine reputation for expertly prepared gourmet meals and a good wine list. The **Bali** restaurant, which occupies a houseboat in a lovely harbor in town, serves up a good rijsttafel. Other restaurants in unique settings include **De Olde Molen**, in an old Dutch windmill just outside of town in the Palm Beach area, and **Papiamento**, which occupies one of Aruba's stately mansions in Oranjestad; both specialize in Continental cuisine. For tapas and seafood, try **Temptation on the Beach**, which you'll find across the street from Talk of the Town.

Out on the Island

The natural bridge along the rugged windward coast just north of Andicouri and south of Bushiribana was formed over the centuries by crashing waves. You can climb to the top of the high sand dunes near Boca Prins and slide down (wear jeans and sneakers). Some caves here have primitive decorations dating to the island's habitation by Arawaks, and others have primitive-looking paintings that are the work of a film crew that shot a movie here recently.

Other points of interest include abandoned gold mines at Bushiribana and Balashi, and the town of Savaneta, the oldest on the island, located between Balashi and San Nicolas. Inquisitive naturalists will enjoy driving through the *cunucu* (countryside), with its varied plant life and abundance of divi-divi trees.

Facilities, equipment, and instruction for a variety of water sports are offered by most of Aruba's resort hotels or by concessionaires on the property. If your hotel doesn't offer your sport of choice, chances are that the staff will be happy to make appropriate arrangements for you. Visibility in the waters off Aruba ranges up to about 100 feet; several sunken freighters just off the coastline make for excellent diving. And the strong tradewinds contribute to the challenging windsurfing conditions that draw afficionados of the sport to Aruba from all over the world.

Anglers can arrange for charter boats from any of a number of operators on Aruba. Typical catches include tuna, bonito, marlin, kingfish, sailfish, and barracuda.

At the **Rancho El Paso**, located close to most of Aruba's hotels, you can rent a horse and go for a one-hour guided ride through the countryside or a two-hour beach ride.

Throughout the year visitors to Aruba can enjoy a diverse array of special events. Every Tuesday evening from May to December the **Bon Bini Festival** in Oranjestad features folkloric entertainment, food, drink, crafts, and general revelry.

For most visitors, though, the key pleasure is simply wandering on the island, which will inevitably lead you to a secluded beach that you can claim as your own for an afternoon picnic—there are lots of them, and they are all public.

Palm Beach, mentioned above as the site of many of Aruba's hotels, is a lovely stretch of sand. You'll also find sparkling **Arashi Beach** to be a pleasant spot for sunning, swimming, and snorkeling. Generally, you can expect pounding surf on the north coast of Aruba, at beaches such as **Boca Prins**; the settings here are inspiring but the currents can be treacherous. On the other end of the spectrum, **Baby Beach**, with its lagoon on the southern tip of the island in Seroe Colorado, is shallow and calm.

Eagle Beach, between Palm Beach and Druif Bay and not far from Oranjestad, is a favorite spot for picnicking.

USEFUL FACTS

What to Wear
Lightweight, casual clothing is recommended for comfort and is suitable for most occasions. Those conducting business in Aruba or planning to visit some of the choicer restaurants and casinos should bring along some dressier clothes as well.

Getting In
The major airlines that serve Aruba with direct flights (check with the airlines or a travel agent for information on other routes available with connections) are: ALM, from Miami and Curaçao; American, from New York and

San Juan; Eastern, from Miami and San Juan; and KLM, from Amsterdam. In Canada, a number of charter flights are available through Toronto and other gateways.

Entry Requirements

U.S. and Canadian citizens must have a passport or other proof of citizenship, such as a birth certificate or voter-registration card. British citizens do not need passports, but must have a British "Visitor's Passport." Visitors from other countries must have passports. Everyone entering the country must have a return or ongoing ticket. There is a departure tax of approximately $9.50.

Language

Papiamento (a local dialect endemic to the Netherlands Antilles) and Dutch; English and Spanish are also widely spoken.

Currency

The Aruba florin; most hotels and the larger shops accept traveller's checks and major credit cards. U.S. currency is widely accepted.

Electrical Current

Same as in the U.S. and Canada—110 volts, 60 cycles.

Getting Around

Rental cars are available from Hertz, Avis, Dollar, Budget, National, Interent, Pelican, Marcos, and JM Car Rental. Driving is on the right. You may drive a car on Aruba with any valid foreign license or with an international driver's license; you must be 21 to rent a car.

Taxis are not metered, so travellers should negotiate rates before embarking on a ride. The approximate cost from the airport to Oranjestad is $7; to the hotels on Palm Beach, approximately $12. (The taxi dispatch office can be reached at 22116 or 21604.) Airport buses also service the hotels, but you must have a prepaid travel coupon (available through your travel agent). Public buses run between Oranjestad and the hotels on Eagle Beach and Palm Beach. Car rentals are also available at the airport.

Business Hours

Most shops are open Monday–Saturday from 8:00–noon

and 2:00–6:30. If a cruise ship is in port, some shops open Sunday mornings. Banks are generally open from 8:00–noon and 1:30–4:00, weekdays.

Festivals

Annual events include the boisterous Carnival celebration, culminating with a big parade on the Sunday before Lent; Queen's Day, on April 30, with parades and sporting events; a wind-surfing festival in May; the Aruba Annual Marathon, held the third weekend in June; an International Fishing Tournament, the first week in November; and the Pan American Race of Champs, a drag race scheduled the second week of November.

ACCOMMODATIONS REFERENCE

The rate ranges given here are projections for fall 1988 through spring 1989. Unless otherwise indicated, rates are for double rooms, double occupancy. The telephone area code for Aruba is 297. All addresses for Aruba are in the Netherlands Antilles (N.A.).

▶ **Americana Aruba Hotel and Casino.** L. G. Smith Boulevard. 83, Palm Beach, Aruba. $90–$160. Tel: 8-24500; In U.S., (212) 661-4540 or (800) 223-1588; in Canada, (800) 531-6767.

▶ **Aruba Concorde Hotel and Casino.** L. G. Smith Boulevard. 77, Palm Beach, Aruba. $100–$250. Tel: 8-24466; in U.S., (800) 223-7944 or (800) 327-4150; in Canada, (416) 665-9500.

▶ **Aruba Holiday Inn and Casino.** L. G. Smith Boulevard. 230, Palm Beach, Aruba. $85–$165. Tel: 8-23600; in U.S. and Canada, (800) HOLIDAY; in U.K. (01) 722-7755.

▶ **Bushiri Beach Hotel.** L. G. Smith Boulevard. 35, Oranjestad, Aruba. $70–$155. Tel: 8-25216; in U.S., (203) 847-9445 or (800) 622-7836.

▶ **Divi Divi Beach Hotel.** L. G. Smith Boulevard 45, Oranjestad, Aruba. $200–$280. Tel: 8-23300; in U.S., (800) 367-3484; in U.K., (452) 813-551.

▶ **Golden Tulip Aruba Caribbean Resort and Casino.** L. G. Smith Boulevard. 81, Palm Beach, Aruba. $115–$240. Tel: 8-33555; in U.S., (212) 486-2996 or (800) 344-1212.

▶ **Playa Linda Beach Resort.** L. G. Smith Boulevard. 83, Oranjestad, Aruba. $180, for up to four people in a suite–$350, for deluxe room accommodating up to six people. Tel: 8-31000; in U.S., (212) 594-5441.

INDEX

Admiral's Inn, 168, 172
Agave Terrace rest., 95
Alcázar, 63
Alexander's rest., 94
Alhambra Casino and Bazaar, 287
Ali-oli rest., 78
Almond Tree Bar and Restaurant, 39
Altos de Chavón, 65
Ambiance shop, 57
Americana Aruba Hotel and Casino, 286, 291
Andromeda Gardens, 225
Anegada, 113
Anguilla, 135–140
Annaberg Sugar Plantation, 101
Annandale, 250
Anse Chastanet Hotel, 214, 218
Anse des Cayes, 129
Antigua, 164–172
The Antiquarian and Trading Co., 47
The Antique Furniture Shop Ltd., 35
Arashi Beach, 289
Arcadia House, 262
Arecibo Observatory, 83
Arie Boutique, 269
Aries Club, 108
Arnos Vale Hotel, 261, 265
Artsibit, 210

Aruba, 284–291
Aruba Concorde Hotel and Casino, 286, 291
Aruba Holiday Inn & Casino, 286, 291
Asa Wright Nature Center and Lodge, 256, 264
Atarazana shops, 63
Atlantis Hotel, 226
Auberge de la Distillerie, 185, 187
Auberge de la Vieille Tour, 181, 187
Au Bon Vivant rest., 94
Au Coin du Port rest., 184
Aux Trois Gourmands, 131
Avila Beach Hotel, 278, 283

Baby Beach, 289
Bagatelle Great House, 224
Bagshaw's shop, 211
Bajan bar, 223
Bakoua Beach hotel, 203, 206
Bali rest., 288
Ballahoo rest., 155
Bamboo Avenue, 38
Banana Bay, 158, 162
Banana Bay Club, 97
Baños de Coamo Parador, 87
Barbados, 219–230
Barbados Museum, 222
Barbados National Trust, 222

Barbuda, 164–172
Bar de l'Oubli, 131
Bartolomeo, 131
Basil's Bar and Raft Restaurant, 240
Basil's Bar and Restaurant, 235
Basse-Terre, 185
Basseterre, 155
La Bateliere, 200, 206
Bath Hotel, 161
The Baths, 111
Bathsheba, 225
Baxter's Road, 223
Bay Gardens, 250
Le Bec Fin, 120
Belham Valley, 176
Belham Valley Restaurant, 176
La Belle Creole, 123, 125
La Belle Creole, 252
Bequia, 238–239
Best of Barbados shop, 222
Bibliothèque Schoelcher, 198
La Biguine, 199
Biras Creek, 112, 116
Bistro Des Amis, 270
La Bistroelle, 279
Bistro Le Clochard, 278
The Bitter End Yacht Club, 112, 116
Blackbeard's Castle, 94, 103
Bloody Bay, 26
Blue Crab rest., 261
Bluefields Bay Villas, 37, 50
Blue Horizons hotel, 252
Blue Lagoon, 45
Blue Lagoon rest., 45
Blue Mountain Inn, 48
Blue Waters hotel, 167, 171
Blue Waters Inn, 262, 265
Boca Prins beach, 289
Bolivar Bookshop and Gallery, 47
Bombay Club, 97
Bonaire, 266–273
Bonaire Beach Hotel & Casino, 269, 272
Bonaire Marine Park, 268
Bon Bini Festival, 289
Boquerón, 82
Boston Bay, 45

The Bottom, 143
Bridgetown, 221
Brimstone Hill, 156
British Virgin Islands, 105–117
Bromley Estate, 40
Buccament Valley, 237
The Buccaneer Hotel, 98, 104
Buccoo Reef, 260
Buck Island, 97
El Buren, 64
Bushiri Beach Hotel, 287, 291
Butterfly People Gallery, 76

Cabarete, 66
Cabrits, 193
Cadet-Daniel shop, 198
Calabash hotel, 247, 252
Calle Las Damas, 63
Camuy Caves, 83
El Canario hotel, 79, 86
El Canario by the Sea hotel, 79, 86
Cane Bay Plantation, 100, 104
Caneel Bay, 102, 104
La Canne à Sucre, 182
Cap Haitien, 58
Cap Juluca, 137, 140
Cap'n Don's Habitat & Hamlet, 269, 272
Captain Hook's Hideaway, 215
Captains' Quarters, 144, 146
Carambola rest., 225
Carambola Beach Resort & Golf Club, 100, 104
Caravanserai hotel, 126
Caravelle/Club Med, 185, 187
Caribbean Casseroles, 107
Caribe Hilton International, 78, 86
Caribelle Batiks, 156
Carib Indian Reservation, 194
Carinosa Gardens, 40
Caroni Wildlife Sanctuary, 258
Carriacou, 250–251
Casa Blanca, 74
Casa de Campo hotel, 65, 68
Casa del Francés hotel, 83, 87
Casa del Libro, 76
Casanova Restaurant, 39
Castelets hotel, 131, 133

Castries, 209
Cathedral of St. John the Divine, 167
Cathedral of Santa Maria la Menor, 64
Cayman Brac, 23
Cayman Islands, 21–29
Centre d'Art Paul Gauguin, 201
Charlestown, 158
Charlo's rest., 215
Charlotte Amalie, 93
Chart House, 79
Charthouse, 212
Chef Tell's Grand Old House, 24
Chez Clara, 186
Le Chic, 270
China Garden, 270
Christ Church, 227
Christiansted, 96
Christoffel Park, 280
Chukka Cove hotel, 41, 50
Cinnamon Bay, 101
Cinnamon Reef Beach Club, 140
Citadelle La Ferrière, 58
Clarence House, 169
The Cloud's Nest Hotel, 217
Club Comanche, 97, 104
Club Lafayette, 131
Coal Pot rest., 212
Coamo, 83
Cobblers Cove hotel, 224, 230
Coccoloba Plantation, 137, 140
Cockleshell rest., 166
Coco-Bef Restaurant, 216
Coco Point Lodge, 170, 171
Cocrico Inn, 261
Codrington, 169
Coffee and Cream, 227
Coki Beach, 95
Colombier, 130
Colony Club, 230
Columbus Square, 210
El Comandante Racetrack, 80
Condado Beach Hotel, 79, 86
Condado Plaza Hotel & Casino, 79, 86
Condado Strip, 78
Cool Corner, 150

Copper and Lumber Store hotel, 172
Coral Reef Club, 224, 230
Corossol, 130
Cotton House hotel, 240, 244
Cove Castles, 140
Coyaba hotel, 247, 252
Crab Hole shop, 239
Cracked Conch rest., 24
Crane Beach, 227, 230
Creque Dam Road, 100
Cristo Chapel, 76
Croney's Old Manor Estate, 160, 162
Cruz Bay, 101
Culebra, 84
Cunard La Toc Suites, 218
Curaçao, 274–283
Curaçao Caribbean Hotel-Casino, 279, 283
Curaçao Museum, 278
Curaçao Plaza Hotel and Casino, 277, 283
Curaçao Underwater Park, 281
Curtain Bluff hotel, 169, 171

Darkwood Beach, 168
Darkwood Beach Bar, 168
DeMontevin Lodge, 44
Den Laman Seafood Restaurant and Aquarium, 269
De Olde Molen rest., 288
La Desirade, 183, 187
Le d'Esnambuc rest., 199
De Taveerne, 279
Devil's Grotto, 26
Devon House, 48
Diamond Estate, 215
Dickenson Bay, 166
Le Diplomat rest., 24
Divi Divi Beach Hotel, 287, 291
Divi Flamingo Beach Resort & Casino, 268, 273
Dominica, 188–195
Dominican Republic, 61–69
Donald Schnell Studio, 101
Donn's rest., 97
Dorado Naco, 66, 68
Duggan's Reef, 98

Eagle Beach, 289
Eden Rock, 26
El Embajador hotel, 68
Emerald Pool, 194
Emeraude Plage, 134
Empress Oceanfront, 80, 87
Eunice's rest., 94
Eurotel Playa Dorada, 66, 68
Evergreen Hotel, 192, 195

Falls of Baleine, 237
Farley Hill, 225
Filao Beach Hotel, 134
Firefly House, 244
Fisherman's Wharf, 221
Folichon, 37, 51
La Fortaleza, 74
Fort Amsterdam, 277
Fort Bay, 143
Fort Burt, 108, 116
Fort Christian, 93
Fort-de-France, 198
Fort King George, 260
Fort Nassau, 279
Fort St. George, 176
Fort Young Hotel, 190, 195
The Fountains, 138
Fountain Valley, 100
Fox's Bay Bird Sanctuary, 176
François Plantation, 130
Frangipani Hotel, 239, 244
Frank's rest., 97
Frederiksted, 99
Frenchman's Cay, 116
Frenchman's Cove, 46
The French Restaurant, 237
Frenchtown, 94
Frigate Bay, 157
Frigate Bird Sanctuary, 170

Los Galanes, 77
Galeria San Juan, 76
Galerie Trois Visages, 57
Gallery of West Indian Art, 34
Galway's Soufrière, 175
Garden Loggia Café, 24
Garuda Restaurant, 278
George Town, 25
Georgian House, 155
Gingerbread shop, 57

Gîte des Deux Mamelles, 186
Gîtes Ruraux de Guadeloupe, 187
Goblin Hill villa, 45
Golden Lemon hotel, 157, 162
Golden Rock Estates, 159, 162
Golden Tulip Aruba Caribbean Resort and Casino, 286, 291
Good Hope Plantation, 40, 51
Gosier, 181
Grand Anse Beach, 247
Grand Case, 124
Grand Case Beach Club, 126
Grand Cayman, 21–29
Grand Etang Forest Reserve, 250
Grande-Terre, 181
Grand Hotel Oloffson, 57, 60
Grand Pavilion Hotel, 23, 29
Grand View Beach Hotel, 234, 244
Gran Hotel Lina, 64, 68
Grassy Point, 98
Greenwood, 40
Grenada, 245–253
Grenadines, 231–244
Grencraft, 248
Gros Islet, 212
Guadeloupe, 179–187
Guanahani, 130, 133
Guana Island Club, 113, 116
Guavaberry-Spring Bay Vacation Homes, 116
Guido's Disco, 145
Gustavia, 131

L'Habitation, 126
Hacienda Gripiñas Parador, 83, 87
Hacienda Juanita Parador, 83, 88
Haiti, 52–60
Half Moon Bay Hotel, 172
Le Hamak, 184, 187
Harmony Hall, 41
Harpoon Saloon, 239
Harrismith beach, 226
Hermitage Plantation hotel, 160, 162
Hibiscus Lodge Hotel, 39, 51

Hilton International Mayagüez, 87
Hodges Bay Club, 166, 171
Hole in the Wall shop, 150
Holetown, 224
Holiday Inn, 87, 259, 264
Horse Shoe Beach, 252
Hostal Nicolás de Ovando, 63, 68
Hostellerie des Trois Forces, 134
Hotel 1829, 94, 103
Hotel Normandie, 259, 264
Hotel Trident, 43
Hull Bay, 95
Hummingbird rest., 215
Hyatt Dorado Beach, 80, 87
Hyatt Regency Cerromar Beach, 80, 87
Hyatt Regency Grand Cayman, 23, 29

Icacos Cay, 83
Ilma's rest., 112
Infinity disco, 279
Institute of Jamaica, 47
Island Harbour, 138
Isla Verde, 80
Ivor Guest House, 46, 51

Jack Tar Village, 66, 68
Jack Tar Village/Royal St. Kitts, 157, 162
Jacmel, 58
Jai Alai rest., 64
Jalousie Plantation, 215
Jamaica, 30–51
Jamaica Inn, 38, 51
Jamaica Pegasus, 46, 51
Jaragua, 68
Jardin de Balata, 200
El Jardin de Jade rest., 65
Jean-Yves Froment shop, 130
Jimmy's rest., 212
Johnnycakes rest., 94
Jolly Beach Hotel, 168, 171
Josef's rest., 227
Jost Van Dyke, 113
Juliana's Apartments, 145, 146
Jumby Bay Resort, 168, 171

Kaliko Beach, 58, 60
Kariwak Village hotel, 261, 265
King Christian Hotel, 104
Kingston, 46
Kingstown, 234
Kralendijk, 269

Lacovia Condominiums, 24, 29
Lafayette Hotel rest., 199
Lance aux Epines, 247
Landhuis Ascension, 280
The Last Stop, 112
Lilyfield, 41, 51
Lina's Restaurant, 64
Little Cayman, 23
Little Dix Bay, 111, 116
Little Switzerland shop, 79
Little Tobago, 260
Littman Jewelers, 269
Long Bay Hotel, 109, 116
Lucy's Harbour View, 137
Luquillo Beach, 81

Mac's Pizzeria, 239
Magens Bay, 95
Mahogany Run, 95
La Maison sur la Plage, 150, 152
Malecón, 65
Malliouhana hotel, 137, 140
La Mallorquina rest., 77
Mama's, 248
Manapany Cottages, 129, 133
Manoir de Beauregard, 204, 206
Man O' War Bay, 260
Maria Islands Nature Reserve, 216
Marie Galante, 183, 187
Marigot, 122
Marigot Bay, 213
Marigot Bay Club, 134
Marina Cay, 110
Marina Cay Hotel, 116
Mariners hotel, 138, 140
Martinique, 196–206
Mayagüez, 82
Mayagüez Hilton, 82
Mayoumba Folkloric Troupe, 138
Mayreau, 241
Meliá Hotel, 87

Mercado Modelo shop, 64
Le Meridien, 184, 187
Le Meridien–Trois-Ilets, 203, 206
Mesopotamia Valley, 236
Middle Quarters, 37
Mikve Israel-Emanuel Synagogue, 277
Miramar, 78
Mrs. Scatliffe's Restaurant, 109
Montaclair shop, 199
Montego Bay Area, 33
Mont Joli, 60
Montpelier Plantation, 160
Montpelier Plantation Inn, 160, 163
Montserrat, 173–178
Montserrat Springs Hotel, 178
Moonraker Lounge, 97
The Moorings, 213
Moorings Mariner Inn, 108, 116
Morne Fendue rest., 249
El Morro, 74
Le Moule, 184
Moulin sur Mer, 58, 60
Mounia shop, 198
Mt. Irvine Bay Hotel, 261, 265
Moxon's rest., 39
Mullet Bay Resort and Casino, 122, 125
Musée d'Art Haitien, 56
Musée de Rhum, 202
Musée Saint-John Perse, 182
Museo de las Casas Reales, 63
Museo del Hombre Dominicana, 64
Museum of Antigua and Barbuda, 167
Mustique, 239–241

Nassaustraad, 287
Necker Island, 114, 116
Negril, 35
Nelson's Dockyard, 168
Nevis, 153–163
Newcastle Pottery, 159
New San Juan, 78
Nisbet Plantation Inn, 159, 163
Nuccio's rest., 39
Nylon Pool, 260

Oasis Parador, 88
Ocean Terrace Inn, 155, 162
Ocho Rios Area, 38
Octagon House Museum, 278
Old Donkey Cart, 261
Olde Yard Inn, 111, 116
Old Gin House, 150, 152
Old Market, 191
Old San Juan, 74
Oranjestad, 147, 287
L'Or et l'Argent shop, 199
Oualie Beach, 159
Outdoor Club of Barbados, 229
Oyster Pond Yacht Club, 122, 125

Pablo Casals Museum, 74
La Pagerie, 203
Palmas del Mar resort, 80, 87
Las Palmas Hotel and Vacation Village, 279, 283
Palm Beach, 286
Palm Island, 241
Palm Island Beach Club, 244
Panthéon National, 56
Papiamento rest., 288
Papillote Wilderness Retreat, 192, 195
Parc Naturel, 185
Parham, 167
Pasanggrahan Royal Guesthouse, 120, 125
El Patio de Sam, 77
Pelican Club, 166
Penthouse rest., 277
Peter Island, 113
Peter Island Yacht Harbor and Hotel, 113, 116
Pétionville, 57
Petit St. Vincent, 242
Petit St. Vincent Resort, 242, 244
Philipsburg, 119
Phosphorescent Bay, 82
Pigeon Island, 212
Pigeon Point, 260
Pineapple Beach, 95
Pine Grove Guest House, 48, 51
Pink Beach, 270
Pink Fancy, 97, 104
Pinney's beach, 158

Pisces rest., 227
Pitch Lake, 258
Pitons, 214
Plage des Salines, 204
The Plantation, 175
Plantation Leyritz, 202, 206
La Plantation rest., 182
Playa Dorada, 66
Playa Grande, 66
Playa Lechi, 270
Playa Linda Beach Resort, 286,
    291
Plaza Criolla shop, 64
Plaza de la Cultura, 64
Le Plaza Holiday Inn, 56, 60
PLM Azur Carayou, 203, 206
Plymouth, 175
Pointe-à-Pitre, 181
Pointe des Châteaux, 184
Pointe du Bout, 203
Point Pleasant, 96, 103
Poisson d'Or rest., 123
Ponce, 81
Ponce Museum of Art, 81
Port Antonio, 41, 44
Port-au-Prince, 56
Port Elizabeth, 238
Port of Spain, 258
Portsmouth, 193
Princess Beach Hotel and Ca-
    sino, 280, 283
Prospect Lodge, 251, 252
Prospect Plantation, 40
Prune Island, 241
Puerta de Tierra, 78
Puerto Plata, 65
Puerto Rico, 70–88
Punta Caña, 65
Pusser's Landing rest., 109

Queenie Simmons's Serving
    Spoon, 144
Queen's Park Savannah, 258

Raffles rest., 224
Rafter's Rest rest., 42
Rain rest., 210
Ramada Hotel El Convento, 74,
    78, 87

Ramada Renaissance, 247, 252
El Rancho, 57, 60
Rancho El Paso, 289
Rawlins Plantation, 157, 162
A la Recherche du Passé shop,
    182
Le Récif, 57
Redcliffe Quay, 167
Reid's rest., 225
Reigate Hall, 192, 195
Relais Creoles, 206
Rendezvous Bay Hotel, 140
La Résidence, 126
Restaurant Indonesia, 278
Restaurant Karacoli, 186
The Retreat at Rum Point, 24, 29
Richmond Great House, 262,
    265
Rick's Café, 36
Rincón, 82
Ristorante Pappagallo, 24
Rivers Meet rest., 48
Road Town, 107
La Robe Creole rest., 191
Rockhouse, 36, 51
Rocklands Bird Feeding Station,
    35
Rockview Holiday Homes, 117
Roger Albert shop, 198
La Romana, 65
Romney Manor, 156
Le Rond Point rest., 57
Roof Club, 44
Roseau, 191
La Rotisserie, 78
Round Hill, 33, 51
The Royal Antiguan, 172
Royal Dane Hotel, 99, 104
Royal Pavilion, 230
Rum Point, 26

Saba, 141–146
Saba Artisan's Foundation, 143
Saba Museum, 144
Sacré Coeur de Balata, 201
Saint Aubin hotel, 203, 206
St. Barts, 127–134
St. Croix, 89–104
Sainte-Anne, 204
Les Saintes, 183, 187

St. Eustatius, 147–152
Saint-François, 183
St. George's, 248
St. James Church, 224
St. James Coast, 223
St. James's Club hotel, 172
St. Jean, 129
St. Jean Beach Club, 129
St. John, 89–104
St. John's, 167
St. Kitts, 153–163
St. Lucia, 207–218
St. Lucia Artists Association, 210
St. Maarten, 118–126
St. Martin, 118–126
St. Michael's Cathedral, 222
St. Nicholas Abbey, 225
Saint-Pierre, 202
St. Thomas, 89–104
St. Vincent, 231–244
Salt Island, 113
Saltwhistle Bay Club, 241, 244
La Samanna hotel, 123, 125
Sam Lord's Castle, 226
San Antoine rest., 212
Sand Dollar Beach, 237
Sandpiper Inn, 230
Sands Hotel & Casino, 80, 87
Sandy Ground, 137
Sandy Island, 251
Sandy Isle, 137
San Germán, 82
San José Church, 74
San Juan Cathedral, 74
San Juan Gate, 76
El San Juan Hotel & Casino, 80, 87
Sans Souci, 58
The Sans Souci Hotel Club & Spa, 38, 51
Santiago's rest., 25
Santo Domingo, 63
Santo Domingo hotel, 69
Sapphire Beach, 95
Savannah Beach, 111
Scarborough, 260
Scott's Café, 212
Scout's Place hotel, 144, 146
Sea Saba, 143
Secret Harbour, 253

Secret Harbour Beach Hotel, 96, 103
Le Select, 131
El Sereno Beach, 131, 133
Seven Mile Beach, 23
Shaw Park Gardens, 40
Shoal Bay, 138
The Sign of the Goobie, 150
Six Men's Bay, 224
Sorobon Beach Naturist Resort, 269, 273
Soufrière, 213, 214
Southern Cross Club, 29
Spanish Water, 281
Speightstown, 224
Spencer Cameron Art Gallery, 155
Spice Island Inn, 247, 252
Sprat Hall Plantation, 99, 104
Spritzer & Furman, 269
Statia, 147–152
The Stone Oven, 150
Stouffer Grand Beach Resort, 96, 104
Strawberry Hill, 48
Sugar Mill, 109, 116
Sugar Mill Restaurant, 34
Sulphur Springs, 215
Sunbury, 227
Sunny Caribee Hotel, 239
Surfside Saba Deep, 143

Talk of the Town rest., 150
The Talk of the Town rest., 288
Tamarind Reef Beach Club, 98, 104
Temptation on the Beach rest., 288
Thelma's, 112
Things Jamaican, 48
Thomas de Rogatis shop, 199
Tiara Beach Hotel, 29
Tivoli Gardens, 97
Tobago, 254–265
Tobago Cays, 234
La Toc Suites, 211
Top Hat rest., 97
La Toque Lyonnaise, 131
Tortola, 105–117
La Toubana, 183, 187

Town House Restaurant, 35
Trafalgar Falls, 194
Treasure Beach, 223, 230
Treasure Island Hotel and Casino at Cupecoy, 122, 126
Treasure Island Resort, 24, 29
Trident Villas & Hotel, 51
Trinidad, 254–265
Trinidad Hilton, 259, 265
Tropicrafts, 191
Trunk Bay, 101
Tryall Golf, Tennis and Beach Club, 33, 51
Turtle Beach Hotel, 261, 265
12 Degrees North hotel, 253

United States Virgin Islands, 89–104

Le Verger, 199
Vesuvio rest., 64
Vieques, 84
Villa Creole, 57, 60
Villa Esperanza Parador, 83, 88
Village St. Jean, 134
Villa Parguera Parador, 88
Virgin Gorda, 105–117

La Vista, 126
Vistamar Parador, 83, 88
Vue Pointe Hotel, 176, 178

Wajang Doll rest., 120
Warehouse, 223
Washington/Slagbaai National Park, 270
Waterfort Arches, 277
Waterfront Café, 221
West Indian Tavern, 120
Willemstad, 275
Wilton on the Sea, 37, 51
Windwardside, 144
Wine Cellar, 279
Witch Doctor rest., 227

Young Island, 237
Young Island resort, 237, 246
El Yunque Rainforest, 81

La Zaragozana, 77
Zeezicht Bar and Restaurant, 270
Zetland Plantation, 160, 163
Zin d'Art, 57

FOR THE BEST IN PAPERBACKS, LOOK FOR THE

In every corner of the world, on every subject under the sun, Penguin represents quality and variety—the very best in publishing today.

For complete information about books available from Penguin—including Pelicans, Puffins, Peregrines, and Penguin Classics—and how to order them, write to us at the appropriate address below. Please note that for copyright reasons the selection of books varies from country to country.

In the United Kingdom: For a complete list of books available from Penguin in the U.K., please write to *Dept E.P., Penguin Books Ltd, Harmondsworth, Middlesex, UB7 0DA.*

In the United States: For a complete list of books available from Penguin in the U.S., please write to *Dept BA, Penguin, 299 Murray Hill Parkway, East Rutherford, New Jersey 07073.*

In Canada: For a complete list of books available from Penguin in Canada, please write to *Penguin Books Canada Ltd, 2801 John Street, Markham, Ontario. L3R 1B4.*

In Australia: For a complete list of books available from Penguin in Australia, please write to the *Marketing Department, Penguin Books Australia Ltd, P.O. Box 257, Ringwood, Victoria 3134.*

In New Zealand: For a complete list of books available from Penguin in New Zealand, please write to the *Marketing Department, Penguin Books (NZ) Ltd, Private Bag, Takapuna, Auckland 9.*

In India: For a complete list of books available from Penguin, please write to *Penguin Overseas Ltd, 706 Eros Apartments, 56 Nehru Place, New Delhi, 110019.*

In Holland: For a complete list of books available from Penguin in Holland, please write to *Penguin Books Nederland B.V., Postbus 195, NL–1380AD Weesp, Netherlands.*

In Germany: For a complete list of books available from Penguin, please write to *Penguin Books Ltd, Friedrichstrasse 10–12, D–6000 Frankfurt Main 1, Federal Republic of Germany.*

In Spain: For a complete list of books available from Penguin in Spain, please write to *Longman Penguin España, Calle San Nicolas 15, E–28013 Madrid, Spain.*